THE
GRIMOIRE
— OF —
GRAVE
FATES

THE GRIMOIRE

OF

GRAVE FATES

CREATED BY HANNA ALKAF AND MARGARET OWEN

Stories by Preeti Chhibber, Kat Cho, Mason Deaver,
Natasha Díaz, Hafsah Faizal, Victoria Lee,
Jessica Lewis, Darcie Little Badger, Kwame Mbalia,
L. L. McKinney, Tehlor Kay Mejia, Yamile Saied Méndez,
Cam Montgomery, Marieke Nijkamp, Karuna Riazi,
Randy Ribay, Kayla Whaley, and Julian Winters

DELACORTE PRESS

Text copyright © 2023 by Hanna Alkaf and Margaret Owen
"2:00 A.M.: WREN WILLEMSON" © 2023 by Marieke Nijkamp
"3:00 A.M.: DIEGO SAKAY" © 2023 by Randy Ribay
"4:00 A.M.: JAMESON 'JB' BRIG" © 2023 by Kwame Mbalia
"5:00 A.M.: TAYA WINTER" © 2023 by Darcie Little Badger
"6:00 A.M.: KETURAH AUSTIN" © 2023 by Cam Montgomery
"7:00 A.M.: BHAVNA JOSHI" © 2023 by Preeti Chhibber
"8:00 A.M.: JIA PARK" © 2023 by Kat Cho
"9:00 A.M.: IRENE SEAVER" © 2023 by Kayla Whaley
"10:00-ish A.M. (Or earlier? Maybe later): SYDNEY MEEKS" © 2023 by L. L. McKinney
"12:00 P.M.: MARIAM ABIDIN" © 2023 by Hafsah Faizal
"1:00 P.M.: XANDER WILSON" © 2023 by Julian Winters
"2:00 P.M.: NADIYA NUR" © 2023 by Karuna Riazi
"3:00 P.M.: DELORES 'LOLA' CORTEZ" © 2023 by Tehlor Kay Mejia
"4:00 P.M.: MAXWELL ASTER" © 2023 by Mason Deaver
"5:00 P.M.: JAMIE ELLISON" © 2023 by Victoria Lee
"6:00 P.M.: DELFINA MOORE" © 2023 by Yamile Saied Méndez
"7:00 P.M.: IVY BARTA" © 2023 by Jessica Lewis
"8:00 P.M.: LUPITA AUGRATRICIS" © by Natasha Díaz
Jacket art copyright © 2023 by Katt Phatt Studio
Map copyright © 2023 by Virginia Allyn
All rights reserved. Published in the United States by Delacorte Press, an imprint of Random House Children's Books, a division of Penguin Random House LLC, New York.

Delacorte Press is a registered trademark and the colophon is a trademark of Penguin Random House LLC.

Visit us on the Web! GetUnderlined.com

Educators and librarians, for a variety of teaching tools, visit us at RHTeachersLibrarians.com

Library of Congress Cataloging-in-Publication Data is available upon request.
ISBN 978-0-593-42745-3 (trade) — ISBN 978-0-593-42746-0 (lib. bdg.) —
ISBN 978-0-593-42747-7 (ebook) — ISBN 978-0-593-70577-3 (international ed.)

The text of this book is set in 11-point Adobe Garamond.
Interior design by Kenneth Crossland

Printed in the United States of America
10 9 8 7 6 5 4 3 2 1
First Edition

For everyone who ever

wanted to feel like they were Chosen:

magic belongs to you, too.

GALILEO ACADEMY FOR

CUPS TOWER

BESTIARY

DINING HALL

SWORDS TOWER

ARCANA TOWER

GYM AND KINETICS PRACTICE

ADMINISTRATION OFFICES

WORKSHOPS
CRAFTING & INDUSTRIAL MAGIC

FACULTY HOUSING

MAIN ENTRANCE

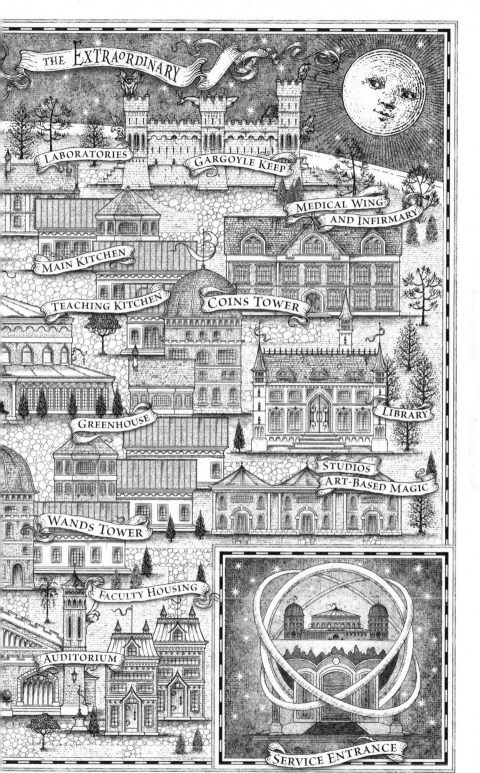

THE EXTRAORDINARY

LABORATORIES

GARGOYLE KEEP

MEDICAL WING
AND INFIRMARY

MAIN KITCHEN

TEACHING KITCHEN

COINS TOWER

GREENHOUSE

LIBRARY

STUDIOS
ART-BASED MAGIC

WANDS TOWER

FACULTY HOUSING

AUDITORIUM

SERVICE ENTRANCE

WELCOME TO GALILEO ACADEMY FOR THE EXTRAORDINARY

THE GALILEO ETHOS

For hundreds of years now, Galileo Academy for the Extraordinary has been educating the future of the Sorcerer world.

With a rigorous academic curriculum, a broad range of extra-curricular activities, and the most cutting-edge magical training techniques, as well as a faculty of highly dedicated staff, Galileo provides students with confidence in themselves and the ways in which they can impact the world around them.

We pride ourselves on the diversity of backgrounds, cultures, temperaments, opinions, and aptitudes in both our faculty and student body, and believe each has their place here. We believe in creating a community that thrives in difference, and allows each member the space they need to flourish. Our aim is to provide an environment in which students learn beyond the classroom, and as much from each other as they do from their teachers.

HISTORY

Originally located deep in the wilds of the English countryside, Galileo Academy for the Extraordinary was founded centuries ago. It was built by the leading astronomy sorcerer, Galileo Galilei, as a secret observatory in which to conduct his experiments, and as he began to take on his own mentees and disciples, the observatory eventually grew into a school dedicated to academic innovation. The school's motto, *Eppur si move,* comes from the legend that after recanting his theory that the Earth orbits the sun, Galileo muttered under his breath, "And yet it moves."

In the last few years, that motto has become literal.

While we are proud of our long and illustrious history and our rich heritage, at Galileo we do not believe in living in the past. Instead we look forward, constantly evolving and embracing innovations in order to always provide the best education that we can for our students. For this reason, Galileo has shed its roots and now roams from country to country, affording its students a more global view of magic. Further, we have overhauled the course structure and requirements to be more inclusive and accessible, thus living up to the most important part of our name: "extraordinary."

THE SCHOOL

The school is open to students aged thirteen to eighteen. In the first two years, students are educated in general magical technique and theory, on top of a robust academic curriculum. By age fifteen, students are encouraged to declare their chosen major (and minor, if applicable) house. At this point, students may choose to move into their respective house tower rather than staying in the general-population Arcana dormitories.

Galileo Academy has five houses, each focusing on a specific area of study.

HOUSE	SYMBOL	AREA OF STUDY
Cups	Chalice	Math & Science
Coins	Five coins	Social Studies
Wands	Two crossed wands	Humanities
Swords	Three swords in a triangle	Kinetics
Arcana	Four crowns in a square	General Studies/ Undeclared

The school typically spends one month docked in a single location before moving to its next destination. In this time, students learn about local history and culture in a nonexploitative way and take part in pre-approved community service projects. We are also very proud of our renowned cultural exchange programs, in which chosen students spend a week with a Neutral family in the culture they visit, while Neutral students spend a week at Galileo to experience life here.

All prospective students must sit for a series of stringent admissions examinations and tests of basic magical ability and aptitude before being considered for admission. Financial aid and scholarships are available; please inquire for more information.

LEADERSHIP

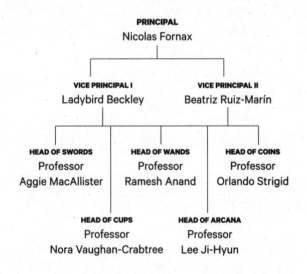

PRINCIPAL
Nicolas Fornax

VICE PRINCIPAL I
Ladybird Beckley

VICE PRINCIPAL II
Beatriz Ruiz-Marín

HEAD OF SWORDS
Professor
Aggie MacAllister

HEAD OF WANDS
Professor
Ramesh Anand

HEAD OF COINS
Professor
Orlando Strigid

HEAD OF CUPS
Professor
Nora Vaughan-Crabtree

HEAD OF ARCANA
Professor
Lee Ji-Hyun

We look forward to having you join our constellation of stars here at Galileo Academy for the Extraordinary!

2:00 A.M.: WREN WILLEMSON, 16, SWORDS

BY MARIEKE NIJKAMP

In a small room in the Swords Tower of the Galileo Academy for the Extraordinary sat a young Sorcerer who—according to their stepfather—had been born under unlucky stars. Wren sat cross-legged on the bed while a dead spider crawled across the bedspread. Despite the late hour, Wren still wore their regular clothes. A dark hoodie, easily two sizes too large. Compression gloves on their hands. A bulky walking brace around their left ankle, which had dislocated again. They tugged strands of blue and silver hair behind their ear, and a small bubble of low magical light that floated above their bed flickered.

The light barely illuminated their bland, narrow room, with its pale walls and looming wardrobe. Wren had never made an effort to decorate. The only signs that a student lived here at all were the stack of textbooks near the door, a stack of sketchbooks on the windowsill—filled with endless patterns and paintings that Wren didn't share with anyone—and the rat skeleton on the bedside table.

The dead spider shivered before its legs gave out from under it, and it curled up again, lifeless and broken.

Wren grimaced. With a wince of pain, they tossed the spider corpse out the open window. The bubble of light above them wavered briefly once more, and their hands trembled.

"Stop it," Wren hissed—and the light steadied.

"Focus," they told themself sternly—but their hands kept trembling.

There was a restlessness inside them that set Wren's teeth and joints on edge. Even though the Swords Tower was quiet and the night calm, Wren felt like their bones were going to crawl out through their skin. Because every time they closed their eyes, their mind replayed the afternoon's encounter at the Gargoyle Keep, and every part of them wanted to disappear.

They'd needed time for themself after spectacularly failing yet another telekinesis test, and the bestiary had been crowded with Cups students and their biology classes. So Wren had kept walking in the direction of the Gargoyle Keep to stare for a while at the majestic stone creatures—only to collide head-long with Professor Dropwort, Galileo's history teacher and the school's prime bully. He was the type of teacher who looked down his nose at any student who wasn't a legacy student, or at the very least a fine young cis man, whole of mind and body. Wren's mere existence as a Sorcerer was an abomination and an offense to his sensibilities.

Just like their appearance in the Gargoyle Keep had been an affront to him, apparently. He'd stepped back, brushed down his clothes, and lifted his chin. "Thinking of adding 'assaulting teachers' to your list of failures, Willemson?"

Wren had mumbled an apology and turned to walk away,

when the professor's voice had stopped them. "I've spoken to your head of house, you know. Professor MacAllister tells me you're last in all your classes, in direct violation of your scholarship. There's no place for a disappointment like you here at Galileo."

The all-too-familiar words had landed like physical blows, and Wren had frozen in place, their hands clenched into fists, and their heart pounding the same rhythm over and over again.

Cursed. Unlucky. Failure.

Professor Dropwort had laughed. "Run along now."

Wren still didn't know how they'd made their way back to the Swords Tower, or their own room. They must've eaten dinner, but the encounter kept plaguing them, even now. It hurt. It hurt so freaking much.

Cursed. Unlucky. Failure.

Professor Dropwort might have been a malicious malcontent, but he wasn't wrong about Wren failing their tests. Professor MacAllister had told Wren the same thing just before the school had made port in Stockholm. Wren's aptitude for kinetics and manipulating approved forms of magical energy was meager, scarcely enough to justify a magical education. If they got kicked out now, they'd be forced to return to an unwelcome home, where their stepfather would know they were all but powerless. There'd be nothing they could do to protect themself or their Neutral sister from his cruelty.

"I hate him, Rat," Wren whispered.

They slammed a fist into their pillow, and they did the only thing they *could* do. They took all their pain and rage and flung their awareness *outward*.

Earlier in the night, the darkness had remained opaque and

impenetrable. But now, it opened up to Wren. It flooded with colors. Neon green and pale orange. The softest of pinks and the deepest of purples. Here a bright blue thread stretched out and led all the way to Professor Ram, the head of Wands and a world-renowned textile mage. It rather looked like the magic thread he used to weave spells. Further, the soft golden threads of Principal Fornax's life force spread like a web across the entire school.

Wren's shoulders loosened.

They'd never found the right word for what they saw, exactly. It was energy and magic, but not like the bland energy they were tangling with in their classes. It was *life,* and whenever Wren managed to get their focus *just* right, it turned Galileo into a kaleidoscope of constantly changing shapes and colors, like the endless patterns they sketched, though they'd never been able to get this sensation quite right.

With their hands in front of them, Wren sorted through the tangle of energy. They reached out beyond their own bedroom toward their neighbor Saga, whose energy was a warm burnt amber, like narrow flames sparking up and away from her. The energy burned radiantly when Saga was casting—or throwing snide remarks in Wren's direction—but it still danced while she was asleep.

Wren tilted their head and reached a hand toward the flames. They summoned their own energy—glinting like sharp silver knives—and cut a piece of Saga's energy away. The flames' warmth seeped into Wren's skin like molten wax. It curled around their ankle and numbed the pain, and on the bedside table, Rat, the rat skeleton, moved. It turned to face them and chattered brightly.

Wren's frown softened. They might not excel in kinetics,

but they had *this* at least. This ability to see and control the magic in the world around them. No one else knew about this aptitude, because manipulating life energy and life force, like all other forms of necromancy, was strictly forbidden at Galileo and beyond. But it wasn't the all-encompassing destructive force that people whispered it was. It helped Wren kill their pain, envision a brighter world, and connect with Rat.

Nothing else.

Until Rat's squeaks made way for a different sound. A voice, as loud as the brightest colors.

Hunger, it whispered, a dozen voices amidst a swirling slate-gray energy, shaped like small rocks and pebbles, and equally rough.

Wren started. They tried to pull back from the energy, but just like it had been impossible to focus all night long, now it was impossible to let go. Wren reached for Rat and cradled the skeleton close. They *saw* energy. They'd never used it as a means to communicate. They hadn't even known that was *possible.* "Who's there?"

Their voice wavered only slightly. Who had they bumped into now?

The room stayed quiet.

Then, *Come.*

Wren shivered. "Show yourself," they tried again. They reached deeper. Desperation turned to determination. They took more of Saga's energy. A haphazard snap of another student's blustery gray. "Who are you?"

Death.

Wren bit their tongue. When Wren had accidentally re-animated a kitten once, as an eight-year-old, their stepfather had made it painfully clear to them that they were cursed and useless. Courting death, he'd called it. Was this what he'd meant? For Wren, their necromancy never felt like a curse. It felt like a comfort.

Wren haphazardly seized a maroon branch of energy and drew strength from it. "Who are you? What do you want?"

The answer came after a torturously long moment.

Wren.

The gray mass swirled together, and Wren reached for more energy still—more than they'd ever tried to hold at once. A ribbon of deep magenta that danced through the air and briefly connected Wren with Bhavna, one of the other students in the Swords Tower. A tendril of soft pink flitted around Wren and reached all the way back to the Wands Tower. Wren gathered as much power as possible, until the voice sharpened and cleared. Energy became image. Pebbles became teeth. Rocks formed claws. Dark cavities where eyes would be. Hungry, ferocious, gleeful grins.

"Gargoyles!" Wren's eyes shot open, and in their shock, they lost their focus. The bubble of light floating above them extinguished. Rat curled up and hissed. And the sound formed a roar that rumbled through Wren's bones before it faded away, leaving nothing but silence and a dark night once more.

Wren cursed softly. Their hands still trembled, and Wren felt worse than they had minutes ago. "What do you want?" Their voice cracked. They didn't expect a reply—their connection to the energy around them was gone. Rat would be awake for a few minutes more at best, and Wren had failed at this— whatever this *was*—too. They hadn't known it was possible for gargoyles to reach out like this. How did they do that? And more important, why? What if they had an important reason to? What if they needed help? What if Wren was the only one who could hear—

Come.

Wren nearly dropped Rat when the voice still echoed around them, the energy not entirely gone. "What's wrong? How can I still hear you?"

Come. A call. A beckoning.

Wren got to their feet. They pushed a trembling hand through their hair. "Why? Do you need anything?"

Come.

The gargoyles didn't elaborate, but Wren realized that the answer was obvious. As far as they knew, there were no other necromancers at school. No one else who knew about the life energy that swirled around them. Wren was the only one who could hear this. That meant they were the only one who could answer, and the gargoyles must need them for a reason.

Was this their curse? Or a chance? They'd learned to shield their aptitude when they were small, but they longed for the day when that wouldn't be necessary anymore, when people would see that what they did was *good*, actually. That their necromancy wasn't to be feared but understood. They longed to find ways to prove themself. To bastards like their stepfather. To the Professor Dropworts of the world.

To themself.

No longer Wren, the failing Swords student, whose only official claim to magical prowess was being able to summon decent barriers and accidentally succeeding in telekinetically moving a pen. Once. Wren, the quiet, *odd* one. Cursed. Unlucky. Failure.

No more. They took every last scrap of their self, their determination, their anger and reached out.

Come.

"I will."

They'd show Galileo exactly what they were worth.

Wren grabbed Rat, pulled their hood up high, and prepared to leave the room, while the voices of the gargoyles still echoed around them.

Death.

Some fifteen minutes later, Wren snuck through the hallway. Rat sat in the pouch of Wren's hoodie, peeking out and squeaking softly.

"It's well after midnight," Wren muttered. "No one is out here anymore."

Rat chattered a protest. She usually became her stiff skeleton self again in the heartbeats after Wren dropped their focus, but right now, she was still awake and full of opinions.

"Fine, you tell the gargoyles I'm not coming."

Rat squeaked.

"Yes, I know, we'll be in trouble if we get caught. So we have to make sure that doesn't happen."

Something else had changed too, Wren realized when they inched past the doorway to Saga's room. It was still shimmering with the same amber light that they'd seen earlier. In fact, if they focused *just* right, every door in the hallway glowed with a different color. The energies that usually dissipated once Wren lost their focus now wrapped themselves around Wren. Tonight they'd reached out further than they ever had before, and it felt as if, as a result, their connection was stronger than ever before too. Wren didn't understand where the power came from, but the sprawling Gothic building, with its gloomy shadows and hard edges, *shone.*

Brass fire behind one door. A copper gleam underneath the next. Blue waves so dark they were nearly black, and amethyst storm clouds. Tendrils of emerald energy crackling like electricity.

Necromancy wasn't just strictly forbidden; it was considered horrifying. But Wren didn't understand how anyone could be scared of this. This was *beautiful.* This was where Wren wanted to belong.

A large staircase led down from Swords Tower to the main hall. Wren took the stairs carefully, little flares of pain bouncing up their left ankle with every step. By the time they reached the bottom, Wren already regretted not taking a little slice of copper gleam or section of amethyst storm clouds.

Even in this place of magic, where staircases turned into ramps and previous principals had begrudgingly accepted accessibility modifications to the ancient building, Wren still hurt. Daily. Constantly. Galileo might be doing its best to be inclusive and open, but that didn't necessarily mean it succeeded. Like that bloody telekinesis test. It hadn't just involved moving things around with their mind, but running and dodging, and Professor Mathews had refused to give Wren a pass. He'd told them they needed to learn how to perform magic under suboptimal circumstances, but how could something that harmed also be educational?

Meanwhile, necromancy wasn't macabre—it helped. So how could something that healed also be harmful?

A whisper caressed the back of their neck. The echo of chuckling bounced through the massive Gothic hall, where dim lights illuminated the solemn portraits of former principals and teachers.

A bright glow appeared at the edge of Wren's vision, and Rat squeaked an alarm. Without time to think, Wren pushed themself into the nearest corner, the darkest spot they could see, and held their breath.

In Wren's strange double vision, ghosts were brighter, their life energy not contained by any sort of corporeal form. But while some ghosts might be lured into curious conversations with a budding Sorcerer in the privacy of their room, the ones that patrolled the school's buildings wouldn't be amused at finding Wren wandering. They kept the halls safe at night, and operated under a strict code of conduct that required them to remain visible to students and staff at all times. In other words, they were serious about their job.

Rat retreated into her pouch.

Wren kept still and reached for the nearest tendril of energy they could find. For a pulse-racing desperate moment, the only things that surrounded them were the thick stone walls of the school and the disapproving stares of its teachers.

Then a collection of dark magenta stars sparkled at the edge of Wren's vision. They plucked a handful of stars without hesitation. One to keep themself standing without trembling. One to ease the tension in their cramped hands. One, two, three to keep them hidden.

Death, the voice called from somewhere far below. Wren

frowned. They'd expected the gargoyles to be outside, near the Keep. Instead the sound was coming from the opposite direction, and below the school, where no gargoyles should be. Where the loading docks underneath the school's gyroscopic structure connected Galileo to the outside world. It was off-limits for students. It was *certainly* off-limits for gargoyles.

And—wasn't the school supposed to be traveling tonight?

Come.

The voice still beckoned.

The patrolling ghost floated closer, his low chuckling louder.

Fear coursed through Wren. They twisted their ankle until pain bloomed, and used the pain to focus. They pulled a barrier around them, like they had a hundred times in their classes, and countless times to hide their true aptitude.

Tonight, though, instead of using their approved-but-meager kinetic talents, they wove life energy itself into their barrier. The magenta grew darker the closer it got to Wren, and that was their intention. The barrier didn't merely exist to hide them. They wove fear into it, and loneliness. Repulsion too, so that everyone who looked in their direction would want to look away.

Pain. Perhaps they should have tried to use pain as a barrier before.

The ghost drew closer, and Wren pushed back against the wall. They recognized the spectral visage of Castelli, one of the oldest poltergeists on the grounds. Castelli had been Galileo's first student, and now spent his days drifting through walls, muttering about the natural order of the world, and being entirely too impressed with himself. Any student unlucky enough to be caught out of bounds by Castelli was invariably treated to a long lecture in barely audible Italian, and Wren had enough sense to stay well clear of him.

Castelli floated in place and stared in Wren's direction for what felt like the longest time, his lips constantly moving. *"E le medesime cose seguiranno quando ambidue fossero corpi calamitici in primo significato . . ."*

Wren held their breath and clung to their barrier.

Rat trembled in her hideout.

And Castelli continued to mutter, while he slowly drifted away to resume his patrol.

Wren breathed out but didn't move. Only when Castelli was out of earshot did they laugh. Rat squeaked and climbed out of her hiding spot, which made Wren laugh again, and they struggled to keep the barrier in place.

"I didn't think anyone could fool the ghost patrol," they whispered. "I didn't think that would *work*."

They stared at their gloved hands and the barrier that shimmered in front of them, and they clung to the feeling of power. A barrier this powerful proved they weren't useless, no matter what their stepfather might say, or what their professors might think. It proved they were worthy of belonging here, amidst the other students. The extraordinarily talented ones they were intimidated by, *and* the ones they wanted to befriend. Like Bhavna in Swords, who moved through the school with such bright grace that Wren didn't know how she did it. Or Nadiya, with her cute berets and even cuter freckles, who sometimes looked at the school around her like there was a potential disaster hiding in every shadow. Wren understood that wariness well. Or Irene, who seemed to be well on her way to taking over the world one day.

Even—even Jamie. The only person in the school—other than Nurse Fibula, of course—whose life force Wren could never quite see or feel. They'd tried, several times, but Jamie remained elusive. Not like he was as lifeless as his wardrobe suggested, but like Wren couldn't get *through*. It intrigued Wren, even as it made them uncomfortable.

But the point was, Wren knew all of them. They *saw* all of them. They wanted to be worthy of them.

Rat squeaked, and Wren petted her. "I know you believe in me."

But perhaps Wren could too.

Come.

The school grounds were a spectacular, vibrant green when Wren stepped out of the Swords Tower. The weeds that pushed up between the stones were surrounded by swirls of flowers, and the handful of midnight birds tumbling through the air left softly colored trails. The stars were like a painting. And Wren was sweating, fatigue and adrenaline battling for dominance. They'd never kept their magic up for this long before, and they weren't sure how to make it stop again. But it was a good type of fatigue. Not from pain or from sleeplessness but from purpose.

Wren crouched and trailed a hand along a cluster of closed poppies that pushed up around the steps to the tower. Their gentle red light clung to Wren's fingers, and Wren smiled when it briefly eased their aches, though the flowers themselves shuddered and crumbled.

"What I do isn't malicious." Wren rubbed a fallen and

unscathed petal between their forefinger and thumb, and sparks flew up around them. "Look at it, Rat. This isn't evil." They never took more energy from others than those others could or would miss either. And if they wouldn't miss it, why shouldn't Wren use it?

Outside, the gargoyles were louder too, but like before, the sound came from below Wren, near the location of the main entrance to Galileo. But what would gargoyles do there? They didn't usually leave school grounds. What would bring them there? Why would they call Wren there?

Death.

Come.

Wren wavered, but they wouldn't turn back. Even if only Rat and the gargoyles knew what they did here tonight, they refused to fail at this too. They plucked a poppy and crushed the flower in their fist.

"I'm coming."

By the time Wren had found their way to the source of the gargoyles' call—with their barrier pulled up high all the way through Arcana Tower, then in the elevator that led down to the main entrance and the loading docks underneath the school—they were swaying and yawning, struggling with their braced ankle, dragging their foot behind them. They'd left a trail of poppy crumbles in their wake.

The school's buildings were suspended above Wren in the magical gyroscope; massive pillars created a stable docking point, and the main entrance and the loading docks provided access to the school, while the school was stationary. From the academy's vantage point just outside of town, a sleepy Stockholm spread out in front of them, the city covered under a blanket of artificial light against the night. Wren stared at it for a second, wondering what the city's energy would look like from within its winding roads and old bright houses. If Wren's powers were strong enough to see all the energies of Galileo, what would a whole city look like?

At the same time, a practical question wormed its way through their mind. The school was meant to travel tonight. Why were they still here?

A large shadow flew past, and Wren ducked, the colors around them dimming for the first time that night. A slender but tall gargoyle, with sharp wings and hungry claws, passed them by and circled around the pillars toward the loading docks.

Hungry.

Its gnashing call nearly drove Wren to their knees, and they covered their ears.

"What is it?" Wren asked. Perhaps the gargoyles could respond properly now that Wren was closer. "I'm here. What do you need?"

Hungry.

Another call. Then, a response, from behind them.

Death.

Come.

With a sinking feeling, Wren put the pieces together.

Hungry.

Death. Come.

It didn't sound like a cry for help; it sounded like a call to come down for dinner.

Wren's hands twitched. Had the gargoyles ever been calling out to them? Or had Wren simply overheard their cry to the rest of their pack? They'd called Wren by name, or—

Had they simply realized Wren was listening in?

Even so, this was a chance to prove their skill and worth. They had to cling to that chance. They refused to give up now.

They kept an eye on the sky above them to make sure no other gargoyles came closer, and they carefully walked around the main entrance and the pillars on which the gyroscopic school rested, in the direction of the loading docks.

Rat hissed, and Wren pushed a trembling hand into the hoodie's pouch to pet the skeleton.

"I don't know what they eat, but I won't let them eat you. Don't worry." A sad smile tugged at their lips. "Not a lot of meat on your bones anyway."

When they circled around the school's entrance, three large gargoyles came into view. They were gathered around something—some sort of shadow—on one of the loading docks, where the service entrance to the school was located. The gargoyle that had passed Wren was circling above them, while a fifth had taken to the skies and now flew up high, back in the direction of the Keep.

Wren pulled the barrier closer. They pulled feathers of energy from the gargoyles. Stars from the night sky. Yearning from their own pain, until they were sure they were as protected as they could be.

They took a step closer to the gathering, and they could hear the same voiceless whisper, over and over. *Hungry*, from the gargoyle that circled overhead.

And the same constant call from the three on the loading dock. *Come.*

Not one of them paid attention to Wren. They clenched their jaw. How very like them, to think someone was calling out to them, when in fact the person was just waving at the person behind Wren or smiling out of politeness.

Rat squeaked, and Wren shook their head. "I know. Thanks . . ."

A subtle hint of sickly yellow energy wound its way around the gargoyles. Wren's focus shifted to the shadowy figure beyond the gigantic stone beasts, and they stumbled when recognition hit them.

A body.

And not just any body.

The tufts of white-gray hair. The mustache. The ever-spotless traditional suit, its creases as sharp as the wearer's tongue, now torn and marred with spots of red. There were claw marks across his face and clothes.

Professor Dropwort.

Professor Septimius Dropwort. Motionless. Without the usual glow of magic clinging to him. Without any sign of life, but for that wisp of color.

Had the gargoyles somehow attacked him? Nervous jitters bubbled up inside Wren, and they choked back a laugh. Professor Dropwort, Wren, and gargoyles. It was a recipe for disaster, and Wren wanted to be anywhere but here. Whatever had happened on the loading dock wasn't good, and Wren was certain that they didn't want to get involved in it.

Except. There was that fading yellow energy, reaching out

from between the gargoyles that planned to feast on the professor, the color growing paler by the moment. Dropwort might not be alive anymore, but he was not completely gone either.

Wren bit their lip. If it hadn't been for their insistence to prove themself, if it hadn't been for their forbidden second sight, they would never have known about the professor—or that there was something left of him.

They could easily do the exact same thing so many others had done around Professor Dropwort. Close their eyes and pretend they hadn't seen his cruelty, hadn't heard his harsh words. Walk away.

"Thinking of adding 'murder' to your list of failures, Willemson?" Wren muttered viciously.

But the moment they asked that question, they knew the answer. Perhaps they *were* failing at all their classes. Perhaps they *didn't* belong here. Perhaps they could only ever numb the pain, never find a way to cure it, and they'd lose all the focus they'd gained tonight. But they were still better than Professor Septimius Dropwort.

They were meant to be here for a reason.

Wren caressed Rat's skull. "Sorry, buddy. You're not going to like this."

With one last-ditch effort, their hands cramping, their knees buckling, and a haze of pain surrounding them, Wren drew energy from all around them, as much as they could handle without combusting. From the ground where the school was docked. From the city beyond it. From the gargoyles. From the echoes of other spells. From their anger at the injustice of it all. From inside themself. Then, in one massive swipe, they shoved the gargoyles aside.

The stone monsters scattered like birds, tumbling over each other and clambering to safety. Wren's hands hummed with power, and every cell in their body felt charged with energy and determination and purpose.

Wren stood in the middle of a sphere of magical energy, shielding not just themself but Rat and Professor Dropwort from the gargoyles.

"Leave him be," Wren demanded, making sure their voice carried. For once, they wanted to be heard.

From a slight distance, the biggest gargoyle tilted its head, and a fierce grin appeared, growing wider and wider, until it seemed as though it cut its face in two. Sharp teeth, made for tearing meat off bones. Stony eyes. Hard, lean muscles.

Behind the first, the other two fixed their gaze on Wren as well.

Wren. The sound went from recognition to challenge, and the message was quite clear. Student out of bed and out of bounds. They were not supposed to be here.

Wren straightened as much as they could. "You're not supposed to be here any more than I am," they replied, their voice wavering only slightly. "You're supposed to protect the grounds, not eat professors."

Hungry.

Wren jutted out their jaw. "So am I," they responded.

One of the gargoyles broke away from the pack and dashed toward them, only to bounce off Wren's shield. The biggest gargoyle snarled, while one of the smaller ones tried to run at them again. It leered at their brace. The fourth, who had remained airborne, called a challenge but didn't come any closer.

"I can keep this up all night," Wren said. They were lying through their teeth, but no one would know that.

They stared up at the gargoyles, Rat squeaking her own challenge from the safety of Wren's hoodie.

The gargoyles hovered near. One flew closer but didn't attack the barrier. The other three remained in a holding pattern above the barrier. And Wren's arms began to tremble.

Wren acted on pure instinct. They took their magic, shaped by curses and hurt and misinterpretation, and flung it in all directions, sending the biggest gargoyle tumbling several feet past the loading dock. When it regained its balance, its grin was replaced by a snarl.

"Try me again," Wren taunted the stone creatures, though the only things keeping them standing were their ankle brace and their spite. "If you don't stop this, I'll call Sally on you."

Sally, the gargoyle keeper, would not like to see the gargoyles here any more than Wren did, and perhaps that would be the last nudge the massive magical creatures needed.

The gargoyles kept their holding pattern, but they moved with a new hesitancy.

Wren held their gaze, fixing their stare on the biggest gargoyle. They felt the seconds tick away. The pain spread. And the gargoyle made up its mind. Finally, facing down Wren with derision, it broke. It slowly led the others away from the dock. It stopped just before it was fully out of sight, and it turned its stony gaze back to Wren.

Remember.

"Oh, I will," Wren promised. They'd never felt this strong and this *right* before. "I will remember."

Wren waited until they were sure they were alone before

they dropped the shield and dropped to their knees next to Professor Dropwort. Wren gagged as they took in the state of him. His clothes were torn, and one of the most enterprising gargoyles had eaten away at one of the professor's eyes. Another had bitten into his cheek and exposed flesh and jawbone. But by the looks of it, that wasn't what had killed him. Dropwort had five deep puncture wounds in his chest, and his shirt was torn and ringed with rust-colored tinges where he had been stabbed, though, oddly, no blood was visible on his flesh.

Wren forced themself to lean in closer for a better look. They reached out and traced the puncture wounds that definitely weren't from gargoyle claws. They checked the professor's pulse. Nothing. Not even the faintest flutter of a heartbeat.

He'd been murdered before being turned into a midnight snack.

"Professor Dropwort?" Wren whispered.

While the faint whispers of yellow energy continued to swirl around them, the light grew fainter, and whatever was left of Professor Dropwort was fading fast. Without a second thought, Wren reached out and grabbed hold of him.

The cries of the gargoyles echoed in the distance, but Wren couldn't pull the shield up again. They needed what was left of their magic. They'd only ever reanimated spiders and rats, and that one time—completely by unlucky accident—a kitten.

But they'd never fought off a group of gargoyles before either. Professor Dropwort had been *murdered,* and Wren knew for a fact what they were meant to do. If they could figure out what had happened, tell their story to one of the other teachers—or, more likely, Nurse Fibula—it would mean something. They could do something right. They could prove their worth to Galileo.

Wren leaned in and nearly toppled over from exhaustion. Rat squeaked her protest.

"It's okay," they murmured. "I'll be fine."

Fatigue made it harder for them to draw on the energy around them. They considered pulling Dropwort's body from the dock toward the shelter of the freight elevator, but the mere idea of that exertion made their head hurt. And if the gargoyles got wind of how weak they were now . . . They needed help, but they didn't have time.

Wren did the only thing that made sense to them. They drew the energy from within themself—countless tiny silver feathers—and transferred it to Professor Dropwort.

An endless current, mixing with the hints of sickly yellow around him.

The edges of Wren's vision went gray. They felt faint.

And Dropwort's body jerked, so they kept pouring.

Their vision narrowed further. A sharp pain took up residence behind their eyes.

Wren could raise an arm—Dropwort's arm. They grinned coldly, and a potent combination of power and relief surged through them. It worked. He would have hated this. "Failure, Professor? Who has the power now?"

Wren's speech slurred, though they hardly noticed, so committed were they to the connection. Just a little more, and they could make him sit up. Maybe they should lie down themself. Keep the energy going, and he could dance and dance to their whims.

Rat squeaked near their ear, and an intense sharp pain shot up their earlobe.

Wren dropped the connection and found themself lying next to the twitching corpse of the professor. They pushed themself up to a sitting position, and the whole world twisted and turned around them. They fought to keep from vomiting.

They glanced at Rat, who'd dropped from Wren's shoulder to their lap. "What'd you do that for? It hurt."

The rat chattered, and Wren frowned. "I was in control of . . ."

Their voice trailed off. Professor Dropwort's body had stopped its macabre dance, and the echo of life energy around his body faded. Briefly it seemed inanimate again.

Then a bright yellow outline shimmered around his body, and a specter clawed its way out. Wren had never before given thought to how ghosts came to be, but they could feel its pull now. Pouring energy into Professor Dropwort's body had done nothing for his physical wounds, but it had strengthened his spirit. Except now the ghost was connected to Wren.

And by the look on his face, he didn't like it one bit.

"Wren." The professor's distaste came through clearly, even in death. His ghost faded and appeared again, his words hard to make out. "Always knew . . . good for nothing."

"I didn't do anything!" Wren snapped. Their voice echoed in the night. "I tried to help."

"Failure . . ."

Wren nearly severed the connection between them, but they hadn't come so far just to let Dropwort chase them away again. There was a murderer at Galileo, and that mattered more than Professor Dropwort's disgust. Even if they currently understood the desire to stab him.

"Who did this? What happened?" Wren asked.

The ghost's lifeless eyes fixed on Wren. ". . . of your business."

"Tell me what happened," Wren insisted. "You were *stabbed*." Wren's mouth was dry, but they met the ghost stare for stare, their frustration for his derision.

"You can't . . . murderer . . . useless." Dropwort's specter wore the same sneer his body had worn in life. ". . . always wants more . . . deserve."

Wren climbed to their feet. Rat squeaked, and the gargoyles cried out again. Wren glanced up toward the gyroscopic school and shook their head. They didn't want more. But they wouldn't settle for less either.

"You'll still be . . . failure," the ghost insisted.

Something snapped inside Wren.

"No, Professor." Wren trembled, Dropwort's words hitting too close to the ones they'd heard at home, but they raised their chin and clenched their hands into fists. Indignation lending strength to their words.

They'd shielded themself from the all-seeing ghost patrol. They'd chased away the gargoyles. They'd reanimated the ghost in front of them. The stars at the edge of their vision swam, but what made stars unlucky anyway? "I'm not useless; I'm powerful. There's still a place for me at Galileo." If there wasn't, they would *make* it. They would claim it. "So you can help me or disappear to whatever afterlife you may believe in, like the coward you are."

Wren snapped their fingers, but the professor's body didn't jerk or twitch as they'd expected it to. Instead it merely shimmered.

"Necromancy . . . Cursed thing." The ghost sounded disgusted, and Wren did the only thing they could do. They laughed. They laughed at the twisted justice of it all.

"Cursed and beautiful and so full of potential. And if you never saw that, doesn't that say more about you than it does about me?" It felt good to say this, to get it all off their chest. Even to a ghost who kept fading in and out of existence.

The ghost stilled. Tilted his head, as though he was honestly considering Wren's words. Then he nodded. "When they ask . . . hourglass."

Wren narrowed their eyes, even as pride surged through them. "What does that mean?"

But the ghost began to fade, muttering much like Castelli the poltergeist had, only a lot less audible and a lot less interesting. "Once they discover . . . an uproar."

Wren asked again, to no avail. Again, but unsuccessfully. At least their question wasn't met with further abuse. The edges of their vision began to narrow, and their head pounded. The bloody specter was right too. There would be an uproar. One of the professors of Galileo, stabbed on school grounds? Tomorrow would be a mess. And the idea that there might be a murderer at school . . .

Wren hated Galileo some days, *most* days, but they still wanted to belong here, to be *safe* here. They wanted this place to be so much better than it was.

". . . revenge . . . important," the ghost muttered.

"Who would avenge you, old man?" Wren scoffed. "Your army of intolerant lackeys, who care about nothing but appearing important? You're a relic." They smiled suddenly, the words so obvious, the relief so strong. "Perhaps I'm cursed. But you'll be forgotten. And it's what you deserve. There's no place at Galileo for *you* anymore."

Wren turned away and started to drag themself back toward the school's entrance. The ghost followed, whether by choice or by connection, Wren didn't know and didn't care. With every step they took, the specter faded further and the pain that lurked at the edges of Wren's awareness crawled closer.

Wren closed their eyes, envisioned the silver feathers floating between them and the ghost, and with a grimace they reached out—

—and severed the bond.

Pain snapped toward them. Exhaustion too.

When they opened their eyes again, Professor Dropwort's ghost was nowhere to be seen, and his body lay lifeless on the loading dock. Wren was alone. The energy around them began to dim, but Rat still chattered. Wren was worn and depleted, but the stubborn power they'd found inside themself was still there, and they would remember what it felt like. No one could take that away from them. Cursed. Lucky. And one day, extraordinary.

For now, they had a murder to report. And they had a clue—"hourglass"—but no idea what it meant. At least it was a start. Tomorrow they had to keep practicing their skills, both newfound and old.

They staggered. They retraced their steps, back to the elevator that led to the Arcana Tower. The darkness that lurked around them began to fill their vision, like spilled ink flowing across endless colors. Wren kept pushing forward, determined, but to no avail. The darkness crawled closer, and suddenly the night felt too large, too overwhelming. Wren reached out a hand to steady themself and found nothing.

They fell—

And the last thing they saw were the shadows that shifted across the ground. The sharp angles of the school, like shards of night. Clouds and shapes that looked like grotesque gargoyles' wings. And for a brief, deadly moment, a human figure amidst the darkness, crossing the dock, carrying a dagger that glistened in the moonlight.

Then the world spun away from Wren. They cradled Rat close, pulled an impenetrable, invisible barrier around them—and fainted.

<u>EVIDENCE EXHIBIT A2</u>
CASE ID: 20-06-DROS-STK

<u>Type:</u>
[X] Communication
[ ] Audio recording
[ ] Spell residue
[ ] Photo or other visual reconstruction
[ ] Object
[ ] Form or record
[ ] Other: _____

Source: Phone records
Relevant Parties: Nicolas Fornax, principal;
Ladybird ("Birdie") Beckley, vice principal;
Beatriz Ruiz-Marín, vice principal; Salbiah
Hussein, groundskeeper
Description: Text messages exchanged after
discovery of deceased

(2:41 a.m.) LB: The loading dock is secured, and
I've put in the call for SNACC-EOs

(2:41 a.m.) NF: Birdie, I just told you to lock down the area. We don't even know if we need law enforcement.

(2:42 a.m.) LB: Principal Fornax, the standard protocol for any death on campus is to contact the Bureau of Sorcerer-Neutral Anti-Conflict Conventions Enforcement. Only the enforcement officers are cleared to determine if the death was natural or

(2:42 a.m.) LB: Hold on

(2:42 a.m.) NF: That doesn't matter, we've discussed this before. I gave you an order

(2:42 a.m.) NF: I will not hold on

(2:43 a.m.) NF: What's happening?

(2:44 a.m.) NF: Answer me right now

(2:44 a.m.) LB: Stockholm PD are here

(2:45 a.m.) NF: Tell them they don't have jurisdiction, the loading docks are part of school property

(2:45 a.m.) NF: Who called them?

(2:46 a.m.) LB: Salbiah says she called them when she found the body

(2:46 a.m.) NF: Tell

(2:46 a.m.) NF: Never mind, tell them to wait for me and I'll handle them.

(2:46 a.m.) LB: It's under control

(2:47 a.m.) NF: Clearly it's not.

(2:47 a.m.) LB: Beatriz is dealing with the Stockholm PD

(2:47 a.m.) LB: I'm waiting to meet the SNACC-EOs

(2:48 a.m.) NF: No, I'll speak with the SNACC-EOs. You go make sure there aren't any students breaking curfew. I don't want any gossip about this getting out.

(2:50 a.m.) NF: That's an order, Birdie.

(2:52 a.m.) LB: Fine.

3:00 A.M.: DIEGO SAKAY, 17, COINS

BY RANDY RIBAY

[Beginning of transcript.]

<u>Vice Principal Beatriz Ruiz-Marín:</u> This interview is being conducted by Vice Principal Ladybird Beckley and myself, Vice Principal Beatriz Ruiz-Marín, and is being recorded via my own casting of the Verbatim spell. The time is . . . three a.m. We are in Vice Principal Beckley's office at Galileo Academy, currently located in Stockholm airspace. Jeff, my cat, is also present. Diego, can you please state your name for the record?

<u>Diego Sakay:</u> You just said my name.

<u>Vice Principal Ladybird Beckley:</u> Here we go.

<u>DS:</u> Does *she* need to be here?

LB: Though I know it might be unusual for you, Mr. Sakay, I would advise you to take this seriously.

DS: "Mister"? You selling me insurance?

BRM: [Sighs.] Please, Diego.

DS: Fine. Diego Protasio Reguero Sakay.

BRM: House?

DS: Coins.

BRM: Year?

DS: About to be outta here.

LB: But it remains to be seen if that will be with or without a diploma.

DS: Masimot ka.

LB: English, please.

DS: Galileo doesn't have an official language, Professor.

LB: That's "Vice Principal Beckley" to you, Mr. Sakay. And if you don't—

BRM: Diego, Vice Principal Beckley found you out of your room far past curfew, cloaked by an Invisibility spell. What were you doing?

DS: Why's this all so official? The office, the Verbatim spell, both of you grilling me like I murdered someone. Usually I get the demerit, then go back to my room and add it to my collection.

LB: The only thing that should concern you right now is answering our questions truthfully. What were you doing sneaking around past curfew?

DS: What were *you* doing sneaking around past curfew?

BRM: Diego.

DS: Fine. If you must know, I needed some fresh air.

BRM: Why?

DS: Clear my head. Everything going on with that other noise is mad stressful.

BRM: For the record, can you clarify what "that other noise" refers to?

DS: My hearing next week.

LB: Ah, yes. Your plagiarism in Professor Dropwort's class.

DS: My *alleged* plagiarism. It's bullsh—

LB: We could do without the language.

DS: Thought you wanted me to speak English?

BRM: So you went for a walk to clear your head. What time was this?

DS: A bit before midnight.

BRM: Where did you go, exactly?

DS: First I stopped by JB's real quick. Wanted to see if he'd go with me. I like to check in on the transfers, make sure they're getting on all right.

BRM: And?

DS: Nah. Said something about how tall people need more sleep.

BRM: Then?

DS: I went to see Changmin. But dude didn't want to roll with me either.

LB: There seems to be a common denominator.

DS: F—

BRM: Diego.

LB: Touch a nerve, did I?

DS: Whatever. Had nothing to do with me. He was busy updating his bird spreadsheet.

BRM: His "bird spreadsheet"?

DS: Yeah, he keeps track of, like, every single one he ever sees. Species. Color. Size.

Location. And a bunch of other details. I
don't get it, but you've got to respect the
dedication. Anyway, I ended up heading down to
the elevator bay by myself after that.

LB: How did you bypass the security
enchantments?

DS: I've got my ways.

LB: Mr. Sakay, I'd strongly advise you to—

BRM: We'll come back to that. But why the
elevator bay, Diego?

DS: To watch the school take off. It's the last
place to detach, so it's a cool view.

BRM: You know students are prohibited from all
levels below the reception hall during launch
due to the danger.

LB: He knows. He just doesn't care.

DS: True. I do it pretty much every time. It's
real nice. I put on my headphones, then sit at
the gate with my legs dangling out into the sky
as we drift away.

BRM: Okay, so you went to the elevator bay by
yourself around midnight. What did you do when
midnight passed and the school didn't leave?

DS: I was gonna ask why we're still here—
does it have something to do with why you're

disrupting my sleep to give me the third degree?

LB: Answer the question, Mr. Sakay.

DS: Rude.

BRM: [Sighs.]

DS: I was chillin'. Figured there was just some kind of mechanical issue and that we'd be on our way soon enough.

BRM: How long did you stay there?

DS: Don't remember.

LB: I don't suppose you were smoking something that might have impaired your memory? Some abracadabra perhaps?

DS: It's not a crime.

LB: Actually, it is. You're underage.

DS: Age is arbitrary when you really think about it. But whatever. I went down there to watch us leave. That's it. If I happened to be hitting a bit of abracadabra—and I didn't say I was—who cares? I didn't hurt anyone.

[Long silence.]

DS: Why'd y'all look at each other like that?

BRM: This is very important, Diego. If you had to guess, how long did you stay in the elevator bay?

DS: An hour. Maybe two. I drifted off for a bit.

BRM: And then what did you do when you woke up?

DS: Headed back toward Coins, but Beckley snatched me up before I got there. End of story. Can I go? I'm mad tired.

[Long silence.]

DS: What? Why'd y'all look at each other like that again?

LB: What are you not telling us, Mr. Sakay?

DS: Nothing.

LB: Then why are you lying?

DS: I'm not lying.

[Long silence.]

BRM: Vice Principal Beckley's Retrace spell revealed that you had not come straight from the elevators when she found you. Rather, you were on your way back from the direction of the Gargoyle Keep.

DS: Retrace? So that's how you got me despite my Invisibility spell, ha? If I'm not mistaken, in 1507, the Sorcerers' High Court ruled that Retrace wasn't admissible evidence. Something about the manipulability of its half-life making the timing unreliable.

BRM: You're not on trial, Diego.

LB: Not yet, at least.

BRM: Birdie, please.

DS: Fine. I'll admit it. I went to the Gargoyle Keep.

BRM: Why?

DS: I'd rather not say.

LB: Tell us, Mr. Sakay.

BRM: Diego, I again assure you that this is an extremely serious matter, and it's essential that you tell us the truth. Why did you go to the Gargoyle Keep after you woke up?

DS: [Mutters indistinctly.]

LB: What did you say?

DS: I said I had to cast some wizardlings into the abyss.

BRM: "Cast some wizardlings into the abyss"?

DS: Defecate. I had to defecate, all right? Like, mad suddenly. The wave was on its way to shore. I should've known better. Those vegan dinners never sit well with me. But for real, that's what went down. I fell asleep waiting for the school to shove off, woke up, then had the sudden urge to poop.

BRM: Then why go all the way to the Gargoyle Keep? It was farther than your house's tower.

DS: It's kind of a secret . . .

LB: You're not in a position to be holding secrets, Mr. Sakay.

BRM: Please, Diego.

DS: Fine. If you must know, the Gargoyle Keep has the best bathroom in the entire school. Hands down. Nice and spacious. Single toilet. Enchanted to smell like your favorite scents— for me: coconut, sampaguita, and the sea. Plus, hardly anyone knows about it, so it's always mad clean and nobody disturbs you when you're in the zone.

LB: But Retrace showed that you didn't actually enter the Keep, let alone go to the bathroom. Instead you suddenly turned around and left.

DS: True.

LB: Why?

DS: False alarm.

BRM: What do you mean?

DS: The wave settled before it reached the shore, if you catch my drift.

LB: How convenient.

DS: You're telling me.

BRM: So then you headed back to your room?

DS: Yup. That's it. So we good?

[Long silence.]

BRM: Diego—

LB: You didn't like Professor Dropwort very much, did you, Mr. Sakay?

DS: [Laughs. Laughs some more. Laughter passes. He catches his breath, then starts to laugh again.] No.

LB: Note, Beatriz, how a single syllable simmers with such hatred.

DS: Dude has treated me like aswang phlegm from the jump. Just like my kuya *and* just like my nanay when she was his student. But what's he got to do with anything?

LB: Tell us, Mr. Sakay—

DS: Wait, back up—you asked me if I "didn't" like him very much. Past tense. Something happen to Dropwort?

BRM: [Sighs.] I suppose you'll find out soon enough. . . . Professor Dropwort has passed away.

DS: For real?

LB: Stop smirking.

BRM: I'm afraid so. His body was discovered tonight near the dock.

DS: So that's why we're still in Stockholm.

BRM: Correct.

DS: Damn. What happened? Heart attack or something?

LB: Or something.

DS: You mean, like, murder?

BRM: We can't say for certain. We're still in the process of investigating.

DS: So if you're still investigating, that means a killer could be walking around Galileo *right now* and y'all haven't told anyone?

[Long silence.]

DS: Why you looking at *me* like that?

BRM: Vice Principal Beckley isn't looking at you in any way, Diego. But since you were out and about around the same time—

DS: I didn't like the dude, but I didn't kill him, Professor. That's the truth.

LB: [Coughs.]

BRM: Of course. But think carefully, Diego.
Did you happen to notice anything out of the
ordinary tonight?

LB: Or any*one*?

DS: Like what? Like who?

BRM: We don't know, Diego. Anything unusual.

DS: Hmm . . .

[Long silence.]

DS: I'm sorry, Professor. I'd help you out if I
could, but I didn't find anything.

LB: "Find anything"? Interesting choice of
words . . .

DS: Yeah, I mean . . . um . . . I didn't find
anything out of the ordinary. Like, I didn't
hear anything weird or see anyone until you
picked me up.

LB: He's lying again, Beatriz. Look at how he's
fidgeting with that ridiculous nose ring.

BRM: You do seem kind of nervous—is there
something you want to tell us?

DS: Yeah, make sure I get my rooster back.

BRM: Excuse me? Your . . . rooster?

DS: It's a Paraokan. Feathers as black as night. Big, muscular bird that looks like he skipped leg day.

LB: Mr. Sakay, can't you be serious for one moment? A man is dead. Show some respect.

DS: I am being serious, Professor. When you roll through Dropwort's place, I'm certain you'll find him.

BRM: Why do you think Professor Dropwort would have your rooster, Diego?

DS: Long story.

BRM: I'm listening.

DS: All right, so most people know about Spain and the US colonizing our islands; maybe they even know about the Japanese occupation during World War II. But the British *also* got their greedy tentacles on the Philippines from 1762 to 1764, during Britain and France's so-called Seven Years' War. We were, of course, a pawn in these petty-ass European tribal wars because—

LB: Is this going anywhere?

DS: Yeah, but first you got to know the context.

LB: We can look up the details later, Mr. Sakay. Get to the point.

DS: You can, but I doubt you will. Whatever. The relevant thing is, that's when the Dropworts first crossed paths with my ancestors. See, my great-great-great-great-great-grandlola was a babaylan. One of the most powerful in the archipelago, and one of the leaders of the resistance—first against the Spanish, and then against the British after they decided to drop by. At one point, she and her crew sank a bunch of raggedy-ass British ships to the bottom of the Albay Gulf. That's why Britain's occupation stopped at Manila. So the next day, this sunburnt, salty—literally and metaphorically—British admiral came by her barangay, pale tail tucked between his legs.

BRM: A Dropwort?

DS: Nah, but he had a Dropwort in the squad. Anyway, they came, negotiated their surrender, stayed the night, and then left early the next morning. The villagers soon realized that a bunch of their ancestral objects were missing. Real powerful ones, practically vibrating with old kulam. There was, like, a really cool enchanted kris sword, a tabo that automatically refilled, my lola's immortal rooster, and some other stuff.

BRM: How'd she know it was Professor Dropwort's ancestor that took the missing objects?

DS: Tracing magic.

LB: If she knew tracing magic, surely she could have recovered the objects easily enough.

DS: She tried, but before she could catch up to him, he enchanted and sold them.

BRM: Let me guess: one of the enchantments was Ahistorica?

DS: We call it something different, but yeah. Didn't want potential buyers to be scared away by the prospect of the original owners vengefully tracking them down someday.

LB: Assuming all this is true—a massive assumption, I must say—then why do you think we'll find your family's rooster in Professor Dropwort's quarters? Didn't you just say that ancestor sold the objects he supposedly stole?

DS: Because ever since then, my family's kept real close tabs on the Dropworts, and we've gathered enough clues to figure out that their family never sold the rooster. They've been passing it down from one generation to the next all the way down to Professor Dropwort. My kuya wasn't able to find it, so the job fell to me.

LB: Why? Does it bring good luck or fortune?

DS: Nah, nothing like that.

LB: So it's simply a really old rooster?

[Something slams against a solid surface, and there's a clattering sound.]

BRM: Everyone calm down. Diego, pick up your chair and lower your voice.

LB: Mr. Sakay, have you forgotten to whom you're speaking?

DS: I know exactly "to whom" I'm speaking!

BRM: Everyone, calm down, please. Diego, lower your voice and sit down. Ladybird, back away from Diego.

[Long silence.]

BRM: Thank you. Now, Ladybird, why don't you take a short break?

LB: This little—

BRM: I'll handle things here for a few minutes.

[A door opens, then slams.]

BRM: [Exhales.] I understand this rooster means a lot to you, Diego—for whatever reason—and I personally promise to keep an eye out for it when it comes time to pack up Dropwort's possessions and return them to his family.

DS: I appreciate that, Professor.

BRM: But now I really need you to tell me the truth.

DS: That was the truth.

BRM: I mean about what you were doing out of your room tonight.

DS: Oh. Um. I was telling the truth about that too.

BRM: Diego, Professor Dropwort is dead. I know you didn't like him—you weren't alone in that—but he was a human being. His children and grandchildren loved him and will miss him dearly. Don't they deserve justice?

[Long silence.]

BRM: And, between you and me, we do suspect murder. So until we catch the person responsible, everyone is in danger.

DS: I didn't do it.

BRM: I didn't say you did.

DS: Beckley thinks I did.

BRM: Which is one more reason to tell me the actual truth. But more important than that, anything you know might help us solve this thing without involving the Neutrals and before anyone else gets hurt.

[Long silence.]

DS: [Takes a deep breath.] Okay. Fine. The truth? I wasn't just out for the view.

BRM: Thank you, Diego. So what were you doing?

DS: I . . . was looking for Dropwort.

BRM: Why?

DS: I heard he had something sketchy going down tonight.

BRM: Who did you hear that from?

DS: Myself.

BRM: How so?

DS: The other day, I dropped by his class early, hoping I could talk some sense into him about this plagiarism thing. Prove I wrote the paper myself, you know. But when I got there, he was talking to someone.

BRM: Who?

DS: No idea. He was on the phone, finishing up a conversation. His voice was all whispery and low.

BRM: What was he saying?

DS: Didn't catch everything, but I heard him say that he'd be at the loading docks at the arranged time last night and that the other person better show up too.

BRM: That's all?

DS: Just about. He promised nobody would follow him, then said goodbye.

BRM: So, you tried to follow him?

DS: Naturally.

BRM: Hoping it might have something to do with the rooster?

DS: Maybe. Maybe not. But I was sure I'd catch him doing *something* mad sketchy. I mean, why else would he be meeting someone in the middle of the night at the loading docks right before we leave the country?

BRM: What do you think he might have been up to?

DS: Don't know. But like my lola always says, "Rotten roots, rotten fruits."

BRM: Wait—were you planning to blackmail a Galileo professor?

DS: Nah, I just thought having some potentially career-ending info about the dude might help me persuade him to drop this plagiarism business.

BRM: That's blackmail.

DS: Ah, okay. Then I guess I was.

BRM: [Sighs.] Let me guess: you asked JB and Changmin to go with you because you wanted someone to be able to confirm whatever you ended up seeing?

DS: Bingo. As you know, I'm not the most trustworthy student in the eyes of the administration. But turns out it didn't matter. Neither could roll with me anyway. It was a bust. I hung around the elevator bank for a while, but nobody showed. Then I went looking around in case I'd misheard something when I was eavesdropping on that conversation, but Beckley snatched me up before I'd covered much ground.

BRM: So you never saw the body?

DS: Nope.

BRM: And you didn't find anything?

DS: Nope.

BRM: Are you sure?

DS: I'm sure.

[Long silence.]

BRM: I appreciate that you've told me all this, Diego. But, to be honest, I can't help but

feel like there's still something you're not
telling me.

DS: Say I did know something else—and I'm not
saying I do. If I told you, then what would you
do with that info?

BRM: Pass it along to Principal Fornax, of
course.

DS: And you trust Fornax?

BRM: I do. He's the head of this institution,
after all.

DS: [Sucks his teeth.] Right. No disrespect
to you, Professor, but like many other
institutions, Galileo hasn't always proven
itself to be a paragon of justice.

BRM: We've made progress.

DS: You and I both know it'll take more than a
few years of *diversity* initiatives to repair
centuries of exploitation, Professor.

BRM: True enough. But you can trust me, Diego.

DS: For real, Professor, I'm not hiding
anything else from you. I didn't see anyone or
find anything.

BRM: [Sighs.] Very well, then. Thank you for
the information that you've provided—it will

certainly help our investigation. Hopefully we can get this resolved before anyone else is harmed. Before I call Vice Principal Beckley back in, I have one more question.

DS: Go for it.

BRM: Is there something magical about the rooster beyond its immortality?

DS: I didn't feel like telling Beckley, but yeah—it's our family's ancestral vessel.

BRM: Really?

DS: Yup.

BRM: I've never seen one in person, but to be able to summon the spirit of any of your ancestors . . . No wonder your family has spent generations tracking it down.

DS: Exactly. Imagine all the knowledge and history the colonizers cut us off from that we'll be able to recover.

BRM: I really do promise to return it if we find it among his things.

DS: Thank you.

BRM: Now let me get Vice Principal Beckley back in here.

DS: Is that really necessary?

[Door opens, then closes.]

LB: Did he confess, then?

BRM: He's not guilty, Ladybird.

DS: And I'm sitting right here, so you can—

LB: [Mutters Cone of Silence incantation.
Turns to Ruiz-Marín.] He obviously is. He was
sneaking around under an Invisibility spell
around the time the murder must have occurred.
And he has *very* strong motives. Let's wrap this
up and detain him. I'll notify the authorities
that I—I mean *we*—have solved the crime.

BRM: I admit, Diego's not our most responsible
student, but do you honestly believe he
killed Septimius over a family heirloom and a
plagiarism accusation?

LB: I do.

BRM: Well, I do not. And we're only at the
beginning of our investigation. If nothing
else, consider how it would look if it came out
that you wrongly accused a *student* of murder.

[Long silence.]

LB: Fine. But he's certainly hiding something
from us. That much is obvious. If only I could
try casting a little something . . .

BRM: I know you're not suggesting anything illegal.

LB: . . . Of course not.

BRM: Look, Birdie, we have his statement, and the school is locked down. We can always bring him back for further questioning, so let's just—

[There's a knock. The door opens. Inaudible conversation.]

BRM: Ay. I've got to run, Birdie. Can you finish up here? Give him one demerit for breaking curfew; then send him back to his room. I doubt it will do any good, knowing Diego, but cast a Stay-Put spell on his room if that'll make you feel better.

LB: Very well, Beatriz.

[The door shuts.]

LB: [Mutters the incantation to end Cone of Silence.]

DS: I hate Cone of Silence. It's mad disrespectful. And where'd Professor Ruiz-Marín go?

LB: She had a pressing matter to attend to. Now tell me, what did you say to her while I was out of the room?

DS: [Laughs.]

[Long silence.]

DS: So I'm gonna bounce too, okay?

LB: Not so fast.

DS: Can you back up? I don't appreciate you
getting up in my face like this again . . .
especially since it smells like it's been
a minute since you brushed your teeth,
Professor.

LB: *Vice Principal.*

DS: You care about that way too much.

LB: I know you're lying, Mr. Sakay. Want to
know what I think?

DS: Not really.

LB: I'm guessing that you told Professor Ruiz-
Marín a fragment of the truth. Not all of it,
but just enough to make her feel as if you
were confiding in her. I suspect that you did
indeed "find something" while sneaking about,
and that's why Retrace showed that you suddenly
turned around. I'd like to know what you found,
exactly, and why you're so determined to keep
it hidden.

DS: I don't know what you're talking about.

LB: I may not be known as the "cool" administrator like Professor Ruiz-Marín, but it would be a bad idea to continue lying to me, Mr. Sakay. I am the vice principal, after all.

DS: You're *a* vice principal. And with no due respect, Professor, that makes you a glorified cop.

[Long silence.]

LB: You know as well as I do that if you were holding on to anything you didn't want me to find, a simple Search and Seizure spell would illuminate it.

DS: And you know as well as I do that ever since 1984 it's been illegal for school officials to cast that spell on students. But besides that, you also know as well as I do that if I cast an Obscure spell before you picked me up, it would have rendered your little cop spell powerless.

[Long silence.]

LB: Very well, then. I suppose I will see you at your disciplinary hearing next week.

DS: Wait—what? But Dropwort's, you know . . . dead?

LB: Fortunately, he already filed the full report.

DS: Like I said, the plagiarism charge is garbage. Dropwort didn't even find the source text I *supposedly* copied from. Just told me the paper was "vastly beyond" my capabilities and that there's no way I could be so "eloquent." I may not turn in every assignment, but that's not because I can't do them. Ask Professor Strigid—he'll tell you. I promise you I wrote every word on that scroll. Not my problem Dropwort thought us brown kids couldn't think for ourselves just because we weren't buying the whitewashed history he was trying to sell us.

LB: Rest assured, there isn't anything about your race in his report, Mr. Sakay.

DS: Oh, okay. Cool. Definitely not racist, then.

LB: Depending on how things transpire tonight, however, it may soon be in my power to drop the charge.

DS: What do you mean?

LB: You don't need to concern yourself with that.

DS: Whatever. So I suppose you'd drop it out of the kindness of your heart?

LB: Hardly.

DS: Then what do you want?

LB: Tell me what you found, and nothing will stand between you and that diploma.

[Long silence.]

DS: I didn't find anything.

LB: This is your last chance.

[Long silence.]

LB: [Sighs.] So be it. You'll receive one demerit for breaking curfew, another for dress code violation, and—

DS: Dress code? It's the middle of the night! These are my pajam—

LB: And a third demerit for disrespect and insubordination.

DS: Cool, a hat trick. Can I go now?

LB: You may. But you are to go straight to your room and remain there for the rest of the night. I will be casting a Stay-Put spell that shall last until classes begin, so I will know if you take a single step past your doorway.

DS: Ooh, scary.

<u>LB:</u> I'll see you at your hearing next week, Mr. Sakay.

<u>DS:</u> Yeah, okay, Professor . . . gago ka.

<u>LB:</u> What was that?

<u>DS:</u> It means "Looking forward to it."

[End of transcript.]

EVIDENCE EXHIBIT GG-8

CASE ID: 20-06-DROS-STK

Type:

[ ] Communication
[ ] Audio recording
[ ] Spell residue
[ ] Photo or other visual reconstruction
[ ] Object
[X] Form or record
[ ] Other: _____

Source: GAE new-student orientation packet
Relevant Parties: n/a
Description: Partial page from student orientation packet found within suspected area-of-origin for unauthorized Decryption spell; significant fire damage

APTITUDES

Each student brings their own special magic to Galileo Academy for the Extraordinary. Maybe you can instinctively speak to the animals around you, or call music from the stars, or turn that fastball pitch into a fireball! In addition to the world-class general education GAE provides, we can help students take their aptitude to new heights. We're also happy to build your skills in different areas, if your aptitude isn't compatible with your career goals!

UNSUPERVISED SORCERY

At GAE, it's our job to help you grow—but also to keep you safe. First-years, transfers, and other students who have not yet obtained their practitioner's license are limited to the approved list of spells (see page 67) when practicing magic without the supervision of a faculty member. Unlicensed students who are found to be practicing spells not on the approved list will face disciplinary measures proportionate to the risk to themselves and others, including but not limited to detention, suspension, and expulsion.

PRACTITIONER'S LICENSE

Students are eligible to undertake the exam for their practitioner's license after one year of attendance at GAE, or earlier with the written recommendation of a senior faculty member. Exams consist of a written test and a practical demonstration, and are administered on the first Saturday and Sunday of each month. Fees are waived for

[charred end of paper]

4:00 A.M.: JAMESON "JB" BRIG, 15, COINS

BY KWAME MBALIA

Incense type: Cored stick

Associated aromas: Stormy sunrise, ozone, cayenne

Traits: Explosive, temperamental

Notes: Rare leadership smokewitches can exhibit mood swings, especially during teenage years, and will always be prone to an explosive temper

—*Excerpted from* Esther Brig's Compendium of Witching

4:52 A.M.

JB blamed the current catastrophe on his hand-me-down clothes.

Every member of the Brig family received an entirely new wardrobe on their sixteenth birthday. Custom designer jeans and polos, tailored slacks, and crisp button-ups, even sweatpants and hoodies, all in several different colors that complemented the hue of the smokewitching that had chosen them. Every single item of clothing, down to the socks, was treated with Great-Aunt Laura's Flame Impervity spell. With the Impervity spell, the wearer's chances of immolating themself and everything around them were greatly reduced. To around one percent, GiGi Laura would say, not zero, because "some fools just couldn't help themselves."

Jameson Brig, "JB" to everyone but GiGi, felt like the fool now.

He was only fifteen for seven more days. His wardrobe was waiting for him back at the Brig family compound, sitting up in GiGi's room. But his transfer acceptance to the Galileo Academy for the Extraordinary wouldn't wait for his birthday.

They'd fought over his leaving. Again. He explained it would only be for a year. Again. And Big James, his namesake, grandfather, and—until a week ago—his future mentor, ended up stomping away, clouds of navy smoke trails billowing from the cuffs of his kaftan as he slammed his office door shut, shouting that Brigs have always taught their own, and that no fancy school had accepted their witching before, why would they start now. Again.

JB sighed, glanced down at his own shirt, passed down from one of his many cousins, smudged with ash and dotted with scorched holes, cuffs that stopped somewhere around his forearms. The fifth shirt he'd ruined since he'd arrived a week ago. Big James Brig refused to give JB his wardrobe early, but, for once, it wasn't his biggest problem.

Something had gone horribly wrong with the ritual, and the crisp rectangular note that Diego had tasked him with enchanting had started sputtering sparks instead of burning. A few had singed his wrist, he'd flinched, and . . . well. He looked around in panic-tinged frustration.

Now four different magical fires burned in JB's dorm room. The area rug passed down from his grandfather, one of two family heirlooms Big James had allowed him to take, the one that should've resisted all burn damage, somehow smoldered. The anti-singe curtains his sister had snuck into his duffel, the ones he'd struggled to install on move-in day, had, inexplicably, developed scorch marks that continued to creep up the heavy purple fabric. Most of his stack of blank incense sticks blazed merrily on his desk, the blood-red flames threatening to spread to his other books and the notes from today's classes. And, if that wasn't enough to send him into a mild panic, all his pencil tips were burning.

Not the pencils. The pencil tips.

How was that even possible? Could things get any worse? At this rate the school would send him home—Big James would love that, and the thought of his grandfather's smug face sent another tremor of frustration through JB's body. Although, as another cloud of smoke rippled out of the curtains, the temptation to beg for help—any help—surged forth, even if it came from his grandfather, who would almost certainly let an *I told you so* slip into his voice.

JB glanced at the bright red stick of incense on his desk, the only one *not* burning, then looked away and gritted his teeth. No. He wasn't calling home for help. Not yet. Not until he'd exhausted all his options. Not until he figured out how to get out from under the shadow of Big James.

And then there was the note . . .

"You did the spell wrong," a gravelly voice said from the corner of his room.

JB ignored it.

"I bet it was the breath control," the voice continued. "You always mess up the breath control. Or maybe it was that juicy sneeze in the middle of the ritual? So *many* mistakes."

"Thanks, that really helps," JB muttered. He climbed out from beneath his desk—those sparks had gotten really aggressive—and began to root around in his duffel bag for the one tool that could handle the fires. The bag overturned in his haste, dumping its contents onto the floor, and he cursed under his breath, then got down and pushed aside a stool with a strange wooden incense holder—what GiGi called a censer—sitting on top of it. The upper half of the censer, carved in the shape of a bare-chested man holding a smoking pipe, reached out and tried to smack JB's hands.

"Watch it!" the censer snapped. "As if you ain't got enough stuff burning in here."

JB ignored it again, though, as usual, that didn't stop the enchanted vessel from talking.

"I swear, I'm not built for this. I'm not built for this. Big James didn't send me all this way just to burn. Now, how would that look? Hmm? Me, burned up on your first week in this flying death trap?" The censer folded its arms and shook its tiny wooden head. "The ancestors will call me seven-times-seven ways a fool."

JB found what he was looking for and pulled out the small brass douter that had been a present from his grandmother. Though it was normally used to snuff candles, she'd used her witching to perform an Extinguish spell on it. Now, as he dropped to his knees and ran the thin tool over the area rug, the douter drew in the oxygen around the burning portion and smothered the glowing cinders. JB felt a tiny bit of tension release from his shoulders. That was one problem solved, at least.

"You *can't* burn, Khep," JB said to the censer. He leaned back and rolled his shoulders, glaring at the carved man. "You're impervious to fire, magical or otherwise. It's the whole reason you're here, the *only* reason you're here, remember? You're supposed to teach me, to help me to not accidentally set anything on fire, you know, like *this*! So you can stop complaining and actually *help* me. You're the teacher, so *teach* me, or we'll both be sent home in disgrace."

He gestured at the scorched curtains as he waved the douter over them, then collapsed back onto the floor and used his grimy T-shirt to wipe sweat off his forehead. "Because I'm off to a great start," he muttered.

The censer glared back. After a few moments, it brushed a speck of ash from the interior of its carved bowl. "Fine. I ain't going back in disgrace, so listen up, and snuff out the rest of them sparks before this whole place turns into ash. This ain't no place for a smokewitch, no sir, not at all."

JB moved toward his incense stash and began to snuff each one out, and Khep cleared its throat and began to take small cubes of incense and stack them in its bowl.

"If you want to learn, you gotta start at the beginning. Great-Aunt Laura's first rule of magic—it's not the vessel but what's inside that counts. You understand?"

JB nodded. "Big James called it magical intent." Just before

JB had gotten his Galileo acceptance letter, his grandfather had been working with him on his control. "It's not the ingredients of the spell but what they represent as a whole when the preparer burns them."

"Exactly!" Khep pointed at the incense cubes. "Let's practice."

Incense type: Coil
Associated aromas: Autumn winds, forest shadows, pine
Traits: Cunning, scheming

Notes: Smokewitches show extreme levels of control and coordination but exhaust easily, and are capable of weaving several trails of witching at once

—*Excerpted from* Esther Brig's Compendium of Witching

4:05 A.M. [ONE HOUR PRIOR]

A knock on the door startled them both. JB glanced at the clock as Khep swept sparkling gray sand over the practice incense protruding from the bowl. Just after four in the morning. Who was wandering around this early? And, even more important, what did they want with him?

JB had only been aboard Galileo for a week, and in that time had managed to meet a handful of people. He tried to forget those encounters—clumsy and awkward were his best attributes in public, and talking? Making conversation? Forget about it!

"You expecting anyone?" Khep asked, smoothing the sand until it resembled a smooth pile of ash. "Maybe that cute girl you accidentally tripped on Monday?"

JB flinched, then hurriedly continued sweeping evidence of his witching out of sight.

"Okay, maybe not. What about that cute boy you elbowed in the jaw on Wednesday?"

Now the only thing burning was his ears. Why'd Big James have to send the censer with him?

Khep scratched his head, then shrugged. "Okay, neither of them. What about that gargoyle you thought was a coatrack? Think they've come to take revenge?"

"You're not helping," JB hissed as he stood. He checked himself over, then walked to the door. Whoever was outside hadn't stopped knocking. Soft, insistent raps. Someone wanted to be discreet. JB licked his lips, then opened the door slightly and peered through the crack. "Yes?"

A short figure with a hood drawn over their head extended a folded slip of paper. "This is for you," they said in a deep voice.

Something glinted beneath the hood, and JB squinted. "Diego? What are you doing? It's four in the morning!"

The hood fell back, and a short boy with light brown skin and a nose ring piercing his septum stared up with a disappointed expression. "How'd you know it was me?" he asked. JB tapped his nose, and the boy rolled his eyes. "Betrayed by bling, the Diego Sakay story."

Despite the lighthearted quip, the shorter boy shuffled from foot to foot, and his eyes kept flicking down the hall, to where the dorm exit lay. Was he in some sort of rush?

"Everything all right?" JB asked. "I thought you were watching the departure?"

He'd first met Diego a few days back when he'd had trouble

72

navigating the dorm. Diego's quick jokes and goofy behavior had been the first thing to make JB feel like coming to Galileo had been the right decision. Earlier he'd stopped by to see if JB wanted to sneak out with him to watch Galileo take off, departing Stockholm for the school's next stop. But a gargoyle messenger had just delivered the small box containing the bright red stick of incense, the message from Big James clear. *For when you realize I'm right and you're ready to come home.* He'd passed on Diego's invitation ("Us tall people need more sleep," he'd joked, dodging the answering punch) and closed the door, collapsing to the floor in frustration before reattempting to practice his witching.

Now Diego was shaking his head. "What? Oh, yeah. Well, not exactly. I need your help. I've got, like, five minutes, but can you take this and see what it says? I need to go." He shoved the note at JB, who took it and, with a raised eyebrow, unfolded it. The paper was a type of thick stationery, the kind that Big James used to burn notes to important clients across the country. Expensive. But when JB unfolded it, the only thing he saw was a curious pattern of swirls in faded black ink.

"This is incredible," JB said. He'd never seen a spell like it before. "How'd you do this?"

"I didn't. Dropwort—I mean, never mind that. Can you read it?"

JB looked up. Dropwort? That bigot? He'd run into the snooty professor exactly once, and that was enough. Dropwort had glared down at JB, sniffed, and then pulled a handkerchief out of his robes and covered his nose, muttering something about secondhand smoke, and stalked away. Jerk. It was people like him who proved Big James right, who made smokewitches keep their talents hidden and stay isolated in their own enclaves around the world.

JB was the first in his family to leave for his training. People like Dropwort wanted to make him the last. If this was his note, maybe it was better to leave it alone.

"Isn't this something the school should take care of? Give it to a teacher or something." JB held out the note, but Diego was already shaking his head furiously.

"Nuh-uh. If they find me with that, I'm in big trouble. I've already been interrogated once this morning."

JB's jaw dropped. "Interrogated? For what?"

"I don't know. Something big." Diego hesitated, as if wanting to say more. "Everyone was on edge. All I know is, it has to do with Dropwort, and I found this note with a Security spell on it in the elevator bay—"

"A Security spell?"

"—and if it's about my rooster, I'm going to war—"

"Where did the rooster come from?"

"—so if you could do this for me, that would be so clutch."

Something rustled down the hall, and Diego jumped three feet into the air. When nothing emerged from the darkness, he turned to JB and started edging away, down the corridor. "Well? Can you use your magic? To figure it out? Burn it like you did before?"

Diego was the only student who knew about JB's witching, and that was only because JB had needed help finding a fire extinguisher a few days ago and had forgotten about the douter in his panic. Honestly, anyone would have done the same after they'd set their doorknob on fire. The doorknob! He and Diego had squatted in Diego's room afterward as JB, desperate to im-press somebody after his three previous embarrassing run-ins with intelligent life (excluding himself, of course), had demonstrated how he could read one of his practice incense sticks by igniting it and deciphering the smoke. He'd even shown Diego how he could make the smoke whisper its message, or become tactile words he could trail his finger though and understand their meaning. They probably *shouldn't* have spent the next few hours gleefully coding messages that would have gotten them suspended for a decade, but Diego had been so excited. It made JB feel like he just might belong at this exclusive school.

Besides, what was magic's usefulness if it wasn't accessible to all?

But this new coded message—this was something different. Something dangerous. JB could feel it in the weight of the paper, in the swirl of the ink, trailing with an impressive flourish. This was Official, emphasis on the capital "O."

"Uh . . . ," JB said. Diego was near panting now, jittery and nervous. This must really be stressing him out. JB glanced at the note, then back up and down the hall. Maybe a little witching wouldn't hurt. Besides, Diego was, like, the only friend JB had made so far. Did he want to sour that friendship, especially when the shorter boy looked like he needed help?

"Fine," JB sighed. "I'll do it."

"Great! It might be important, way too important to hand over to the school Feds. They'll never be honest about what's inside anyway. You're the only one who can read it. Let me know, okay? Thanks!" Diego took off sprinting.

And just like that, JB was alone.

Well, almost alone.

Khep spoke before JB even turned around. "I say go for

it," he whispered excitedly. "Light it up. Let's see what sort of gossip we've got here. Oooh, the brazier back at the compound is going to ash itself when it hears about this. Uppity piece of copper thinks it's better than me just cuz it burned a few notes to the mayor. This'll fire its pan. Do it."

"Are you sure?" JB turned the note over in his hands. *Could he do it?* Diego would be impressed. So would Ivy, the cute girl he'd accidentally tripped while trying to lean nonchalantly against the wall during an orientation tour. Heck, *JB* would be impressed himself if he could pull this off.

And so he started the ritual . . .

Incense type: Powder
Associated aromas: Gale-force winds, sea coves, ginger
Traits: Patient, stubborn

Notes: Powerful smokewitches capable of maintaining high levels of witching, though spell diversity remains low

—*Excerpted from* Esther Brig's Compendium of Witching

4:55 A.M. [THE PRESENT]

JB wiped sweat from his brow and sat back in frustration. "I can't do this," he muttered. The note sat in front of him, stubbornly indecipherable.

"What? Sure you can. I won't tell." Khep looked exhausted, as much as a carved wooden figurine with only an upper torso *could* look exhausted. It pulled a T-shirt off the desk next to the stool and draped it over itself. "Let me just get some more protection."

"No, I can't keep going," JB said.

Khep slapped the sand in its bowl. "Don't get soggy on me now, kid. A minute ago you were begging me to teach you, and now you can't—"

"I mean I've never burned anything like this," JB shouted. He stood and paced his room, long lanky legs poking out of his too-short apron, his strides covering the length of the space within two steps before he pivoted and stomped to the other side. His hands clenched and unclenched, raising in the air, only to drop back to his sides. "This is why Big James wanted me to stay home. Because I can't focus. I can't remember everything I'm supposed to do. First this, then that, it's all a jumble of shouting and instructions when I start calling the smoke."

This was it. *For when you're ready to come home,* his grandfather had said—and he was right. JB didn't belong here. Even Dropwort, who didn't even know him, had shown him that. JB had done nothing but make a fool of himself all week. Diego was the only one who'd befriended him, and JB couldn't even help the guy out when he needed a favor.

He snorted in sarcastic amusement. It was almost like the note was protected by GiGi's Impervity spell. Whoever had written it must have wanted to make sure their note didn't burn. In fact . . .

JB narrowed his eyes. Lifted the crumpled note from the carpet. Ran his index finger over the swirling ink.

"What if I've been going about this all wrong?" JB asked himself.

Khep groaned from under the T-shirt. "And now he's not even making sense, ancestors *help* me! What did I do to deserve this?"

"I'm serious! What if I've been too generic with the witching?" JB got up and began to pace again. He studied the carpet as he walked. Examined the curtains. Both items were supposed to resist all but the most high-level magic. So, what if . . .

The censer peeked out from beneath the T-shirt. "I'm listening."

But JB was focused. Determined. He lifted the note to his face and inhaled, filling his lungs with oxygen, enough for both him and the cinders that lived inside him, because they both needed to breathe, to grow, to get a chance to travel and consume, him knowledge and it fuel, both trying to prevent their sparks from being extinguished.

He *had* been going about it all wrong. JB slowly began to trace along the pattern (not random patterns of ink but a symbol! magical intent!) that swirled on the weighted stationery.

Ink that wasn't *specifically* included in the note's enchanted protection. Careless, really.

Slowly, wisps of smoke rose into the air, and JB heard a message.

Dropwort . . .

Focus, JB thought.

Dropwort . . . meeting . . . tonight . . .

Focus!

Dropwort—

Meeting's set up for tonight, where we discussed.
You have until midnight to deliver the goods. If

you send it by courier, mark them with a unicorn symbol so we know they're the real deal. Either way, come alone. And just remember, if this goes sideways: the prophecy says anyone who tampers with this artifact will meet their doom at the hands of the Chosen One. This whole thing will go up in flames.

JB collapsed, the note falling from his still-smoking fingers. Khep peered down from the stool and opened and closed his mouth repeatedly. *That's interesting,* JB thought, his eyes blurring and refocusing. *The censer's finally speechless.*

Warm ash scattered on his lips, a few flakes slipping inside to fill his mouth with the taste of lukewarm racism. JB sat up and retched, then wiped his mouth with his sleeve. Suddenly the air popped around him, and sound rushed into the emptiness.

Go up in flames.

The note had been a warning, among other things. A warning *to* Dropwort. It mentioned someone powerful challenging him if he messed with something. An artifact. And that things would go up in flames if the artifact was tampered with. But that couldn't affect JB . . . could it? No. Of course not. There's no way a note would've been able to predict his actions tonight . . . right?

"Brig! Get your butt up before you burn this place down!" Khep yelled, banging his hands on his ash bowl repeatedly. "Get up, get up, get up!"

Weak from exertion, JB crawled up onto his hands and knees and looked around, then froze. Smoke billowed throughout the room! He scrambled to his desk for the douter and

79

hurriedly swept it back and forth, sucking up fragments of Dropwort's message before he suffocated. He hissed in pain as his arm scraped against a door hinge.

"What are you grinning for, you sandbag!" Khep yelled. "You almost died!"

He *was* smiling from ear to ear, wasn't he? And why not? He'd done it! He'd deciphered the note, a highly encrypted magical message; he'd heard the smoke, and hadn't burst into flames! JB laughed. He could really do this smokewitch thing!

He swept the room one more time with the douter, but a few traces of smoke escaped into the vents. JB shrugged. Maybe everyone would think someone had put foil in the microwave again.

A knock sounded on his door.

JB looked up. Diego, again? Well, at least he could give him the good news. He looked at Khep, who'd pulled the T-shirt back over itself. Coward. JB tossed the douter back into his duffel and winced as a few more trails of smoke slipped beneath the crack of the door, the message still faint in his ears.

Dropwort...

The knocking intensified. JB dusted off his hands and crossed the room.

"Hey, man, I was just—" he said, pulling open the door, then stopped, confused. It wasn't Diego.

A short girl (although everyone was short to him these days, silly growth spurt) with brown skin, freckles, and glasses smiled at him. "Hey, JB!"

"I-Ivy," JB said. "What are you—why are you—how are you doing? I mean, how can I . . ."

"Stop talking," came a muffled whisper from inside the room.

JB clapped his mouth shut and raised his eyebrows, hoping that sufficiently posed his question.

Ivy's eyes twinkled even as she handed him a hexagonal note with "DETENTION" written in blocky red letters across the top.

"Sorry," Ivy said, "but the school reported hazardous magical activity in your room." JB frowned—how the heck did they know already?—but Ivy went on. "I guess I'll see you in detention later. Beckley will be expecting us."

"Us?" JB said, taking the note.

Ivy grinned and shrugged. Wow, she was cute. "I'm the aide on call for Beckley today. So . . . see you at four p.m.?"

"Sure," JB said, and watched her slip back down the hall. He closed the door, pulled the T-shirt off a still-grumbling Khep, handed over the note ("It's a detention slip, not a love letter," the censer grumbled), and hurried over to his desk.

It was time.

He snatched up the bright red incense stick from his grandfather, the one that awaited his reply, the only magic that *apparently* wouldn't get him another detention, and he thought of the words he wanted to say. Hopefully Big James would understand.

If he didn't . . .

JB shook his head, focused, pinched the tip of the stick alight, and waved it to extinguish the flame until only a cherry-red spark smoldered at the end. The smoke billowed up, splitting, curving, outlining, until the harsh image of a face appeared. Two eyes opened, then narrowed.

Big James glared out at him.

"Yes?" the smoke-visage asked in Big James's voice. "Oh, it's you. 'Bout time. Ready to come home?"

JB leaned forward. "One year," he said firmly. "I'll see you in one year."

Big James's eyes widened; then he scowled. He glanced behind JB to where Khep sat, the T-shirt discarded, but the censer didn't say anything. Just folded its arms and raised an eyebrow. The Brig patriarch studied the room. The scorch marks. The burns. Dropwort's note, a gray crumbling pattern where the ink used to be. The detention slip JB didn't bother to hide. His grandfather then turned back to JB and—was that a hint of approval?

"One year?" the smoke finally said.

"One year." JB nodded.

Another beat of silence, then: "One year. That's it."

JB grinned, only to freeze as his grandfather continued.

"Oh, and JB?"

"Yes?"

Big James nodded. "I'll have your wardrobe airmailed to the school's next stop."

The smoke began to separate as the message ended, and JB reached for the douter. But just before the message completely disappeared, one last comment filtered through, filling JB's chest with pride and purpose, two things he'd never realized he wanted and needed until that moment.

"Show them what a Brig can do."

EVIDENCE EXHIBIT T8

CASE ID: 20-06-DROS-STK

<u>Type:</u>

[X] Communication

[ ] Audio recording

[ ] Spell residue

[ ] Photo or other visual reconstruction

[ ] Object

[ ] Form or record

[ ] Other: _____

Source: Phone records, multiple

Relevant Parties: Students, multiple (see attached list)

Description: Text messages exchanged by students in various conversations following the dispersal and circulation of the unauthorized Decryption spell

ARCANA NORTH CORNER 4TH FLOOR GROUP CHAT:

Katie: hey Claire:) can you turn your volume down? It just woke me up

Claire: what

Katie: the movie you're watching, I just heard something about a prophecy and chosen ones and doom, but it was SO LOUD Claire, it felt like it was right in my ear

Claire: um

Katie: and I know you don't mean it but it's kind of inconsiderate

Katie: also you're not supposed to smoke in the dorms and I don't really care if you smoke but can you not do it in your room

Claire: UM??? I'M NOT WATCHING ANYTHING. I literally just woke up???

Hinako: Hold on, I heard something too, but all I got was "Dropwort" and "unicorn" and "meet their doom"

Claire: EW dropwort?? WHY

Nike: Oh good, it wasn't just me! I got something about an artifact, and the Chosen One and a prophecy, and I smelled smoke too, Katie

Greta: I think I saw some smoke come through the vents, and then I heard something about a courier and a unicorn, and then "doom at the hands of the Chosen One" came through super clear.

Katie: :(were you guys watching a movie without me again

Claire: omfg Katie

Hinako: No, we all heard a voice saying random things just now, and I think some of us heard parts of the same thing

Claire: OMG

Claire: SAGA JUST TEXTED ME SHE FOUND WREN PASSED OUT IN THE ELEVATOR BAY AND BROUGHT THEM BACK TO THEIR ROOM

Nike: oh no are they okay???

Claire: YEAH. THEY JUST WOKE UP, BUT LISTEN

Claire: WREN SAID DROPWORT'S DEAD

GALILEO STUDENTS ASSOCIATION CHAT:

Hinako, treasurer: Hey, sorry this is so early, but I think you should know, there's a rumor going around that Professor Dropwort is dead

Hinako, treasurer: @Lupita @Mortimer If it's true, we should be ready to make sure there's grief counseling for the students, right?

Mortimer, president: That's ridiculous.

Mortimer, president: This is all just a prank. I'm sure it'll blow over by

Mortimer, president: hold on I'm getting a call from Birdie

Alessio, secretary: LMAAAAO DROPWORT DIED

Alessio, secretary: didn't know you could die of being a dick

Hinako, treasurer: Well, it's just a rumor right now

Alessio, secretary: nah I heard it from someone who heard it from the VPs themselves

Alessio, secretary: REST IN PISS OLD MAN

Mortimer, president: A great man has died. Alessio, if you do not show some respect, I will remove you from your position as secretary. Am I understood?

Alessio, secretary: dude

Hinako, treasurer: Then it's true?

Mortimer, president: Birdie confirmed the professor's passing.

Mortimer, president: He gave EVERYTHING to this school and its students. He personally mentored myself and my brothers and asked for nothing in return. The LEAST we can do is honor his memory.

Alessio, secretary: He refused to read aide applications from girls because he said they were too emotional

Alessio, secretary *has been removed from the chat.*

Hinako, treasurer: Mortimer, you can't do that without Lupita's approval as the student body vice president

Hinako, treasurer *has been removed from the chat.*

GSA MORTIMER-FREE ZONE CHAT:

Alessio: holyyyyy

Alessio: Mortimer's on a power trip

Hinako: He was Dropwort's aide last year, so

Hinako: Anyway, sorry Lupita, whenever you wake up, you'll have to add us back to the chat

Alessio: whatever, he's just pissed Dropwort can't write him a recommendation letter

Alessio: [DROPWORT GOT DROPPED meme]

Hinako: I mean, before we got kicked out of the chat, I was going to ask if anyone knew how he died

Alessio: with my hands around his throat

Hinako: Don't even joke about that

Alessio: right, for the SNACC officer reading all my texts right now, I super didn't do it

Hinako: Wait, so he really was murdered?

Alessio: uh

Alessio: you didn't hear it from me

Hinako: SO THERE COULD BE A MURDERER ON CAMPUS?? RIGHT NOW???

Alessio: probably not on campus? the dude was sketchy as hell, probably just caught up to him

Hinako: oh my god wait, the smoke message, what if that had something to do with it?

Alessio: you heard it too?

Hinako: my whole dorm wing did, we all got different pieces

Hinako: but it mentioned Dropwort by name, and said something about him delivering an artifact, or a Chosen One would be his doom

Hinako: and now Dropwort's dead

Alessio: so . . . who's this "chosen one"??

Hinako: and what was worth killing for?

5:00 A.M.: TAYA WINTER, 16, SWORDS & WANDS

BY DARCIE LITTLE BADGER

On a typical day, the phantom voice might have beat Taya's alarm clock. Sure, as the daughter of farmers, she was a born-and-raised morning person, but Taya didn't make a habit of waking up before sunrise. However, she'd been throwing back fruit sodas and reviewing formulas all night long, her body cradled in the fold of a grungy red beanbag chair. There was a calculus exam coming up later that morning, and—to the dismay of many first-years—magical students still had to learn math. With an exhausted groan, she completed the final practice question and closed her personal Mimic Tome, which was helpfully imitating a four-hundred-page Calc 201 textbook.

"I wish I had a memory like yours," Taya said. Allegedly, Mimic Tomes could store an infinite number of pages, although a claim like that could never be tested.

After a long yawn, Taya gazed at her twin-sized bed. She could attempt a nap before basketball practice, but her brain was humming with so many equations, it'd be difficult to fall asleep. "Have I fed you any comics?" she asked the Mimic Tome, and in response, its bland gray cover transformed into a neon-bright image of three teenagers skateboarding on a flying saucer. "Skaters vs. Aliens? I forgot I had this! Thank—"

That's when a ghostly voice hissed, "Dropwort . . . midnight . . . deliver the goods . . . remember . . . prophecy . . . who tampers . . . artifact . . . doom . . . the Chosen One."

"Gyah!" Springing upright, Taya spun three-sixty, searching for the voice's source. Although the room smelled faintly of smoke, there was no other sign of an intruder in the two-hundred-square-foot dormitory. "Who's there?" she asked, resting a hand over her thrumming heart. "Hello?"

Her questions were met by silence. She sniffed the air, disappointed to find that the smoke had completely dispersed. It seemed like answers weren't forthcoming.

Unless she uncovered them herself.

First things first: What the hell was that? A magical prank? They weren't exactly rare on school grounds; just last month, a jokester had charmed the Sword Tower's ground-floor bathroom mirrors to display images of monster faces instead of reflections. (All fun and games until somebody—not Taya, honest—screamed like a banshee and punched the mirror.) But the ghostly message had been too ominous for a joke. Plus, it was clearly intended for humorless old Dropwort.

Truthfully, Taya barely knew Galileo's illustrious professor of history and ancient civilizations, but she was aware of his reputation. During her first year at Galileo, eleven different students (and a gossiping log imp) had approached her with warnings about the man, encouraging Taya to avoid Dropwort's classes like they carried the acid-sweat plague. The imp had even joked that the deadly plant known as hemlock water dropwort had been named after his poisonous personality. Considering that there was an active whisper network dedicated to protecting first-years from Dropwort, Taya wondered why he hadn't been sacked years ago. The guy had to be blackmailing somebody, right?

Point was, the message seemed legitimate. And, more important, familiar. She'd heard those words before. . . .

"No way," Taya said, flopping back onto the beanbag and cradling the Mimic Tome. "Please show me the elder's prophecies." Wide-eyed with anticipation, she watched as the tome's cover became an off-white rectangle of paper with a handwritten title: *Dreams for Taya.*

As she flipped through the pages of that tight, precise handwriting, Taya vividly remembered the day Galileo had accepted her as a student. Almost everyone in her community had been overjoyed. Everyone but her big brother, Sam.

"You could still go somewhere else," he'd reminded her.

"Yeah, but I want Galileo. It's got the best program for art-based magic."

"Says who? Their school pamphlets? Don't be impulsive."

That one had stung. Taya, despite her tendency to charge through life, had dreamed of Galileo for years, envisioning its place in her future, her place in its classrooms. "Can't you just say 'Congratulations' like a nice person, Sam?" she'd asked.

"Congratulations, Taya!" he'd mockingly responded. "You want a gold star too?"

Taya couldn't remember whether she'd flipped him off, but she did recall accusing Sam of being jealous, and storming away in a huff toward her family's mesquite field. She'd expected solitude, since work on the farm typically ended at noon. However, a shawl-draped figure with a silver bob had been standing among the rows of trees. Taya had immediately recognized the finely wrinkled visage of Councilwoman Maria Gessup, the tribe's magical policy officer.

"Councilwoman! Um, did you hear any of that?" Taya had asked, pointing to the house where she and Sam had been fighting.

"It was hard to miss. You and your brother have powerful voices."

She'd blushed. "Sorry. Everything's an argument with him lately."

"Mm-hmm. But are you sure he's jealous?" the elder had asked. "He's always bragging about you, Taya. His magical little sister."

"Wh . . . Really?"

"Mm-hmm." She'd closed her eyes. "Taya, did I ever tell you about my sister?"

Taya wondered where the councilwoman was going with this. "Uh, no. Never."

"Once, we were inseparable. Until she met a young man—a Neutral doctor—and announced plans to marry and move to Ireland. My sister would put a whole ocean between us! And for what? Love? Her fiancé was such an annoying man! He chewed with his mouth open. He talked too loudly. He laughed at his own jokes. I only noticed flaws, flaws, flaws. It wasn't until later that I realized . . . I was being unfair, focusing on the negatives to justify my selfish desire to keep my sister at home. In the process, I drove her away. If I could change the past, I would, Taya. Someday Sam may feel the same way."

For a moment, they basked in thoughtful, companionable silence.

"I'm sorry about your sister," Taya finally said.

"Me too."

"Would you like to come inside for sweet tea?"

At that, the elder shook her head. "Another time. I have a dentist appointment in fifty minutes."

"Just came here to drop a wisdom bomb and leave, eh?"

She chuckled. "Somewhat. I also have a gift for you. A book of dreams."

"Dreams? You mean . . ."

Maria nodded. "Portents." The elder was a powerful foreshadower, gifted with dream-sight of important futures. With a gravely serious expression, Maria handed Taya a thick spiral notebook labeled *Dreams for Taya*.

"Are these about me?" she asked, flipping through page after page of handwritten prophecies. "All of these? Wow. It's a lot."

"There's no certainty in my art," Maria explained. "No future that cannot change. We sacrifice confidence for specificity. Vague prophecies are probable but mostly useless. Specific prophecies are easily recognizable but unlikely to occur." She paused, waiting for Taya to step nearer. Once they both stood in the shadow of the same mesquite, Maria continued. "I sense that there is a hero's journey in your future, a lifelong path winding through a thousand adventures."

"I'll be a hero?" Heroes of old were known to befriend spiders and wrestle monsters, among other feats. Taya stood a bit taller. If that was her future, bring it on.

"Possibly."

"When does my journey begin? And how?"

"You're asking very specific questions." Encouragingly Maria patted the spiral notebook. "I've dreamed of your futures, recorded them here. Become familiar with all my prophecies, but remember: only one will come to pass. You cannot take two first steps."

"And if I miss my chance," Taya asked, "or horribly mess up, can I still be a hero of a thousand adventures?"

"Of course," Maria smiled, shrugging. "But it won't be very likely."

In the journal, there were exactly 371 different prophecies, none longer than a paragraph. Some were written like stream-of-consciousness poetry, others were more cryptic than riddles, and one prophecy was just two words: "pink backpack."

Every couple of months, Taya read the notebook to refresh her memory . . . and she swore there was something about artifacts and doomed chosen ones near page sixty.

There! On page 57, Maria had written:

> On the day you intercept
> the warning carried on fire's breath,
> a message meant for Dead Man's ears,
> identify the artifact and
> share your discovery with them all
> lest doom follow the Chosen One.

Fire's breath. That could mean smoke! And the dead man? Dropwort, of course! After all, the poisonous hemlock water dropwort was also known as dead man's fingers. She wasn't sure what the final line referred to. Who was the Chosen One? *Her?* Somebody else? Either way, doom wasn't good, and now Taya knew how to start the hero's journey Maria had portended.

It would be easy. She just had to identify one artifact.

Closing the Mimic Tome, Taya rushed over to her sewing table on the other side of her bedroom. In her excitement, she stumbled over a laundry basket. Dirty socks, sports bras, joggers, and jerseys exploded across the floor, contaminating the piles of clean clothes she'd kinda planned to fold and hang later in the week. Some kids tackled their chores with magic, but Taya's spells were so time-consuming, it wasn't efficient to use them for daily labor. Luckily, the piece of clothing she needed wasn't crumpled on the floor. Her denim jacket hung from a copper hook on the wall. Covered in embroidered patches, the jacket resembled a fabric jigsaw puzzle.

Taya flattened it chest-up across the sewing table. Her strongest stitched spells—the largest, most intricate patches—were sewn to the back, where there was plenty of room. In contrast, she fastened casual spells to easily accessible regions. For example, a two-inch-wide embroidered pair of winged sneakers were sewn to the lower part of the right sleeve. Taya activated that patch when she needed a burst of speed. Judging by their frayed quality, the shoes had a couple more uses before the threads popped loose and all their magic leached away, causing hours of delicate work to unravel. No worries. She could embroider more. Plus, Taya wasn't hungering for swiftness at the moment, though she might eventually run through the halls. Assuming the midnight deadline in the smoke message referred to tomorrow night, she had precious little free time to find and identify the artifact. Approximately eighteen point five hours.

She supposed she could skip basketball practice at six-thirty a.m., since Coach was generally understanding of extenuating circumstances like prophecy fulfillment.

What stitched spell could help track down an unknown item? Her gaze shifted to seven cherry bomb patches sewn to her jacket. Explosions were fun in sparring matches during magical combat practice, but this would need to be a stealth mission. She passed over the bullhorn patch, which amplified her voice to the "lead singer at a death metal concert" level. Yeesh, did she have any more subtle spells? There were the door and the pair of owl eyes, both of which might prove useful later. The former let her walk through walls, and the latter heightened her eyesight in dim conditions. But Taya was otherwise out of luck. Neither the tornado down the right side of the jacket nor the burning broadsword down the left side were remotely appropriate for her current mission. Even her masterpiece, a green-eyed, snarling lioness stalking up the back of the jacket, seemed presently unhelpful, although her familiar might come in handy if the artifact was hidden on a roof or in the bestiary.

As she thought, she stroked the lioness's cheek, running her fingers across thousands of fur-like stitches, comforted by the static-spark tingle of power within the fibers.

Professor Anand, a master of textile magics (and fashion), might've had a point when he'd told her, *Taya, your spell arsenal is unbalanced. Simply put, it's all offense. Isn't there room on that jacket for a Healing spell or shield?* Thing was, Taya excelled at offense. That's why she played point guard in basketball.

For now, she'd have to improvise.

With an annoyed grunt, Taya pulled open the supply drawer

in her sewing desk. She grabbed a needle and a spool of brown thread. As she threaded the needle, she mentally pictured a Y-shaped stick. The new patch would depict a divining rod. Traditionally such rods were used for pinpointing underground water or minerals, but in the twenty-first century, skilled diviners could locate everything from missing pets to bank robbers with the elegantly simple tool. Although Taya wasn't into divination, she hoped that the symbolism would conform her magic into a spell that could locate the artifact. She'd learned that trick from Professor Anand. Magic, like art, could be interpretive, poetic, metaphorical. That's why—in Taya's completely unbiased opinion—Galileo's most badassery-capable sorcerers were the arts and humanities faculty and students. If she'd known that earlier, Taya might have picked Wands instead of Swords as her tower of residence. Unfortunately, her double major didn't come with double dorm rooms.

"Find my desire," she muttered. "Divining rod."

There'd be no time for a proper patch; the stitches went straight into her jacket. With the first pull of needle and thread, Taya connected her will to the rhythm of sewing; thread up, thread down. Needle in, needle out. The rhythm seized her heart, hastened its beats. Her hair—gathered into a sloppy black bun—crackled with static electricity, and loose strands bobbed in the air.

One hundred stitches later, she tied off the thread and inspected the Y-shaped embroidery on her sleeve. Most effective stitched spells required hours of work. The divining rod had taken seven minutes. There was a big chance that it would fail or malfunction, but at least a faulty twig couldn't cause much harm. In contrast, Taya would never try to rush a cherry bomb.

It's go time, she decided, taking a quick swig of strawberry soda. Although the can had been open for hours, its remnants still fizzed. (Magical schools had the best snacks.) With that, she slipped into the jacket and popped its collar. The move normally made Taya feel tough, but its wow factor was dampened by the rest of her outfit: cotton pajamas covered with cartoon unicorns. No time to change. At least the pajamas were comfy. Plus, they matched the rainbow sneakers she pulled on.

Concentrating, she touched her new spell. It crackled, and then Taya felt a delicate pull, as if an invisible toddler had grabbed ahold of her sleeve and was gently tugging her forward. The divining rod urged her out the door and through an empty common area. Her pals must have been studying late too, since they'd left mugs of imp-roasted coffee on the table, and every chair was dusted with cheesy popcorn crumbs. In the hall, Taya became impatient and broke into a jog, but the pull slackened. She resigned herself to a slow and steady pace, descending the Swords Tower only one step at a time.

As she stepped onto campus grounds, the pull drew her toward the administrative offices. Was that where Dropwort worked? No. He had an office in the Coins Tower; it was rumored to be decorated with rare curiosities. Allegedly even a rooster. Was she remembering that story correctly? It sounded a bit far-fetched, but Taya was currently living in a flying gyroscope school, so who was she to judge?

Suddenly all the tension on her sleeve vanished, as if the intangible thread pulling her forward had snapped. "No, no, no. Come on." Taya tapped the divining rod, urging its threads, which were now frayed with the strain of magic, to give her just a few more steps. She hoped that the lack of pull meant she was close to the artifact, not that the power was sputtering out. "Find my desire."

"Heeeey, Taya! I like those pajamas. Unicorns, nice. What's up?"

A five-foot-nine, gym-shorts-wearing, gum-chewing, gray-haired girl named Nike Noelle jogged out of the Arcana Tower and, in the blink of an eye, appeared inches in front of Taya. Dang space-skipping Sorcerer! Sometimes Taya swore that Nike used her transportation magic to cheat in games. She rarely missed a pass. Luckily, Nike was always on Taya's team.

"Shhh. Keep it down," Taya whispered, "or we'll get written up for disturbing the peace."

"I'm heading to the gym." Nike started jogging tight circles around Taya, swinging her arms vigorously. They were alone on a brick path between two admin buildings, surrounded by pink roses. "Gotta get laps in before practice. That's a legitimate reason to be outside. What about you?"

"It's a weird story," Taya said, still tapping the divining rod, desperate to salvage her half-baked plan. "Remember my notebook of prophecies?"

"Yeah. It's impressive." Last year, Taya, Nike, and several friends had met up to drink coffee and swap prophecy stories. Unsurprisingly, everyone in the group had the portended capability for greatness (or infamy, in one case).

"I heard a disembodied voice this morning," she continued. "It matched a prophecy in my book about—"

"A Chosen One?"

"Yeah! Doom and a Chosen One." Still unable to feel any pull on her sleeve, Taya glanced at the administrative offices. Perhaps the divining rod had completed its job before losing power, and the artifact was hidden in the building. "Long story short," she continued, "I need to identify an—"

"Artifact?"

"Okay. How did you know?"

Nike shrugged innocently. "I took a class in divination last year."

"Divination isn't mind reading, Nike. . . ."

"I might have heard the disembodied voice too." Well, that explained it. Taya had been worried for a second. It's hard enough to play basketball against a teleporter. A telepathic teleporter would be all but unbeatable. Thankfully, Nike still only had one godmode power.

"So you want to identify the artifact in the message?" Nike asked, and for the first time that morning, she stood still. "As in . . . the message for Dropwort?"

"Yes?"

"That seems really dangerous."

Taya stood tall in an attempt to seem convincing when she said, "I'm not scared of Dropwort."

"Oh, whoa. You haven't heard?" Nike grabbed Taya by the shoulders and squeezed them tightly. Her voice dropped to a bubble-gum-scented whisper. "Dropwort is dead. Some people think it was murder!"

"Murdered?!"

Maybe it was Taya's shock that did it. Or maybe it was Nike's touch. Whatever the case, the divining rod sparked, and the pull returned. But this time, instead of tugging politely on her sleeve, it grabbed Taya by the lapels and flung her into the air. Her body flipped around, rising, falling, as if gravity was flickering on and off. The world spun in a kaleidoscope blur of shapes and colors. The last time she'd felt so obscenely disoriented was after she'd begged Nike to teleport her across campus in order to reach class on time.

But why was this happening now? And more important, where was she going? Luckily, Nike couldn't teleport anything or anybody more than a hundred miles, and her average was usually less than five. She often complained that she couldn't drop into New York City or Tokyo on a whim. So as long as Taya reappeared on or near school grounds, everything would be—

Splash!

A millisecond after the swirl of colors coalesced into towering pines, Taya was dropped into ice-cold water. She thrashed, disoriented, reaching for Nike, but Nike wasn't there. The whole world became a murky brown, with no indication of up or down. Taya frantically kicked her legs, following the bubbles that rose up around her. Soon her head burst into chilly morning air. With sputtering coughs and snorts, Taya cleared her nasal passage, thankful that she hadn't inhaled too much water.

As she caught her breath, Taya took stock of her surroundings. She was bobbing in a picturesque lake: a dark lima-bean-shaped pool of water that was surrounded by the deep green pines of a majestic Swedish forest. The sky was a silvery blue-black, that liminal color between night's darkness and the blush of sunrise. The world seemed to be holding its breath.

"Dammit," Taya gritted out. She'd been zapped into the wilderness outside of Stockholm. *Thanks a lot, Nike.*

No, that wasn't fair. This mess had to be Taya's fault. She'd rushed a stitched spell, assuming that a malfunctioning divining rod couldn't do any harm, but the spell must have combined with Nike's transportation magic and sent Taya hurtling into the nearest lake.

All this time, the ridiculous thing had been leading her to drinking water.

"Lesson learned," she groaned, swimming toward the nearest bank. Her jacket was completely waterlogged, but she powered through the strain, unusually grateful for her month on the synchronized swimming team. Finally Taya dragged herself up a muddy bank.

If she hurried, she might get back to the city and then school grounds before her calculus test. There was just one big problem: she was lost in a freaking forest.

Heck, Taya could barely see beyond the pines bordering the lake.

Grimacing, she fished her cell out of her pocket. Water trickled from the gaps in its protective cover, and when she extracted the phone and waved it in the air, muddy drops sprayed her face. It had been charged that morning but now wouldn't turn on. Why hadn't she shelled out extra for the waterproof cover?

Because she'd rather spend her money on never-flat sodas and tennis shoes. Because she'd never expected to take a dunk in a lake. Because she always took her friends for granted, too confident that—with some of the world's most talented young sorcerers on the campus—she could sweet-talk somebody into fixing a broken machine with the snap of their fingers. Look where that mindset had gotten her: utterly unprepared, with nothing but her soggy pajamas, shoes, and jacket.

At least she was wearing an arsenal of spells.

Considering the news about Dropwort, Taya might not be alone. The forest was the perfect hideout for a violent criminal—vast and full of hiding spots. It still shocked her that a man like Dropwort could have been killed. How had that happened? When? And what did the artifact from the smoke message have to do with any of it? According to the rumor mill, he'd had sticky fingers, had permanently confiscated items from kids in his class. Perhaps Dropwort had stolen from the wrong person this time.

Taya knew one thing. The artifact she had to identify? A man had probably died for it.

She wrung out her hair, cold and uncertain.

Looking up, her neck cricking with the strain, Taya gauged the height of the nearest pine. Somebody in its upper branches could probably see for miles. But Taya wasn't a child of these forests. She'd grown up climbing squat, sturdy mesquite with gnarled branches and plenty of handholds.

Just one small, quick spell could help. A summons. It was better than dying out here where nobody would know her fate.

Taya peeled the soggy jacket off her back and held it in front of her face, staring directly into the lioness's emerald-bright eyes. This was her greatest accomplishment at Galileo, the result of a year working under the tutelage of Professor Anand. When Taya had come to Galileo, she'd only known that her stitches could burn holes through fabric and fizzle like firecracker threads. She'd learned so much since then. Now, as Taya called the lioness's name—Ketesl—her voice was carried into a realm of spirits through filaments of magic as fine as her thread, as widespread as radio waves. She could not demand the lioness's presence, though. That was not how a summons worked. Familiars chose their sorcerers, and that choice could be revoked anytime for any whim.

"Ketesl. My friend, please help me."

When Taya lowered the jacket, she made eye contact with two green flames in the darkness between trees. From the shadows crept Ketesl. She was twice the size of a worldly lioness, with fur the color of bright straw. With every step, Ketesl's muscles sent ripples of movement throughout her body; Taya was reminded of wind bending the stalks in a golden field. Fitting, since her familiar was like the wind, capable of gentleness, swiftness, and fury. Ketesl yawned, stretching like a kitten, her heavy paws—each the size of a catcher's mitt——flexing against the ground.

"I'm in trouble. Lost," Taya said. The lioness listened. Her whiskers collected dew from the heavy air. "I'd really appreciate your help. Could you climb a tree, find a road or the city, and point me in the right direction? Shouldn't be far."

Ketesl licked her lips.

"What, really? You can't wait to collect till I'm out of this forest?"

In response, the lioness turned and returned to the shadows. . . .

"Fine! Okay!" Taya held out her left hand, closing her eyes. She'd never get used to the acid-sharp sting of claws, but all spirits had their price. At least Ketesl was satisfied with a taste. As quick as a viper, the lioness pawed a razor-wire cut across Taya's palm and then lapped up the blood, as pleased as a four-hundred-pound kitten with a fresh bowl of milk.

"I should have chosen a wolf familiar," Taya said, yanking her hand back. "They'd be happy with a pat on the head."

With a high-pitched yowl of disagreement, the lioness pounced upon the nearest tree, her hind legs throwing her ten feet into the air. Bone-white claws, some still bright with Taya's blood, pierced the bark. She didn't even need branches. She simply scrabbled up the vertical trunk, and her body quickly vanished above a million slender needles. Five minutes later, a domino-tumble succession of crashes announced the return of Ketesl, who landed feetfirst in front of Taya, completely unfazed by the drop.

"That's one way to get down, kitty."

Unconcerned, Ketesl padded northwest. With no better choice, Taya followed.

"Is Galileo close?" she asked.

The lioness grunted.

"I have to get back quickly. Gah. Nike—she's my friend, the one who always wears pigtails—thinks Professor Drop-wort's been murdered!"

Ketesl indulgently picked up the pace, allowing Taya to jog. As they drew away from the lake, the forest's canopy blocked the emerging sunlight, and a thin fog swirled between the trees.

"Poor man. Like, I know he was a jerk, but murder? That's messed up. I wonder who did it."

Somewhere, the bushes rustled. A startled rabbit, maybe.

"Oh damn. What if the artifact killed him? It could be volatile. Or a weapon! Maybe that's why I need to identify the artifact. . . . Galileo could be in a lot of danger." If she hadn't already been soaking wet, Taya might have broken out in a nervous sweat.

CRACK!

Taya jumped, startled by the sudden noise, and turned in the direction of the sharp sound. Sometimes, in the bitter cold, trees snapped apart, their sap freezing, expanding, and splitting them lengthwise. That's what the noise had sounded like.

But it wasn't winter. Not even close.

Then there was another sound. Louder. Closer.

CRACK.

Pine needles showered from shaken trees, and shrubs crunched as if flattened by a giant's footsteps. A lanky, long-armed figure approached from the south, visible only as slivers of stone-gray fur in the gaps between trees. He was taller than a T. rex, with fists the size of boulders. Ketesl slunk back, her fur standing on end.

Before the school had landed over Sweden, Taya had learned about its wildlife in Introduction to Natural Magical Animals, her favorite elective course. Trolls were endemic to the region, but she hadn't expected to encounter one. They were more reclusive than bigfoots, particularly during the daytime. Most subspecies couldn't survive direct sunlight.

Taya ducked behind a tree, held her breath, and waited. She could think of a couple of reasons why a troll would be crashing around near school grounds—maybe he was sick or just territorial. Either way, he was dangerous.

So she waited, willing her heart to beat more gently, preparing to sprint toward the direction of the school as soon as she had an opening. About thirty feet away, a sapling fell with a shrill *CLICK!*

Then the footsteps stopped entirely.

"Where did you go, young lady?" the troll rumbled, his voice an auditory rockslide. "I hope you have an exceptionally good reason for wasting my time."

Wait, he could talk? And he had a British accent?

A *thud, thud, thud, crack* rang out, as if the troll had whaled on a tree until it had splintered under his fists. "I know you're here. Stop hiding."

This encounter didn't make sense. According to her intro to

magical creatures textbook, trolls reeked of smelling salts, moss, and basalt. This one didn't seem to reek of anything except locker room BO. Furthermore, trolls respected their homes: mountains, forests, and valleys. What kind of troll would obliterate a tree, even during a tantrum?

"Dammit!" the troll roared. "Where is the artifact Dropwort promised us? Why did he call the meeting off? Tell me now, courier, or I'll transform into your doppelganger and strangle you with your own hands!"

Taya gasped with sudden understanding. Her Scrying spell had led her to somebody who could identify the artifact, the person Dropwort was supposed to meet in the middle of the night. *Last* night, not tonight!

Even worse, the troll wasn't actually a troll. *I'll transform into your doppelganger,* he'd said.

He was a *shape-shifter.*

Some sorcerers danced between bodies, transforming into animals with subtle human features. But only the exceptionally powerful ones could take the form of a magical creature.

Well, at least he wasn't Dropwort's murderer. However, judging by his temper, he might want to murder her.

CRACK!

The Sorcerer, in his rage, snapped another branch off a tree.

"Okay!" Taya shouted. "Don't kill me!" He seemed to think she was Dropwort's courier, a student sent to deliver the notorious artifact. Maybe Taya could use that misunderstanding to her advantage.

There was a difference between impulsiveness and quick thinking, and Taya hoped that her plan was the latter. Stepping into view, she held up her hands and asked, "What is the artifact?"

The troll-shaped Sorcerer grimaced down at Taya, scrutinizing her unicorn pajamas. Honestly, he had no right to judge her fashion choices; he wore the biggest, most ill-fitting pair of overalls she'd ever seen. "Excuse me?" he snarled.

"Sorry for the inconvenience," Taya said, clasping her hands together so they wouldn't shake. "There was an incident last night. It . . . nearly ruined this exchange. For security, I cannot give the artifact to anyone—even you—unless they identify it first."

He gritted his slate-gray teeth. "The egg."

"Right! It's an egg. I'll grab that for you . . ." She patted her pockets, feigning surprise. "Errrrm. Don't be upset, but . . . I might have accidentally dropped the egg in the lake. Can you transform into a fish?"

"Such nerve!" he roared. "No! You won't waste my time twice!"

The shape-shifter lunged, Taya dodged, and Ketesl charged into the forest with a shrill yowl. Taya ran after her familiar, but the Sorcerer's thudding footsteps sounded close behind. She smacked her hand against the embroidered winged sneakers, and launched forward in a burst of preternatural speed. A pine toppled forward, nearly crushing her like a flyswatter.

Great news: she'd identified the artifact.

Terrible news: she might not survive to warn the others.

"If I die, Ketesl," she panted, leaping over a fallen log, "warn Galileo . . . about the egg. Tell Professor Anand . . . he's a great teacher. Tell my friends . . . and my family . . . I love them. Sam . . . him too. Love him too. Take my jacket home. Make sure that I'm buried . . . beneath a mesquite tree."

Her foot snagged on a root, and Taya tumbled. She didn't

pause to brush dirt from her scraped knees. Instead she wrapped her arm around Ketesl's bowed neck, let the cat help her stand, and then continued running. She'd never used the winged sneakers in an obstacle course as tricky as a pine forest, its uneven ground full of natural hurdles. Clearly her boost in speed came at the cost of agility. Taya ducked under a low branch, dodged a trunk, and slid down a shallow trench, the corpse of a dried-up stream. The shape-shifter's footsteps echoed her racing heartbeat. Then there was silence. Taya chanced a glance behind her, and saw nothing but trees. Before she could feel relief, Ketesl looked up, hissing.

The shape-shifter was plummeting earthward. He must have hopped into the air like Spring-Heeled Jack! A breath later, his impact on the opposite bank shook the ground and launched a cloud of debris into Taya's face, momentarily blinding her. She scrambled back and narrowly dodged his blurry, grasping hand, which was large enough to crush her ribs with a single squeeze. His thumb grazed her arm, bruising like a baseball bat.

"Got you," he said.

However, when the shape-shifter grasped for Taya a second time, Ketesl unleashed a guttural roar and pounced upon his hairy arm. She bounded from wrist to elbow to shoulder, her claws dislodging clumps of fur, and was teeth-deep in his neck before the shape-shifter could react. He cursed and swatted at the cat, but she scampered up his head and scratched at his eyes.

"Thanks, Ketesl!" Taya bounded up a bank and charged through the forest, using every thread of the winged sneakers to boost her speed. The pines began to clear; she had to be nearing the outskirts of the forest. Unfortunately, between Taya and the school's current location was a final hurdle: a twenty-foot-high sheer natural wall of rock.

Dead end.

Steely-eyed, she turned, squaring her back against the wall. Taya's right hand hovered over seven cherry bombs, and her left hand twitched beside the tornado; she was a gunslinger ready to draw. As the Sorcerer approached, trees swayed, the mist magically thickened, and birds scattered into the air with screams of displeasure. In a deep human voice, the Sorcerer taunted, "Nowhere to run."

"That's right!" she shouted. "I have a tornado, lotsa bombs, a sword that'll melt the skin off your face, and I'm done running. So leave! Me! Alone!"

A quick shriek rang out, its pitch banshee-sharp. The mist between the pine trees stirred, as if something was approaching with great speed, but there were no cracking leaves or snapping twigs. Only the silhouette of a floating body sailing closer. The shape-shifter had taken another form.

"Bring it!" Taya shouted, plucking a sizzling bomb from the patch over her heart. Against her body, a million stitches hummed with power. Years of preparation, all for this moment. At her side, the lioness waited, and Taya reared back for the throw of her life.

The mist parted around a ghoulish floating head with a wide mouth of fishhook teeth. Its howl vibrated through her bones, her eyes, and her scalp. The sound plucked at Taya's body like a thousand needly fingers pinching her. Hissing with pain, Taya chucked the bomb and covered her ears; an explosion of fire and heat burst against the shape-shifter's cheek.

With a warbling screech, her bodiless attacker spun in the air and retreated back into the fog.

"The next one's going into your mouth!" she bluffed, rubbing tears from her eyes. "No more warning shots! You think a banshee wraith can fly in a tornado?"

She squinted at the vague silhouette in the forest. Was it shifting, changing? Growing arms and legs? Or were her eyes—still burning—merely playing tricks?

No. The mist-veiled shape-shifter was now a tall man in a black wool suit; his lower face was hidden behind a checkered scarf, and the size, shape, and color of his eyes changed fluidly, constantly shifting, as if demonstrating his power to be anyone. Taya could never have picked him out of a lineup. The Sorcerer took a step forward. His movement seemed hesitant. He stopped, swaying. Considering. She'd hurt him, if only superficially. Hopefully, that would be enough motivation for the Sorcerer to cut his losses and leave her the hell alone.

"Tell Dropwort," he said, "that he will pay dearly for this failure. He was once a fine smuggler. How did it come to this? An egg in a lake and a courier in pajamas."

Dropwort . . . a smuggler? Taya bit back a gasp.

Shaking his head with bitter disappointment, the shape-shifter transformed into a stag and fled into the forest. Soon the birds began to sing again.

Taya finally let out a breath. "Is he gone?" she whispered. "Is he really gone?"

Ketesl's tail twitched slightly. With that, she prowled around the rock face. Her relaxed movements suggested that the Sorcerer was no longer a threat, so Taya shoved the inactivated cherry bomb into her pocket, where it promptly unraveled into a mess of red, black, white, and yellow threads. Then she followed her familiar.

"Let's hustle," she said. She had to warn everyone about this artifact, the egg—whatever that was. And the bizarre revelation that Dropwort was a smuggler! Was that related to his rumored murder?

Suddenly a ding rang out. "My phone!" Taya pulled it out of her pocket, delighted to see its screen glow. "It's alive!" She could contact Nike and ask for a quick teleport home, no need to hitchhike or puzzle out public transportation in Stockholm. With a swipe, she scrolled through several message bubbles.

Nike (5:21 a.m.): WHATS UP

Nike (5:30 a.m.): TAYA WHERED YOU GO

Nike (5:34 a.m.): IM SO WORRIED

Nike (5:40 a.m.): DUDE WTF

Nike (5:51 a.m.): IM TELLING COACH U NEED HELP

No! Not good! Taya fired off the quickest text she could muster.

Taya (5:54 a.m.): im ok

"We made it, Ketesl," she sighed. "Thank you."
Her familiar became momentarily translucent, a lioness

spun out of sunbeams. Then Ketesl vanished, returning to her home among spirits.

Nike (5:55 a.m.): WHAT HAPPENED??

Taya (5:56 a.m.): Explain soon. Prophecy fulfilled. Sending coordinates. Pls come get me.

Nike (5:56 a.m.): On my way!

Taya (5:57 a.m.): Thank you! Dude I think the artifact is an EGG

Taya (5:57): It may be dangerous. Need to warn EVERYONE!

Nike (5:58 a.m.): AGREED

Taya sat down and wrapped her arms around her folded unicorn-clad legs, waiting. A final ding chimed.

Nike (5:59 a.m.): Are you really OK?

Taya's thumb hovered over her phone. Was she? Was anyone? With Dropwort murdered, her school at risk, wounds to heal, a thousand adventures in the future, and a calculus test at nine, Taya had a few doubts.

However, she responded:

Taya (6:00 a.m.): Yes <3

CASE ID: 20-06-DROS-STK

Type:
[X] Communication
[ ] Audio recording
[ ] Spell residue
[ ] Photo or other visual reconstruction
[ ] Object
[ ] Form or record
[ ] Other: _____

Source: Email records of Nicolas Fornax
Relevant Parties: Nicolas Fornax, principal; Mortimer Plunk III, Esq.; Mortimer Plunk IV, student; Ladybird ("Birdie") Beckley, vice principal
Description: Email exchange concerning Stockholm Neutral police detention of a student

From: Mortimer Plunk III, Esq. (plunk@plunkandhyde.law)
To: Nicolas Fornax (nicolas.fornax@galileo.extra)
Subject: Mortimer

Fornax, do you want to tell me why the hell I woke up to a 3 a.m. call from my son, *your* student, from a Stockholm police station? Since when do you allow Neutral police to detain Sorcerer students? And over the apparent murder of one of the few respectable faculty GAE had left? I'm beginning to question if my donations are being put to the best use at this circus you seem to be running. And don't you dare try to call me with some mealymouthed excuse—I want your replies in writing for my records.

———
MP, III
Plunk & Hyde Law Group
With Us, You're in Elite Company
Note: I will be on holiday in Reykjavik from June 20 to July 15 and unable to respond to email.

From: Nicolas Fornax (nicolas.fornax@galileo.extra)
To: Mortimer Plunk III, Esq. (plunk@plunkandhyde.law)
Subject: re: Mortimer

Mr. Plunk,

I want to assure you that GAE's staff is doing everything they can to manage a difficult and sensitive situation.

Unfortunately, due to the incident with Professor Dropwort, the Stockholm Neutral police force have set up a checkpoint outside the school's entrance to detain and question anyone who leaves school property. We will be advising all students to stay on campus for the time being, and staff are posted before the checkpoint to intercept them. Mortimer disregarded our staff's instructions and attempted to leave school grounds. He was briefly questioned by the police before our student advocate, Kevin Vaughan-Crabtree, intervened and returned him to campus. Given his time as Professor Dropwort's student aide, he may be additionally questioned by SNACC Enforcement Officers, but only under the supervision of Mr. Vaughan-Crabtree.

Please let me know if you have any further questions.

Best,

—————————

Nicolas Fornax
Principal of Galileo Academy for the Extraordinary
SNACC-Education Advisory Board Chair, Social Ethics
School Network President, 2013 Educator of the Year,
2003 Forces Obscura 30 Under 30 Honoree, 2019 Open
Paths Award Recipient
"What you are will show in what you do."
—Thomas Edison

From: Mortimer Plunk III, Esq. (plunk@plunkandhyde.law)
To: Nicolas Fornax (nicolas.fornax@galileo.extra)
Subject: re: Mortimer

| he may be additionally questioned by SNACC
Enforcement Officers

He damn well better not be, or you'll be selling GAE for
parts when my lawyers are done with you.

Furthermore, even if it wasn't a gross violation of
Mortimer's freedoms to restrict him to campus, you're
telling me your entire staff couldn't keep one sixteen-
year-old inside for a few hours? Disgraceful. The board
will hear about this.

———

MP, III
Plunk & Hyde Law Group
With Us, You're in Elite Company

From: Nicolas Fornax (nicolas.fornax@galileo.extra)
To: Ladybird Beckley (ladybird.beckley@galileo.extra)
Subject: Fwd: re: Mortimer

Birdie

Fix it

6:00 A.M.: KETURAH AUSTIN, 18, WANDS & SWORDS

BY CAM MONTGOMERY

It began as a tremble of silk across the right side of her face.

Dropwort . . . meeting . . . tonight—

The prophecy . . . artifact . . . will *meet their doom . . .*

Keturah startled awake in the least attractive way possible. Her silk bonnet had come off, her locs were askew, and one of her fifty facial piercings had snagged on her top sheet.

It took some time to put everything back in order—bonnet tucked under her pillow, lip ring detached from bedsheets, goddess locs doing . . . whatever they wanted, which was typical and not something she could fight. Not with hair as long and thick as hers.

Bring this artifact . . .

There.

There it was again. What *was* that?

A tickle across the right side of her face that swam into her ear.

. . . artifact.

On occasion, Keturah liked to imagine that the blotches across her umber skin were trying to communicate with her. Sort of a tap on the shoulder. Like somehow the vitiligo could act as a sixth sense or something. A seventh, eighth, or even ninth, technically, what with all the magic she'd learned here. It wasn't true, but it wasn't out of the realm of possibility.

Maybe that sense was trying to alert her now.

Midnight.

It sounded like black keys on a piano, pausing and then beginning again, and pausing once more. It sounded like ice that'd sat in the back of a dark freezer for too long. It sounded like a heavy, densely weighted smoke.

A text hit her phone, and with a clumsy swipe of her thumb, she squinty-eyed the message from her suitemate, Heather.

> bruh! are u up? i'm hearing some mess about dropwort rn. it's wild. somebody went all Jason vorhees on him text me when youre up. 😬

And that wasn't even the first text on her phone. There were half a dozen from her circle of friends. One from a number that wasn't even saved in her contacts. All of them said some semblance of the same thing. Dropwort was on a permanent TKO.

She exhaled. "What in the hell?"

Artifact . . .

This smoke thing again.

It made her think of Gaia witches and their Questing moment.

The Questing was the thing she'd come here to Galileo Academy searching for. That pivotal moment in a witch's life that changed her, gave her purpose. And Keturah had hoped against all hope that being here at this academy might jump-start her own Questing moment—her path as a Gaia witch and her eventual ascent to high priestess, as her Vovó, the current high priestess (not just in her small Louisiana parish but in *all* of New Orleans), had foretold.

Any Quest given to a witch of her people demanded that they hunt down and obtain an object—some unspecified object, because nothing could ever be easy—that had some value to the Gaia. An object that would help the Gaia help this earth. Completing a Quest was the way a witch fated for priestess-hood made a mark in her people's culture.

Because their Quests were inherently tied to their ancestors, to a chaotic and pivotal history, some Gaia witches completed their Quest and felt a *literal* removal, a decimation of their generational trauma. The trauma that clung to Gaia from past lives, from multiple incarnations.

Other witches failed their Quests, carried that strain through their lives, and passed it on.

She'd heard rumors, whispered by her cousins and aunts, that an incomplete Quest would cause a small piece of your soul to wilt.

Ma had never confirmed or denied when Keturah had asked about the rumor's validity, but it was clear: failing a Quest had critical, world-bending repercussions.

Was this it?

She shook her head once, twice, a third time. But the smoke stuck close to her eardrums.

this artifact . . . midnight . . . will *meet their doom*
the prophecy—

. . . the Chosen One

. . . the Chosen One—

flames.

She'd been taught that when you weren't certain about a decision, you asked the ancestors for help. And so that was what Keturah did now. She'd taken a few minutes and made prayer jars full of sand that she kept on hand, noting how it felt odd in her hands; just a little warmer than usual. She used a ball-peen hammer to smash several bits of quartz into smithereens. Added them to the jar.

And, as a last resort, she swallowed her requisite handful of Wellbutrin.

In the words of Nike: *Just do it.*

She was up now, after all that, had pretty much launched herself out of bed, and was moving about her small room with slightly more finesse than was usual for her at this hour. The whispered message behind the smoke was something that scared her and thrilled her in equal measure.

What kind of magic user would hurt someone for . . . an artifact? Who could possibly do that? And how had they possibly been anywhere near Galileo?

It all made her think of Ma and how she sometimes spoke about her own Questing moment. She had been wary too.

Vovó would have told Keturah the smoke whisper was a kiss. Welcome, subtle, the beginning of something more.

And those were things her Vovó would urge her to follow.

Oh, gods. This was *exactly* the kind of thing that would be the beginning of her Questing. Because she felt Vo in all this. The smoke was a facet of nature, was exactly the kind of thing her people used to bless newborn babies, build up couplings and throuplings . . . give a boost to shitty SAT scores.

The smoke was the ticket. She'd *never* felt anything like it.

And, the thing was, hearing Dropwort's name in any kind of vision, message, or whisper was *obviously* something to listen to. Especially with the word going around school.

But how dope would it be if she were the one to find out the truth about the whispers—both on her phone and in the smoke?

She was unnerved—*but only just a little bit*—by the fact that her Questing was tied to Dropwort. To someone who'd possibly been murdered. In life, the man had been this messy, absolute butchery of a human.

In death, he was the same. And she wanted nothing to do with that. She loved true-crime podcasts just as much as anyone else, but this was something else entirely.

Then again, it wouldn't stop her from rising to the occasion.

Another notification hit her phone. This time, it was a DM on IG.

> GWORL! YOU HEARD ABOUT DROPWORT DROPPING DEAD?????

There was so much pinging and vibrating from that stupid device, she wished she'd paid better attention in her Technopathy class. What she wouldn't give to never need the thing at all. Instead she silenced it. Calls, texts, social media, emails. All silent so that she could breathe for a second.

She stretched her arms above her head, felt the pull on the

muscles in her back, inhaled, held it, exhaled. Keturah had really hoped it would center her.

It did not.

She was inclined to follow the smoke, even knowing that if her texts were anything to go by, there was likely an actual, literal, more-than-technically-speaking *murderer on the loose, hello!* Keturah felt like she was about to be that horror flick stereotype: follows the voices, too dumb to live.

But if she didn't? If she played it safe and kept her Black behind in the dormitory and continued counting those sheep like a good little witch . . . The alternative fate was unthinkable.

Still, Keturah hesitated. There was the small fact that she'd broken one too many rules of late, and wandering around campus grounds after curfew could be the final straw that would land her in the counselor's office. She'd had three strikes already. Three strikes that had led to three detentions.

The first one had happened when they'd docked in Tokyo. Keturah; her suitemate, Heather; a few kids from Wands; and a handful of wild cards had snuck out to go exploring. When they'd returned, they'd found a host of professors waiting for them.

The second had been when she'd told Professor Ramesh that his tie reminded her of her auntie Cheyenne with the loud mouth. Then she had mixed an ink potion and *accidentally* spilled it on his loudmouthed neck rope.

She'd been told she had to write an essay on respecting the use of magic *and* respecting people's property and *also* respecting one's professors enough to not call them by their first names. Instead of writing the essay, she'd snuck into her favorite dance room and written *I did you a favor* all over one of the

124

mirrored walls. It had made for great selfies, and the Sharpie had come right off after. But that had been strike number three and Ramesh had made her clean it off herself.

Keturah wasn't much of a follower, and since she'd been studying at Galileo, she'd learned that following was the foundation to a lot of this kind of learning. It required her to, essentially, rewire her I'm-Southern-and-mouthy brain into something else.

Assimilation. And that burned her but good. It was a colonization of her Sass Mouth and everything else about her upbringing.

It was why so many of these rules were difficult for her.

Still, Professor Ram had offered her a fourth chance to get her game together. The head of Wands was such a vibe. The coolest of cool old dudes, even if Keturah gave him crap sometimes. Stylish to the effect of thick horn-rimmed glasses, pants that were maybe a little too tight, ties with explosive yet delicate designs that Keturah had seen *actually* moving. Except that one tie. All the others were like a symphony of fabric. Professor Ramesh Anand was That Guy. It would suck to let him down again, almost as much as it'd suck to lose her magic privileges.

Because they'd bind her. For a week, they'd said. Which would pretty effectively put Keturah behind the rest of her Music & Movement Conjuration class in a way that would make it ridiculously difficult to catch up. And it wasn't that she had to be the best in her class. But she, like, *needed* to be the best.

There was never a time when she didn't hear her mother's words in her ears. *Twice as good, babygirl, for half as much. You remember that now.* Whenever Ma said this, she would grip

Keturah's arm tightly, as though she could press and bind the words right into her skin.

Okay, focus. Artifact, artifact, artifact.

An artifact could be *anything* in this giant Howl's Moving Education System. But knowing that this Quest was meant for her, that this was a piece of prophecy her Vo had seen, the artifact was likely to be something of value to the Gaia.

A stone, a gem, a feather or leaf, even a skeleton's tooth if she were that freaking unlucky. Anything that might stem from nature, from the earth, from life or even death.

But before she went searching for it, she had to get dressed.

She picked up the bone tusk off her desk, whispered over it, and then pushed the thing back through her septum. Recklessly donned a pair of probably-gonna-get-her-in-trouble hole-in-the-knee jeans she couldn't remember throwing into that particular corner. A crewneck with the school's logo blazed across the front. She actually liked those for more than their comfort and convenience.

The logo was dope.

Back home, she might have weaponed up with a little more than her blessed statement jewelry and some gold links in the loc'd strands of her hair. She might have thrown a black dagger or two into her chest holster, an ode to all the greats. She might have used some forbidden magic of the Chosen Ones. But she needed to play it cool—stay out of trouble.

Keturah stood on the threshold of her dorm room. The floors were wooden. Most of the flooring here was.

Kneeling, she formed a fist and pressed her knuckles into the ground. The second the carnelian ring on her middle and index fingers touched the wood, her intention became clear.

That was the best part of being Gaia—nature was inescapable. *Everywhere* and in *everything*. And the wood that had once belonged to great trees from thousands of different places on earth over the course of just as many years showed her flickers. Not quite a vision, but enough visual flashes in the back of her eyes that she knew exactly where she needed to go first.

The docks. She saw the docks.

Leaving the residential floors was the work of a moment. And even though the anxiety of knowing full well she was breaking *yet another* rule was heavy in her stomach, still—this was the easy part. Because if this artifact was as important as the whispers made it seem, as her Quest made it seem—then there was a more-than-decent chance Dropwort had been killed *because of it.*

What *thing* could be so important?

It had to be all tied together. The artifact, the murder, her Quest. The feeling in her gut told her so.

Past the ornate wall decor, the gilded balustrades and the probably-real-gold ginormous picture frames featuring the greats of Galileo.

This had to be a quick and careful exploration. Quick because the rest of the school would be waking soon. Careful because, with the crackdown of professors and security catching students where they shouldn't be, detention assignments were being handed out like on-sale candy the day after Halloween.

But she had to find the artifact. And with all the magic of the Gaia, she would. Because she had to prove 'em all wrong back home, had to show all her cousins who'd been so sure they were going to be the next high priestess when Vo was gone, that this was hers. Her birthright. Her claim to that title.

The *baddest witch.*

With a shake of her head to clear the thoughts the way she used to clear her Etch a Sketch, Keturah exhaled. Reminding herself once more about the message she'd picked up. About the smoke whisper.

Dropwort . . . artifact . . . Meeting . . . tonight.

There was a good chance that taking the elevators down to the main entrance, alone, at that hour, would gain her a great deal of unwanted attention. From both staff and the potential John Wayne Gacy cosplayer lurking about school. Still, it was the quickest way. As she crept down the hallway toward the elevator, she very nearly stumbled into a couple of SNACCs and two professors she knew from Arcana. She pressed herself against one of the shadowed concrete columns that were found all over campus.

". . . student accessing the lower entrance will be stopped and detained for questioning."

"I understand the SNACC policy, but we believe the teachers here need to have some involvement in this. By all means, please do halt any student you find coming or going through here. But a professor *will* be present at questioning."

Sweet chocolate Christ, what in the world . . .

They were detaining students who came through here? *Detaining?*

Which meant . . . stairs it was. And there were a lot of them. Why were there so many of them? A StairMaster on steroids and a twenty-ounce Red Bull would have been kinder to her heart rate.

But she made it. And she didn't have a single second of

hesitation. None of that sweaty-pits, dry-throat, trembling-stomach business.

Keturah was relatively levelheaded to begin with. Her mother hated it. Called her "careless." Vovó called her "careful with her emotions." She liked that one better.

Vo always knew the right words. Except for when the right words were the ones Keturah wasn't trying to hear. Ones like, "To truly love this earth, you must acknowledge and respect every soul that feeds it."

Like, okay, fine. Everyone had value. Except fans of Oasis, right?

Still, people always listened to her grandmother. She was the kind of Afro-Brazilian woman who demanded that the world stop its breath the moment she opened her mouth to breathe words into it herself.

Keturah wanted to be that kind of person. She *would* be. Want it or not, she would.

She arrived at the main entrance, and just as she was about to—

Keturah laughed.

She'd recognize those French braids anywhere. Taya was walking at a pretty fast but measured clip, hands held slightly away from her body as though trying to protect an injury. Her badass punk jacket, pins and clips and patches oozing with magic, stood out even in the dim morning light. She looked . . . pissed? Like, truly heated about something as she grumbled to Nike, a friend of hers Keturah had met only recently, about "adults and their eggs," whatever the heck that was supposed to mean.

Nike, on the other hand, seemed focused on what Taya was saying.

Where were they even coming from? Because clearly Keturah wasn't the only student up and about and getting into something kinda grimy. There weren't a lot of places Taya *could* have just come from. Not in that direction.

The docks, maybe. Which was where Keturah herself was headed.

The image of the docks flickered in her head again. Barely clear now, but she could swear she *felt* the docks pulling her. Professor Vaughan-Crabtree—whose Black Girl Magic magic was different from Keturah's, but it still spoke to her, and solidarity was everything—would have pushed her to follow that feeling whether she was comfortable or not.

With a quick glance at her watch, Keturah breathed a single, centering breath, refocused, and kept going.

As she started toward the docks, she realized the area was cordoned off. Yellow tape and red cones and what she thought might be a flare sitting used up and lifeless on the ground.

Getting in there, behind the tape . . . she knew that was unwise. Hours and hours of *The First 48* had taught her that.

She grabbed the necklace containing her scrying stone, which sat warmly against her sternum, held it away from her body, and cleared her mind of everything but the smoke whispers.

She stopped thinking about how much studying she'd need to do for Precision Telekinetics, stopped worrying about her sisters back home, stopped thinking about breakfast and her bed and all the sleep she'd missed and Teyana Taylor's abs and—

Gods, there it was.

Another path to the docks. Just ahead of her and to the right was a cobblestone alleyway between two structures that looked like oversized gardening sheds that had long ago waved their white flag to the devils crawling all over it. Less scenic for sure, not as dressed up as the rest of the school, but also lacking all the yellow tape. She didn't come here much. Once, maybe, on one of her excursions off campus.

Her raw quartz crystal sang and pulled the chain of her necklace taut. Right in the direction she needed to be going.

Here, where the docks were, it was colder. The air felt somehow both dry and wet, which might have a little to do with the fact that this area of the school saw more action from the outside world than any other part of it.

Or maybe the loading docks and all the stairs and smooth ramps and such were just meant to be that way. For *aesthetic* purposes. This school was extra on every level.

She was cataloging the surrounding area when her booted feet scuffed across something. A shiver ran up her leg and into her bones like ice.

Was that . . . sand?

On bended knee, Keturah pulled her sleeve back, closed her eyes, and carefully waved her hand over the sand. It lifted and whirled, like the world's tiniest tornado, almost pretty in its burnt-orange hue. She'd learned to do this fairly early on, when she'd first come to GAE. To move the earth's inherent energy. Hand below the dancing sand now, she released it, and a small palmful settled in her hand the way honey would trundle off a ladle and back into its jar.

Oh, this was interesting. The moment it touched her hand, it just . . . yeah, wow.

As a Gaia witch, Keturah's power lay in her ability to work the roots, to know the earth and connect with it. To preserve it and protect it from the headlong death the planet was tumbling toward. To know which pieces and parts of the earth could help people. And which parts could hurt. Sometimes she even manipulated them herself—crystals in jars full of sand, rotting tree roots, weeds growing in unusual places at the front of a dilapidated house—into what she needed them to be for her own purposes.

This sand was . . . not *any* of that. It was nothing like the sand she'd used not long ago in her dorm. This sand was coated in earth magic she'd never seen.

This sand felt, deep in her marrow, like swollen skin—

Rusted

Red

Breath

Dew

Wild

A riot.

This magic was a quiet undoing that made her feel as though she were going to cry.

The last time she'd felt like this . . . The last time she'd felt like this, Dropwort had been trying to institute a new policy about uniforms, and he'd yelled about it to such an extent that most of the staff had pushed back in a very public way.

Skirts no more than four inches above the knee. Necklines of tees no more than two inches below the collarbones.

She'd drawn the line on him shouting about "boy clothes" and "girl clothes." Clothing was not binary.

Of course, he'd only twisted their words, made them into something that wasn't being said, and had done it all while trying to make himself look like the hero.

The hero of what? Decrying religious garb as indecent? Offensive?

He'd used the term "segregation" to talk about how religious and cultural clothing pushed the students of Galileo apart instead of unifying them.

That was the last time Keturah had felt this kind of unnamable, too-big, hooked-up-to-a-power-saw's-battery kind of emotion. She'd gone wordless and felt the frustrated sting of tears in the backs of her eyes.

He'd been a stain on her school. And Galileo Academy was very much hers.

Keturah's whole opinion on the rumor of Dropwort's death was this: *So whaaat, man??* So what if ole Septi might have bit the dust? Oh flippin' well. Keturah ascribed to the major philosophy of "Don't start nothin', won't be nothin'."

Septimius Drops-his-pants had a very bad habit of starting things unnecessarily, unfairly, and—worst of all—annoyingly.

Vo's voice struck hard and fast in her head. *To truly love this earth, you must acknowledge and respect every soul that feeds it.*

Every soul that feeds it.

Bodies that died became the earth, no matter how they were cremated or buried. They always returned. They always fed the earth. They always gave something back, even if in life, all they did was take.

Keturah hated that. Hated it so much. She didn't want to admit that this man gave value to anyone or anything. She didn't want to admit the severity of a life lost. To admit that this death had meaning.

But a person's life had been lost.

Which was scary to her on a level that her bravery couldn't quite combat.

And that life would feed this earth that she and her people protected. *That* was big and important too.

Vo had been trying to teach her that lesson for years. Had been pleading with her to understand that any high-priestess-to-be would know this and understand it.

Soul-deep.

Soul-deep, where Keturah took in the truth of this situation.

On a whim, with her chest burning, she pulled out her phone, snapped a picture of the sand, and sent it to Vo with the words: Ashes to ashes.

Vovó wrote back immediately. Dust to side chicks.

Keturah held in her laughter, feeling a sharp pang of home-sickness. She quickly wrote a text back: Eu te amo, Vo

> Eu sei, minha luz

Keturah squeezed the magic earth in her palm so tightly that it hurt. She shut her eyes so firmly that she imagined she might disappear into herself.

The tainted magic came to her in a rush that blew her locs back off her neck.

There was no way *this* was the thing her Quest was leading her to. No way.

Keturah wrenched her eyes open.

Oh.

She knew. She knew where she was meant to go. Oh, gods. She knew where she needed to go next.

Keturah turned, hand still full of sand, and found a line of it at her feet, a trail leading her away from the docks, around the way she'd come in.

The vibrancy behind the sand changed. It was like having a claw reach into your chest, slowly wrap itself around your lungs. And tug.

She broke into a run, following the sand trail with her eyes but feeling a pull from within her chest. The air she drew in was sharp and biting, her lungs screaming, her calves beginning to burn as she pushed herself to run faster.

Then, with a stuttering halt to her steps that almost had her biting the dust, Keturah went still.

She heard something. She swiveled her head slowly, eyes scanning. Gods, if she was caught . . .

She had to be more careful.

She came back up the stairs at the north side of the Arcana Tower, careful not to step in the sand trail, and smelled the pastry cooking in the kitchens somewhere off to the right of her position. Her stomach rumbled, cursing her out for not having eaten last night. Shoot.

There were two sets of stairs leading to the Cups Tower, and Keturah followed the set on the right in hopes that some divine being who looked like Beyoncé would swoop down from the kitchen heavens and deliver a raspberry creme pastry.

No such luck, though. She pushed out of the Cups Tower, through a set of glass doors, and into the labs.

Everything was dark here, but the sand trail was hard to miss. It smelled a little like formaldehyde, but also, disturbingly, a little bit like burning sugar, and also her favorite flower—sunflowers. Sweet death. It smelled like a sweet, sugary death.

The exit on the back side of the labs was a difficult door to move. It seemed airlocked somehow, and only slid open after she swore and cursed and threatened to take its mother back to Ikea or something.

And there. There it was.

The Gargoyle Keep.

She let go of the sand the second she stepped through the short wrought-iron gate surrounding the Keep's small garden. But the moment she looked down and noticed that the trail she'd been following had stopped, she also realized its color had changed. It had gone from rusted orange to this. To white.

"The color of death," she whispered.

And the burst of energy, the immediacy—that had all changed too. Her body felt cold, especially the palm she had been holding the sand in.

Kneeling once more, she pressed her carnelian-ringed fist to the ground and concentrated.

The flickers she got here weren't nearly as clear as the ones she'd seen while kneeling on her room's threshold. But they were clear enough.

Dropwort had died *here.*

At the docks, she'd felt energy in the sand. She'd felt . . . well, not vitality. But she'd felt life. And as she thought about it, holding that sand felt like being . . . pushed backward? A tugging in her chest, like someone had just given her a great shove.

Moved, she thought. Dropwort's body had to have been moved! From point A to point B.

And Keturah had found point B first, at the docks.

Her head craned up, taking in the dark, monstrous building with its higher-than-God brick walls and turrets. A dark flag with a blue gargoyle on it waved at her as it danced in the wind. As did the winged gargoyles overhead. She wasn't a fan. The gargoyles creeped her right the hell out.

Keturah took her phone out of her back pocket, glanced at the time, nodded. She was close to something big.

She could taste the success. Of finding answers, of using her magic well, of rising to the occasion her Quest had demanded of her. She really believed she could figure this out, could find that artifact.

She could see her Vovó's smile, so wide and big and proud.

And her legs carried her forward with a mind all their own. They carried her forward right into Max.

She gasped, caught off guard, and they grabbed one another, trying to steady the other.

Max Aster was one of her favorite humans. They sometimes got paired together on group assignments because of how close together their last names were. On occasion, she called him the Slenderman because of his aesthetic, the way he walked and moved and gestured with grace and purpose. And because he had arms and legs that seemed almost too long for his body.

He looked surprised, flustered. She hadn't exactly been paying enough attention to see him, but hadn't he seen her?

Clearly not, what with the *How the hell did you get here?* look he was giving her.

At the same time each of them muttered "Yo! My bad" and "Ope! Soz" before heading away from the other.

Before he could get too far, Keturah paused and turned to him.

"Aster!"

His head whipped in her direction, his eyes growing large. Those expressive eyes said pretty much everything. Right now, it was something like, *Who? Me?!*

She smiled.

"What's up?" he said on an exhale.

"Are you okay?"

He nodded, wet his lips, then smiled back at her. "Sorry about that," he said, pointing over his shoulder to indicate their collision. "I was off somewhere in my head."

"Dream-walking?" she countered.

"No, no. Nothin' like that. Just . . . preoccupied. None of that walking stuff involved me. Trust me, I have way too much else going on."

Keturah had heard that a cabal of Cups students had come up with some complicated spells to dream-walk. To enter and exit any person's dream at will. It was a thing *professionals* did in many mental health programs, but it wasn't super welcome at Galileo, particularly because none of her peers were qualified to do so.

It would be dangerous.

She rocked back on her heels. "Just thought I'd ask."

"Just thought you'd find out some tea, is more like it."

"Guilty." She grinned.

She glanced at the watch on her wrist and caught him doing the same.

"It's pretty early to be out here."

Max brought a hand up and ran it across the top of his head. "Yeah, I just—what are you doing here?"

"I was looking for something down at the docks—"

"You were at the docks this early?"

"Don't interrupt; it's rude. I found this trail of sand."

"Sand?"

"Sand, bruh," she confirmed. "I followed it. And it wasn't *just* sand. I could feel some magic around it."

He nodded, thoughtful.

"Do you think it means something?" she fished, lowering her voice. Stepped a bit closer. "You've been hearing the rumors, right?" Keturah hugged her arms around herself. The bitter chill of intuition was really starting to set in.

"Yeah, I've heard some stuff. And to be honest, I'm pretty sure whatever power you followed has something to do with Dropwort."

"How do you know? You saw him? Here?"

"I don't. And no. But . . . just. There's this whole situation with the Keep and the gargoyle eggs, and in the lunch hall the other day I was having *a simple conversation* with Dropwort, and he said—"

They both turned like deer in headlights when a voice boomed, "Maxwell Aster!"

It was one of the SNACC-EOs. Keturah didn't stick around to find out what they wanted with Max. She never stuck around when they were involved.

Pivoting, she whispered, "I'll text you later" to Max. He nodded back at her, and then she made her way into the dining hall.

Gargoyle eggs, Max had said. Was this the artifact she had been looking for?

Keturah looked at his retreating back only once, wondering if maybe she *should have* waited with Max. Solidarity and all that. But the SNACC-EO walked fast. And it was very clear Max was being *escorted* somewhere.

She faced forward and kept moving. Just like she always did.

Gargoyle eggs.

Surely the high priestess of New Orleans could help her work this out.

She pulled her slim phone from a back pocket and dialed her Vo.

EVIDENCE EXHIBIT S-4
CASE ID: 20-06-DROS-STK

Type:
[ ] Communication
[ ] Audio recording
[ ] Spell residue
[ ] Photo or other visual reconstruction
[X] Object
[ ] Form or record
[ ] Other: _____

Source: Crime scene technician
Relevant Parties: n/a
Description: Indeterminate sandy residue collected from the immediate ground around the deceased's body; please see toxicologist's report for full analysis

[IMAGE: a baggie containing a very small amount of sand]

Per supervising officer's request, sample has been tested and confirmed to contain human DNA.

7:00 A.M.: BHAVNA JOSHI, 15, SWORDS

BY PREETI CHHIBBER

Bhavna Joshi was not a morning person. She heard the clock chime seven times. . . . Did seven a.m. even count as morning? If she couldn't see the sun and the sun couldn't see her, it was still night, as far as Bhavna was concerned.

Then she felt the heat of sunlight beating through the covers over her face, and the scene behind her eyelids went from deep gray to pink-orange, as if she'd summoned the sun just by thinking about it. She sighed. It was time to get out of bed and start the day.

Bhavna flung the covers off her and groped in the space next to her for her dandiya, or as her brother helpfully (not helpfully) called them, her magic dance sticks. Instead of her dandiya, with the back of her hand she hit the heavy, familiar weight of the book she'd fallen asleep reading, stinging the skin there. She groaned. It wasn't her fault that the fourth volume of the Good Knight series was basically the best thing ever put to page. Not cool of the universe to punish her for reading.

She finally opened her eyes and sat up. She could do this. She glanced around at her dorm in the Swords Tower. The sun shone through a stained-glass window at the top of the eastern wall and left a pattern of three swords in a triangle on the center of the floor. The silhouette of the swords rotated slowly, mirroring the magical laced glass work. She rubbed her hands against her face and pushed up from the bed.

While mornings usually sucked, this morning felt even more difficult, which was not surprising. Bhavna thought back to the phone call she'd had the night before with her mom.

"Beti, we're all counting on you! I hope you're doing well. You don't know what it's like for us poore, these days. So much easier for you poore-aur."

Bhavna's stomach had lurched. At school she usually got teased for the other side of things. How could she, a Sorcerer from a family of Neutrals, ever really be a part of the magical culture?

But she'd just rolled her eyes and bitten her tongue.

"Ah, Ma, don't worry. I'm doing well in my classes."

She shook off the memory and squared her shoulders. She had to get to the gym so she could practice the twelve-step ras movements in time for the Advanced Precision Telekinesis test at the end of the week.

She quickly changed into a pair of jean cutoffs and a loose T-shirt with the words "Hero in Training" emblazoned across the front. And she finally picked up her dandiya. The wooden cylinders were covered in a swirl of deep brown and burnt orange; they were long and thin, slightly thicker at the base, not unlike candlesticks you'd find on the table at a fancy banquet— not that she'd ever been to a fancy banquet, of course—and they fit comfortably in her loose fists. She twirled outward with the left and right sticks and said the words "wash and style." The magic covered her, pulling her hair into a ponytail and the sleep from her eyes, and putting a minty taste into her mouth. She grinned. Morning ablutions done, sort of. She made her way to the door to exit the dorms quietly, noting that most of her dorm mates were still sleeping. It was early, but if the bacon wasn't ready by the time she got to the dining hall, there were going to be words.

She headed out the dorm door and down the stairs toward some delicious, delicious fried foods.

"The truth is actually stranger—"

"Is this related to Dropwort? And, you know, what happened?"

That was Nike Noelle's voice, and it sounded like she was talking to Taya Winter. Bhavna didn't really know Taya or Nike very well, but they did have a few classes together. What was really weird was that they sounded really far away. Like they were fighting over walkie-talkies or something? Was there a Walkie-Talkie spell? Bhavna hesitated but then moved forward a few feet to see what was going on.

When she saw them, she came to an abrupt halt, her eyes wide and mouth open.

It was Nike and Taya . . . but she could see *right through them.*

Even for someone who knew that ghosts existed, this was still *very* unnerving. But Taya and Nike weren't *dead.* She watched as Taya's mouth opened in slow motion, the words coming out garbled and strange. She could only make out a few words—"prophecy . . . call . . . action. . . . Chosen One!"—

and then nothing until Nike's hands came up and grabbed Taya's shoulders.

"Dropwort . . . murdered . . ."

Bhavna gasped. Then Nike fell backward and Taya disappeared in a shock of light, and Bhavna realized what she was looking at was the result of some powerful magic. The scene started again, but this time there was even less sound. Big and wild magic sometimes left behind remnants of scenes for a few hours after the fact, but she'd never seen one in real life before. She'd just read about them. She took a step back and put a hand over her chest. Professor Dropwort . . . dead? No, not just dead. *Murdered.* Had she heard that correctly? And was a Chosen One involved?!

Could this seriously be true? She pulled out her phone and scrolled through Cantrip, the Sorcerer equivalent of Twitter. And then she saw it:

EPHEMERA WORDSWORTH (@SORTED_OUT)

OH heard the principal in the hallways. Dropwort is 💀.

Bhavna wasn't surprised by the cutting way it was reported. Dropwort hadn't exactly been beloved by the students. Then it hit her that that was a pretty decent confirmation of his death.

She gulped and thought back to the night before. It must have been around ten or eleven. She'd been out late to see if she could find any of the rumored secret passages in the school. She'd been just near the entrance to the school, crouching and searching for what she thought was the imprint of a pigeon's foot in the hard stone of the walls—which was *just* weird enough for her to want to see it—when a shadowed figure had moved quickly past her. So of course she'd done what every good Good Knight fan would do. She'd gone to investigate.

But instead of an adventure, she'd found Professor Dropwort, who'd furiously bitten out, "You're out after lights-out, Joshi. Get to bed before you get demerits." And then he'd glanced around and added, "Or worse." At the time, she'd groaned. Dropwort had not been her favorite teacher; he'd kept his favorite legacy students close, and any new students—especially new students with no magical relations to speak of—at a distance. He'd never been particularly kind, that was for sure. But last night he'd been clearly agitated and ruder than usual. She also remembered him fidgeting with something in his hand; she hadn't been able to see it clearly, just a hint of silver. Looking back, the "or worse" felt less like he'd been trying to scare her and more like he might have actually been scared.

What if she'd been the last person to see him alive?

That was macabre, but it didn't sound like Nike and Taya knew what had actually happened to the professor. . . . Maybe this was Bhavna's chance to do something big! In the Good Knight series there was *always* someone who fixed the problems—the Chosen One, as it were. And in her head, sometimes, Bhavna liked to think of herself as that person. Or she liked to think that she *could* be that person.

Without the Chosen One, there's no *story*.

Now she waited a beat in case anyone else was coming, and then snuck out from behind the column to head to breakfast. While walking toward the dining hall, she ran through the pieces of the rumor in her head.

146

Possible Facts:

Professor Dropwort: Deceased.

Something* on his person.

* "Random piece of silver junk"

Bhavna might have been the last person to
see him alive.

She shivered a little at that last one, then shook her head.
Thinking about it wasn't going to help anything. What she
needed was to find some clues to see if she could find out *who*
did this. Maybe she could retrace the professor's steps?

She couldn't remember if she'd seen Dropwort at dinner . . .
though, granted, she'd been reading and practicing a new Ras
Step spell in her head. Retracing his steps might be harder
than she'd anticipated. She reached the end of the staircase and
stepped out into the wide hallway of the school's ground level.

"JB's *gotta* figure out that note . . ."

Oh no. A voice she recognized floated around the curve of
the wall. It was *Diego*. Diego, who she had been in serious like
with for three full semesters! She looked for somewhere to hide.
Just then her stomach gave a great growl, and she pressed her
sticks against it as her eyes widened in horror. She glanced left
and right, panicked.

"Hello? Is someone there?" Diego's voice had gotten closer,
and Bhavna's desperation grew. Where was she going to
hide . . . ?

Oh, right. Bhavna could do magic.

A quick three-step should do it. She brought her hands up over her head and tapped the dandiya together softly, then turned a quarter step and tapped the sticks again just next to her left hip. One more quarter turn, and one more tap down near her knees.

"Float and disappear," she whispered. Her whole body tingled for a second as the Invisibility spell took effect, and then she was rising into the air. Right as she hit the high ceiling with a soft thud, Diego came around the curve of the wall. She bit back a sigh. His dark hair was disheveled as usual, and his walk was purposeful. She wondered if he'd heard about Dropwort yet—if Dropwort hadn't cared for Bhavna, he'd been downright antagonistic to Diego. It was one of the reasons for her truly epic crush. Diego never let Dropwort push him around! She still remembered his caustic *Because colonialism, Professor* after one history class where Dropwort's perspective had felt particularly limited.

Now, however, she was glad to see he was passing by without noticing her. She released the breath she'd been holding, only for Diego to spin around, brows furrowed.

"I know there's someone there! If you're spying on me, I already told the vice principals everything. I didn't have anything to do with what happened to Dropwort." He sounded angry, then muttered under his breath, "His note is with JB now, anyway."

Bhavna silently put a hand over her mouth. How did Diego know about what had happened to the professor? And who thought he was involved?! And what did the note that new kid JB had have to do with it?!

Diego threw a nasty look in Bhavna's general direction, as

if daring whoever he thought was spying on him to come out and admit it. But Bhavna *wasn't* spying and *wow* did she not want to explain that gargantuan stomach growl to the cute boy in front of her, so she kept her body perfectly still until Diego finally shrugged.

"Okay," he said, "if you want to stay quiet, stay quiet. I'm going to go take a nap." Then he stalked off toward his dorm.

For safety's sake, she moved several feet in the opposite direction before twirling her dandiya above her head and saying, "Drop." She looked back the way Diego had walked off in, thinking about how his face had looked handsome and furious in the low light of the hallway, and wishing she could go talk to him. But what would she even say? *Hi, Diego. I was invisible and floating above you, and I heard that you were thinking about figuring out what happened to Professor Dropwort—me too!* She rolled her eyes and groaned.

Then she froze. JB! Diego had mentioned that he had given him a note. She could find JB and ask him how this note thing played into it all. But before she could take that line of thinking any further, her stomach growled again.

She looked down and glared.

"Okay, fine, stomach. You win. Breakfast first, then figuring out where JB is."

She followed the hall north in the direction of the dining hall, nestled next to the Cups Tower entrance. The doors came into view, and despite her wandering thoughts about the mystery at hand, she couldn't help but grin. It was one of her favorite places in the school. First of all, it was *huge*. Every single one of the thousand students who went to the school could fit in it at the same time if they wanted to. The room was shaped into a shallow arc, and the longer wall was lined with these beautiful, enchanted windows. Bhavna pushed through the doors and grinned at the brightly colored stained glass that flipped through the symbols of all the school houses. Just then it was featuring a row of swords spiraling upward. The room itself was pretty empty; most students hadn't gotten out of bed yet. She thought again of Diego's comment about JB. He wasn't in the dining hall, but that didn't mean she couldn't ask around.

First she walked through the empty buffet line, filling up her plate with delicious breakfast foods—including the ever-necessary single pancake to balance out the eggs and sausages. Chewing her lip, she looked at the long walnut tables, debating where to sit. There was a group of older students huddled together on one end, and a few younger students sprinkled throughout the room. There was no one Bhavna knew by name. Was it her imagination, or were people starting to stare? Had she been standing and looking around for too long? It was moments like these when Bhavna wished that she already felt like she really was meant to be at this school. If she was, it would have been so easy to just plop herself down with any of these kids and ask some questions. She took a deep breath and let it out in a heavy sigh before sitting a few seats down from the group of older students.

While she ate, she considered next steps. If she were JB, where would she be? It was still early. . . . Maybe she should head over to the Coins Tower—she was pretty sure that was his house—and ask around. She tapped a fork against her plate absently. And then, like fate, she overheard JB's name from the very group she'd sat down near.

". . . saw JB and Ivy headed to the infirmary. There is something in the water, for sure."

The infirmary!

She shoved the last piece of sausage into her mouth, jumped up from the table, hit her dandiya together with a quick "Clear," and ran to the exit as her dirty dishes vanished behind her.

Coming to the Galileo Academy for the Extraordinary had not been an easy experience for Bhavna. The trouble wasn't even the school or her acceptance, not really. It had all started way earlier.

In November during her seventh-grade year, Bhavna had been allowed to go to a Navratri celebration with her older cousins, instead of having to wait for her mom and dad to take her. She never got to hang out with the older kids, and she was excited—garba and ras were probably her favorite things in the entire world. After an hour or two of garba—dancing in circles and pounding her feet, giant leaps, and twirling her heart out—it was time to pull out her dandiya for ras. She found a partner, they joined the line, and the dhol started. Bhavna raised her stick and tapped her partner's on beat once, twice, and then brought it back to hit her other dandiya as she stepped forward. But when her sticks touched each other, instead of her hopping forward, she flew straight up into the air and ended up spending two hours stuck in the rafters, waiting for emergency services to arrive and help her down.

Afterward, her family pulled her out the door and into the car before erupting into nervous laughter.

"Meri bachi! A Sorcerer! Poore-aur!" Where she'd grown up,

people without magic were called poore, or whole. And people who had magic? "Poore-aur"—"whole-and." There hadn't been a Sorcerer in the Joshi family since, well, ever. Her parents were thrilled, of course, but that night an invisible line had been drawn between Bhavna and the rest of her family. They loved her, but now she had this whole other piece of her they couldn't understand. But it was okay, Bhavna thought—she'd have understanding when she got to Galileo.

She thought she'd have people who got it.

But then she came to Galileo and it was different. She started a year late, so while the kids her age were in the midst of their third year, she was still in her second. A lot of the students had already known each other. And being the only kid who had no Sorcerer family whatsoever *mattered*.

She had a few friends, of course, but there were unwritten rules and inside jokes and familial Sorcerer relationships that she just didn't understand. Plus, because her magic involved dancing and big movements, she'd gotten a bit of a reputation. People avoided her, like they thought she was going to put out someone's eye. (Even though it only happened once, and the kid's eyeball grew back in five minutes!)

All in all, it had turned Bhavna into a bit of a loner.

But solving this mystery? If she could pull this off, no one would be able to say she wasn't supposed to be here.

"Joshi! Watch out!"

Bhavna looked up from her mad dash away from the dining hall just in time to avoid running directly into Professor Anand.

"Bhavna!"

"Sorry, Professor!"

Professor Anand had one hand to his heart and the other clutching a piece of silk fabric. He took a deep breath and lowered his arms, frowning at the silk in his hand.

"Oh, well that's going to need steaming now." He turned his attention back to Bhavna. "And where are you running off to so early in the morning?"

Bhavna tried not to let her nerves show. Professor Anand always had on a perfectly tailored suit. Today it was deep blue—fully covered in a subtle paisley pattern—with a matching shirt and a solid red tie. He always looked as if he belonged wherever he was, and he always pronounced Bhavna's name perfectly. It didn't help that when her mother had learned he was a teacher there, she'd said, "Bhavna! You'll have an *uncle* at school, Ramesh Uncle!" Her mom still asked about "Ramesh Uncle" every single time Bhavna called home. Every time she saw Professor Anand, she was terrified she would slip and call him Ramesh Uncle by accident.

"Bhavna?"

"Oh, nowhere, Professor! Just . . . going to practice some spells in the gym."

Professor Anand gave her a knowing look. "The gym that is in the opposite direction"—he pointed—"behind you?"

Get it together, Joshi. Why had she said the gym?! Panic was never her friend.

"I just wanted to ask Nurse Smith something, so I was going to go to the infirmary first."

"Hmmm, okay. Be careful about running—you're lucky this silk is the only thing that got hurt today." He held up the brightly colored fabric and Bhavna winced.

"Yes, sir." She started walking slowly toward the infirmary again before hesitating. "Professor?"

Anand turned around.

"Yes?"

"Do . . ." Bhavna paused, unsure of how to ask about the murder. "Is it true about Professor Dropwort? That he's . . . dead?"

Anand's eyes went wide with shock.

"How did you—?" Then his face softened. "Ah, I should have known the rumor mill would get to the students before we could. Nothing stays quiet long here. I'm sorry to say that he was found this morning. The principal will be addressing the students soon. It's a little early still, so I can't tell you much. I don't know too much myself. But . . ." He hesitated for a moment before starting again. "You know, Bhavna, if you ever want to come by during office hours for chai and a chat, my door is open."

This was not what Bhavna had expected, but she found herself warmed by the idea. It was an unexpected kindness, and a welcome one.

"Oh, uh, thank you, Unc—*sir*. Thank you, sir."

He gave her another one of his looks, but just waved her off.

"Have a good day, Joshi."

It took everything Bhavna had not to dash away, but she kept herself to a slow gait until she was sure Professor Anand was gone. Then she ran the remaining length to the infirmary.

Bhavna opened the door to the medical wing and made her way into the infirmary. It was a big room, with high windows and curtained beds placed sporadically throughout. Not the most efficient or ordered, but Nurse Smith wasn't exactly what you would call traditional.

The waiting area was quiet; Bhavna didn't see Nurse Smith anywhere. She stepped further into the room. Bhavna noticed Ivy lying on one of the beds near the entrance. Only, instead of the smiling, freckly brown-faced girl Bhavna usually saw in the halls, there was an oozing mess of pustules wearing a pair of glasses. Bhavna paused near her bed, eyes wide, but Ivy interrupted before she could speak.

"Don't ask. But if you do want to ask, it was Birdie's fault." She groaned. "I always forget how flighty she is. She asked me to go to her office but forgot to turn off her alarm! And by 'alarm' I clearly mean 'horrible curse.'" Ivy leaned her head back against her pillow and screwed her eyes shut.

"I'm going to just put my headphones on, listen to some soothing music, and sit here quietly now, okay?"

Bhavna blinked. "Okay, Ivy. Hope your face feels better soon. I'll . . . just leave you to it, then."

Ivy gave her a thumbs-up.

"Argh!" A voice cut through the air, and Bhavna's head swiveled in its direction. Next to her, Ivy didn't react. Her music must have been *loud*.

"Hello?" Bhavna called. There were curtains drawn around one of the beds at the other end of the row. Another yelp came, loud and fast, and Bhavna could tell it was coming from behind those heavy green drapes. She snuck closer and paused right near the side of the bed. There was a crack between the post and the curtain, but Bhavna couldn't see anything. "Um, hi?" she asked again. Before anyone could answer, she heard Nurse Smith's voice from near the entrance to the infirmary.

"Just follow me, Officer! I'll be right with you!"

A dark brown hand shot out from behind the curtain and

155

gripped Bhavna's wrist, then pulled her whole body into the dark space.

"Ahh—" is all Bhavna got out before a hand slapped across her mouth and JB hissed, "*Shhh!* I want to hear this, and I don't want Ole Nurse Bones to remember that I'm here!"

Bhavna raised both her hands in a placating manner. JB removed his palm, and Bhavna frowned.

"You could have just told me," she whispered back, wiping at her chin. There was some kind of gooey substance all over the bottom half of her face. "What the heck is on your hand?"

JB grimaced. "Ah, sorry. It's the burn meds Fibs put all over me." She noticed now that JB's arms were covered in a thick translucent salve. "And sorry, I . . ." He hesitated before continuing. "I couldn't remember . . . your name," he finished, glancing away awkwardly. Bhavna felt a little bad for him. She didn't know him well, but she understood feeling uncomfortable in a new place!

"Don't even worry about it—"

Nurse Smith's voice interrupted before Bhavna could say anything else to JB.

"So, what else can I help SNACC with?" she asked.

"Is there anything you can tell us about the victim's body? You examined it, right?"

Bhavna and JB said, "Dropwort!" under their breath at the same time. Then they both pointed at each other with surprise.

"Wait," Bhavna said. "Let's keep listening." JB nodded in agreement. Outside of the curtains Nurse Smith was speaking.

"Yeah, it was a doozy of a crime scene. A real skull scratcher, if you catch my drift." She paused, like she was waiting for something. The pause went on for much longer than Bhavna would have expected. "Aaaanyway," Nurse Smith finally said. "I can see that you're a real fun guy to be around, Officer." There was an unamused grunt from Nurse Smith's conversation partner. "*Fine*. I'll give you the details, really get down to the bones of it all." Next to Bhavna, JB dropped his head into his hands and let out a soft groan.

"The puns are always so bad," he said.

Bhavna shrugged. "She thinks they're funny."

"What I can tell you is that the wounds on Dropwort? They don't match whatever you guys think killed him. That's for sure. *Way* too many stab wounds for a single weapon." Nurse Fibula's voice started getting quieter, like she was walking away from the infirmary. Bhavna couldn't even hear what the officer said in response. JB exhaled loudly, and Bhavna turned to him.

"*What* is going on?" Bhavna asked.

"I wish I knew. All I know is that Diego asked me to figure out what some secret note said—"

"What'd it say?!" Bhavna interrupted.

"Just someone telling Dropwort about a meeting last night to pass along the goods, basically. And some threats." Bhavna felt JB shiver next to her. "Listen," JB said suddenly, gripping her shoulders. "I'm stuck here. Can you tell Diego what we heard? We're trying to figure out what happened." A small thrill shot through Bhavna. She nodded. She was going to talk to *Diego*.

"Yeah, yeah. I can do that." As the last word left her lips, the curtains around them were flung open.

Nurse Fibula Smith was always a sight to behold. Bhavna wasn't sure where she came from, but rumor was that she'd *always* been in that school, after one of the original founders had spied an old pile of bones and thought, *What a great option for our school nurse.* You know, *totally* normal. Nurse Smith was just that: a tall skeleton who wore a candy striper smock over her bones and a traditional nurse's cap on her smooth ivory skull. The resulting image was hilariously macabre but somehow fit right in with the rest of Galileo in a way that Bhavna couldn't help but be envious of.

"Eep," Bhavna let out.

"Was that a peep or an eep, dear? You'll have to speak up because I haven't got any ears." Nurse Smith let out a big laugh at her own joke. JB just groaned again. "What are you doing in here, anyway? I don't remember leaving two skeletons behind . . ." Even though the nurse didn't have eyes, Bhavna could somehow feel Nurse Fibula's penetrating gaze. She scrambled for something to say.

"Oh, I was just asking JB if he wanted me to take notes for him today," she blurted out.

"Thanks, Joshi," JB said. He flinched as Nurse Smith squeezed a tube of something called Mr. Burns's Burns Off all over his arm. "Fibs, is it supposed to hurt?"

"Humor us, Mr. Brig." Nurse Smith paused. Bhavna and JB stared blankly at each other. Nurse Smith let out another big laugh. "Humor us? Humerus?!" She pointed at her upper arm bone, then shook her head. "My wit is wasted on the uninformed. Now, Mr. Brig, I'm going to give you some extra ointment. Use it once an hour for the next four hours, and you should be as good as new. In the meantime, you can rest here."

JB nodded, then narrowed his eyes at Bhavna. "Hey, Joshi, don't forget about that *other assignment.*"

Bhavna grinned and nodded. She didn't want to get ahead of herself, but this was starting to feel like a secret club.

Then the skeleton nurse ushered Bhavna away from JB's bed and back toward the entrance. "Is there anything else I can help you with, Ms. Joshi?" Nurse Smith asked. Bhavna gripped her dandiya tight in her hands.

"Nurse Smith, did you see Professor Dropwort's body this morning?"

The skeleton fixed her eye sockets on Bhavna. "Well, it's only been morning for a few hours, and what is time anyway but a fading construct?"

Bhavna's thick brows furrowed. "What?"

"Ms. Joshi, Professor Dropwort had too few grains of sand left, if you know what I mean. Time waits for no man, but this man lost time. All of it." That time she did laugh, and Bhavna awkwardly joined, even though she didn't totally understand what Nurse Smith meant. She decided to push on.

"I saw him late last night, and I was just wondering if you knew what happened."

"Wish I did, dear! When I saw Wren—that's who found the body"—Bhavna shuddered, but Nurse Smith went on—"they just kept talking about some hourglass." Then she shrugged her shoulder bones, and Bhavna could see the scapula moving behind her chest cavity. "It's reminding me of something, but I can't quite put my phalanx on it."

What could Wren have meant by "hourglass"? Bhavna belatedly wondered if JB or Diego might know what it meant. What could an hourglass have to do with Dropwort dying? Was that the thing he was passing along? Who would kill over an hourglass, even if it was silver? Bhavna shook her head, trying to clear her thoughts. It was definitely important, but she couldn't figure out *how.*

"Ms. Joshi!" Nurse Smith was calling her name. "Earth to Ms. Joshi!"

"Ah! Sorry!" Bhavna's face was warm. She had to stop getting so lost in her own thoughts.

"Now, why are you asking all these questions? You know what curiosity did to the cat, don't you?"

"Killed it?" Bhavna asked hesitantly.

Nurse Smith twisted her skull to look at her again. "What? Is that what it did? I always wondered. Anyway, why all the questions?"

Bhavna shrugged, suddenly uncomfortable. Her plan to solve the murder had sounded good before, but now it all seemed very real. Was this a reason to bond with people? Did that make her even weirder?

Nurse Smith put a cold bony hand on Bhavna's.

"Ms. Joshi, you can tell me. We have nurse-student confidentiality. I promise."

"I . . . I thought if I could help figure out what happened to Professor Dropwort, it would mean that I was supposed to be here."

Nurse Smith chuckled. "Bhavna, you're supposed to be here, because you're supposed to be here."

"But—"

"No, no buts, and no butts, incidentally. I'm a skeleton! Do you think I'm not supposed to be a nurse?"

"Of course you can be a nurse!"

"Then why can't you belong here?"

Bhavna scrunched her nose.

"So . . . I belong here, because I'm here?"

Nurse Smith's skeletal grin seemed to get wider.

"You belong here because you belong here. Fitting in or fitting out doesn't mean you're not supposed to be somewhere. It just means there's more to come."

Bhavna grinned. She was already poore-aur—whole-and. Maybe she could be whole-and-more-to-come too. She thought of Professor Anand and his chai, and she thought of JB and Diego—*Diego!* She'd go see him next and tell him everything she'd learned here. And maybe they could work on what came next together. She liked the sound of that.

[Beginning of transcript.]

[Pleasant ding indicating start of announcement.]

Principal Fornax: [Clears throat.] Is this . . . Hello? Is this thing on?

Vice Principal Beckley: Yes, Principal Fornax.

Principal Fornax: Right. Good morning, students. It is with a heavy heart that I must inform you all of the sudden and untimely passing of one of our esteemed colleagues, the honorable Professor Septimius Dropwort. Many of you will be familiar, of course, with the good professor, who has long served on the faculty of Galileo, and was highly respected in his field.

I am sure you will all want to pay your respects, so please note that a memorial service will be held later this morning, at eleven a.m. in the auditorium. Your attendance is mandatory. Please do not be late. [Papers shuffling. Pause.]

Vice Principal Beckley: . . . Furthermore, SNACC Enforcement Officers are conducting a standard review-[Muffled.] You weren't saying anything, so I— It's fine. [Coughs.] As I was saying, the school's departure to Turkmenistan has been delayed so that SNACC Enforcement Officers can conduct a standard review. You may be pulled out of class to answer a few questions, and we encourage you to cooperate so that we may move on as quickly as possible.

Kevin Vaughan-Crabtree: Hi, just gonna jump in here—this is Mr. Kev. I will be available to sit in on any meeting with the officers as your advocate, if you so choose. Also, Nurse Smith and I are on hand should you need a listening ear. I can provide grief counseling for any students struggling with Professor Dropwort's passing—

Nurse Fibula Smith: And I suppose I could, well, take a stab at him. [Chuckle.] I mean it.

Kevin Vaughan-Crabtree: . . . Maybe just come to me for grief counseling, actually.

Principal Fornax: [Clears throat multiple times.] We know this is terrible news, but we believe in the resilience of our students, and trust that you will carry on about your day as you usually would, despite the circumstances. Thank you, and again, attendance at the memorial is mandatory. [Pause.] Birdie, can you . . .

Vice Principal Beckley: [Sighs.] Again, it's the red button—

[Pleasant ding indicating end of announcement.]

[End of transcript.]

8:00 A.M.: JIA PARK, 15, UNDECIDED

BY KAT CHO

Jia Park hated running behind, especially today. Because today was the day she was going to prove her worth to her parents. Not only had a professor been found dead (murdered, according to the whispers going around, and Jia was inclined to agree—Professor Dropwort was disliked by almost everyone) but she had heard a smoke message that called out a "Chosen One."

Jia was determined to be that person.

Let's just get one thing straight right off the bat. Jia wasn't glad that Dropwort was dead (even if he had been a backward, bigoted blowhard). But if *someone* was going to be the Chosen One, it was going to be Jia.

Ever since her parents had sent her away to Galileo, Jia had been trying to show them they'd made a mistake. That she should be learning back home at Chosun Academy, like they had, like all the Sorcerers in her family had before they'd gone on to run Chosun Academy itself. If Jia wasn't chosen as a headmaster of Chosun, she'd be breaking a legacy that had spanned five generations in her family. But once Appa made a decree, Jia was always expected to obey. And the day they'd dropped her off at Galileo, he'd gripped her shoulders and said, "You represent Chosun while you are here. Make us proud."

Jia wasn't quite sure why she had to come all the way here to "represent Chosun," but maybe this was her chance. After all, who wouldn't be proud to have raised the Chosen One? The only problem: she wasn't quite sure *how* the chosen one would be, well, chosen.

The dining room of Galileo Academy for the Extraordinary was bustling as kids rushed around, gossiping about the mystery of Dropwort's death. The large wood-trimmed room was five times as large as her beloved Chosun's dining hall.

Everything here felt so different from what she'd grown up with. The moving school, the food, the way classes were taught. It had taken Jia an embarrassing amount of time to get used to it. Luckily, she was a great student, so her grades hadn't suffered. Sometimes she wondered if her parents would call her back if her grades did slip. But she was too chicken to try that tactic. She'd get home by proving to her parents that she was worthy instead.

Every table was overflowing with students. Ugh, this was why Jia liked to come to breakfast earlier, when there weren't other students to bother her as she reviewed her day's assignments. Jia scanned for a seat as she pulled her tight braid over her shoulder, running her fingers over the smooth loops; it helped calm her when she was feeling anxious.

"Jia!" someone called from behind her.

It was Layla Longfeather—tall, perky, and utterly odd. The

kind of girl who wore a second pair of glasses because she'd forgotten that she'd put her first pair on top of her wildly curling mahogany hair. Which is what she happened to be doing right now.

"You can sit here!" Layla patted the seat next to her. She was sitting with a bunch of other third-years. Jia wasn't particularly friendly with any of them. Then again, Jia wasn't particularly friendly with anyone.

She craned her neck, looking for any other open seat.

It's not that Jia disliked Layla. It's just that whenever she was near the girl, her skin felt all itchy and her chest got all tight. It made it hard for her to think, and since Jia's brain was her pride and joy, she rejected anything that muddled it.

But there were no other seats available. And without a good escape, Jia finally sat down.

"How are you?" Layla asked at the same time that Dan Corbin leaned his pale blond head across the table and said, "Did you hear the announcement?"

Jia didn't really like talking to Dan. He was a legacy, and he made sure everyone knew it.

"Apparently they took so long to move the body, some magical creatures *got to it*," Dan continued, looking around eagerly. Jia just lowered her gaze.

Aretta Musa's eyes widened. "Ew, really? I think I'm going to be sick. Maybe Nurse Smith will let me skip my first class . . ."

"I wouldn't go to the nurse's office. I saw that Ivy girl in there, and she looked gross. Like, cursed gross," Dan said.

"Should we really be talking like this? Dropwort was a professor," Layla said, her gaze drifting toward Jia, who purposefully avoided eye contact. Dreadful Dropwort wasn't someone she liked discussing. Still, Jia watched Layla out of the corner of her eye. The other girl's frown scrunched up her nose, making her look like a cartoon rabbit. It was . . . sort of cute. If you were into that kind of thing.

"He was a jerk and a snob." Aretta shrugged.

"He was just a traditionalist," Dan argued. Jia tried to hide her scowl. Dan was one of the students that agreed with Professor Dropwort's *conservative* (ahem, racist) views of "tradition."

Jia had never been a fan of the professor, though she'd never said so aloud. Dropwort had had distinct ideas about what elite Sorcerers looked like (hint: more male, straight, and white than Jia).

But Jia knew better than to let that get to her. She'd been raised in one of the top schools for sorcery in the Pacific, run by her family for generations.

"What do you think that prophecy thing said?" Aretta asked.

Jia drew herself up, interested in the conversation for the first time. Were they talking about the smoke message?

"I heard someone will 'meet their doom' at the hands of the Chosen One," Aretta continued.

Jia frowned. She didn't want to hurt anyone to prove herself to her parents.

"Maybe this 'Chosen One' will make Dropwort's killer pay," Dan said.

Jia saw Layla roll her eyes at that. But Jia reluctantly thought there might be something to what Dan said. Not to avenge Dropwort, but maybe to find a killer? A murderer was a threat to the school, weren't they? Exposing their identity would be kind of heroic.

And who wouldn't want to bring their hero daughter back home to celebrate her?

Layla shifted in her seat as the other kids continued discussing the mystery of Dropwort's death. She turned to Jia and said, "So, Jia, have you decided what major you're going to declare?"

It was clear that she didn't want to participate in the gossip anymore. As Layla leaned in closer, Jia could smell the scent of parchment on her. Probably because she was always pulling out sheets to write her music down on.

"I haven't decided," Jia said. She was going to be out of this school before the deadline came anyway.

"You know you were a natural in Introduction to Magical Music Studies last year. And I bet you'd love the Wands Tower," Layla said with a smile. This close, Jia could see the freckles that splashed across Layla's nose. They made the green in her eyes appear brighter.

Jia felt herself flush. Had the room suddenly become ten degrees warmer? Maybe someone had cast a Heater spell?

Jia cleared her throat and leaned away. "I just learned piano because my parents claimed it would help my magical calculations studies," she said with a frown she hoped would discourage more questions. "And the central tower works just fine for me."

All magic schools (not just Galileo) focused on preparing students to receive their magic license after their first year, which would allow them to practice their aptitude independently. But while other schools stuck to a core curriculum, Galileo encouraged students to branch out into the different specialties. It was a freedom that scared Jia sometimes. She liked structure; it's how she knew that she was succeeding.

"Noona!" Jia's bumbling younger cousin Changmin rushed over, almost tripping over his own feet. He was gangly and already taller than Jia, but he never knew what to do with his limbs. Currently his long arms were clutching one of his many magical birding charts that he meticulously updated. Jia really hoped he wasn't coming over to ramble about his latest sighting. "I have to talk to you about something of utmost secrecy."

Jia cringed. Changmin was a little much, even on his best days. It was like his body and mind always wanted to be in three completely different places at once—he was constantly flailing about and talking in circles. Unless he was talking about magical creatures; then he was too hyperfocused. When Jia's samchon and aunt had decided to send him to Galileo Academy this year, her parents had told her that Changmin was her responsibility. She'd known immediately what that meant: if Changmin got in trouble, then Jia would be to blame.

"Noona, I need to talk to you," Changmin repeated in an urgent whisper that was still loud enough for everyone to hear.

"Who is this first-year?" Dan glared down his thin nose at Changmin. "What are you doing on this side of the dining room?"

Jia gritted her teeth. She wanted to put Dan in his place, but she knew she had to keep her cool. If she got into a fight, it could reach the ears of the principal. And then her parents.

"There are no sides in the dining room," Layla said, then turned to Changmin. "Hi. I'm Layla."

"Hi!" Changmin gave Layla one of his wide, bright smiles. Layla immediately smiled back. Changmin was always way friendlier than Jia could even wish to be. "I'm Jia's cousin. Park Changmin."

"Park Chang?" Dan scoffed. "What kind of a name is that?"

"It's not," Changmin said with an unaffected laugh. "Those are both last names. Who would go by two last names? That sounds ridiculous!"

Dan looked stunned. But Changmin, ever oblivious, continued. "Oh, I shouldn't have used the Korean way of introducing myself. I guess you'd call me Changmin Park. Anyway, the more you know, right?"

Dan's eyes were wide, his mouth opening and closing like a silent fish's. But Aretta muttered under her breath, "Who is this kid?"

Jia was burning up with embarrassment. And then she noticed that Layla was shaking with laughter, her hand pressed hard against her mouth. Oh great, now Layla thought her family was a joke.

Jia stood up quickly and pulled Changmin away by the arm. She yanked her cousin into an empty study room and shut the door firmly behind them.

"Okay, Changmin, what did you do this time?" Silently she prayed that it didn't involve any property damage. Once he'd hidden a gumiho in one of Chosun's towers, and it had broken through the roof, costing the school a pretty penny to repair it.

"Will you promise not to get too upset?"

Jia didn't want to make a promise she couldn't keep, but she realized that her cousin didn't just look contrite—he looked scared. "Changmin, what is it? What happened?"

He took a deep breath. "So last night, after lights-out, I left my room, and I saw him. His *body*." Changmin didn't need to clarify who he was talking about. There was only one "body" he could have seen.

"Are you okay?" Jia asked. "Do you need to talk to someone?"

"No." Changmin shrugged childishly, and it reminded Jia that her cousin was younger than her. That she was supposed to be protecting him. "I've seen a body before."

"That was harabeoji. He died of a heart attack. That's different."

"I'm fine, Noona!" Changmin insisted. "This isn't about that professor guy. It's about Sami."

"Sami?"

"My samjokgu puppy."

"What?!" Jia burst out, any concern she felt for her cousin evaporating in an instant. If she knew one thing for sure, it was that unsanctioned magical pets were not allowed at Galileo. "Please do not tell me you smuggled a magical creature into the school. That's against the rules."

"Well, if I can't tell you, then I can't finish my story."

Jia sighed. "Fine. Tell me, and quickly."

Changmin took a deep breath, which was a signal that he was about to launch into one of his long and meandering stories. "So, I found Sami by the woods by my house. She's so cute with her three legs. She looks kind of like a Jindo breed dog, but more gray, like the moonlight. I found her at night, did I mention that? So she blended in with the flora at first."

"Changmin!" Jia said, growing frustrated.

"Right, so, yeah, Sami was so small that I knew I couldn't just leave her at home all alone. Eomma and Appa don't really love the strays I take in."

Jia knew "don't really love" meant "often despise and try to kick out." In fact, Jia had a sneaking suspicion that Changmin had been sent away because of his predilection for finding and harboring magical creatures.

"So, I know that the Galileo rules say no unsanctioned magical creatures are allowed on the premises. But I had this thought—maybe Sami could grow up to be my familiar."

Jia was pretty sure that wasn't how choosing a familiar worked, but she didn't say anything.

"I usually keep her in my room," Changmin continued, "but the other day, Sami became all listless and wouldn't eat. So, I thought maybe she was lonely all day in my room. I decided to bring her to class with me. She was being super good most of the day. But you know how samjogku can sense evil, right? And she hated Professor Dropwort. Like, would not stop growling at him. I tried to tell him it was my stomach, and I swear he almost bought it. But then Sami just leapt out of my coat pocket and started snarling at him, and Dropwort confiscated her!"

Jia dreaded where this story was going.

"So, last night I snuck out after Diego Sakay checked in on me. Nice guy. Do you know him?"

"Changmin," Jia said again in warning.

"Right, so as soon as I opened Dropwort's office door, Sami took off. I chased her, and she led me right down to Dropwort's body." Changmin shuddered. "I had to be really quiet, because that other person was there—"

"Wait!" Jia held up a hand, finally interested in Changmin's story. "You saw someone? It could have been the killer!"

Changmin frowned thoughtfully, then shook his head. "I don't know. They were just hovering over him . . ."

"Doing what?" Jia asked, her eyes wide.

Changmin shook his head again. "Sorry, I can't really remember. I was mostly focusing on finding Sami."

Jia sighed in disappointment.

"Anyway, Sami took off again, and I never found her. That's why I need your help."

"To find a magical three-legged dog?" Jia scoffed. Then she paused. "Wait, you said samjokgu are good at finding evil, right?"

"Yeah," Changmin said slowly.

"And whoever killed Dropwort must be evil. I mean, come on. Murder is, like, the number one evil thing." Jia was starting to form a plan.

"What are you getting at, Noona?"

"I'll help you find Sami," Jia announced.

"Really?"

"And then you and your dog—"

"Samjogku."

"Right. You and the samjogku will help me find the culprit."

Jia was really starting to wonder if she'd bitten off more than she could chew as she followed her cousin through a tight vent. She hadn't planned on spending her morning staring at her cousin's skinny butt as they shimmied through musty air ducts. Changmin claimed this was the last place he'd seen Sami, and Jia was pretty sure this vent led to the forbidden storage area under the school. Only faculty could summon the service elevators to access it.

As she was debating calling the whole thing off, Changmin stopped. Jia halted just in time to avoid slamming into him.

"What are you doing?" she asked.

"Gotta get this grate off." Changmin grunted. There was the rattle of metal against metal, then a loud crash. "Success!"

Changmin shimmied forward. Before Jia could react, he dropped from view.

"Changmin!" Jia called, crawling forward. He didn't answer at first, and a dozen worst-case scenarios flew through her mind—most of them featuring Changmin with horrible injuries from his fall. But as she reached the opening, Changmin's face popped up again. Jia screamed and jumped, her head slamming into the top of the duct.

"Oops, sorry, Noona. Let me help you."

Jia had no choice but to let him help her down.

The storage space was filled with a bunch of wooden shelving, lit by low lamps hanging from the vaulted ceilings. And just beyond the shelves were multiple archways leading to hallways that stretched so far, she couldn't see the ends.

Jia had read up on Galileo's history. It was said that this area was magically enhanced to hold all the odds and ends of the school. The further down the halls you went, the odder the things you would find.

"I guess we should just start . . . looking in rooms?" Jia said, choosing a hallway at random. Her hand shook as she reached for the first knob. Warnings about this area holding rogue magic and being off-limits echoed in her head. But she took a deep breath and told herself that if she wanted to be taken seriously by her parents, she couldn't be a coward.

When she opened the door, she saw that the room was filled with a garden—a literal garden with giant tree trunks that soared overhead and flowers competing for room between their roots. There was even some kind of artificial light shining down through the branches.

"Whoa," Changmin whispered. "Why do you think the school needs to store a whole forest?"

"I don't know."

Before Jia could stop him, Changmin plucked one of the flowers and twirled it between his fingers.

A rumble sounded from below them, and the large tree roots started to move.

Jia pulled him back just as a root shot out of the ground right where he'd been standing. She slammed the door shut. "Maybe we shouldn't touch anything in these rooms."

Changmin nodded, his eyes wide.

The next room held dozens of desks. And each desk was somehow enchanted. Some were frozen in blocks of ice. One kept on spontaneously combusting, scorch marks all over its battered wooden surface. Another was leaking some kind of syrupy substance. And at least half a dozen were floating overhead, bumping into each other like wayward balloons. Changmin pointed with a laugh to the one that kept catching on fire. "That's the desk that Dhruv Ahmed accidentally put a combustion curse on in our magical charms class. I wondered what they did with it."

"Maybe we should split up and cover more ground," Jia suggested.

Each room was weirder and weirder. One was stark white, with a single potted flower in the center; when Jia tried to step toward the flower, she came across a magical shield so strong that it pushed her back with an electrical buzz. Changmin found another one that turned you black and white if you stepped inside. Jia found one that screamed when she opened the door. But none of the rooms held a samjogku puppy.

Until Changmin called for Jia from outside a room that leaked grape juice into the hallway. He pointed to a purple set of pawprints leading further down the hall, where the lights faded into darkness. "It's her! She was here."

Jia had a bad feeling about this. But before she could voice her concern, Changmin took off after the tracks—so Jia reluctantly followed. The lighting grew dim as they followed the prints down the hall, which were becoming harder and harder to see. Changmin turned to Jia. "Do you have a flashlight?"

Jia rolled her eyes, then whispered a glow charm into her palm. A light emanated from her hand. It was the first spell they were taught here.

"Oh yeah!" Changmin said, and repeated the charm into his own hand. He started forward again, but Jia grabbed his shoulder and pointed up.

"We shouldn't go further." The walls ahead were ragged like a cave, not smooth like the stone-covered walls of the storage area. Jia's bad feeling grew more insistent.

"The tracks lead down there," Changmin whispered, his voice wavering.

"No." Jia had to take charge of this situation now. The storage area was one thing, but this led to the tunnels under the school. There was a mere one-page entry about the underground tunnels in *Galileo Academy for the Extraordinary: Official History and Records.* It simply read: *Do not enter the tunnels under the school. They were made by wild magic that is not friendly to visitors. Many who have ventured inside have never found their way out.*

"I'm sorry, Changmin, but if Sami went down there, then she's probably lost forever." Jia winced a little as she said it, but it was the truth—Changmin might as well hear it from her.

"We can't give up now!" Changmin wailed. His voice echoed down the tunnel, and Jia took a step back as if the noise would wake a beast or a specter.

"Maybe we can tell someone on staff. They could help you find Sami."

"And then they'll send her away." Changmin sniffled.

"Maybe it's for the best?" After all, those were the rules. And weren't the rules supposed to be there for a reason?

"Sami's my best friend here."

Jia frowned at the thought that her cousin's best friend was a samjogku puppy. But then again, who was she to judge? She had no friends at all.

Jia was about to take Changmin's arm to gently lead him back to the exit when they heard a keening howl from the cave.

"It's Sami!" Changmin shouted, and took off down the tunnel.

"Changmin, come back," Jia called after him. But it was useless. His magical light faded away as he sprinted toward the sound.

Jia hesitated. Maybe she should go tell a teacher, ask them for help. It was the responsible thing to do. But by then Changmin might be lost forever. And he was her responsibility. So, cursing her cousin, she took off after him.

* * *

Jia had a new plan. She was going to catch up to her cousin, and she was going to wring his neck. Then she was going to use a Stay-Put spell so he could never leave his room again.

Jia's eyes darted around the cave as she ran, and she couldn't help but feel like the walls were somehow . . . breathing. Like they were more than stone and mineral. Like these tunnels were somehow alive.

Jia caught sight of a light bouncing along ahead of her, zooming to the right with the curve of the tunnel.

"Changmin, slow down," she called, but the light raced on without slowing.

Jia was wondering if she could aim an Immobilizing spell well enough in the dark, when she realized that she was no longer following just one light but two.

What the heck? Was there someone else down here?

Jia suddenly imagined a murderer killing Professor Drop-wort and then ducking into the secret tunnels under the school to hide. She sped up her pace.

Changmin finally stopped, and Jia raced to his side and grabbed his arm, intent on pulling him away. But he pointed and exclaimed, "Sami!"

Jia looked up, and sure enough there was a small, white samjogku puppy . . . floating in the air!

No, Jia realized, she wasn't floating; she was caught in a tangle of tentacles. And whatever they were attached to let out a bioluminescent glow—the extra light Jia had seen.

"Air jellyfish," Changmin said, his eyes widening.

Then a dozen more lit up, floating lower until Jia could see that they did look like jellyfish, their tentacles hanging low beneath them as their glowing bodies wobbled and floated through the air.

"I've never seen them outside of a magical zoo before." Changmin lifted his hand toward the low-hanging tentacles.

"Changmin, no! They'll sting you!"

But he just laughed and said, "They don't sting like normal jellyfish. It's more like a static shock that kind of tickles. But how did Sami get so tangled?" He frowned as he lifted his hand toward the puppy, like he could reach her. But she was too high up. "Maybe I could climb?"

Jia shook her head. "Let's think about this. You know everything about every magical creature."

That seemed to puff Changmin up with pride. "Well, not every magical creature. There's the elusive bunyip, and of course no one's seen a firebird in who knows how long."

"Focus, Changmin," Jia said. "What do you know about air jellyfish?"

Changmin pursed his lips in thought. "They're usually very gentle. They live in dark spaces like caves, and they communicate by humming."

Jia paused. "They like the dark? Or they hate the light?"

"Isn't that the same thing?"

"Maybe. I think I have an idea." Then she recited the incantation to create light in her palm, but she combined it with a magnification charm she'd just learned last week. She wasn't sure if it would work, so she said a little prayer and then opened her palms. A beam of bright light soared out from each hand, like a crash of lightning that lit the entire cavern. Jia could see dozens of air jellyfish floating above, before they all zoomed away, seeking out any dark crevice they could find. The one holding Sami released her so quickly that she fell with a yelp. Changmin cried out and leapt to catch the puppy before she dropped to the ground. The glow from Jia's hands slowly faded until she only held a small ball of light again.

"Noona!" Changmin said. "You should have warned me first."

Jia winced. "Sorry, I didn't think they'd drop her so quickly."

But before Jia could congratulate herself, she saw the glow of lights overhead, zooming ten times faster than the jellyfish had been moving before. "Changmin!" Jia called a second before a jellyfish descended on him, its tentacles weaving around him.

Jia tried to run forward, but another jellyfish latched on to her arm. When she'd been eight, Yoon Minho, the son of one of the Chosun professors, had used a Static spell on her—that's what the air jellyfish stings felt like now. But when Jia tried to pull free, they tightened and her feet began to lift from the ground.

"Noona!" Changmin called in alarm. Sami let off another rapid set of barks.

Jia was trying to stutter out the Magnification spell again when another burst of light—a giant golden beam—appeared. It was coming from the opening to a far tunnel. Jia felt the jellyfish drop her, and she hit the ground with a thud.

"Come on!" a voice called, and Jia didn't have to be told twice. She grabbed Changmin, who was still holding Sami, and pulled him along.

They raced away from the jellyfish, following the golden

light. Once they'd gotten clear of the creatures, Jia leaned against a wall, gasping for air and clutching a stitch in her side.

When she finally straightened, she found herself face to face with a bird with dozens of beautiful mismatched feathers, like it had borrowed the plumage of others to cover itself. Jia let out a squeak and took a step back before she noticed that the bird was perched on a staff, and that staff was held by a cloaked figure, their hood pulled so low Jia couldn't see their face.

"It's a cu bird," the mysterious person said.

"Whoa," Changmin said, stepping forward. "I've never seen one in person before." He started to reach out, but the bird snapped its beak in warning, and Changmin darted to Jia's side.

"How did you make such a bright light?" Jia asked, staring at the newcomer, unsure what to make of them.

"My staff holds the feather of a firebird. This orb dims it so that it is not blinding." They pointed to the resin-like glowing bulb at the top of the staff. "I merely used an incantation to peel back that magic."

"A firebird," Changmin whispered reverently. And Jia understood—even she knew what a firebird was. They were rare and powerful, and their feathers glowed like fire. Even when they molted, the feathers never stopped glowing.

Jia stared at the orb in wonder. She'd heard rumors of firebirds being hunted for their precious feathers, or eggs being stolen and sold on the black market for millions. How had this person come into possession of something so valuable as a firebird feather? Had they gotten it through nefarious means? Were they dangerous?

"How did you find us?" Jia asked, eyeing the figure and pushing Changmin behind her in case they needed to run.

The figure finally pulled their hood back to reveal short-cropped gray hair, a weathered tan face, and sharp brown eyes. "I heard your shouts. You shouldn't be down here. It's dangerous."

"And how do you know your way?" Jia frowned.

"I'm Professor Ayala. I do independent study down here with a select few advanced students of my choosing. We document the magical creatures."

"Creatures?" Jia asked. As in, more than the angry air jellyfish? She looked around at the shadows warily.

"Yes, which is why you shouldn't wander down here alone," the professor replied. "Plus, the wild magic that created these tunnels makes it unsafe for anyone who doesn't know their way. The tunnels have a tendency to shift and change."

"We didn't have a choice!" Changmin said. As if on cue, Sami poked her head up and gave a little whimper.

Professor Ayala's eyes widened. "Ah, a samjogku puppy. I haven't seen one in years."

"We had to rescue her," Changmin said, putting Sami down so she could sniff at Professor Ayala's shoes.

"If you teach here, how come I never see you?" Jia asked, still eyeing the professor suspiciously.

"I like to spend most of my time down here. Come on, I'll lead you out." Professor Ayala turned and started down the tunnel, obviously expecting Jia and Changmin to follow. Jia caught her cousin's eyes, still unsure if she could trust this person. But Changmin just shrugged and jogged to catch up to Professor Ayala.

"Do you live down here?" Changmin asked chattily, no malice or suspicion in his voice. Jia rolled her eyes as she followed after them. Without her, Changmin would never survive this school.

Professor Ayala laughed. "Even I'm not brave enough to live down here. But I spend most days here. I like animals more than humans."

"How did you get a firebird feather?" Changmin asked, his wide eyes highlighted by the soft glow from the orb.

"By chance," Professor Ayala said vaguely.

"Did you actually *see* a firebird in real life?" Changmin asked. "Did the bird give you the feather? Are they as smart as legend says?"

Professor Ayala stopped walking, and Jia and Changmin had to stop too or risk ramming into the professor's back. They turned, and their gaze was dark and sharp as they took in Changmin. "You're a bright boy. Don't waste your time chasing after a bird that almost no one has ever seen. Remember, firebirds are harbingers of doom, and often tragedy befalls anyone who tries to possess one." Then they muttered to themself, "Strange how people are suddenly so interested in firebirds."

"Who else is interested?" Changmin asked.

Professor Ayala laughed. "You really have no filter, do you?"

Changmin grinned and said, "My mom says I'm still bordering on precocious, but that I'd better watch my butt."

That made the professor chuckle again as they said, "Well, I'm afraid Professor Dropwort will never get a chance to see a firebird now."

"*Dropwort's* the one who asked?" Jia blurted out so loudly that it echoed against the cave walls.

"Mm-hmm. Why does it matter to you?" Professor Ayala

asked, climbing over a large boulder. They reached back to help Changmin over, then Jia.

"Because I want to know what happened to him," Jia said, trying to figure out how to wheedle more information from Professor Ayala. "Why did he want to know about firebirds?" Jia tried to keep her voice casual, like she was merely curious.

"The same as most people. How I came across the feather. If I'd ever had a firebird in my possession. How to care for them. If I'd ever hatched one. I told him the same thing I'm telling you, that it's not worth wasting your time looking for a firebird. No matter how powerful they are, they're too rare. You could waste your whole life just trying to get a peek at one."

"Did you talk to Dropwort a lot?" Jia asked. "Were you . . . friends?"

Professor Ayala threw back their head and let out a rumbling laugh. "Oh, definitely not. Dropwort wouldn't ever hang out with a queer nonbinary Sorcerer. Not that I'd want to hang out with him either. Found him an insufferable bore."

Jia was shocked at that. It seemed wrong to talk badly about the dead, no matter how bigoted the dead had been. "Ah, okay, so you didn't see him after he asked about the firebird?" Jia was starting to deflate.

"The last time I saw Professor Dropwort, he was talking with that kid who helps with the gargoyles. They were having some kind of disagreement."

"What did they look like?" Jia asked eagerly.

Professor Ayala thought about it a moment. "Tall, gangly boy. Blondish hair, I think."

Jia didn't recognize the description, but she made a mental

note to look into him. "And you didn't think to tell anyone this?"

Professor Ayala raised their eyebrows. "I told Vice Principal Beckley what I saw. Sometimes the smartest thing to do is trust the experts to do their job."

Jia frowned. Maybe that worked for Professor Ayala, someone who was content playing with their animals all day. But Jia knew that she had to take the lead on things if she was going to succeed her appa as headmaster at Chosun someday.

"Sami! Stop that," Changmin said to the puppy, who'd begun furiously digging at a corner, growling low in her throat. Changmin frowned as he moved toward her. "Sami, what is it?"

But before he could pick her up, the cave began to rumble. It shook the ground so hard that Jia almost lost her footing. Jia let out a shout as a shower of stones fell right over Changmin's head. She raced forward and wrapped her arms around him, letting the rocks hit her in the shoulder. They both tumbled to the ground.

The two cousins held on to each other until the cave finally stopped shaking. Slowly Jia lifted her aching body, rubbing at a spot on her shoulder where a large stone had struck.

"Are you okay?" Jia asked.

Changmin nodded, scooping the whimpering puppy into his arms, and said, "Sami and I are both fine." Then he looked around and said, "Wait, where's the professor?"

Jia spun around in surprise. Where Professor Ayala had been standing a moment ago there now was only stone.

"Kids!" came a muffled call, and Jia let out a breath of relief. The professor hadn't been crushed by the rockslide, but they *had* been cut off from Jia and Changmin.

186

Jia pressed her ear against the stone. "Professor?"

"Are you two okay?" the professor's muted voice called.

"Yeah," Jia replied. "Just shaken up."

"Stay there. I'll find a way to get you out."

The rocks rumbled again, and Jia stepped back, worried another rain of stones would fall on them.

"Who disturbs me?" said a voice that creaked like aged wood.

Jia spun around, readying to fend off another creature. But she didn't see anything at first. Then the rock wall that Sami had been pawing at started to *move.*

No, not a wall, Jia realized, but the shell of an enormous turtle-like creature. Its face, now poking out of the shell, was distinctly human, like an old Asian man with a long white beard, bushy eyebrows, and wrinkled gray skin.

"Jinsilmadi," Changmin whispered reverently.

Jia's brow lifted at the word. She had heard her halmeoni tell stories about such a creature.

"We're sorry to disturb your slumber," Jia said, bowing at a ninety-degree angle. She grabbed Changmin's hand and pulled him down into a bow as well.

"You should show him respect," Jia whispered.

The jinsilmadi shifted its giant body. "It has been so long since I've seen others. What truths do you hide?"

"Excuse me?" Jia said with a frown.

"Don't you remember from Halmeoni's stories?" Changmin reminded her. "Jinsilmadi likes to uncover hidden truths."

"Oh yeah." Jia nodded as the tales came back to her. A jinsilmadi was a creature that could find the truth no matter how deeply buried.

"Touch my shell. Show me what you hide," the jinsilmadi said.

Changmin stepped forward.

"What are you doing?" Jia hissed.

"You said to show him respect," Changmin said. Before Jia could stop him, he pressed his palm to the large shell, and it began to glow.

"You do not have many hidden truths," the jinsilmadi hummed. "But there's one hidden even from yourself."

Jia watched as her cousin let out a gasp.

"I saw a figure. It had on gloves. With spikes? It took something. I couldn't see it. I was too far away. I was scared." Changmin looked panicked, his eyes darting around at the shadows of the cave.

"What are you doing? Why is he reacting like this?" Jia asked the jinsilmadi.

"He is reliving a memory."

Changmin closed his eyes and began muttering to himself. "Gloves with spikes. They took something from the body. I can't see it."

The body? Jia thought. *Dropwort's body?*

Changmin began to shake, tears falling from his eyes. "I'm scared," he whispered shakily.

"That's enough. Let him go. He told you his secret." Jia pulled on Changmin's hand, but as her knuckles brushed the shell, it glowed again and she felt like she was plucked off her feet.

One second she was in the cave beside her cousin; the next she was in pitch black surrounded by fog.

"Hello?" she called. The dark space absorbed her words.

Nothing echoed back. Out of the darkness a figure appeared, an old man in gray robes with the dark eyes of the jinsilmadi.

"Where am I?" Jia asked.

"In a space between your conscious mind and subconscious. The place where humans hide their truths." The jinsilmadi frowned. "You search for answers."

"I—I'm trying to solve a murder," she stuttered. "To find justice."

"Is that the truth?"

"Yes," Jia said weakly.

"Not all of it." The jinsilmadi's eyes narrowed even further.

Jia could feel the force of the stare, like it pushed at her brain. And soon she found herself blurting out, "I want to be seen!"

The jinsilmadi's large dark eyes widened, and Jia felt more words tumble free. "For once, I want to be seen as someone worthy."

"And why do you want that?" The jinsilmadi's stare started to make Jia's skin heat.

"Because I have to be the best."

"No, that's not all of it."

Jia shook her head as something pushed against her chest. Like words she'd long buried were fighting to be free.

That pressure built and built until she could barely breathe.

"Because maybe once I'm seen as worthy, I won't have to be perfect all the time. It's exhausting and . . . lonely," Jia gasped out.

"And why do you have to be perfect, Jia Park?" the jinsilmadi's booming voice asked.

She shook her head again. This was too much. She didn't

want to think about this. How the effort to appear as if she knew every answer, could ace every test, could navigate every problem felt like a crushing weight. How she feared that people would figure out she was a fraud because no one could be as perfect as Jia pretended to be. How she had to be the one and only representative of an entire complicated group of people. How she felt like she was failing at it all. And that's why her parents weren't bringing her home.

"Because if I'm not perfect, they won't love me."

"Ah." The jinsilmadi smiled, his eyes disappearing under wrinkles.

And finally, Jia let out a single sob. And with that small release, the wall she'd built to keep all her insecurities at bay collapsed. And the pressures she'd lived with her whole life came crashing free like water breaking out of a dam. Jia folded in half as the sobs overtook her. And the harder she tried to stop, the more her body shook.

"Stop!" Professor Ayala's voice broke through. "You've got your truths from them. Let them go."

Suddenly Jia fell backward, her hands digging into rock and dirt. Changmin was sprawled beside her, blinking owlishly, tears still damp on his face.

"Thank you for your truths." The jinsilmadi towered above them, huffing, before it receded back into its shell. Its large body shifted and lowered, the rocks rumbling precariously above them.

Jia gazed at the professor in astonishment. "How did you get to us?" she asked. "We thought you were trapped."

Professor Ayala nodded toward an archway that almost looked like a natural formation, even though it hadn't been there five minutes ago. "It took me a minute, but my magic was finally able to work its way through," they said. Then they took Jia's hand gently. "Come on, I'm taking you back to the school."

Jia nodded weakly and let the professor lead her and Chang-min like children through the archway. Her cousin recovered more quickly than Jia. And he started chirping questions at the professor. Jia would have told him to leave the professor alone, except she had a headache and was too exhausted to rein him in.

"How many magical creatures are down here?" Changmin asked, shifting to cradle Sami closer.

The professor thought a moment. "No one really knows, but I find a couple of new ones every year. Just today I ran into a peculiar girl looking for a new catlike creature called a perl. Apparently it sheds sand."

"Whoa." Changmin looked like he'd never want to leave the tunnels. Which would be difficult for Jia to explain to her samchon and aunt.

As they emerged back into the storage hallways, Changmin slowed to walk beside Jia. "Noona?"

"Hmm?" she replied, still huffing a bit with exertion.

"I'm sorry you feel so lonely sometimes."

"You heard that?" Jia asked, surprised.

"Some of it." Changmin shrugged. "But it's okay, I get it. I don't really fit in either."

"It doesn't matter," Jia said. "I'm going to catch whoever killed Professor Dropwort, and then my parents will see that they were wrong for sending me away. Then I can go home, to where all my old friends are."

"That's why you want to catch the killer? So you can leave?"

"Oh, don't worry," Jia assured him. "I'll make sure they bring you back home too."

"I don't want to go home."

Jia frowned. "But you just said you don't fit in here."

"But maybe one day I will. Besides, I like it here. Don't you?"

"It's not about liking it here. Every head of Chosun graduated from there. It's a tradition." It's why Jia had been so upset about being sent away. In her heart she always worried it meant her parents didn't think she was up to the task of running Chosun one day.

"You know your appa wasn't the one who wanted to send you here."

Jia stopped in her tracks at that. "What?"

"Yeah, I heard samchon talking to my appa before they sent me here. He said your eomma was the one who wanted to send you. She said she wanted you to 'see more of the world so you'd have no regrets,'" Changmin said.

Before she could unpack that thought, they emerged into the loading area by the service elevators. Professor Ayala waved their hand over the magical lock pad, and there was a hum as the elevator was summoned.

"Thank you," Jia said with a grateful nod.

"It was nice to meet two bright students." Professor Ayala held out a hand to Changmin, who shook it eagerly.

"I had an amazing time! I never thought I'd see a cu bird or an air jellyfish or a firebird's feather." He hesitated. "I'd love to be able to see more of your creatures. Maybe one day you'll find a real firebird!"

The professor smiled kindly, and Jia was afraid they were going to remind Changmin of the school rules and break his heart. But instead the professor said, "You know, I've been thinking of getting a new apprentice. My last one graduated two years ago, and I've been feeling a bit lonely, taking care of the creatures all on my own."

Changmin's eyes widened with glee. "Yes!" he shouted just as the elevator doors dinged open. "I'd love that."

Professor Ayala laughed and then turned to Jia as she was stepping into the elevator. "I hope you find what you're looking for." It didn't sound like they were talking about catching Dropwort's killer.

"Um, thanks," Jia said awkwardly as the elevator doors closed.

The last thing Jia saw was Professor Ayala's kind and knowing smile.

Sami had fallen asleep in Changmin's arms. He gently placed her into his pocket, petting her lightly on her dozing head. Jia just watched him. The only moments Changmin seemed still and calm were when he was with his magical creatures. Had this always been the case and she'd just never realized it before?

There's so much Jia had never noticed before.

Changmin's words came back to her. That her eomma had wanted her to see the world. To have experiences outside Chosun. And she'd spent the last two years refusing to think of anything but getting back home. She felt ashamed that she was squandering the gift that her mother had tried to give her.

She'd been so focused on seeing her time at Galileo as a punishment, she hadn't let herself really live.

It might have hurt to be forced by the jinsilmadi to tell her deepest secret. But now that it was out in the open, Jia could see that her pursuit of perfection had stopped her from really living. It stopped her from putting down roots at Galileo or making friends . . .

Well, maybe there was one student who still wanted to be her friend. Or maybe more than friends? Odd, bright, perky Layla Longfeather, with her kind green eyes, ink-stained fingers, and an ever-ready smile for Jia.

But was it too late?

No, she wouldn't think that way. She was Jia Park; when she set her mind on doing something, she accomplished it. Besides, if even her little oddball cousin could find a place here, then she probably could too.

And when the elevator dinged open, she started walking with a newfound purpose.

"Noona, don't you want Sami to help you with your investigation?" Changmin called after her.

"Maybe later. Go to class, Changmin."

Jia walked straight for the music rooms, where she knew she'd find Layla. The other girl was just walking out of a room with a couple of her friends in tow. It stopped Jia in her tracks. She wasn't sure if she had the guts to interrupt the laughter and conversation. Would Layla think she was rude for suddenly wanting to talk after avoiding her so hard earlier? But Layla looked up, and her eyes widened when she saw Jia.

"What happened to you?" She rushed over and grabbed Jia's hands.

"What?" Jia asked with a frown, looking self-consciously at Layla's friends, who'd started giggling the moment Layla had taken her hands. She tried to pull free, but Layla held tight.

"Hey, guys, go on ahead. I'll catch up to you," Layla said. Her friends nodded and linked arms, walking toward the stairwell, their heads bent close together as they chatted.

"You could have gone with them," Jia muttered, suddenly feeling uncertain, standing alone with Layla. The other girl's hands were still wrapped around hers.

"I didn't want to go with them. I wanted to see if you're okay. You have dirt everywhere, and you're cut!" Layla lifted her thumb to run over Jia's cheek.

Jia stepped back, realizing she'd forgotten to clean up first. She'd let herself get carried away and hadn't even thought about her appearance. This was not the perfect facade she was used to showing to the world.

But maybe she didn't care.

Jia smiled shyly at Layla. "Well, I could tell you about the wild morning I had, if you'd like. Maybe during a study date?" Layla's eyes opened wide in surprise.

"And," Jia hurried on, "maybe you could tell me more about Wands. I hear some great magical philosophers have come out of that house. That's a good skill to have for someone in a leadership role, right?"

Jia practically held her breath, waiting for the reply. She told herself she'd be okay if Layla said no. After all, how many times had Jia brushed Layla off in the past? But instead the other girl blushed. It made the freckles that danced across her nose darken, and she smiled shyly as she said, "Yeah, a study date sounds nice."

Layla held out her hand, and Jia took it, letting their fingers link. She felt that same spark itch down her skin. But this time she let it spread, and she realized it felt good.

When they turned the corner, they almost collided with a girl. Layla put her arm out protectively, pushing Jia back as the girl barreled past them without so much as an "I'm sorry."

Layla tsked. "Some people are too focused on their own stuff to take a look around."

Layla's arm was still half around Jia. They were practically hugging in the middle of the hallway. Jia let out a nervous laugh, her heart racing. She didn't know where to look, so she glanced at the girl who'd raced by; then Jia narrowed her eyes.

The girl was in all black, with a choppy haircut, one patch dyed a faded blue. She definitely seemed like she was in a hurry—something that wouldn't have struck Jia as odd, except that she saw something glinting on the girl's hand: a black glove with silver studs.

Changmin's mutterings to the jinsilmadi came back to her. He'd seen someone with "gloves with spikes" hovering over Dropwort.

"Who is that?" Jia asked. She internally cursed herself for being so antisocial that she didn't recognize the student's face.

Layla looked toward the girl and said, "Oh, she's in my charms class. Cortez or something."

Jia started after the girl, but realized her hand was still firmly clutched in Layla's. Crap, was this bad date etiquette? Leaving before the date had even begun felt like a no-brainer faux pas.

When Jia looked back again, the Cortez girl was nowhere in sight.

Maybe it was for the best. What was Jia even planning to say? *Did you murder our professor?*

"Hey, where'd you go?" Layla asked, and Jia turned back

to face her. Layla was watching Jia with worried eyes, her nose scrunched in concern.

"Nowhere. I just have to . . ." She trailed off, unsure how to explain to Layla what was going on.

Layla frowned and let go of Jia's hand. "Oh, you don't want to do the study date anymore?"

"No. I do," Jia said, shaking her head at how silly she was being. Figuring out who the killer is was not her sole responsibility.

Jia took Layla's hand again. "Let's go."

She would tell the principal about Dropwort asking about firebirds. About the gloves and Cortez.

But it could wait, until after her date.

And Jia let Layla lead her toward the library. Feeling, for the first time since she'd come to Galileo, that she was excited to be here.

CASE ID: 20-06-DROS-STK

Type:

[ ] Communication

[ ] Audio recording

[ ] Spell residue

[ ] Photo or other visual reconstruction

[ ] Object

[ ] Form or record

[X] Other: Excerpt of bird spreadsheet

Source: Park Changmin, student

Relevant Parties: Park Changmin, student

Description: Excerpt of bird spreadsheet found in school cafeteria, composed by Park Changmin, student.

Investigator's note: connection to missing artifact may be coincidental.

Bird	Rarity	Home	Notes
Cenderewasih	Intermediate	Southeast Asia	Guardian of sacred jewels, drinks only dew and eats only clouds
Martlet	Common	Great Britain	They never land, said to represent quest for knowledge and adventure
Caladrius	Common	Western Europe	Can detect illness, and heal people! So cool!
Firebird	SUPER rare	Central Europe	Feathers give off light, supposed to be a blessing, but omen of doom for anyone who traps them
Alicanto	Rare	Chile	Eats precious metals, feathers match the metal it eats, nocturnal

9:00 A.M.: IRENE SEAVER, 16, CUPS/COINS

BY KAYLA WHALEY

The first ever Sorcerer-Neutral Anti-Conflict Conventions Conference on Climate Change (SNACC-CCC) was being held in Turkmenistan in two days' time, and Irene Seaver had been chosen as the Youth Sorcerer Ambassador. The recognition was nice, sure, but more important, she was going to use the platform to introduce her Ten Steps to Climate Stability, the plan she had spent most of her life putting together. Years of poring over every piece of Neutral and Sorcerer research, pulling together the disparate strands from both worlds, conducting her own research as Galileo flew to every climatological region, trying to form a more unified—and useful—approach to climate change.

Except now Dropwort had gone and gotten himself murdered, and if the school didn't leave Stockholm as planned, Irene would miss the conference entirely.

She'd been born prematurely during an ill-advised skinny-dip in the Gulf of Mexico, slipping from womb to storm-frothed waters before her mom could even head for shore. Irene should have died in those waves, but the gulf had spat her out onshore, wrapped snug in seaweed and clutching a pearl in one tiny hand.

So, no one was surprised when her magic showed up. Tiny but potent gusts of wind whipping through the kitchen during a mealtime tantrum. Localized lightning storms in their backyard whenever Irene had a nightmare. But no amount of *Raising Magical Children for Neutral-Born Parents* could have prepared her mom and dad for the blizzard that swept through Mobile, Alabama, when Irene was six. They'd found her sitting on the floor of her closet, her wheelchair abandoned outside the door. Her hands were on her lap, and in them rested the pearl. Her parents knew enough not to force her to stop whatever summoning she was doing, so they simply asked her why. "Global warming," she said. "Our teacher said the earth is too hot. I'm fixing it." By the time they convinced her she couldn't single-handedly reverse climate change, five feet of snow had dumped across the coasts of Mississippi and Alabama, and into the panhandle of Florida.

Nowadays her strategies involved policy and politics as much as meteorological magic, but that instinct to protect, the overpowering need to heal this world, was still always at the forefront of her mind. The ocean had chosen to spare her, had saved her for some reason when it should have swallowed her whole. She had a debt to repay and a mission to accomplish. Her speech at SNACC-CCC was the opportunity she'd been waiting for. She was not about to let one pesky murder get in her way, even if she had to solve the damn thing herself.

"Babe, this is extremely above our pay grade," Irene's best friend, Viv, said. "I'm sure the authorities are handling it."

Irene scoffed. "I'm not."

They were outside Dropwort's rooms, which happened to be right next door to Irene's room. As a rule, no students were allowed in faculty housing. Irene was the disabled exception.

"You didn't hear the junior professors talking about the tip line," Irene said.

She'd been in the faculty break room that morning filling her thermos with coffee (the good, freshly roasted kind, not the stale garbage they served in the dining hall; faculty housing did have *some* perks) when she'd overheard two of the newest teachers chatting. Complaining, more like.

"They were saying how all the tips were prank calls from students," Irene said, "and they couldn't believe they had to waste their time wading through them all."

"See?" Viv said. "They *are* handling it. Reluctantly, maybe, but still."

Irene slammed her hand onto her armrest. "You're not listening. The calls are mostly nonsense, but they mentioned one that felt . . . wrong."

"Wrong how?"

Irene tried to remember the zap of awareness she'd felt earlier, tried to turn the feeling into words. "Like a black sky tinted green on an April afternoon."

Viv was from Oklahoma. She knew that such a sky meant danger—and soon.

"The tip said to search Dropwort's quarters. Said the killer was sloppy, left a trail. But the teachers figured it was another joke call since his rooms are so far from where his body was found."

The hallway around them felt narrower than normal, and Irene's palms tingled as she thought about someone coming around the corner while they were loitering outside a murder victim's door.

"Can you get through the locks or not?" Irene asked, sharper than she meant to.

Viv bit her lip, a gesture Irene normally found adorable but that at the moment was beyond frustrating. "He's dead, though," Viv whispered dramatically. "Like, the man *just* died. Doesn't it feel wrong to break into a dead man's rooms like this?"

Irene snorted. "No."

"Wow. Okay. I didn't realize I was best friends with the ice queen of Arendelle."

"Hey, keep your voice down!" Irene sighed and scooched closer. "Did I ever tell you what Dropwort said when Mom and I moved in?"

Viv shook her head.

"We were still unpacking when he showed up in the doorframe, looming there all creepily, as he does. He didn't even mutter a hello when Mom went over to introduce herself. The only thing he said, I shit you not, was 'Faculty housing should be for *faculty.*'"

Viv's mouth dropped open. "He did not."

Irene nodded. "He sure did. Didn't even bother trying to hide the disdain on his face either. Like, listen, buddy, I would love to live in student housing with my actual peers, but unfortunately this school somehow can't manage to build any accessible housing whatsoever, so suck it up, buttercup."

Viv gasped. "You *said that*? To *Dropwort*?"

Irene slapped her friend's arm. "Of course not. I just thought it really loudly."

Her relationship with her imposing neighbor hadn't improved

any from that first meeting. Dropwort had constantly been finding reasons to complain about Irene, and even more so about her Neutral mom, Irene's caregiver. Irene had learned quickly how to avoid the worst of his capricious moods, both in the classroom and outside it. It was either that or be utterly miserable until graduation—*if* she managed to graduate. She wasn't sure he'd had enough power to actually stop her from finishing school, but she hadn't wanted to test that assumption.

So for two years she'd kept to herself, stayed out of everyone's way. Not just Dropwort's but all the faculty. Her classmates for the most part too. Every time a class had a trip into Amsterdam or Cairo or Yellowstone or anywhere else she was likely to have trouble getting around without help, she stayed put. The school had already made so many exceptions for her to even attend that she didn't want to ask for anything else. What if they realized they had already given her too much? What if they decided she was too much trouble?

She'd only met Viv because the other girl, perpetually being punished for one infraction or another, had been banned from the Angkor Wat trip in their first year. The two of them had been the only ones from their class left aboard. Irene had found Viv pouting in the library. Without preamble, Irene had sat across from her, glad to have someone to pass the day with, even if that someone *was* a sulky mess. They—along with Viv's other friends, Nadiya and Xander—had been close ever since.

Irene clasped her hands together in front of her chest and looked up at her friend with every ounce of sincerity in her. "Viv. Please. Just help me with the breaking part, and I'll handle all the entering, okay?"

Viv stared at Irene for a long moment, hesitation painted

more heavily on her face than her signature cat eyeliner. "I still think we should let the police or whoever deal with it."

"Oh, please. I don't trust any of those petty bureaucratic asses to handle anything on their own. You know how many years Neutrals and Sorcerers have been arguing over the cause of climate change? Not the solution, mind you. The *cause*. Neutrals say magical runoff and excess arcane energy buildup are responsible. Sorcerers say carbon emissions and greenhouse gases are responsible. Meanwhile, the earth just gets hotter because—spoiler alert!—you're *both* to blame. Now please shut the hell up and get to fixing things before we all bite it."

Viv stared blankly down at her friend. "I hope that's not how you're opening your speech."

"Oh, shut up," Irene said, cheeks flaming. "The point is, adults can't be trusted. Listen. Someone straight-up murdered Dropwort, and now they're wandering around with no one the wiser. We can stop that."

Viv rolled her eyes. "I think you're vastly overestimating our detective skills, but . . . Fine." She knelt down in front of the door to get a better look at the lock.

Irene fist-pumped. "I knew being besties with a mechanical engineer would come in handy one day." She turned eagerly back to Dropwort's door, conscious that speed was of the essence.

"Yeah, yeah, just don't get your hopes up. These locks look really compli—" Viv stopped suddenly and leaned back on her heels. With Viv kneeling like this, Irene sat a bit taller than her, a rare treat, given her friend's nearly six-foot frame.

"What is it? What's wrong?" Irene asked.

"It's open."

Irene tilted her head. "You cracked it that fast? Are you sure this is your first time lockpicking?"

"No. It was *already* open. Like, he forgot to lock up when he left."

"That doesn't make any sense," Irene said, leaning in to stare at the door's unwieldy system of custom locks, more like a bank vault than a teacher's dorm room. "I've seen him stand here for five whole minutes locking up all the different parts of this contraption."

Irene shrugged. "Maybe he was distracted? I don't know what to tell you, babe. But there's no B required for this B and E."

Viv stood and picked up her book bag. When she turned to leave, Irene grabbed her arm. Viv looked down, eyes narrowed. "No," she said.

Irene put on her best puppy-dog face, the one that Viv could never, ever resist.

"*Babe,* I'm not trying to get expelled, okay?"

"Five minutes. Just come in with me for five minutes. What if there's something important that I can't reach? I can't just levitate it to me. He's probably got all sorts of anti-magic wards up, and I'm terrible with wards."

Viv groaned loudly enough that Irene worried her mom might hear from next door, where she was eating breakfast and catching up on her late-night shows. But then Viv grabbed the door handle and said, "If I get kicked out of school, *you* have to explain why to my dads."

Irene saluted. "Yes, ma'am. Now let's get to burgling—I mean, *investigating*—shall we?"

* * *

Dropwort's living quarters were somehow both exactly and nothing at all like what Irene had expected. The couple of times she'd been in Dropwort's office, she'd been struck by the disciplined extravagance of it all. Gaudiness with a ruler strapped to its spine. His office was an oppressive space. Made you want to hold your breath. His living quarters, while equally full of endless and various *stuff,* felt less like a "Please Don't Touch" museum and more like a storage room. A well-maintained storage room, but a storage room nonetheless. The living room was mostly overfull bookshelves, with a few stacks of overflow on either side of the couch. Which shouldn't seem so strange, except even from a distance there didn't seem to be any *intent* behind which books went where. The bookshelves in his classroom and office proper put the good old Dewey decimal system to shame. Here the books seemed . . . haphazard. Even the furniture (black leather couch, inexplicable wicker basket chair, tufted love seat) was a mishmash. Nothing felt like it belonged.

Now that they were inside, Irene realized she didn't actually know what she was looking for. Something suspicious? A flashing neon sign with an arrow pointing to a smoking gun? She loved nothing more in life than a well-thought-out, detailed plan. This was neither, and it made her itchy.

3 Steps to Solving a Murder:
Step 1: break into murder victim's home
Step 2: ???
Step 3: solve climate change

How did detectives in movies investigate a crime scene? All she could remember was that they always wore gloves.

"I didn't think to bring any gloves," she muttered to herself.

"What's that?"

"Nothing! Just, uh, strategizing our approach."

Dropwort's apartment, like her own, had an open floor plan. Off to the left was the dining room, which would be attached to a small kitchen. To the right of the living room was another slightly smaller room Dropwort was clearly using as a home office. Beyond that should be a short hallway connecting to the master suite. *Okay, start with the obvious.* Irene straightened into her best presenter posture—shoulders back, head raised, spine as straight as her scoliosis would allow—and gave out her orders.

"You check the bookshelves first, and I'll go through his desk."

Viv nodded and made her way to the far side of the room. In Irene's dorm, that wall was covered in the macramé hangings her mom had started making when they'd moved in. "You're learning about cryptozoology and the history of necromancy," Mom had said. "I want to learn something too!" And she had. The pieces she'd made at the start had been simple one-knot affairs, but now her work was elaborate and detailed. There was something soothing about coming home after a particularly long day to find her mom curled up on the couch slowly turning a pile of rope into a geometric, colorful piece of art. Irene mostly resented not being able to live with her friends and classmates, but she had to admit how nice it was to have her mom here.

"Gross," Viv said, running her finger along one shelf. "They're so dusty." She swiped her hand against her dark-wash jeans. *Storage room,* Irene thought again. Maybe this was where he kept all the items he deemed not quite important enough to display on campus. The rejects of his collection. Now that she thought about it, it shouldn't be surprising that Dropwort would hoard hundreds of books and never even open them. Everything about him was for show.

Irene headed into the adjacent room. Dropwort's desk, a giant mahogany monstrosity, sat square in the middle of the space like an altar, complete with candelabras on each end (still lit) and an overgrown throne of a chair. The small room's walls were absolutely *covered* with artifacts: masks, swords, wands, chalices, dolls, staves, jewelry. They were each on their own floating shelf, all in relative shadow. The effect was eerie. "Probably how serial killers display their trophies." She shuddered and turned her focus to the desk.

A few more stacks of books (also dusty); a slim pile of students' assignments, with signature red felt-tip pen waiting to be uncapped lying on top; and an honest-to-God typewriter.

"You think he spelled this to do his work for him?" Irene called out.

Viv didn't turn around from the bookcase. "Don't even need to know what you're talking about to say yes."

Irene laughed, then stilled. Next to the inexplicable typewriter was a plate of half-eaten steak and untouched asparagus. The meat was rare and bloody, the asparagus in a puddle of long-melted butter. Perhaps the most jarring thing, though, was the fork lying next to the plate, a cube of steak still speared on the tines and leaking pink juice onto the otherwise pristine desk.

"Look at this," Irene said. Viv snapped closed whatever book she was reading and bounced over. Irene pointed at the dinner plate. "Do you know how long it took me to convince Fornax to let me eat in my room when I have a pain flare-up? And Dropwort just has a whole steak delivered apparently whenever he wants?"

"Ugh, that's so typical."

Irene shoved the small plate, and butter sloshed over the edge onto the wooden desk. She hoped it would soak into the grain, leave an oily stain. "Why would his food be here, though?" she asked, her annoyance nowhere near placated by her tiny rebellion.

"He didn't feel like doing dishes?"

"There's nothing out of place in this whole apartment. It's not *clean*—"

Viv looked at her fingers in disgust. "That's for damn sure."

"—but it's not messy. So why leave this here? And how could he just forget to lock the door? None of it makes any sense."

"He must have been in a hurry."

Irene nodded and ran a finger absently on the rim of the plate. The porcelain felt . . . gritty. "Oh, come on," she said, pulling her hand away. "He doesn't even wash his dishes? That's so nasty."

"Didn't," Viv corrected.

"Sorry?"

"He *didn't* wash his dishes. We should probably get used to the past tense, right?"

They looked at each other, an uncomfortable silence falling as thick as a valley fog over the room. Irene cleared her throat first. "Right, well, regardless, there's dust all over this plate." She held her finger up as proof but stopped short. "Viv, arm?"

Viv picked Irene's arm up the way she always did when her friend needed to tuck her hair behind her ear or adjust her glasses. Irene liked to joke that she gauged the closeness of her friendships by how comfortable she was asking for positioning help. Nadiya and Xander were both foot friends, people Irene didn't hesitate to ask to pull her sneaker an inch this way or that when her leg started hurting. Viv was her only foot *and* arm friend. She sometimes wondered how many more she'd have if she weren't so literally separated from everyone.

"What's wrong, babe?" Viv asked, holding Irene's arm steady.

Irene stared intently at her finger, then gestured to let Viv know she could set her arm down. "That isn't dust. It's sand."

"What? Where?"

"On the plate. I've been on beaches my entire life, and *that* is definitely sand. The really fine, shimmery kind that's so reflective, it hurts to look at on sunny days."

They both leaned over Dropwort's abandoned plate. Sure enough, tiny particles of sand littered the surface, mixed with the bloody runoff and butter sheen like the gritty dregs in a shucked oyster shell. When Irene picked up the fork, a small pile of sand fell onto the table. The sight made her shiver, and the fork slipped out of her grip. It hit meat-first and bounced off the desk's surface before cartwheeling straight onto the floor.

"Don't worry, babe. I got this." With a wink, Viv bent and crawled under the desk. "Huh," she said, her voice muffled. "That's weird."

Before Irene could ask, Viv popped back up with the fork in one hand and an ornate silver flask in the other. Irene gasped. "Is that . . . ?"

"Sure looks like it, doesn't it?"

Dropwort's flask was legendary. Students could gauge his mood for the day by how often he took a swig from it in the first five minutes of class. No swigs meant "distracted, won't bother teaching anything but probably won't antagonize anyone either." One to two swigs meant "snippy, but keep your head down and you'll be fine." Three to four meant "*You* get a scolding, and *you* get a scolding, everybody gets a scolding!" Four to five meant "probably should've conjured yourself a stomach flu and dealt with a day of Nurse Fibula's puns instead." More than five meant "you're screwed, sorry, can't be helped."

There were even bets as to what was inside, but no one expected those bets would ever be collected. He never even left it on his desk, let alone unattended.

"I've never seen it this close up," Irene said. She held out a hand, and Viv gently placed the small flask down. The outside was engraved with a strange swirling design. Almost like filigree but . . . off. The pattern seemed kinetic somehow. Irene suddenly felt dizzy.

"I don't think we should try to open it," Irene said slowly.

"What? Of course we should! We can finally figure out what he was always drinking. My money's still on whiskey. Everyone thinks it's this or that fancy potion or whatever, but I bet he's just your basic old white man drinking on the job. Was. I bet he *was* your basic old white man."

Irene carefully set the flask in her lap. It felt important not to lose track of it. "Fine, but let's let Nadiya do it instead. I felt . . . something when I held it. Something wrong. Nadiya'll be able to tell if there's anything weird going on with it."

Viv nodded, and Irene started sifting through the papers

piled up next to the typewriter. Most were indeed their assignments. (Viv shuffled through them until she found her worksheet on the history of Sorcerer-Neutral conflict, which Dropwort had marked with a C-. "Bastard," she muttered, then crossed herself in apology. Irene laughed. "You aren't even Catholic, you weirdo.") There were some memos from Principal Fornax and Vice Principal Beckley, a few notes from Nurse Fibula excusing students from class.

The only suspicious thing they found was a small leather ledger, its pages filled with columns of cryptic code and indecipherable numbers.

"Some kind of log?" Viv asked.

Irene made a noncommittal noise. "Maybe a budget or something?"

"Oh my God," Viv said with a dramatic gasp. "Dropwort's bullet journal era?"

Irene was about to give in and tell Viv they could wrap up their pitiful investigation, when a piece of paper sticking out from under the typewriter caught her eye. She tried to pull it out, but the damn typewriter was too heavy. Seriously, who has a hulking beast of an antique instead of a laptop? Viv noticed her struggling and picked the typewriter up while Irene snatched the paper out from under it.

"What does it say?" Viv asked, peeking over Irene's shoulder.

"Nothing I'd want to say in front of my mother, that's for sure." She read out a few of the choicest turns of phrase, honestly worried her mom would hear the cursing from the other room and come in ready for a good old-fashioned scolding sesh. "But look at the end part. 'Return what you stole.' Signed, LC."

"Well, that's . . . ominous," Viv said. "'What you stole.' That's gotta mean the artifact from that prophecy we heard this morning, right?"

"One would assume, yeah. So whoever wrote this is probably the Chosen One the smoke mentioned. I guess the anonymous tip wasn't a joke after all. Pretty bold move for the murderer to come into Dropwort's rooms and—"

"Irene May Seaver! What in God's name are you doing?" Her mom's voice sliced through the entryway, the living room, and straight over to where Irene and Viv huddled over Dropwort's desk.

Irene cut a glare at her best friend and hissed, "You didn't close the door?!"

Viv held up her hands. "I mostly closed it! Just not all the way. I didn't want it to lock again. I never technically unlocked it in the first place, remember? I didn't want to test my skill from the inside."

Irene's mom strode over from the front door so fast and hard that Irene could swear the swords on the walls around them started rattling. Thankfully, Irene had parked angled slightly away from the door, so she had just enough time to ball up the tiny incriminating note and slip the flask that was still in her lap down into the side of her chair, right between the seat cushion and the frame. It should be safe there until she could get it to Nadiya. As for the note . . . maybe if she gave it to Xander, he could search Dropwort's on-campus office. The killer might have left some clues there too. Or maybe the stolen artifact would be hidden there since it clearly wasn't here.

"Mom! We, uh, we were just . . ." Irene looked to Viv for help.

"We were sad!" Viv shouted. The sudden volume made

Irene's mom screech to a halt a few steps away. "We were—we *are* sad. We're in shock! Dropwort dying and everything. . . . It's a lot to process, you know?"

Irene resisted the incredibly strong urge to face-palm at her friend's truly horrendous excuse, and her even less convincing facial expression, but instead she snatched Viv's discarded term paper from the desk and held it up. "We wanted to know what we scored on our midterms. We were worried with, you know, everything, that we'd have to wait forever. And, well, the door was open, so we didn't technically do anything wrong."

"Trespassing, my loves, is definitely wrong. And you two are terrible liars." She took a deep breath, and Irene could *feel* the lecture coming. But then her mom leaned forward and whispered, "But that bastard gave us hell for years, so your secret's safe with me. Just this once."

Irene smiled while Viv nearly started crying in thanks. Their secret was safe with her mom, and just as soon as Irene had a chance, Dropwort's mysterious flask and the strange note would be safe with Nadiya and Xander. With any luck, two days from now she'd be wearing her Galileo finest in front of the exact people who could put her plan for climate stability into action.

They might not have solved Dropwort's murder, but maybe she would still have her chance to solve something so much bigger.

CASE ID: 20-06-DROS-STK

Type:
[X] Communication
[ ] Audio recording
[ ] Spell residue
[ ] Photo or other visual reconstruction
[X] Object
[ ] Form or record
[ ] Other: _____

Source: Personal residence of Septimius
Dropwort (dec.)
Relevant Parties: Suspect 3 (name withheld
for privacy/age restrictions), Septimius
Dropwort (dec.)
Description: Note found in the residence of
Septimius Dropwort (dec.), left by Suspect 3

Dropwort

We all know you're a dirty, sad old bastard who would dig the gold teeth out of his own mommy's grave, but this time you've gone too far. I'm sick of watching you dote on every little prep school shitbird who crosses your path while bullying and robbing everyone else. I'm coming for your ass, and I won't rest until I see it six circles deep in hell. You want to save yourself from me?

Return what you stole.

LC

10:00-ish A.M. (Or earlier? Maybe later): SYDNEY MEEKS, 16, IT'S COMPLICATED

BY L. L. MCKINNEY

One minute Sydney Meeks was trying to get extra credit in Mystozoology by grooming Mr. Jeffries's prized perl, Uno, and the next she was tripping face-first into the sudden brightness of an unfamiliar corridor in what was probably a pocket dimension. At least, she thought it was a pocket dimension. Maybe a portal to an alternate dimension?

Semantics.

The first thing Sydney noticed? This wasn't her school. Oh, she recognized the unenthusiastic way people shuffled around, that half trot that signaled they were in a hurry but didn't want to actually reach their destination. But these halls weren't her halls, and these walls weren't her walls. This wasn't the weathered stone she stared at every other day when her thoughts started to drift during Mythic Mechanics. These weren't the same dingy high windows that let in the Rose's light. And, most noticeable of all, no one was wearing the stuffy but somehow not-that-bad gold-and-black uniform that marked them as Wyldon students.

The *second* thing Sydney noticed was the familiar green form of Uno winding her way between dozens of legs, then around a corner and out of sight. And like that, Sydney's day had gone from boring-but-aight to bitch-why-*me*.

Sydney hurried to press her back to the nearest wall, in part to get a better look at her surroundings, but mostly to escape the flowing press of bodies around her. A few people glared and muttered at her in passing, but thankfully kept moving. She took a slow, deep breath to try to calm her racing heart. The cold kiss of brick through the thin fabric of her T-shirt helped take the edge off the flush of panic swelling in her chest.

"Okay, you're okay," she whispered to herself. She glanced up and down the hallway, her eyes touching against unfamiliar faces briefly before dancing away.

What was it Dr. Morrow had said about pocket dimensions? Sydney could imagine the statuesque Black woman behind her lectern, her hair swept up into a crown of patterned fabric and twists, her long hands punctuating her sentences as she spoke to the class.

"If you find yourself suddenly sliding between realities, don't panic. Interdimensional phasing is a rare phenomenon still being studied, but what we *do* know is that anything that passes from one plane to another remains tethered to its home dimension, for a time. The best thing you can do is find a safe place near your entry point and wait. Don't leave. Remain inconspicuous, don't interact with that dimension's native inhabitants if you can help it, and await the echoing flux that will pull you back through naturally, or wait for the Division to execute an extraction."

Don't panic. Easier said than done. Especially since Uno

apparently didn't know the rules and had bolted immediately. Stupid lizard-cat.

Stupid lizard-cat that's your responsibility. She couldn't just leave the critter to die, or potentially wipe out some smaller local species. That definitely counted as interacting with native inhabitants. If she didn't want to potentially tear a hole through space-time, or fail *another* class this term, she was gonna have to go after the little monster.

"Uuuuuuuuuuugh," Sydney groaned. A few people pitched curious glances at her, but thankfully they seemed to be caught up in . . . she wasn't sure. Now that she had taken a second to get her shit together, she noticed the almost frantic energy in the air. People gathered in groups here and there spoke excitedly to one another in rapid-fire whispers.

"He's dead!" someone hissed nearby, snatching at her attention.

"They don't know who killed him."

"Maybe another teacher?"

"Bet it was a student."

"Whoever it was, I'm not mad at 'em."

"Did they say how?"

Dead? Who the hell is dead?! You know what? No. Never mind. Pocket dimension drama was not on her list today. She had a perl to catch.

Before she could talk herself out of it, Sydney hurried in the direction she'd seen Uno vanish just a few moments ago. Her mind raced ahead of her, trying to recall her lessons. Given the sudden, jarring way she'd just appeared here, she must have jumped dimensions via teleportation. Technically, Uno had done the teleporting. Sydney was pulled along for the ride.

"One of the ways we're able to study interdimensional phasing is due to perls," she remembered Mr. Jeffries explaining earlier this week, while running his hand along Uno's back. The feline-esque creature had arched into the touch, its body shimmering a pearlescent green.

"Perls possess an ability akin to basic teleportation," Mr. Jeffries had gone on to say, "but what we've discovered is that they actually jump into a pocket dimension, which is essentially a crossroads between realities. Now, time passes much more slowly in the pocket than it does here in our dimension, and likely anywhere else. From that pocket, perls leap back into their home dimension seemingly simultaneously, and voila! This takes almost all of the perl's energy, leaving it vulnerable, which is why this particular trick is usually a last-ditch effort to avoid danger."

Danger had been Sydney's lab partner and friend, Desha, bursting into the room with the force of a Mack truck propelled by excitement.

"IT HAPPENED!" Desha had screamed, the only sound louder than her voice being the door slamming against the wall. "MARQUEZ ASKED ME OUT!"

Uno had yowled and thrashed in a way that had mimicked Sydney's beating heart.

"Really?" Sydney called over her shoulder, trying to calm the agitated creature she'd been focused on brushing. Perls had a coat of what looked like scales but acted like fur, and it took a bit of concentration to groom, if you didn't want your arms torn up.

"Sorry!" Desha said, her shoulders hunched. She stepped up beside Sydney, peering into the open pen with wide, curious eyes. "It's bigger up close."

"Most things are," Sydney said, smirking.

Uno settled but continued to eye both girls, a low sound in the back of her throat.

Desha swatted Sydney's shoulder. "You know what I mean. How long you gonna be playing Dr. Dolittle? I need to talk to you about Marquez!"

"You can talk while I do this."

"Not in here." Desha glanced around the classroom, mistrust crinkling her light brown face. Not without reason—in a place where people could take a potion to turn invisible, or enchant a mirror to be one-way, you never could be certain you were 100 percent alone unless you were in the dorms.

"Fiiiiiine," Sydney huffed. "Just let me get her a bath, and I'll be ready."

"A bath?" Desha dropped her head back and grumbled. "Class starts in twenty minutes!"

Sydney shrugged. "It's *for* class."

Now Desha huffed. "Here, it'll go faster if we both—"

"Wait, no!" Sydney shouted, but it was too late. Desha's hands were already outstretched, reaching into the cage, her movements quick.

Uno, decidedly unhappy with this recent development, hissed and then twisted between both girls' reaching fingers, and bolted to freedom.

Sydney whirled and raced after the perl. Desha sputtered an apology that was cut off when a sudden flash of light filled her vision. Sydney barely managed to close her eyes, the brightness already driving pain into her skull. When she blinked the world back into focus, everything she knew was gone. Everything but Uno, who was still on the run.

Uno, who *now* slipped around a white girl's ankles and out the door behind her.

"Oh!" The girl danced on the balls of her feet like she'd stepped in something. "What was that?!"

"Something from the towers got loose?" An Indian boy walking with her glanced around as well.

The girl gasped, her bright blue eyes lighting up. "What if it killed Dropwort?!"

"Excuse me!" Sydney brushed between the two of them, heading for the door.

The boy's voice followed her. "Is she new?"

"*I've* never seen her before today."

"You think *she*—" Sydney didn't hear the rest of the conversation as she raced out onto what had to be the school grounds. High structures circled the patch of grass laid out before her. Pale light wrapped everything in the faint haze of midmorning, and there, at the far end of the lawn, a lithe green form bounded toward a smattering of trees.

"Awww hell!" Sydney huffed. If Uno got lost in the woods, she would never find her! Without thinking, Sydney twisted her hands around one another. Her fingers ticked through the necessary movements to tap into the ether, like typing in the password for a computer. The sequence came together, and she felt the sudden rush of wind as it came under her control.

Push. The word flowed out from her mind and down through her limbs, filling her and emptying her out at the same time. She took a step, then another, a stuttering stop-and-go before her legs broke into a run.

The strange world whipped past her, her feet thudding against the ground as she chased the small figure flitting in and out of sight as it unfurled a pair of gossamer-thin wings. The panic from earlier gripped Sydney's heart again.

Please don't fly, please don't fly, please don't fly! She would have shouted, but talking while running this fast was a good way to get bugs in your teeth.

She held her arms out, her fingers ticking through new movements, opening new pathways in the ether.

Ignite. The air between Sydney's fingers caught fire. The flames whipped and wound about one another, flickering in the rush of wind as she ran.

Uno leapt. Sydney hurled the fireball. It arched through the air, and just before the flaming orb found its target, Sydney clenched her fingers into a fist. The fireball exploded in a burst of blue and pink. The perl, startled but unharmed, hissed in a very catlike manner as it dropped to the ground—its ears pinned to the top of its head, its forked tongue lashing out, tasting the air for signs of enemies it could not see or hear.

"Uno!" She chanced a shout now, shielding her mouth with her hand and muffling her words at the same time.

The perl perked, turned, spotted her, and tilted its head, looking her over almost questioningly—which gave Sydney the chance to catch up. Her steps stuttered to a halt before she could get too close, though. Out of breath, and fighting to keep from doubling over, she lifted her hands and approached Uno with slow, careful strides.

Uno, thankfully, remained still, watching Sydney with wide, slitted eyes. She chirped in wary curiosity.

"That's it . . . you know me!" Sydney pressed her palms to her chest. "I'm Sydney, from fourth period? I've been brushing you this week."

Uno sniffed the air, head lifted.

"Thaaaaaat's it. . . ." A few more steps. "Good Uno." And a few more. "Nice Uno. Stay your ass right there."

The perl shifted back and forth, its spine undulating with the movements, before taking a few steps toward her. Sydney had to bite down on the delighted noise that threatened to burst forth.

She held out a hand, and—

FWOM!

Something *exploded* behind her. Or at least it sounded like it, but when she whirled around to face the campus . . . there was nothing. The cluster of buildings and the surrounding grounds looked deceptively undisturbed, with bright blue skies overhead peppered by floofs of white.

"I *know* I heard . . ."

And it seemed she wasn't the only one, given the hiss that sounded over her shoulder.

Uno scrambled back and forth over the tree roots, her back arched, her hackles raised as she bared her teeth in a hiss.

Alarm twisted tightly between Sydney's lungs. *Oh no.* She darted forward, bending into a swipe.

Uno dropped low and skittered to the side juuuuuuuust enough, and Sydney's fingers brushed against her slithery body. She couldn't keep hold.

"No!" This time she *did* shout, her voice echoing among the trees. After sliding to a stop in a spray of dirt and grass, she spun in circles, glancing around in hopes of finding a trace of the creature, but there wasn't one. Not that she could see.

"Dammit!" Irritation buzzed between her ears and through the rest of her. "Dammit, dammit, *damn. It.*" She stomped back and forth, the frustrated energy having nowhere to go.

Without thinking, her hand went to her wrist and the circlet of gold metal wrapped around it, a single bangle with a flat connector, the letter *S* engraved in it. It had been a gift from her mom when she'd set off for school this year. A reminder that all things ebb and flow and come back around to one another. The river. The balance.

"Whenever things get to be too much, try to focus on something else. Like this." Mom had tapped the bangle after slipping it onto Sydney's wrist. "Use this as a focal point. Concentrate, breathe, let it pass. Then get back to work."

Concentrate. Breathe. Let it pass.

Deep breaths helped to take the edge off the anger, but Sydney could still feel the thrum of it inside her. It wasn't passing anything.

Just go home, the anger told her. *You don't know where you are, you don't know what's going on, and apparently people think you might've killed somebody!*

So, she wasn't a hundred on that last one, but the conversation between those two students had sounded like folks were looking for murder suspects. Dead teacher, dead student, dead whoever, she wanted no part of it.

You need to focus on getting home, especially if people are about to start acting scary about new faces.

And the further she moved from the flux point, the further in the extraction team would have to come to find her. She should just let the Division handle things. She'd take the L on this one, and the F on this assignment if she had to.

She couldn't help feeling a little guilty about abandoning a poor scared creature, though.

"Dammit." With another burst of anger, Sydney kicked at

the ground with the toe of her boot, digging a bit of dirt free and sending it flying into the air. She turned to stomp back in the direction she'd come, then paused while her eyes played over the earth as it settled back among the grass. Dirt . . . didn't act like that. At least, not this kind of dirt. That spray had been too loose, too fine.

A thought occurred to Sydney then, a heavy, troublesome thing that had emerged from the back of her mind, pushing and shoving its way toward the front.

"Sand?" Sydney said to nothing and no one. Crouching low, she ran her fingers through the blades of grass, pinching and then lifting to inspect what she'd gathered. Sure enough, caught between the pads of her fingers were grains of sand.

That's when the pushy, shoving thought finally reached its destination and settled in.

"Sand!" she said, louder now. She waved her hand through the grass quickly, watching as the granules bounced into the air. The perl was shedding sand! She had a trail she could follow!

Whooping and pumping a fist, she laughed. Then the smile dropped from her face like a lead weight as a second insistent thought settled in beside the first.

The perl was shedding sand. That meant . . .

Oh no.

The thing about perls? They're adorable and kinda sweet. Just big, bright lizard-cats that don't do much but lie in the sun, chew on shiny things, and fall asleep on your desk when you need to do some work. They're pretty much harmless, most of the time! It's the rest of the time you gotta worry about, particularly when a momma perl is pregnant. She'll start shedding dust or dirt or mud, whatever earth is most abundant in her natural habitat. Then she'll use that to make a protective mound where she can have her babies all cozy like. It's real cute, unless you get too close. Then perls will rip your arms clean off, rightly so. Don't mess with a momma and her babies.

But that's not what worried Sydney in that moment, oh no. Arm ripping wasn't the problem. If a momma perl can't make a mound and is forced to have her babies in the open? She explodes. Literally. She blows out a wall of fire and kinetic energy so strong that it decimates all potential predators within a mile or so, and everything else along with it.

Uno was a desert perl. And she was shedding sand for her mound.

Sydney had to find the creature before that happened, or:

(A) Uno would go underground to give birth and raise her babies for a month. Introducing a species to a new plane of existence without prior clearance was a class four violation, and she did NOT need that hanging over her head going into the Ring. Or over her family, period.

(B) Uno would explode, killing Sydney and everyone in this place.

Fan-freaking-tastic.

Her heart fluttered with the swift return of her previous panic, which made her hands a little shaky as she set about keying in yet another connection to the ether. She messed it up twice before finally getting it right.

The rush of wind and the burn of fire faded under something far steadier. She latched on to the weight, to the force of simply being. Earth.

Sydney liked this element, liked the way it made her feel

rooted and strong. The way it steadied her wandering mind and calmed her frantic heart.

Rise. She wove the command into being and lifted her hands. As she did, the granules of sand lying in the grass floated into the air, a rising tide of dust that formed a clear path, cutting to the side, then arching back toward the cluster of buildings in the distance.

Sydney followed that trail as best she could, which did indeed bring her closer to the school, but then veered off sharply, circling around the outermost structures of the campus. The sun was higher in the sky now, and the sounds of life started to pour over the walls and buildings.

A third thought made its way forward, squeezing in between those first two and plopping itself down at the forefront of Sydney's mind. What was she going to do if someone else noticed her? They were bound to, if they had eyes or ears or any other senses available to them. They'd start asking questions she didn't have answers to. And just what do you say when you officially meet someone from another dimension for the first time?

Hi! My name's Sydney, Sydney Meeks. Of the Baltimore Meekses. Don't let the name fool you. I'm anything but. So, I was chasing this magical critter called a perl from my class—I've been helping my teacher look after it for extra credit, and I was gonna give it a bath when it got loose!

Actually, Desha scared it by reaching for it without knowing what the hell she was doing, and it bolted. Pissed me off. Desha, not the creature. Well, it too, I guess. Anyway, I was chasing it when I fell, or I think I fell, into your world. It's a pocket dimension off my world. That happens sometimes. Maybe. I don't really know; this is the first time I've heard of it happening. To a person, I mean. Perls do it all the time.

All the same, I fell into your world, and I've been looking for what brought me here so we can both go home. Her name's Uno, and she's real sweet. She's also about to have babies! Which would be cute as hell if'n it didn't mean your school might burn to the ground. Sorry?

Yeah. That would go over *real* well.

Shoving all thoughts aside, Sydney focused on the task at hand. The sand shivered where it remained suspended in the air, parting like water as she stepped through it. The trail sloped down a hillside and back out toward another patch of wood, or so she thought.

Something snapped ahead in the brush. A quick *pop!* followed by a grunt.

She froze. That didn't sound like Uno.

A rustling of leaves and branches preluded a low, rough "Confound it all!"

Definitely not Uno. Though, according to the trail of sand, the perl had definitely gone this way.

"Hold still, you—"

The voice was cut off by a sharp hiss that was nearly a growl. *That* was Uno!

Sydney hurried forward, her previous caution thrown aside. "Hello?" she called, one hand lifted to protect her face from grasping branches as she hurried through the underbrush.

No one answered. She couldn't hear anything, save her own quick pants and the thud of her shoes against the ground.

"Hello!" she tried again. "That's my—" She broke into a

clearing, an empty clearing, with no sign of anyone or anything no matter which way she looked.

The irritation from before threatened to flare into full fury. Part of her *wanted* to let the fire rise up inside her, then burst free, if just to be rid of the feeling. But then she spotted a small dome of sand near the far tree line. It looked like Uno had started to build her nest, but something had interrupted her. Or someone.

But that wasn't the weird part.

As Sydney approached the mound, she could make out not one but *two* distinct sand trails. One came in from the trees to the left of the clearing. The other went off ahead, once more into the brush.

Well, hell. If she didn't know better, she'd say she had *two* desert perls on her hands. That, and she'd definitely heard what sounded like a person a moment ago, but they were gone too.

And Sydney was, technically, right back where she'd started. But Uno wouldn't stop to mound again near where she'd been frightened off. This place would be considered dangerous.

Which gave Sydney a bit more time.

A seed of hope. Maybe she could fix this after all.

With a wave of her hand, she dispersed the mound, just in case, then hurried on after Uno's trail. At least she thought it was Uno's trail. Prayed it was.

Within a few moments she cleared the brush to find she'd come around the other side of the hill. Right up to a pair of large double doors set into the rocky terrain at the base of one of the larger campus buildings.

She groaned. A building meant people. People who could notice her, people who could spook Uno, and people who could end up hurt if the perl literally went off. She couldn't stop now. She took a breath and pushed through the doors.

Instantly the roar of a crowd flooded her senses. She'd stepped into another hall, but there were more kids this time, more shuffling, more whispering about killers, with some talk of chosen ones and prophecies thrown in.

But there was no sign of Uno. Not a chirp. Not a glimpse.

She . . . she'd lost her. Genuinely lost her.

Sydney let go of the door, stepped to the side, and sank to the floor. The pounding in her head blossomed, mirroring her heart. What was she going to do? She shut her eyes tight against the sting of tears. A gnawing in her middle seemed to sharpen—she'd used so much energy casting, and now she was hungry and lost, and Uno was gone and . . . and . . .

Her fingers went to her bangle and twisted it furiously about her wrist before she drew up her legs, wrapped her arms around her knees, and buried her face in them.

What was she going to *do*?

"Hey," a voice said nearby.

Sydney ignored it, still wallowing. And hungry.

"Hey?" the voice said again, louder this time.

She wondered if she could find a way back home and then bring Mr. Jeffries *here* to look for Uno. That . . . that might work. Why hadn't she thought of that before?

"Excuse me!" This time when the voice spoke, there was a tap against Sydney's shoulder.

She jerked upright, and someone standing entirely too close for her liking jumped in response.

"Oh!" the girl gasped, a hand pressed to her chest. "Sorry, I didn't mean . . . I only thought . . ."

Sydney stared at the girl as she stumbled over her thoughts, which was fine because that gave Sydney time enough to gather her own.

The girl was short—well, shorter than Sydney—with a soft cashmere hijab wrapped over her head and around her shoulders. The rest of her body was draped in silk. The folds fell around her beautifully. She was gorgeous, and any other time Sydney might have found herself fumbling her words, too, but right then she didn't have the calories necessary to be flustered.

Plus, she got the distinct impression that this one wasn't gonna leave her alone until she said something. "Can I help you?"

"No, I, it's just, I thought *I* could help *you*?" The girl folded her fingers together and fidgeted with her nails. "You looked like you needed help."

And she did. Saints be, Sydney needed all the help she could get. But she knew better than to go getting involved with people from pocket dimensions, especially when she didn't know if they knew they were in said pocket dimension. Folks could be a bit tetchy about stuff like that.

"I'm fine," Sydney said, her lips pulling into an automatic smile.

The girl's eyes moved over her. "You don't . . . look . . . fine . . ."

"No? Prolly just me being tired, then." Sydney rested her cheek on her fist. She felt her smile fraying at the edges. "I'll be all right, though. Don't let me keep you."

Back home, anyone would have taken the hint and likely skedaddled with a quickness. But this place was brand-new, with people who just didn't know better. Like the girl, who continued to stand there, though she looked to be thinking twice about it.

"It's just . . . things aren't the safest right now . . . ," the girl continued.

The breath Sydney let out was slow and careful, and she tried to let the buzzing of her irritation go with it. This girl didn't know what was going on with Uno. She had no idea what had happened before and what would likely happen after. She didn't know just how sore, tired, worried, and DONE Sydney was. None of this was her fault.

That's what Sydney told herself. And it did nothing to curb her growing ire.

"Thank you. Really." She propped her smile back up as best she could. It had to be near to beaming with all this effort. "But I'm okay. In fact." Sydney pushed her way to standing, and the girl—who had crouched beside her by now—did as well. "I need to be on my way, class and all, but thanks."

"You're not going to the assembly?" the girl asked as Sydney started down the hallway.

"Nope!" Sydney kept walking, relieved to be done with the conversation.

Though that relief faded as the girl hurried to fall into step beside her.

"Maybe if you ate something, you'd feel better."

Okay, now that almost got Sydney to smile. For real. This girl was clearly the mothering type. It was sweet, and unyieldingly loving in a way that just made your heart warm when you thought about it.

It reminded Sydney of how Desha was always wanting to help, even when no one asked for it. Even when it wasn't needed. Even when she didn't know that helping would make things worse.

Thoughts of Desha and how this whole fiasco had gotten started in the first place slammed down over the blossoming warmth Sydney had felt for this unknown girl. Who was still talking.

"Usually when you eat something, it makes everything better, and I—"

"Look, ahhhh . . ." Sydney trailed off, gesturing for the girl to fill in the blank.

It took a moment before she gave a soft "Oh!" then cleared her throat. "I'm Mariam."

"Mariam," Sydney repeated before stopping in her tracks and spinning to face her unwitting companion, who stopped as well with lips pursed and eyes wide.

"You're nice," Sydney went on to say. "But I really, really don't have time right now."

Mariam nodded, glancing around as people shifted to step past them. Some of the students tossed ugly looks or muttered indignantly, likely because Sydney and Mariam were now standing in the middle of the hall.

"I've got something to do, so if you don't mind." Again Sydney turned to go, hoping that was the end of it.

"I could help!"

Clearly it was not.

Mariam shuffled alongside her again. "I'm sorry, I don't mean to be pushy, but there's this aura around you? And I . . . it's . . . you need help." Her voice lowered.

Sydney stopped again, this time making sure to step off to the side, and pressed her fingers to her temples. "Okay, I need help. But I don't NEED help!" Her voice rose a little bit. "I need . . . I need to be able to think, and this?" She gestured between them. "Is the opposite of help, for me. So, again, I appreciate it, but—"

"But I can—"

"Thank you!" Sydney said, a little louder than she meant. A few people turned to look at them. She ignored them, though she did speak a little softer. "Thank you, for your generous offer, really, but I promise I'll manage."

She spun to go, hoping to put some actual distance between herself and Mariam's rather sweet intentions, though she didn't get more than a few feet before a hand caught her shoulder again.

"Look, I seriously need you t—" Sydney started, but she turned and found herself craning her neck back in order to stare up into the face of a middle-aged white man. His gray-and-black robes put Sydney in the mind of the mantles worn for graduation back at her school. They hung on his body like fabric caught in the branches of a dead tree. His face was all sharp angles and hard lines, excepting for the one receding from his brow. His almost too-wide smile was juuuuust the right side of creepy.

"Principal," Mariam said quietly, her shoulders hunched as she eyed him.

Sydney stared at where his narrow fingers gripped her shoulder then at him. There was something . . . off about this guy. Something about the energy around him pushing against Sydney's skin like sandpaper dragged against the grain. While Mariam was a bright and, albeit, inconvenient burst of eager apprehension, he was a cold spot of twisted anxiety, despite his seemingly calm demeanor.

"Run along, Miss Abidin," the man said, his voice stretching the words out like taffy. "I need to have a word with Miss Meeks."

The fact that this white man in another world knew her name sent a shudder through Sydney, and a quick kick of fear. She went to shake off his touch, to tell him that she didn't know him. That he needed to stop touching her, but . . . she couldn't.

She couldn't really do much of anything but stand there, the need to move and speak an impotent desire withering in her bones.

This . . . this is fine. I don't have anywhere to be.

. . . But wasn't I just . . .

Mariam didn't look too keen on walking away, just yet.

Then, as if to taunt her, a familiar wiggle of movement caught Sydney's attention. Just over Mariam's shoulder, she could see down the hall to where Uno slithered into a doorway. The creature paused and lifted its head, eyes locked with hers. It was as if the perl knew that their game of hide-and-seek was over, and it wanted to know why.

Then Sydney blinked, and Uno was gone. Again. Only, this time the air wavered in the perl's wake, superheated and faintly blue. A new flux point. Uno wasn't just gone; she was gone *home*. And with her return, the Division would have no reason to come here searching. Sydney would . . . would be stranded here.

Her entire body *vibrated* with fear.

Fear that took hold of time and space and stretched them both out impossibly. The moment seemed to hang for an eternity, but was shattered when this white man patted her shoulder. Who was he, again? And why was he *touching* her?

More important, why was she letting him?

"Sydney and I simply have a few matters to discuss concerning some . . . ahh . . . extra credit she asked for," the principal said through a smile that was all teeth. Despite his smile, she could feel his fingers trembling. "It won't take but a moment. That'll be all, Mariam."

"Yes, sir." Mariam lingered briefly, her eyes dancing between Sydney and the principal a few times before she eventually turned and walked away.

And it was funny, because now Sydney didn't want her to go. She wasn't sure why, wasn't sure about a lot of things all of a sudden. A sort of haze settled over her mind, and trying to think was like trying to run through water; slow, clumsy, with a feeling of not being anchored in any meaningful way. That mental buoyancy left her torn between the odd assurance that this principal could help her—being head of the school and all—and the small though still very present revulsion at being left alone with Creepy McCreeperson here and his bad vibes. She needed to find Uno, needed to get home, to . . .

His fingers tightened their hold, and an unpleasant tingle moved through her body.

"This way, please," he said, and gestured with his other hand.

Sydney's legs started moving.

They were walking in the opposite direction of where she'd seen Uno.

"Th-that's it, Miss Meeks, n-nice and steady," the man said, his voice finally matching the shaking in his hand. He nodded to a few people in passing, the two of them moving along, easy as you please. "We need to have a chat."

His words were deceptively quiet, reserved, but tight with unease. He kept glancing over his shoulder between half-hearted greetings to others.

"What do you want, sir?" Her voice sounded way too calm, monotonous almost. And why was she calling him "sir"? She ain't know him!

"Oh, I—I want a great many things, M-Miss Meeks." The man smiled and waved at a Black woman standing in a nearby doorway, then pulled out a handkerchief and mopped his brow with it. He licked his lips and released a shuddering breath. "But we must hurry, yes?"

Their pace picked up.

Sydney stared straight ahead. Her fingers curled into fists, her arms shaking with the foiled effort to *move*! But they stayed locked at her sides. Her legs wouldn't listen to her either. They kept going even when she wanted to stop.

The quaking in her limbs got so bad that she felt the familiar slide of metal against skin as the bangle wrapped around her wrist slipped free. She heard it tink against the floor when it fell but couldn't stop to pick it up. Couldn't even look back at it as they continued forward.

"What do you want, sir?" Now she was repeating herself in that same silly elevator-lady voice, and it—

Wait a second.

Elevator-lady voice.

Where had she heard that before?

The fog over her mind choked the memory that tried to surface, forcing it back, but Sydney latched on. Her hands, trembling as badly as they were, managed to tap through another sequence.

Reveal . . .

The memory exploded against the backs of her eyes. She was seated in Dr. Morrow's class, and they were discussing the various means by which a person's will could be usurped by magical means. Not for the sake of teaching the students how to do it, but how to recognize when it was being done to them.

"You may notice yourself questioning why you're doing something over and over, but be unable to think of a reason to stop," Dr. Morrow had said as she pushed her glasses up her nose, her brown face serious. "Another sign is speaking strangely, slowly, sort of like this, pronouncing every syllable in soft, even tones." She demonstrated with her explanation, her own voice flattening out.

Desha had snorted, resting her cheek in the palm of one hand, the other pretending to take notes but really doodling *D+M* in different styles in the margins of her notebook. "If I ever sound like some boring-ass elevator lady, something is wrong with more than my will."

"Right you are, Miss Newton." Dr. Morrow aimed a finger in Desha's direction, and Desha sat up straighter. "Having your will controlled is physical in nature. Your body acts out, but your mind is aware of what's happening on some level, no matter how small. If you are able to recognize this awareness for what it is, the source of the outside influence is easier to fight off or detect and thus dispel. But having your will enchanted? That's more subtle. It tricks the mind as well as the body into thinking it wants what the caster wants. This is powerful magic that only works through transfer or touch. Some enchantments have been known to last days, weeks, months . . . even years in the very rare instance. But once the enchanted becomes aware of what's happened, the spell loses its hold on them."

The memory faded, and Sydney's mind snapped back to the present. She was still walking. *They* were still walking, and the man's voice had turned sort of tender, almost remorseful. ". . . while your presence is indeed a surprise, it's one I can use quite freely."

Sydney's panic returned, slamming into her like a wrecking ball as the enchantment started to fall away. First the mind clears, then the body regains control. That's how it would go. The shorter the time under the spell, the faster it would fade. She'd be free of it, now that she'd realized what was happening, but would it be soon enough? Her limbs still refused her commands.

No. . . .

They stopped in front of a door, the words "PRINCIPAL FORNAX" embossed across the front in bright golden script.

The man muttered something, and Sydney felt the familiar brush of magic as a spell was cast. The knob twisted and the door swung inward into darkness.

"I need a suspect," the man said, pushing the door wider, revealing more nothing. "And a girl no one will miss because she was never supposed to be here in the first place."

With that, they stepped through the door.

The last thing Sydney Meeks was aware of was the thunk of wood and the click of tumblers, before the pain in her body folded around her, and everything went black.

EVIDENCE EXHIBIT TRANSCRIPT-A-2

CASE ID: 20-06-DROS-STK

Type:

[X] Communication

[ ] Audio recording

[ ] Spell residue

[ ] Photo or other visual reconstruction

[ ] Object

[ ] Form or record

[ ] Other: _____

Source: School announcement archives

Relevant Parties: Nicolas Fornax, principal; Ladybird "Birdie" Beckley, vice principal

Description: Transcript of schoolwide announcement broadcast to students at 11:23 a.m.

[Beginning of transcript.]

[Pleasant ding indicating start of a school-wide announcement.]

<u>Vice Principal Beckley:</u> Good morning, students. Thank you for your patience with this slight delay, as the principal was running a little bit behind schedule. You may now make your way, with minimal disruption, to the auditorium for Professor Dropwort's memorial service. Please enter the auditorium in an orderly fashion, take your seats, and wait for the service to begin at 11:45. Teachers, please supervise your students accordingly. Thank you.

[Pleasant ding indicating end of announcement.]

[End of transcript.]

EVIDENCE EXHIBIT T8
CASE ID: 20-06-DROS-STK

<u>Type:</u>
[ ] Communication
[ ] Audio recording
[ ] Spell residue
[ ] Photo or other visual reconstruction
[ ] Object
[X] Form or record
[ ] Other: _____

Source: School medical records
Relevant Parties: Fibula Smith, school
nurse; Student "Jane Doe" (name withheld for
privacy)
Description: Prescription for medication
issued to Jane Doe; possible side effects may
render her testimony inadmissible

**GALILEO ACADEMY
FOR THE EXTRAORDINARY,
INFIRMARY**
FIBULA SMITH, HEAD NURSE

Patient name: ███████ *"JANE DOE"*
Date: June 28
Prescription: Extract of Hornbeam, diluted
Disp: 3 fl oz with 10 ml measure
Refills: none
Instructions: Take 10 ml once every four hours,
for as long as symptoms persist.

NOTE: Since this is for a head injury, please
return to the infirmary ASAP if symptoms worsen
or persist for more than two days.

Possible side effects: Confusion, paranoia.
Please note that hornbeam has hallucinogenic
properties when taken in conjunction with
certain medications. Refer to your primary care
sorcerer for further details.

―――――――――――――――――――――

Date   Signature

June 28   *Fibula Smith*

12:00 P.M.: MARIAM ABIDIN, 16, WANDS

BY HAFSAH FAIZAL

Mariam's pulse spiked with every glimpse of a silver badge. The police were everywhere—stone-faced Stockholm police outside, SNACC-EOs inside, their badges glinting like fangs in the dark, steel-handled wands doing nothing to set her nerves at ease.

She *should* feel at ease. These were folks sworn to uphold the law. Their wands were meant to protect people like her, but every time she caught sight of the officials escorting a student for questioning, it felt like a snare tightening a little more around her. She finally exhaled when they turned the corner.

Wait.

Where had Sydney and Principal Fornax gone? Mariam turned a slow circle—neither of them was in sight. Almost as if they'd never existed in the first place. Just like Dropwort, just like the blood beneath her fingernails this morning.

Today was shaping up to be quite horrendous.

You see, the problem with an entire school knowing how much a man hated you became evident only when he was dead.

Rather, the problem only really *arose* after he turned up dead and you yourself woke up with crimson stains beneath your fingernails. A terrible predicament for a girl whose contact with a weapon was limited to the shears she used to trim flowers for her painting nook.

Her knuckles still stung from the frantic force she'd used to rap at the door next to hers. Daphne had assured her there was nothing but creamy skin beneath her fingernails—a feat, considering how there were always bits of some paint or another—but *she* hadn't spent an entire dawn scrubbing her fingers raw because her eyes had shown her something else.

Mariam had proceeded to avoid eye contact all morning, but she'd seen the looks students had been giving the other Muslim girl in her year, Nadiya, and knew they were only a twin to what she was trying to ignore.

Normally it would rile her, but today her hair was a little too damp beneath her hijab, her heart a drum . . . because she herself wasn't sure what she'd been up to last night when Dropwort had been gasping out his last breath. When the SNACC-EOs eventually called her in for questioning, the way she'd seen them doing with students all morning, she wouldn't be able to give them an alibi if she couldn't remember a thing. *Oh no, I don't really know what I did last night! What? Why do I keep rubbing at my nails like there might be blood crusted beneath them? Not sure, but that's not the point in this murder, is it?*

The truth sounded far more suspicious than any lie she could create.

Mariam rubbed at her head where a lump sat just beneath her hijab, after Diego had punted the ball at her so hard during rugby that she was *still* seeing stars. She couldn't even blame her strange predicament on *that,* because she'd gone straight to wisecracking with Nurse Fibula when it had happened and she'd gotten herself fixed.

Something shot across the floor, and Mariam leapt back with a yelp. A . . . cat? No, that couldn't be. It was too green to be a cat. It vanished, leaving behind nothing but a faint trail of something that looked suspiciously like sand.

Mariam's palms dampened.

"Cats don't shed sand, Mariam. Get a grip on yourself," she muttered. First she'd imagined blood crusted beneath her fingernails, and now a green, sand-shedding cat?

But wasn't that the essence of a painter? They were made to entertain ideas that were a step from the practical. Galileo pushed that further, prodded them not only to think beyond the practical but beyond the mundane. It was one of the things she loved about the school, one of the reasons she'd eventually accepted the invitation to follow the strangeness in her blood and leave her family of Neutrals behind. She was a collection of differences, an assembly of splintered ends society didn't want to deal with.

And now she was imagining things. Who knows what else she'd fabricate?

Being Dropwort's murderer.

A chill dragged down her spine.

What she did know was this: she hadn't killed Professor Dropwort, but until she cleared the fog in her head and remembered what had happened last night, she wasn't safe—not even from herself.

Nurse Fibula. Mariam had to find her. She'd know what was wrong.

Someone jostled Mariam, and didn't even bother to apologize before joining the swath of students streaming for the auditorium and the memorial service of a man she loathed. Golden sunlight flooded the wide windows hanging parallel in the corridor, painting a lie, for the air was worrisome and concerned and *afraid*. Mariam knew this atmosphere well, and despite the fact that any one of them could be the killer, every last student made sure to slide an accusing look at her as they passed.

She turned, nearly slamming into another student right at her heels.

"Oh, I'm sorry!" Mariam exclaimed.

The other girl waved off her apology, and Mariam tried to remember her name. In fact, Mariam tried to remember what she'd been doing all this time—panicking about something. Something important. Her fingers felt sticky, the kind of stickiness that came with blood, but she was too terrified to look.

"No worries," the girl said, seemingly in a hurry. She narrowed her eyes. "We share a class, right? I'm Lola."

Mariam quickly shoved her hands behind her back, clasping them with a tiny laugh that was always a dead giveaway whenever she felt guilty. That was when Mariam noticed *Lola's* hands. She was wearing a single studded black glove and an ornate ring that was far too fancy for the day after a teacher had been murdered.

"Nice ring," Mariam said, partly to break the awkward silence and partly so Lola could hurry on her way and Mariam could find Nurse Fibula. *Ah. That* was what she'd been meaning to do.

"Thanks," Lola said slowly, spreading her fingers. The studs caught the midday light. She was hesitating, watching in a way that said Mariam was supposed to know *why* Lola was wearing the strange thing.

Mariam frowned and pointed past her. "I'm just—"

"You know what, never mind," Lola snapped suddenly, and stormed away, disappearing into the gaggle of students.

Mariam tilted her head and scrunched her mouth.

"What just happened?" she asked aloud. Had she imagined Lola and her strange glove? She glanced down at her fingernails—they were clear still, no blood. Nothing out of the ordinary. It was becoming a sign, she realized with some satisfaction: blood when she couldn't trust her mind, clean when she could. If only she'd checked when that green cat had darted across the hall.

No, she hadn't imagined the other girl.

Mariam hurried past the Coins Tower, ignoring anxious professors and murmuring students in the halls. She stumbled to a halt in front of the medical wing.

There was a line. Actually, "a line" was stating it mildly because it was *huge*, students pale-faced and worried, clutching stomachs or heads or simply wandering in shock. She even spotted a couple of girls she knew from rugby. A murder was no small deed. It was smart of them to be taking their mental health seriously, but if Mariam got in line now, she was very likely to be seeing a SNACC-EO before she even reached the nurse's office.

Fibula couldn't help her.

Tears burned in her eyes, but Mariam refused to let her spirits sink.

A commotion echoed from the hall just beyond, and Mariam leaned back to see a first-year yelling at a pair of SNACC-EOs. Her heart picked up speed. They were looking for their next mark, their next student to grill about Dropwort's murder.

That could very well be her.

Mariam threw open the nearest door and ducked into an empty classroom. She shivered in the dark, clammy space. Squinting, Mariam realized it was an old art classroom. Part of her felt a distant pang of sorrow at the sight of it, abandoned to dust and age. When she blinked, she could almost imagine her painting nook at the far end, flowers drooping in a vase.

Her hands trembled, as they had been ever since she'd learned of the professor's death. It was one thing to have a teacher die, and quite another when one you hated thoroughly was *murdered*.

Serves him right, being dead.

That had been her first thought when she'd heard the news, moments after she'd seen the blood beneath her nails. It was a sin to think it, but she couldn't help herself. It wasn't a sin to pity him, but she couldn't help that either, and she hated it.

Mariam used to sleepwalk as a child. She'd wake up in the morning and realize she had gone and done exactly what she'd thought of doing the night before, like removing the frame from her wall or going downstairs to fetch some milk, only for her mother to find bloody bits of glass in the morning and cuts on Mariam's arms when Mariam herself had no recollection of what had happened.

It was why she was so afraid now. What if she *had* murdered Dropwort because of how terrible a man he'd been?

No. Focus, Mariam, she thought.

She hadn't done it, and now she was going to find a way to cure herself of this ridiculous predicament. If only she had some of her mother's gritty basbousa and mint tea to settle her nerves. Mariam pressed back against the door with a sigh.

And heard a very embarrassed, suspiciously familiar cough.

A silver septum ring flashed in the dark, and Mariam's stomach dropped even lower as the rest of a student's floppy-haired silhouette finally separated from the shadows of the room. *Diego.* The very same Diego who had packed quite a kick during their last game of rugby.

"Hi," he said, and she resisted the urge to rub at the bump on her head. She'd forgotten and accidentally poked her hijab pin into it this morning, further souring her mood. At least he sounded apologetic. "I guess you can say I'm not keen on memorials."

Mariam swallowed and forced herself to nod. "Neither am I."

Diego gave her a sheepish smile. "How's the, uh, head?"

"Not that great," she admitted. "I was hoping to see the nurse, but there's a crowd out there, and I don't think that'll happen."

Diego tilted his head, dark locks falling over one eye. Mariam squinted, and he disappeared altogether for a fraction of a second. "What's wrong?" he asked.

"Well," she said wryly, splaying her fingers, "this boy I play rugby with sort of—"

Diego laughed. "I mean *now.* What are your symptoms? You might be able to find help in the library if Fib's unreachable. Between you and me, she can sometimes mix up tinctures that do the trick, but with horrible side effects."

Mariam *had* been surprised by how quickly the pain in her skull had numbed. She'd attributed it to Nurse Fibula's finesse, not the possibility of Mariam taking one too many tinctures that would cause something worse. Could that be the reason for her hallucinations and sudden loss of memory? She couldn't even remember what Fibula had prescribed for her.

"I'll do some research," Mariam said with a nod. Looking through a list might help jog her memory. Not only that—she might find an antidote.

"Speaking of research," Diego started, waiting for her to turn back. "You know Bhavna Joshi, right?"

Vaguely, but Mariam nodded anyway.

"Apparently Wren found the body and was muttering the word 'hourglass' or something. No clue what that could be about, but it might have something to do with Dropwort's death, you know?"

He was waiting for her to do something more than just nod. "I . . . I don't know anything about it. You mean the little thing with sand that you can invert?"

Diego shrugged. "Dunno. Just thought you might know more about it."

Mariam didn't. She needed to find out what in Galileo was wrong with her.

She had opened her mouth and started to tell him as much, when he flickered in her line of sight and disappeared again.

"Mariam?" Diego asked. "Are you okay?"

She rubbed her thumbs across the tips of her fingers. They felt wet.

Diego was blabbering now, sounding far off. "An echo—Wren raised his spirit—said a lot of stuff—Bhavna—"

Mariam glanced down at the dark smudges beneath her fingernails, yawning wide in the darkness of the room. *It's happening again.*

"I'm fine," she said, half to herself. Her voice cracked. "I'm fine."

Diego didn't reply. He didn't even make a sound.

She lifted her head, and Diego was . . . nowhere to be seen. The room was empty. *Completely* empty. Mariam took a few steps back and the hard edge of the door met her heels. She stumbled back into the hall and threw up her hands. The tips of her fingers shone bright crimson in the light from the windows.

No. Her breath caught as scarlet bled from the crescents of her nails, like fresh paint along the edge of a surface. *No, no, no.* She blinked and blinked again.

The red disappeared.

Mariam took off down the corridor, her willowy figure slipping between a throng of second-years and a cleaning cart. She bumped past the girl who usually sat by her in second period—*Dropwort's class*—who was whispering furiously to her friend.

Mariam stopped. "What did you say?"

The girl she knew stared with wide eyes, her hair coiffed like an old movie star's, spooked by the demand in her voice.

"Hourglass," the girl's friend said. She was confused, her dark cropped hair highlighting the cut of her cheekbones.

"It's all that girl Bhavna keeps repeating," said Mariam's classmate.

Vaguely she recalled Diego mentioning the word. He'd said something else too. Given her a task that she'd said she'd handle in the library.

"We think it's code for the artifact. Smugglers do that kind of thing, don't they?"

Mariam didn't think it was code. One of them dropped her gaze to Mariam's hands, and Mariam curled her fidgeting fingers out of sight. She didn't want to ask if the girl saw it too.

The other one looked like she'd finally figured Mariam out. "You're the one who got hit in the head, right?"

Mariam gave her a tight smile. "That's me. I, uh, have to go. It was nice seeing you."

The pair of them didn't stop staring, and Mariam picked a direction and went with it. *The East Wing Library it is.* She crossed to the west corridor, sprinting for the swath of sunlight that always bathed the recessed water fountain the deepest gold. Mariam forced her breath to calm, scraping the short nubs of her fingernails along her palms. *Left, right. Left, right.* Her mind flashed to the blood beneath them, her morning spent frantically scrubbing them raw.

Murder was no small thing. It wasn't a sin to bounce back from; it wasn't— *Focus.*

She'd had nothing to do with Dropwort's death, and she was going to prove it to everyone else *and* herself. She snuck a glance down each end of the corridor before cutting across. No one was here. Everyone was in the Great Hall for the memorial. Everyone *should* have been in the Great Hall.

So why did she feel a chill across her shoulders, as if she were being watched?

The library doors rose before her, the whimsical carvings enticing her while most of the school did the opposite. Breath held, she eased open one of the double doors and slipped inside, her flats as silent as the silk of her abaya. The place was ice-cold, and Mariam dipped her chin into the bundle of her hijab, breathing in the soft cashmere and a comforting whiff of her favorite gardenia perfume.

It was too cold. Necromancy cold.

Stop thinking. Trailing a hand along the old oak shelves, Mariam looked around for a librarian, but there wasn't a soul in sight. She was on her own. With a careful inhale, she strode to the starburst set into the center of the library and studied the shelves around her. An endless array of tomes stared back, chock-full of dust and words and age and wisdom.

After a quick glance through the catalogs, she made her way to the shelves she needed: the wing dedicated to medicine. When she glanced down, she saw a flicker of red and was surprised by a lack of panic. It was crusted now, the red nearing a dead shade of crimson.

Gripping the arbitrarily trimmed note cards she'd collected from the front desk, Mariam shuffled to the section on herbs and tinctures and everything in between. What she loved about the libraries of Galileo was the way they urged students to learn, making it easy at every turn. Rather than hefting a stack of books to the lonely oak tables in the room's center, Mariam simply slid free the two little latches and unfolded a nifty desk from beneath the sixth shelf. There was one along every other bookshelf, making for tiny—standing—study corners throughout the magnanimous space.

Learning? There was really no excuse *not* to at Galileo.

After propping up the desk and adjusting the attached light's flexible neck, she began pulling books off the shelves, racking her addled brain for the name of the two vials Fibula had given her with instructions on how to consume them. *Think, Mariam.* Her recollection was fuzzy, as if she'd been partly asleep, or watching herself from afar. There was a song involved, wasn't there? Along with a few obscenities, as the nurse was wont to do. *Yes.*

"It didn't start with an 'A,' that's for certain," she murmured to herself, flipping page after page of entries. It started with an "H." Mariam paused at the sudden zap of that recollection. Something strange like "hornbeam." *Hornbeam?* Mariam sighed. The sciences had never been her strong suit, much to her mother's dismay and her dream of her only daughter becoming the world's next great surgeon.

Spying the *Encyclopedia of Phytomedicine,* Mariam pulled it free and frowned at the lack of dust along the upper side, unlike the scraggly coat of it atop the books on either side of it. Something wriggled near her toes, and she jumped, only to see that it was a dust bunny.

Whoever had last pulled this book out had done it recently. She flipped to the letter she needed and slid her finger from one entry to the next. Dark stains rimmed the undersides of her nails. She blinked and they disappeared. She blinked again, and they returned, as gruesome as the moment when she'd killed Dropwort. *As gruesome as* what?

Mariam shook her head and began reading, a newfound urgency worming through her veins.

> *Horehound,*
> *Hornbeam.*

Oh, so there *was* something called hornbeam. If she'd been right about that, then the second tincture was, if she remembered correctly, something from the mint family. Hyacinth? No, that was purple. She'd get to that later.

Mariam squinted at the entry.

> *For many, seeing stars is a most whimsical*
> *experience. The stars associated with a nasty blow*
> *to the head are considerably less welcome. This is*

where hornbeam comes in handy. When distilled,
the aromatic oil will assist in the recovery—or
shall we say reduction—of a bump on one's noggin.
It should be noted, however, that hornbeam
does not play well with others. It converts to a
hallucinogenic when taken with materia medica
such as middlefog, feverleek, dragon's breath,
beetlebrush, and hyssop.

"*No.* Nurse Fibula, what have you done?" Mariam said beneath her breath.

Judging by the way "hyssop" stood out to Mariam, it was probably the second vial the nurse had given her. Mariam started down the list again, to make sure hyssop was indeed from the mint family, as she suspected.

If it was, Mariam was in deep, deep trouble.

When did a hallucinogen, warned about in an encyclopedia, wear off? Before or after one's professor's murderer was discovered? Or after a hallucinating Muslim girl outed herself during a mindless state of delirium when a silver-badged officer pulled her in for questioning?

Mariam swallowed a shaky laugh and forced her gaze to clear.

Houqure
Hourglass—

Mariam stopped and backed up, dragging her light closer, flooding the bolded entry with a blaze of flickering yellow. It was the very last term on the page, dangling like a promise, like a warning.

Hourglass

"It can't be," she told herself. It was only a coincidence that she'd heard the word more than once today. Was it code, like the girls had said, or was it the artifact itself?

Curiosity overtook her. Something in her bones compelled her to pay attention.

Mariam hurried to the next page and stopped.

There was no entry for "hourglass"; the page was gone. Mariam blinked, certain she was hallucinating this too, but her nails were clean—there was a neat tear down the page as close to the spine as possible. It looked dangerously, frighteningly intentional.

A thud from somewhere in the library echoed the quick drum of Mariam's heart. Someone was in the library with her.

She flipped to the front of the book, and cringed when it slammed shut from its own weight. "Hourglass" wasn't the name of an artifact. They had it all wrong. It was the name of an herb or a tincture. *Or poison.* Whoever had checked out this book before she'd gotten to it might even be Dropwort's murderer.

Mariam lifted her light to the scrawls on the inside of the front cover. She recognized the handwriting of the final entry from her days trying to decipher it on his chalkboard: *Dropwort.* Professor Dropwort had been the last to check the encyclopedia out of the library.

That didn't make sense. Had he torn the page out of the book, or was someone else trying to cover up their tracks?

Something dragged along the old wood floors, deliberate and slow. She shoved the books back onto the shelves before folding the desk away and tucking her notes into her pocket. She gripped her nubby pencil tight because she couldn't summon a single Defensive spell. Her throat had gone dry, her mind blank, the edges all jagged like the missing page.

She needed to get word to Diego. Would he believe her? He had to, even if she'd completely ignored him and disappeared without a word earlier.

The sound came again, and Mariam caught sight of the warped branches scraping the wide windows at the opposite end of the library. *No, M. It's not . . .* Another scrape. It was a lot closer this time, a lot more . . . *inside.*

But Mariam had a task, a job. She threw herself into the shadows and stared down at the clean crescents of skin beneath her fingernails. The entrance to the library wasn't far from here, and Diego not too far beyond. If Dropwort's murderer was here, she knew one thing was certain:

Mariam Abidin wasn't going to be next.

<u>**EVIDENCE EXHIBIT L3**</u>

CASE ID: 20-06-DROS-STK

<u>Type:</u>

[ ] Communication

[ ] Audio recording

[ ] Spell residue

[ ] Photo or other visual reconstruction

[ ] Object

[X] Form or record

[ ] Other: _____

Source: Library records of GAE

Relevant Parties: Septimius Dropwort (dec.)

Description: Records of library materials requested and removed by Septimius Dropwort in the month prior to his death

PATRON: DROPWORT, SEPTIMIUS

CLEARANCE LEVEL: UNRESTRICTED, Faculty

LENDING RECORD MAY 30–JUNE 30

Lending Date	Title; Author	Multiversal Decimal Classification	Status
6-12	*Tiny Terrors: An Encyclopedia of Nests, Eggs, and Young of Magical Beasts;* Cybelle, F.	401.7.59 Zoology, Magical	OVERDUE
6-13	*Field Observations of Beasts of Central Russia;* Tsarevitch, I.	401.7.59-A Zoology, Magical, Regional	OVERDUE
6-13	*Lost Treasures of the Mundane World: Neutral Society's Greatest Mysteries;* Croft, Hon. L. H.	903.04.02 Artifacts and Antiquities	OVERDUE
6-13	*Treasury Records of the Winter Palace Under Nikolai II Alexandrovich Romanov, 1912–1913*	930.25.07 Records, Public and Historical	OVERDUE
6-29	*Agrippina's Extended Poison & Antidote Compendium;* the Younger, A.	615.31.90 Alchemy, Chemistry, Toxicology	Returned, defaced/ damaged

1:00 P.M.: XANDER WILSON, 15, UNDECIDED

BY JULIAN WINTERS

Destiny always sounded so deeply promising when it was narrated by a true film legend, like Morgan Freeman.

Unfortunately, the voice in Xander's less-than-epic story didn't belong to another Black Brit like Idris Elba, or even an icon like Sir Patrick Stewart. No, it was Mum.

Your father named you Alexander. "The one who comes to save." "Protector." *That's you.*

Her words echoed loudly in his head as he leaned against the heavy oak door of Professor Dropwort's faculty office. Their hidden meaning—*you're meant to do great things*—shifted and curled in his stomach like a tidal wave seconds from ripping him off his feet. His heartbeat thudded in a noisy, unwanted cadence. It distracted from the lyrics on his lips. The ones he'd barely strung together to keep himself hidden from anyone's vision before he'd snuck onto the third floor of Coins Tower at 1:30 p.m.

Softly he sang, *"You always see the stars, but never the dreams behind them."*

POP!

It was like a massive chewing gum bubble finally bursting in his ears. One of his favorite sounds—the first indication that his magic was working. Cool, swift rivers flowed through Xander's veins, followed by a fleeting heat like the breath of a baby dragon.

He was safe . . . for now.

An Invisibility incantation was one of the few spells most first-years learned before ever stepping foot on school grounds. But Xander had modified it so he could remain hidden from the ghost patrol traversing the corridors outside Dropwort's office. Considering his magic had been a bloody mess since arriving on campus, it was quite the gamble.

Song magic was the Wilson family's legacy. Spells were cast through voice and lyrics. The perfect harmony of brain (what the Sorcerers wanted) and heart (what the Sorcerers needed). Each lyric Xander uttered had to correlate with the kind of spell he wanted to cast. He couldn't very well recite the ABCs and hope for a miracle. There had to be intent.

Fortunately, he'd been exceptionally versed in what it was like to be invisible to people.

Except to one boy.

"And that's why you're here," he whispered, shoulders falling. "Well, mostly."

Xander pinched between his fingers the partially crumpled note Irene had passed to him.

In hindsight, he should've immediately rejected Irene's earnest idea of sneaking about his dead professor's office. Even Viv had looked downright doubtful about Xander's covert abilities. But Irene had promised to involve Nadiya, going on about stolen goods. Solving a murder. How Dropwort's death was ruining all their futures. He'd known that the last bit was more about the climate change convention she was meant to attend in a few days than anything else, but he'd heard something else in her words:

Dropwort's unsolved murder meant the end of the future *he* wanted with a Neutral boy.

He should've consulted with Nadiya first. Knowing her, she'd probably say, "It just doesn't feel like a good idea." Then again, her portents were about as reliable as his magic, most days.

With a deep sigh, Xander heaved himself off the door. Time was short. He merely needed to find *something* of value connected to Dropwort's death before potentially being called into Fornax's office for questioning by the SNACC-EOs. Were his past issues with Dropwort big enough for them to consider him a potential suspect? Certainly the authorities would accept "daydreaming about a beautiful, unforgettable boy who I might not ever see again, thanks to someone offing my arrogant professor" as a proper alibi, right?

(He doubted that.)

Either way, Dropwort's death was mucking up his plans. According to Fornax during the memorial service, *With the murderer still unidentified and potentially on school grounds, we shall have to bring the Sorcerer-Neutral exchange program to an end before our usual post-dinner gathering.*

Xander couldn't let that happen. He needed that extra time. He was so close to something he'd thought impossible.

"But no pressure to save the world or anything, mate," grumbled Xander.

The last time he'd been inside the office, it had been a posh display of history and maps and texts. Undoubtedly stolen. Books had been shelved properly. The walls had been lined with authentic pieces or impressive replicas of famous artwork done by the great Sorcerers—all white, all male—of the past. The curtains had been drawn to allow only a slender gold bar of sunlight in, the rest lit by lamps or floating candles. Every piece of furniture angled to provide Dropwort a position of power over whomever stood in front of his antique desk.

To Xander, the office had been boring and predictable, just like the speech Dropwort had delivered to him.

And now he'd been killed.

Xander fought off the chill crawling up his neck. As he scanned the room, it was clear someone had been there long before him.

The curtains had been split open like a lion's jaws before a meal. Starved sunlight devoured any meter of space it could reach. Books were everywhere, spines cracked, pages torn. Papers scattered across the floor. Both chairs knocked over as if they had been in a brawl.

A kettle of spilled tea forged a swamp on the carpet. Xander's heart knocked against his chest. His mind spun to an evening six days prior:

Of all the students at school, how had *he* ended up on the school's welcoming committee? Viv, that's how. All he'd had to do was formally introduce the faculty to the Neutral exchange students at dinner that first night. Nothing more. And yet, when his eyes had caught on one boy, he'd turned into a right disaster, bumping into an entire tray of cups.

Three different flavors of tea soaking his trousers.

The boy's laugh had been like a melody waiting for accompanying lyrics in his ears as he'd helped Xander clean the chaos.

His words—"I'm Chris Park"—colliding so clumsily with Xander's—"I'm such a mess."

Every detail of Chris had hit Xander like staring into the heart of a star:

The fall of his auburn hair across his brow. His oval face, complemented by long cheekbones. Brown eyes, rich like summer soil. Standing still, he looked like a baby bird—all uncertain limbs, growing out of his awkwardness and into his feathers.

If Dropwort's killer wasn't found soon, Chris would be taking a flight back home to his family before dinner.

Before Xander could say all the things he'd forgot to last night.

"I can't believe it's already been a week," Chris had said under a blue-gray moon, down in the courtyard. His lips were a ruby pink, arresting whether coaxed into a smile or a pout. His voice was a deep, honeyed sound, unlike Xander's own, which felt too light and came out obnoxiously pinched when he was nervous.

Chris's laugh was an unforgettable chorus that begged for an encore.

What Sorcerer falls for a Neutral boy? In less than seven days, at that. Chris was supposed to be nothing more than an exchange student in Galileo's program where non-magical students visited for a period while a group of GAE's prodigies spent time studying at a Neutral school.

It was ridiculous.

Xander could only think of the moments—both quiet and loud—they'd shared. Hours spent unlocking fragments, carefully piecing Chris together. In classes. During lunch breaks and dinners. Over late-night texts.

A beginning being rushed to an unexpected end thanks to Dropwort's murder.

Now Xander whispered, "At least the décor in here looks proper aces now" as he gingerly stepped over the papers and tea. He'd only recently healed from a sprained ankle, thanks to Nadiya's last, mildly incorrect prediction. If he was being honest, a sprained ankle was far less bothersome than Nadiya's original "broken" portent suggested.

Still, there was no time for another mistimed accident. Anyone could've noticed him sneaking out of the memorial service at 1:15.

Back in the auditorium, after Fornax's exchange program announcement, Xander had murmured to Bhavna that he needed a loo break. Not that she had seemed to care. She'd been too busy asking where Diego was. Xander quite liked that about her. While all of Galileo Academy for the Extraordinary was transfixed on uncovering who'd offed Dropwort, Bhavna was thinking about a boy.

Xander had . . . similar issues.

It was the perfect reminder that he needed to get moving. He closed his eyes. These days, spell reinforcement was a necessity. Xander mentally scrolled through songs in his head. He always needed somewhere to start.

"According to your heart, my place is not deliberate . . . ," he sang softly.

Nothing happened.

No noise. No rush of coolness under his skin.

Xander huffed. Why had he even bothered "borrowing" someone else's words? That never worked. Song magic only thrived when the Sorcerers used original lyrics. But he'd lost confidence in his musical abilities while at GAE. Every other student was ten steps ahead of him. Legends in the making, Dropwort had liked to remind him on far too many occasions.

Then came Chris.

Just before dawn, after the smoke magic had woken him, Xander had written the most beautiful lyrics. *His own words.* Voracious magic had poured from him. It was the strongest he'd ever felt. And the most terrified.

Inhaling deeply, Xander brushed Dropwort's voice from his head. He yanked his own lyrics from the warmest parts of his stomach.

> *"And so I linger in the dark, like the sun waiting
> for permission from the moon to rise . . ."*

POP!

He hadn't needed to focus this hard to maintain a simple Cloaking spell before. As a wee one, he'd scamper into Auntie Imani's kitchen. Steal two fistfuls of still-warm lemon bars, undetected. His magic had been a dusting of snow then—fun and safe. Now it was a blizzard—thick and unpredictable.

As Xander rounded the desk, he examined the note Irene had pressed into his palm earlier. He mouthed the last lines repeatedly:

Return what you stole.
Return what you stole.
Return what you stole.

Xander had no clue *who* LC was. Or why any of this had been enough to get Dropwort killed. His professor had been a pillager. His office was a museum of items he'd no doubt plucked from the various places GAE had visited. He'd seized students' belongings. Their confidence too.

And now he was snatching Xander's chances with Chris.

Tingles spread across his lower lip. A voice in his head breathed, *Are you giving me permission?*

Xander shook off the crash of sensations while inspecting the desk's surface. The carnage made it clear that the intruder had wanted something specific from the office. The artifact maybe?

Pens lay on their sides, drooling onyx ink over essay papers. Stacked books had been punished by thoughtless hands. Xander had not known Dropwort to care so deeply for Russian folklore and culture, especially since his subject was history of ancient civilizations.

At the heart of the chaos was an unrolled map of Stockholm weighed down by an iridescent crystal pyramid and a single black fingerless glove. Sunlight glittered off the paperweight onto a pattern of steel studs that adorned the glove's knuckle and hand area.

A weapon? Or just dodgy fashion sense?

He ignored the itch to touch the glove. While the Invisibility incantation gave Xander freedom to remain unseen, his uncertain magic couldn't guarantee untraceable fingerprints. Besides, it was only a glove.

It wasn't listed on the note from Irene.

"Come on, Dropwort." Xander's eyes narrowed. "What's your favorite hiding spot?"

A soft *tick* stole his attention. On the wall, next to a bookcase, hung a clock. The positioning of its hands said he'd wasted nearly five minutes staring at a disorganized desk and a meaningless glove.

He was quite horrible at the whole amateur detective business.

Mercifully, unlike the professor's standard-issue classroom desk, Dropwort's personal one didn't have a switch to activate the PA system. Nothing to trigger an alarm as Xander palmed along its belly. This luxurious monster with its gilded accents—another way for Dropwort to flaunt his wealth—was in the center of the room, unlike the classroom ones that professors kept off to the side, preferring to teach from behind a podium. Xander frantically tugged open drawers. Still, his search came up empty. Only student files and a tin whose aroma filled him with vivid memories the moment he popped the lid.

Dark cocoa. His mum's favorite.

It was the kind she'd sip on long, cold weekends while they holidayed in New York. She would stare out the frosted windows of Gramps's cabin, watching the sugared snow dusting treetops. Waiting on a ghost that would not return.

A Neutral father Xander had only known through her stories.

On instinct, his right hand slipped beneath his shirt collar. Anxious fingertips stroked a stone set in a lattice of gold hanging from a necklace. The amulet, a purple sapphire gradually dulling over the past month, was a family gift. A focus for his magic.

Another memory chased the buzzing in his ears.

"As long as you have a song, you can create whatever you want," his mum had said while helping Xander pick out his outfit for his first day at GAE. "Dreams inside here," she had continued, tapping his temple, then his chest, with that mischievous smile he loved, "are lyrics waiting to manifest."

How had his mum seen all that in Xander? When he looked in the mirror, all he saw was a boy with gold-brown skin, his long limbs impatiently waiting on his muscles to become defined. A short, thick crown of dark curls. He hadn't felt like the powerful gay Black Sorcerer who would one day come to save anything, let alone *anyone*.

The problem was, he struggled to find the words to say what he felt.

What he wanted.

Xander swung away from the desk, moving toward the art along the walls.

"Like a new moon in the night's sky, I'm here, but you never see me," he sang quietly, once more strengthening the Cloaking spell.

He waited for the rush through his blood, the hot, beating glow against his chest, the POP! before cautiously pinching the frame of each painting, shifting them to search for hidden panels.

Nothing there.

If he'd only been as strong as the women of his family, he'd cast a Search-and-Find spell to unearth clues. While Summoning incantations were quite easy, Xander struggled to command more than one spell at a time. Once he'd found a song in his head, jumping to another felt near impossible.

At fourteen, his mum had been casting two, three spells simultaneously.

Dropwort's voice rang in his head: *But you're not her.*

Dariela Wilson had been well-known—and well-loved—during her time at GAE. There was a photograph in Professor Anand's office of the two of them, grinning in their uniforms. House of Wands's finest. Now Xander was meant to carry on the tradition.

He quite liked the school. He'd made friends. Was gradually getting better at invocations. But there was something he desired: *courage.*

Dariela swam in magic, diving deep into its endless core until he was certain she'd drown. Xander merely dipped a few toes in, uncertain if he could handle its depth.

He gravely wanted to be like his mum and aunties. But on his own terms.

Another *tick* from the wall. Twenty minutes had gone, unveiling nothing but time wasted.

The murderer could be long gone if you don't hurry, you dolt.

On a shelf just below Dropwort's window was a gathering of trinkets. They stood guard around a piece of paper. The edges were clean as if sliced free by a sharp blade. Xander studied the headline.

Antidotes for Hourglass Poison

Poison?

A tight crinkle formed along Xander's brow as he skimmed the page. He didn't retain anything. Not ingredients. Nor measurements. Not the step-by-step instructions.

His brain rotated on one question: *Why would Dropwort need this?*

Tick.

Hurriedly Xander folded the page into thirds and stuffed it into his pocket. Once he'd finished here, he could pass it on to Nadiya, who knew—or could use her portents to find out—more about these things than he did.

Familiar laughter from outside the open window broke Xander's concentration. It reignited the panic living inside his rib cage.

The fear of losing something you'd only just found.

"Chris," breathed Xander, staring into the courtyard. His hand pressed to the window's cool pane as if he could touch the boy from a distance.

As if he needed to be rooted to the memories tugging on him.

Last night Chris had whispered, "You're full of music." They'd been beneath the branches of a walnut tree in the courtyard. Xander had begun to call it *their tree.* A hidden universe in plain sight.

"Would you write me a song?" Chris asked as Xander hummed.

He wanted to tell Chris there should be film scores composed to his laugh. Soundtracks about the ways Xander was not yet ready to let this boy disappear in twenty-four hours. But he didn't.

"If I did," said Xander, cheeks warm, "my magic would be tied to it. It'd be unfair to you."

"Because you'd make me fall in love?" teased Chris.

The fire spread down Xander's jaw, through his neck. Against his chest, the purple sapphire flushed. "No. Compulsion is forbidden."

"Could you make me," Chris said, inclining closer, "kiss you?"

"To be quite honest, I don't think you understand the definition of 'compul—'" But Xander didn't finish.

Chris held his gaze. A soft, repetitive melody buzzed in Xander's ears. Jeweled moonlight broke through the leaves. It circled Chris's face. The lyrics raced up Xander's throat, almost shattering his teeth, trying to escape.

If I promised more time, would your lips be mine?

"C-can I kiss you?" Chris said with a frantic stutter.

Xander nodded.

But Chris, persistent and respectful, said, "Are you giving me permission?"

Those unsaid lyrics sank back down into Xander's chest, igniting his breaths. He whispered, "Yes."

The kiss was gentle and deep. It hummed with music that filled Xander's head for hours. He thought he'd never be able to cast a proper spell again if he tried.

"Foolish," said Xander now as he broke away from the window. He moved to the bookcase. Skimmed his fingers along the spines of ancient tomes.

It had not escaped him that this was a familiar trap. One his mum had carelessly walked into when she'd met his father—ironically—while studying abroad in the States. Their love had been a crash of constellations, bright and dangerous at once.

It had ended in tragedy.

Xander pulled at novels as if they would unlock a secret passage behind the bookcase. He would never put it past Dropwort to have things like that—hidden, dark passageways running throughout the school. Places no one else could see, where he could be openly dismissive of students who were anything like Xander.

"You'll be *good enough*," Dropwort had said the last time they'd spoken in the office. "Never exemplary. Nothing remarkable. Simply average."

"You'll never be the"—Dropwort heaved a deep breath, as if his next words took effort—"the Sorcerer your mother was."

"*Is*," Xander mumbled angrily, wishing he'd said it to Dropwort that day.

He ripped a book off the shelf. It thumped against the carpet. He toed it away. Dropwort's words were a superfluous reminder. Xander'd done quite fine carrying all his family's expectations with him over the years, waiting for failure to snap at his skin.

You're the first magical child born to a Sorcerer and a Neutral in our entire bloodline! Dariela had exclaimed so many times during his childhood that he thought it a myth.

His mum loved to leave off the most important detail: her Neutral husband, Xander's father, had died exactly seven days to the minute after Xander was born.

His birth wasn't destiny. It was a curse.

Yet here he was, trying to help solve a crime for a boy.

"And they lived unhappily ever after," sighed Xander.

Knobby fingers tugged at random books. Nothing. No hidden corridor. Only the occasional exhale of dust motes taking flight to sparkle like gold in the sunlight.

"You've single-handedly failed at your one job," he muttered, punching a collection of magical poetry books.

They didn't shift or topple. A hollow thud echoed in the office. Xander arched an eyebrow. He grabbed the "books," and they came out as one unit. Their insides were gouged out. A casing for a maroon, rectangular box accented in gold leafing.

Xander smiled.

Finally!

Cautiously he made room on the desk, then sat in the high-backed chair. He ran his thumb along the gilded *SD* on the box and lifted the cover.

Inside, beneath a sheet of papyrus paper, lay several items. *Confiscated contraband,* Xander thought almost giddily. The paper's text, scribbled in Dropwort's handwriting, was a confiscation record.

Briskly Xander compared the contents to the list:

A posh beginner's wand, the kind parents of privileged

students bought to show off their wealth. A marble-sized garnet stone. *My First Enchantments,* a how-to sorcerer's guide for novices. A scratched golden compass, and—

"Wait . . . where's the dagger?" Xander asked almost breathlessly.

His eyes flitted between the box and paper again.

"What the actual f—"

Xander cut himself off, eyes narrowed at the missing item Dropwort had described at the bottom of the record.

An ornate ceremonial dagger. Leaf carvings along the hilt.
The blade shiny, not a speck of dullness in its steel.

Xander ran a hand down his face. Another wave of dizzying realization smashed against him.

Though there weren't any names listed next to each itemized object, he *knew* that dagger. Memories caught him like a hungry viper's bite. Only one student had spoken of it repeatedly. A cursed family dagger.

With a sharp breath, Xander slowly whispered, "Shit. Julietta."

Just as quickly as he'd snatched it up, the paper slipped from between Xander's fingers. It floated on a calm breeze onto the desk. Was that the weapon that had killed Dropwort? Had Nurse Fibula's overdramatic stabbing puns during the announcements been about . . . *that?*

Shaking his head, Xander said, "This was *not* what my mum was talking about when she said I was destined for great things."

He stood, delicately picking up the confiscation record.

"Nadiya will know what to do. All I have to do is give it to her." He slipped it into his trouser pocket—the one that didn't already hold the page of antidotes and Irene's mysterious note. It was starting to feel slightly ridiculous, the amount of paper he was collecting, but everything seemed important. His eyes peeked in the direction of the window. No laughter greeted him, but Xander was certain Chris was still in the courtyard. He could feel it like the magic beneath his skin. "She'd bloody well better sort this out."

After arranging the confiscated items back in the box, he shelved it among the books again, ready to leave the office behind. First find Nadiya. Then have a brief panic attack in front of Irene and Viv for putting him up to this. Finally, meet Chris before their time ran out.

Xander needed to show him the song he'd written.

He needed another kiss.

Another reason to chase rather than avoid his destiny.

The comforting silence in the office was broken by a jingling noise. The door. Xander fumbled for new lyrics to strengthen his Invisibility spell. They raced up his throat, and were so close to his tongue when another noise betrayed him.

Xander's phone blared from his back pocket. *Not now.* He was going to ruin the Wilson family legacy, be expelled from GAE for snooping around his dead professor's office because he'd forgotten to turn his ringtone to vibrate!

Xander's clumsy hands fumbled for the phone to quiet it.

It was too late.

A muffled voice from the other side of the door interrupted that fleeting moment of quiet he'd found his confidence in.

"Xander?"

EVIDENCE EXHIBIT X5

CASE ID: 20-06-DROS-STK

Type:

[ ] Communication

[ ] Audio recording

[ ] Spell residue

[ ] Photo or other visual reconstruction

[X] Object

[ ] Form or record

[ ] Other: _____

Source: Faculty office of Septimius Dropwort (dec.)

Relevant Parties: Suspect 3 (name withheld for privacy/age restrictions)

Description: Glove found in office of deceased; matches glove found in possession of Suspect 3

[IMAGE: a single black fingerless glove with silver studs]

2:00 P.M.: NADIYA NUR, 15, WANDS/ARCANA

BY KARUNA RIAZI

It felt like everyone but Nadiya had gotten Murder 101.

At least, that was how it felt as she sat on the edge of her bed and stared at the door, hearing the slight murmur of voices behind it, slowly plodding feet and the occasional squeak of a rolling backpack.

Was it weird to be holed up in her room during a murder?

It wasn't like she'd been in here *all* day. She'd sat there with the rest of them, heart pounding and mouth open, through that agonizing assembly. She thought she'd kept her head lowered in respect—but had she?

Had she looked up too long toward the front to see if she could spot her friends Xander and Irene? Or—before the memorial—when she'd seen Mariam and they'd done that furtive *You know I got your back* hijabi nod that was the foundation of their polite acquaintance as schoolmates, had any faculty member noticed and thought it was suspicious rather than a reassurance?

Well, at the time, she'd *thought* that was what they were doing. Now she wondered if Mariam had been trying out telepathy: *We tend to take the fall for stuff like this, so be careful.*

If that was what she'd been was doing, she didn't need to waste her time. No one was more careful, ever, than Nadiya.

But maybe she'd slipped up, at some point. Had drawn the attention of the SNACC-EOs. She knew she had to talk to them eventually, but what Black girl wanted to have herself singled out for extra scrutiny and more rough handling than she was already in for?

So, yeah, it probably didn't look good that she had scrambled right back to her room without so much as a glance over to the lukewarm pastries and equally unappetizing circle of long-faced professors who had volunteered themselves as "trauma counselors."

But she hadn't been able to think about how it looked. All she could think of, in that moment, was how much she needed to get away.

Nadiya groaned and sank her head into her hands.

She needed to go outside. But she couldn't get herself to move.

Not with that word in the back of her head.

Fluid.

Anyone else might not be bothered by having just one word repeating itself through their subconscious. Maybe it was just their favorite word of the day, or something they'd heard a few times in passing.

It would leave, eventually—knocked away by another passing thought.

But that wasn't how it worked for Nadiya. Not ever.

"Fluid," Nadiya chanted. "Fluid. Fluid?"

What the heck did that even mean, and why—of all words in the English language—was it the word she'd had to notice tucked away in the overwrought mahogany curlings and etched flowers of the picture frame at Dropwort's memorial service?

She roughly shoved a stray lock back under her hijab, fuming at herself. She couldn't stop thinking about it. It was like the obsessive thoughts had snagged their claws, kitten-like, into a skein of yarn and were determined to drag it out and torment her as much as possible.

When a word was stuck in her brain like that, it was because she'd seen it somewhere she shouldn't have seen it.

And she needed to worry about it.

Most Neutrals would call Nadiya a professional worrywart. "It just doesn't feel like a good idea," tended to be her catchphrase. And she used it a lot.

One of her cousins, as cousins usually do, had actually laughed at her when she'd proposed that her catchphrase was actually "Keep it real" back in middle school.

"'Keep it real'? Please, Wednesday Addams. You're more like . . . 'Keep it gloomy.'"

It had given her very wicked pleasure the following week when that particular cousin hadn't listened to her warning about "something being off in the living room" and had stepped into a whole patch of Legos.

Not just one. A nice, solid, painful mass.

Because, unlike other worrywarts, Nadiya was unnaturally accurate with her worries, as evidenced by the number of extended family grievances and unanticipated ills that she had predicted at dinners, wedding receptions, and the occasional baby shower.

"Was she born with the caul?" her grandma would marvel.

Her aunt would cluck and shake her head. "It's downright unnatural."

And she was right. Well, kind of.

It was unnatural for Neutrals. It was very natural for Sorcerers, though.

Nadiya could read bad news in someone's freckle, could work out a storm coming from a leaf brushing against her window. She refused to get on a train if she read the wrong word on the timetable, and wouldn't buy a pizza slice from a particular food truck because—just once—the word "ew" had formed clearly in the ooze of oil and cheese on her friend's plate.

It might sound like she had nothing to worry about. After all, the world was handing her warnings of ill fortune, right?

With all that foresight she could sidestep that hole in the pavement or avoid biting into the single, unnoticed pebble in a plate of rice, couldn't she?

Except it didn't work that way.

It was always just one word, vaguer than a crossword puzzle hint and as ephemeral as smoke. "Slip" could mean something as minor as an embarrassing near-fall in front of a crush, or something as major as a broken leg after ignoring a Wet Floor sign.

And since she could never tell, Nadiya had to keep worrying. Always.

But it had never been as bad as it was today.

The word—the *portent*—had to relate to Dropwort and his murder. But how? And why her?

She hadn't liked Dropwort, or gotten along with him. To be honest, no one really had. Nadiya thought of the meme she'd seen earlier on the school discussion board—a little wink of defiance from an anonymous student before a fast-acting faculty member had given it the banhammer: *Someone got the DROP on DROPwort, huh?*

But for her, it had always felt more personal. He'd had a very Orientalist perception of Muslims, and an anti-Black sensibility that had always struck her the wrong way—even though, thankfully, none of the other faculty had seemed to support him and had always been stern when it had come to his "all lives matter" and "I got this from a bazaar in Turkey where no one else would have appreciated it" nonsense.

She was pretty sure that one time she'd told him to "read some Edward Said and stop looting other people's magical heritage" and had gotten points docked for it. But how was she supposed to feel when he'd been waxing poetic about magical colonization and theft?

Not just waxing poetic about it either.

Likely involved in it too.

There were portents she'd picked up, here and there—not clear enough words. But feelings could be good enough.

No matter what way she looked at the situation, it just gave her the creeps. Her warnings had always been targeted at her, or at least someone she cared about or was related to in some way. Why would she be getting a warning for a man who had already suffered the worst fate possible?

Or . . . was it something else? Was it a warning that she could be next? Or one of her friends? A shudder ran down her spine.

It didn't help that the school felt oddly still around her as she sat here. The thick walls of her room muffled any noise that could have seeped through and reminded her she wasn't the only one left alive. It stirred up the unease even more.

Nadia shook her head fiercely. No. She couldn't do this today.

She needed some air.

It took Nadiya a moment to paw through her berets. She finally chose one with rabbits, because the one with cutesy little daggers and the sweet script *Warrior Woman* felt a little . . . daring today. It didn't feel right to tempt fate when it was already trying to warn her that something was off. She slung her messenger bag over her shoulder.

Maybe she needed to hang in the dining hall for a while, or circulate somewhere with a lot of people. Maybe she just needed to pick up on that confident *Everything is cool at our magical school* energy everyone else gave off.

Maybe "fluid" meant "stay hydrated and you won't get murdered."

Ha. As if it could be that simple.

Nadiya opened her door, fumbling with her pocket to make sure she had her key.

And bumped into someone.

She reached out to balance herself, and grasped a handlebar. A wheelchair?

"Irene? What are you doing here? Are you okay—"

"Shh!" her friend warned, and tugged her toward an alcove. Nadiya yelped, having no choice but to follow.

"What is it? What's going on?" Nadiya had never seen Irene, always so cool-looking and efficient at the worst of times, utterly flustered. "Your face is red! What—"

"I said keep it down!" Irene hissed, then muttered, "I'm fine. Viv said something, and I thought it was going south for a moment, but my mom . . . never mind. We don't have time for this. I'm not even sure how much time we have, period. Look at this."

She reached into the side of her chair, rummaging between the cushion and the frame. After a moment, she shoved something forward.

"Recognize this?"

Nadiya gasped.

"That's not . . ."

It was a battered, scraped-up silver flask. *Dropwort's* flask. He'd always carried it with him during classes, and taken sips of—well, they never had been able to figure that out, though it had always been a topic of hot debate. There had even been bets, and once or twice someone had teased that they would drop a match in there, just to see if it was really water like he'd claimed.

(Actually, that may have also been her. Why in the world was she opening her fool mouth so often?)

"Where did you get that?"

"I didn't coffin-rob, if that's what you're implying," Irene said with a roll of her eyes. "Look, I know worrying is your thing, but I need you to pay attention to me. This . . . is valuable."

She brandished the flask again. Nadiya looked at her blankly.

"I'm pretty sure I saw, like, a whole discounted shelf of those two cities ago, but . . . okay . . . ?"

"Not like that." Irene sighed harshly and reached out. She grabbed hold of Nadiya's hand and smacked the flask into it.

"There. Go ahead."

Irene was eccentric at the best of times—really, who wasn't at a magical school?—but this was the most confused Nadiya had ever been by her actions.

"What am I supposed to be doing with our dead professor's flask?"

"Read it," Irene ordered. "Find the portent in it—maybe it will tell us something about the murder. Quickly, please. My mom will cover for me if someone realizes I have this . . . I think. Parents find the weirdest times to be loyal to oppressive systems."

"Irene, we've talked about this." Nadiya held the flask back out to her friend. "I can't do this on command. And why me? Somebody else must be able to . . ."

Irene shook her head. "There's no somebody else, not right now. Come on, Nadi. At least try. We need to solve this. *I* need to solve this. And I think you can help."

"I . . ." Nadiya furrowed her brow, staring down at the flask. And then her eyes widened as finally, wonderfully, the word snapped into place.

Fluid.

"Fluid!" She shook the flask at Irene. Irene hissed at her, fanning her hands. "Sorry. Um . . . fluid! This must be the fluid!"

"Fluid?"

"I saw a word earlier in Dropwort's funeral portrait. I didn't know why I saw it. I still don't. Why see a portent for a dead man? What does that mean?"

Irene looked at her, face grave.

"Nothing good, that's for sure."

"I was hoping you wouldn't say that."

Nadiya inhaled, staring down at the flask. She wasn't lying to Irene. Even with a year of magical education under her belt, harnessing her portents felt as impossible as reaching out on a foggy day and catching some of the mist in her hand.

Before school, she hadn't even had a proper term for it.

"Bad vibes," maybe.

One reason her parents had taken to Galileo more quickly than even she had was the confidence with which a faculty member (Nadiya couldn't remember who or at what point in the flurry that was her entrance interview, as anxiety made everything a blur at the best of times) had leaned forward and said, "So it's portents you're struggling with? We can help with that!"

It had soothed them at least, that someone had been able to put another label to what Nadiya still felt was a messy, cloudy problem in the back of her head.

But even with that label, she felt no closer to understanding it, what she was meant to do with it.

Why she'd been chosen for it.

"Is that helping?" Irene asked, nodding to Nadiya's hands.

Nadiya hadn't even realized she was rubbing her thumb over the neck of the flask. She looked down—and then gasped.

"Irene! Look!"

Irene glanced down, and then shook her head.

"Nadiya, I don't see a thing . . . Wait, are you seeing a portent?"

Nadiya's heart pounded. Of course. If Irene couldn't see it, it had to be.

There, where previously she'd seen nothing but blank metal, was one single word in small, neat script.

"Office," Nadiya read slowly.

Irene mouthed the word after her, and then frowned. "There's only one office that could be, and . . ." Her eyes widened. "Xander! I sent Xander to check on Dropwort's office. Could he be in trouble?"

She stared at Nadiya.

As it turned out, it was just as easy to read portents from faces as it was from objects. Nadiya could read it on every inch of Irene's face: *Go and help him.*

She shook her head.

"Oh, no, no, no. It's not like I want to leave Xander hanging, but . . . no. He's fine."

"Nadiya. You know it has to be talking about Dropwort's office. And you've got a knack for finding things that are out of place."

"You mean bad luck. That's all I ever pick up on. Portents aren't like clues, Irene. They're . . . they're signposts telling you which direction you don't want to head toward. What if it's telling me that going to the office will be what gets Xander into trouble? Besides, this was just a fluke. It never works on command like this. What . . ." Nadiya threw up her hands. "What if I run across the officers who are investigating there?"

"I'm pretty sure I saw them down another corridor, so it should be totally dead down there." Irene winced. "Okay, bad choice of words. Look, Nadiya . . . you're the only one I could think of who I could come to about this, besides Xander. And if he's in trouble, you're the only one I trust to get him out of it."

Irene looked at her urgently.

"I trust your instincts. I trust you. And I need you to trust and listen to yourself right now, because it doesn't seem like faculty or even . . . well, I don't know what the rest of us are up to besides me and Viv, but it seems like right now is the time to be able to trust our own aptitudes."

Nadiya looked down at the flask her friend was pressing into her hand.

She thought back to the hissed rumor she'd heard during the announcement: *Do you think this means the Newts will be cutting us off?*

At the time, the main reaction she'd had was flinching at the slur against Neutrals—the casual, calm way it had been delivered.

Any other day, she would have leaned over and said something loudly, tugging on the confident Timbaland-clad tones of her favorite Brooklyn cousins: "You want to repeat that? No, I want to hear you say that again."

But now the rest of the sentence was sinking in. What if the normal world—her other world, even if so many at the school didn't see it that way or feel the same way about it—cut Galileo off, or the other way around?

What would that mean for her?

She swallowed hard. And then nodded.

"All right. I'll see what I can find out."

She pulled back slightly, but Irene reached out. They clasped hands for a moment.

"Stay safe," Irene instructed.

"You don't have to tell me twice," Nadiya said, rolling her eyes. "You know who you're talking to."

Irene rolled her eyes too but squeezed her hand a little tighter. "Seriously."

"Okay. I will."

Irene was right. It was mostly quiet as she crept down the long hallway of faculty offices. The few doors that were open revealed subdued instructors staring down at their desks or engaged in quiet conversation with equally droopy-faced students. Dropwort's office wasn't hard to miss—surrounded by caution tape, though there was no sign of the officers that Nadiya had been sure would be posted there.

Where was the ghost patrol?

A familiar snatch of verse—Ed Sheeran?—made her startle, along with a scuffling sound and a soft "Ow!"

That voice was familiar too, but it couldn't be . . .

"Xander?"

Nadiya reached out and tried the handle.

The door swung inward.

She swallowed hard and stepped in.

It felt super creepy to be in Dropwort's office, knowing he wasn't coming back. Nadiya inched forward, wrinkling her nose as she took in all the Orientalist artifacts lining the walls. Well, they weren't Orientalist in origin, but definitely stolen by someone who considered himself more worthy of wielding them than their original peoples. Some were definitely cheap knockoffs pressed on him by people in the know who weren't above scamming some colonizer coin, but others looked very, very real. She stared at the large black rooster and made a note to look up some of these curiosities later. Someone might be owed reparations from Dropwort's estate.

That wasn't her concern right now, though. She was sure

she'd heard Xander's phone in here. She was leaning down to check under the desk when a hand landed on her shoulder.

"Miss Nur. Care to explain to me why you are in here?"

Great.

It was Vice Principal Ruiz-Marín, looking as formal and stern as always. Perhaps even sterner, Nadiya realized—there was usually some lingering kindness in the depths of Ruiz-Marín's eyes, some acknowledgment of extra care and affection.

Nadiya swallowed hard. A worn-down, already frustrated Ruiz-Marín wasn't going to be easy to handle.

"Oh! Vice Principal," Nadiya greeted her nervously. "I . . . uh . . ."

"Indeed," Ruiz-Marín snapped. "I thought I made it quite clear that this office and hallway were off-limits, Nadiya Nur. Why are you here?"

"I thought . . . well, it looked like the investigation was done."

It was the most ridiculous thing she could have said, and the assistant principal's face made it clear she was equally unimpressed.

"The officers are conducting student interviews. Incidentally, you were next on the list." The assistant principal's eyes narrowed. "I had been assured by my office map that you were in your room before I left to see how things were with the investigation. Strange now to be informed by the ghost patrol that you're poking around here."

"I was just . . ."

Ugh. She was never good at coming up with excuses on the fly.

Great. Just great.

Ruiz-Marín had her arms crossed, waiting.

"I just couldn't be by myself in my room anymore," Nadiya finally forced out. "I wanted to help."

"By sneaking into a professor's office? Honestly." Ruiz-Marín looked weary, shaking her head. For a moment, Nadiya felt a prickle of guilt. The vice principal looked so tired.

And then the assistant principal cocked her head. "And what is that?"

Nadiya had forgotten about the flask. Her stomach dropped. "That? I . . ."

Ruiz-Marín flexed her fingers, frowning.

"Nadiya, you know better than this. I believe it was explicitly mentioned that we didn't want students poking around and getting in trouble while we're all caught up in other matters. And I can recognize that as Dropwort's flask. Now, please . . ."

Reluctantly Nadiya held out the flask.

Ruiz-Marín's hand was cold, and Nadiya—without even meaning to—pulled back from the shock. Fortunately, though, Ruiz-Marín had already grasped it. She gave Nadiya an exasperated look before trying to uncork it.

"Oh, I—oops!"

She gasped as the cork shot off and the flask spilled between them. It was just a drop or two, but that was enough. The liquid bounced off one of Dropwort's silver vases. As it landed on the floor, it spilled out in dark grains. *Sand.*

The liquid had become sand.

Ruiz-Marín looked from the sand to Nadiya's face. She looked shaken. Nadiya stared down at the little patch on the floor, feeling unsteady herself. She could see something in the grains.

A portent? An omen?

It was too smudged to see properly. She narrowed her eyes.

L . . . o . . .

But then Ruiz-Marín was scuffing at the sand with her smart-looking leather heels, and the letters vanished.

"Goodness, what a mess," the woman mumbled.

Nadiya gritted her teeth in disappointment. Not being able to finish a portent always bothered her, particularly on an anxiety-disorder level—what was she going to stumble into because she hadn't been warned?

But the fact that Ruiz-Marín had seen her looking, and had made a point of covering it up . . .

What had it been trying to tell her?

"Listen," Ruiz-Marín said sharply, and Nadiya looked up at her, startled. The woman was always stern, but this was a new level, even for her. "What you just saw . . . I'm already investigating, all right? Everything's under control, and I don't want any of you worrying or coming up with theories that could make things worse."

Worse? What could be worse than a murder?

There was a scuffle under the desk. Ruiz-Marín's lips drew even tighter.

"You can come out now, Xander. I'm well aware that you're here too."

Xander sheepishly rose up, rubbing the back of his neck. Nadiya stared at him, taking in the rug burn already forming on the side of his hand and the wide-eyed expression on his face.

What was he up to?

Ruiz-Marín's eyes were narrowing, so Nadiya blurted out a question.

"Is it true? What everyone's saying about the normal . . . I mean, Neutral world?"

"What?" Ruiz-Marín looked surprised, apparently not noticing Nadiya's slip. Any other time, she might have narrowed her eyes and coolly said, "This *is* part of the normal world, Miss Nur." Which, of course, Nadiya knew.

But it didn't always feel like the same world where her mom put a cool palm on her forehead and recited over her after she had an anxiety attack, or her dad gave her driving lessons in the parking lot of the masjid after prayers.

"Nadiya," Xander said softly, reaching out a hand toward her as though to soothe her.

"What are they saying?" Ruiz-Marín prodded.

"That this could jeopardize Galileo's ties . . . that Neutral parents may start pulling their kids, and Neutral authorities might become more keen on policing the school. I mean, the Stockholm Neutral police already have that checkpoint outside, and . . ."

As the words left her mouth, Nadiya realized it was bothering her more than she had thought it was.

Her parents were already worried about her being here, what this could mean for her future. They wanted her to be able to focus on her own world too—*their* world. Not realizing that for Nadiya there were multiple possibilities, and she was terrified of being locked into one and losing other opportunities she didn't even realize she could lose.

Ruiz-Marín's face softened slightly, and she put her hand on Nadiya's shoulder.

"I know everything that has happened is upsetting, Nadiya. I know this is a lot to ask of you, and the whole student body.

But for now, it's crucial, so crucial, for you to listen to your teachers. Just listen, and trust us, and things will be all right."

It was the same advice Irene had given her earlier.

Just listen.

Everyone was telling her to listen—but when there were so many voices trying to get into her head, how was she supposed to sort through it all?

Ruiz-Marín looked like she was about to say something else, but then her gaze drifted toward Xander—no, *near* him.

The vice principal's eyes hardened.

"Xander. Where is it?"

Xander blinked. "Excuse me, ma'am?"

"This is no time for games. I see the box on the shelf is facing the wrong way. The dagger. Where is the dagger?"

"The . . ." Xander shook his head. "It was gone when I got here. This was the only thing I found."

There was a crackle from his pocket.

As the vice principal held out her hand expectantly, he pulled out a carefully folded piece of paper.

At the same time, something else fluttered to the ground. A note, handwritten and crumpled, and signed . . . *LC*? Nadiya craned her neck, but it was hard to see what else was written on the page before Ruiz-Marín snatched both the note from the floor and the page from between Xander's fingers, and began to scan them both.

"Xander?" Nadiya hissed.

"Later," he muttered. Surprisingly, he didn't look as concerned with being caught as she thought he would. The vice principal's face was pale as she raised her head to look at them.

"Where did you get these—you know what, never mind.

The less I know what rules you were breaking, the less I have to punish you for." Ruiz-Marín stared at him hard and then sighed. "I'm sorry. I guess we're all jumpy today. Please. I just . . . need you both to return to your rooms. This will be over soon."

Ruiz-Marín shepherded Nadiya and Xander out of the office. Nadiya let the vice principal's anxious chatter—"Things will be okay, Nadiya, really"—wash over her and accepted one last, stiff pat on the back before the woman rushed off.

She turned her head to look around the hall, and then jumped as Xander laid a hand on her shoulder.

Relief and irritation battled inside Nadiya, and all she could do was give her friend a sharp shove.

"Hey!" he protested.

"That's my line. What was that all about? You nearly got both of us in so much—"

"Look. There's no time."

Nadiya started at the sharpness in her friend's tone. Xander looked washed out, worried. She leaned in, grasping his arm.

"What happened? Are you okay?"

Xander glanced up and down the hall, and then leaned in even closer.

"I found this." He pressed a page into Nadiya's hand—not the crumpled textbook page the vice principal had taken, but a rough, handwritten list. "Dropwort had some weird dragon's hoard of stuff in that box on his shelf. Confiscated items. And then I found this."

Nadiya stared at the page, which read: *Log*. Once it registered, she gasped loudly.

"So it was true. He was really smuggling and stealing all that stuff in his office?"

"Shhh!" Xander waved his hands madly at her. "Girl, do you want Ruiz-Marín back here? Look, let's just go to your room."

A few moments later, the two of them sat across from each other—Nadiya on her bed, Xander on her desk. He tilted his head toward the torn page.

"So what do you think? I wish I could have kept the note Irene gave me, and that other page she got—it was something about poison, and the way she reacted . . ." He shook his head. "But this is something too, right?"

"I think this is a huge mess of trouble," Nadiya mumbled, rubbing her temples. She could feel a headache coming on. "I have no idea what's going on. Every time I look at it, it's just . . . so blurry."

"You mean your aptitude?" Xander asked.

"I thought we all agreed to not call it an aptitude! It's not an aptitude. It doesn't even listen to me."

Never mind the fact that it was the first thing faculty always mentioned when they talked about her talents and where her gifts could take her.

Never mind that, more often than not, it seemed like this was the only thing she was really good at—no matter what else she tried to cultivate.

Xander leaned in and put a hand on her shoulder. "Listen. I believe in you. You know that."

Nadiya nodded, looking down to hide the wet sting in her eyes. Why was she being such a baby today?

"Yeah, I know."

"Irene believes in you. And Viv."

"I know that too."

"And right now . . . we all need you to believe in yourself. Galileo needs you to believe in yourself."

Nadiya turned the page between her hands and took a deep breath. "What do you think the dagger has to do with all this, anyway?"

"It's missing," Xander said. "Dropwort was stabbed. You do the math."

It was like Irene had said earlier. Dropwort had been killed. Someone had killed him.

Someone she knew, or ate meals with, or sat next to in classes and was taught with—or by.

Someone who laughed with her over the weird texts her dad sent, or gently stopped her in the hallway to compliment her hijab choice that day, or always gave her weird looks in that grudging way some "old money" magic kids did.

Someone who might be holed up in their room now.

Or maybe, wandering around out there.

If she looked back later and realized she could have done something to keep the tenuous bridge between Galileo and the outer world—between her magic and her home—intact, would she regret it?

Nadiya closed her eyes and inhaled.

What was it that Mama always told her?

You need to stop expecting the worst and start believing in the best. Keep an eye out for the good.

"The good," she whispered to herself.

What even was good in this situation?

I am not a Chosen One.
(But what if I am?)
What will that mean?
What can I change?

For a moment, she sat in that safety. That denial. That nothing would change when she opened her eyes. That there would be nothing on the page but the tight scrawl of a dead man. That, for once, the portents that ran her world would leave her alone.

She exhaled. And opened her eyes.

And the world exploded in red.

"Nadiya?" Xander gasped as she buckled over, but she could hardly hear him. She was too focused on what was behind her eyelids—a wild, vicious afterimage.

So bright that it was painful.

No. No. No.

"Oh my God, Xander. What do we do?"

Xander grabbed her hand. Any other time, the warmth of his grasp would have been reassuring, but now Nadiya couldn't feel it.

The word on the page made her blood run cold.

"What? Nadi, what's happened?"

Nadiya looked up at Xander, tears stinging the corners of her eyes.

"The LC who wrote the letter . . . It's Lola. They're going to arrest Lola."

CASE ID: 20-06-DROS-STK

Type:
[ ] Communication
[ ] Audio recording
[ ] Spell residue
[ ] Photo or other visual reconstruction
[ ] Object
[X] Form or record
[ ] Other: _____

Source: GAE administrative records
Relevant Parties: Suspect 3 (name withheld for privacy/age restrictions); Julietta Monroe, student and associate of Suspect 3; Septimius Dropwort (dec.); Beatriz Ruiz-Marín, vice principal
Description: Record of weapon confiscated from associate of Suspect 3

CONFISCATION RECORD

Date: 6/28/2020

Faculty Name: SD *Septimius, please put your full name on these.—BRM*

Student Name: Julietta Monroe

Description of item: knife [Note from Beatriz: "Please be more detailed in the future, so we can make sure the student's property is returned to them or their family."]

Why was the item confiscated?

[] Disruptive use in class

[] Weapon and/or potentially hazardous

[] Controlled substance

[X] OTHER (please describe): *IT'S A KNIFE_____*

THIS IS A WASTE OF TIME

Your objection has been noted, but please continue to follow the school's new policy regardless.—BRM

3:00 P.M.: DELORES "LOLA" CORTEZ, 16, COINS

BY TEHLOR KAY MEJIA

Lola Cortez had never been too concerned with labels. So far in her life she'd been a truant, a delinquent, a dropout, and (more than once) a "well of untapped potential."

Today she would add "suspected murderer" to the list—if someone would just *catch* her already, dammit.

The corridor was strangely dark for midafternoon as she made her way toward the deceased Professor Dropwort's office for the third time that day, dressed in her slinkiest all-black outfit, her long, dark hair stuffed down the back of her shirt for maximum stealth. The whole ensemble practically *begged* someone to notice how suspicious it was, even without the sinister smacking of a thick lead pipe into her ungloved hand.

No one did.

Lola's movements were exaggerated, like a person pantomiming sneaking. She couldn't have been more obvious if she'd tried. But still, even this close to the professor's office in the midst of an *actual murder investigation,* no one stopped her. No one even seemed to *see* her.

Incredible, Lola thought, that she'd been caught for at least thirty minor infractions at six schools (and their surrounding parks, graveyards, and convenience stores) so far in her life, but today, when she desperately needed to be arrested in connection to a professor's death, the authority figures (who had been drawn to her like flies since prekindergarten) were occupied elsewhere.

Lola thought of Julietta, hauled off for questioning early that morning, her eyes darting one last time to where Lola was hiding under the bed, before Julietta was escorted out of her dorm room. Icy dread began to gather in the pit of Lola's stomach, just as it did every time she pictured the scene today.

Julietta's face in that moment had been proof enough of her innocence—even if Lola *had* been too deeply asleep to know where Julietta had been last night when Dropwort had been murdered. If she couldn't provide an alibi for the girl she loved, she could at least draw suspicion away from her. Force her captors to realize that they were holding an innocent girl . . .

And if Lola had to cause some trouble on the road to that goal—well, it was nothing she hadn't done before. Not even close.

Lola continued to prowl the hallway, the nausea dissipating slightly as she recommitted to her plan. It might sound ridiculous, she knew, risking getting your third strike at magic school and a bus back to non-magical Nowheresville for a girl you'd only been dating three weeks, but Lola and Julietta were greater than the sum of their twenty-one days, seven hours, and nine minutes together. Bigger than anything else Lola had ever felt.

It had been this way since the moment they'd first locked eyes. The deep chestnut hair brushing Julietta's shoulders, the perpetual faraway look in those fathomless brown eyes. The circles and curves of her that seemed magical themselves . . .

Lola had fallen before Julietta had ever spoken a word, her center of gravity obeying a new force, every neuron in her brain sparking with infatuation rather than electricity.

It had taken Lola months—*many* months—to work up the courage to sit beside Julietta at the library. To introduce herself in a voice that wouldn't stop trembling. To smile, and to hope.

Lola had been at the Galileo Academy for over a year by then, but Julietta's hand sliding into hers during their first date—stargazing in the astronomy room—had been the first thing she'd experienced here that felt like *real* magic. The kind worth believing in.

And there had been more, after that. Long nights on the forbidden west rooftop, where Julietta painted the air around them with light and color, picnics by the lake, where they talked about Lola's troubled past and Julietta's worry over the priceless family heirloom Dropwort had his eye on. There had been a kiss, then two, and Lola had thought her heart would burst with the feeling of that longing finally fulfilled. . . .

Julietta had made it all worth it. The troubled years since elementary, the fights with Lola's father, the juvenile court dates, the endless suspensions and expulsions. Even the cursed letter that said her genius IQ and talent for anything mathematical weren't just anomalies (that barely made up for her dismal grades and behavior) but were actually evidence of a hidden magical ability that could be shaped and trained by some of society's greatest minds at a school for gifted students.

It had been an ultimatum that landed her here: Galileo Academy for the Extraordinary, or some military school for the violently unmanageable, and now Lola was risking it all. But Julietta had changed Lola's life, and Lola wasn't going to let her go without a fight.

Everyone in this school felt *chosen* in some way or another—because of their parents' names or money, because of their talent or achievements—but Lola never had. Not until last night, when they'd been wrapped in each other's arms, drifting off to sleep, and Julietta had told Lola she loved her. That's when she knew, without a shadow of a doubt, that this place *had* chosen her. That *magic* had chosen her.

And not for some grand good-versus-evil plot, but for the love of this girl. As simple as that.

But Lola had closed her eyes on a dream that night, and awoken to a nightmare.

"Quick, hide," Julietta had been saying, the sun barely rising out her dorm window. "If they catch you in here . . . if my parents find out . . . Whatever happens, don't let them see you."

Lola had been half-asleep, but she'd rolled under the bed with the dust bunnies and lost scrunchies anyway, as two figures opened the door and walked to Julietta's bedside.

"Recognize this?" one of them asked, holding out something Lola couldn't see.

"It's my family's dagger," Julietta said, her voice scratchy from sleep. "Professor Dropwort took it a few weeks ago. I've been petitioning to have it returned."

Lola knew how much Julietta had dreaded telling her

parents about the loss of the dagger. How angry she was at the man who had taken it from her—stating that weapons weren't allowed on campus, when there was a *clear* exception in the bylaws for objects of power handed down within families. Her petition had been a last-ditch effort, and it had been denied a few days ago.

Julietta had been devastated.

From her position under the bed, Lola thought for one wild moment that these people had come to return Julietta's dagger. That the petition had been reevaluated, or Dropwort had come to his senses. She was just thinking of how they would celebrate, when:

"That made you angry, didn't it? Having that petition denied?" The voice was suspicious, cold. Goose bumps chased themselves up Lola's bare arms.

"I . . . ," Julietta began, clearly sensing the shift in tone. "It's a very important family heirloom. My parents will be devastated to lose it."

"You didn't answer my question," the cold voice said. "Did it make you angry when he denied the petition? Did you want revenge?"

Lola couldn't make heads or tails of this question, and clearly Julietta couldn't either.

"Revenge?" she asked, bewildered. "I don't know what you mean. I only wanted what was mine returned—"

"Where have you been all night?" a second voice interrupted. This one was rough, too loud. The barking of a dog.

"I . . . ," Julietta began. "Here. Here in my room."

"Is there anyone who can corroborate that story?"

Lola was about to say something. Show herself. No matter

how much Julietta feared confessing their relationship to her parents, it had to be better than this. But before she could, Julietta said firmly:

"No. No one. I've been alone all night."

"Then you'll need to come with us, young lady," the cold voice said, and Lola waited for Julietta to call out to her. To let her fix it. But she never did, and the cold voice and the barking voice took her, and Lola was alone beneath the bed.

She left the moment it was safe, and scoured the ever-shifting school for Julietta, asking anyone she could think of where Julietta had gone. No one knew. Lola was lost, confused, her heart—so full of love the night before—deflated now.

And then the announcement of Dropwort's death went school-wide, and it all came into horrifying focus. *Did you want revenge?*

The brisk, clinical words of the announcement rang in Lola's ears until she was sure she'd go mad. Julietta being questioned, with a motive for murder. And Lola the alibi she didn't want shared. Lola couldn't barge in, not after Julietta had begged her not to tell. If things got dire enough that Julietta needed her, she'd tell them. They'd call Lola . . .

But hours passed, and no one came. Lola was invisible, dragging her broken heart through the halls, thinking of the girl she loved, who would rather be thought a murderer than admit they'd spent the night together . . .

That's when Lola decided, standing alone in a deserted fourth-floor corridor: if she couldn't share their alibi, if she couldn't save her love that way, she would save her another way.

Julietta hadn't killed anyone. Lola knew her, right down to her golden-bright core. She was angry about the dagger, yes.

Terrified of what her parents would say. But she would never have done something like this.

And if Julietta hadn't done it, that meant someone else had. This was a school full of magicians, dammit; they could find the real killer if they weren't so busy trying to pin the whole thing on Julietta. So all Lola had to do was convince them that the *real* killer was still out there.

If new evidence was popping up even with Julietta being held for questioning, they'd have to admit it wasn't her. Let her go. Look for the real suspect. Sure, there was a risk they'd catch Lola instead, but she'd been in trouble like this before. She could get out again.

The rightness of her plan burned in her chest as the whispers of prophecy began to spread through the school. *If the rumors could be believed, Dropwort's killer had been chosen.* Well, Lola had been chosen too. Chosen by Julietta, their fates sealed in a different kind of prophecy.

Who was Lola to deny fate?

So, an hour after the school-wide announcement, her heart heavy and still somehow burning, she returned to her room. Paced as the school whispered and seethed with secrets. Turning herself in would never work. There was no evidence, and an obvious false confession would lead to questions . . . maybe witnesses who could tell about her whereabouts last night.

She would have to be more subtle. To act like she didn't want to be caught. To draw them into the chase and delay her capture until Julietta was released. To give them time to find the *real* killer.

And so she wrote, as the first step in her plan, a letter condemning Dropwort. Her fiery, passionate language was full of hate, not to mention creative threats that established a clear motive to anyone who would read it.

Afterward, the damning missive in her hands, Lola reflected on her year at Galileo Academy, the way she'd learned to lay the groundwork for spells and algorithms and formulas while so many of her fancier classmates were seeing the future, or making things fly, or changing their hair stupid colors on command.

All in all, she could boil the *real* lesson she'd learned here down to one concise thesis:

Magic was nothing more than another hoarded privilege of the wealthy. It wasn't worth worshipping. It wasn't worth chasing. The only real magic was love.

And with that, she signed her letter with an elaborate *LC* (initials shared by at least five other students in the school), dressed in the slinky black catsuit she'd never imagined she'd need when she packed it, and snuck into the hall.

Dropwort's room was unguarded. *Some murder investigation,* Lola thought. She left the letter peeking out from under a typewriter on the desk. As insurance—and because she plain hadn't liked the guy—she took an ornate sealing ring from its little porcelain dish and slipped it onto her thumb.

If she needed to, she'd use it later. If she didn't, maybe she could sell it. Buy Julietta something nice when they were free of all this.

Once she was clear of the room, Lola prowled the halls again, listening to every hushed conversation. None of them mentioned a letter. Maybe no one had found it. Well, Lola understood well enough how things like this worked. She found the first girl with big hair and furtive eyes near the doorway to the main hall.

"Did you hear?" Lola asked, vindicated by the hungry look in the girl's eyes. "They say someone wrote a confession letter. It's sitting in Dropwort's room right now."

An hour later, when her gossip had spread and students whispered all throughout the halls about the absolute ransacking going on in Dropwort's private room, Lola barged into his predictably empty office. There she dropped her own studded black glove onto a map of Stockholm across his desk.

I won't stop until you're free, she vowed to herself, and to the impression of Julietta that lived rent-free in her heart.

On her way out, for good measure, she knocked over a few chairs, pulled down a heavy velvet curtain from the window. Of course, she'd drop a rumor or two as well. These people needed all the directing she could give.

Lola spent the next few hours pacing various busy hallways, doing her best to find the place where the action was, to start rumors that the killer was still free, still doing incriminating things. . . .

She worried, once or twice, that someone had noticed her hallway stalking, or realized she'd been at the center of the swirling mill of rumors since this morning. . . .

There'd been a flicker of interest from a professor from the physical magic branch whose name she'd never learned. A suspicious head tilt from a pretty girl in a hijab who Lola didn't know. But both times, her relative anonymity within the walls of Galileo had won out. The eyes had slid away.

The investigation moved from Dropwort's room to his office. But still Julietta was nowhere to be seen.

And so, with her heart fluttering, Lola returned to her room and readied herself to enact the final phase of her plan. The one that would *prove* the killer was still out there, and that Julietta's capture had been unnecessary.

The one where she actually let herself get caught. The authorities would release Julietta because they had a new suspect. An infinitely more guilty-looking one.

Julietta had motive. The dagger was a clear line connecting her and Dropwort. If Lola let herself be caught, she'd have a much easier time getting out of custody than her girlfriend would. All she had to do was say it had been a prank. With Lola's record, they'd more than believe it of her . . .

But the plan wasn't without its risks. Lola—as she'd been told by every teacher, counselor, judge, and principal who'd ever had the misfortune of spending an hour with her—was a delinquent. A criminal. Perhaps, instead of believing her a prankster, a troublemaker, the people investigating Dropwort's murder would believe she'd *really* killed him. . . .

Could Lola run that risk? The risk of finally achieving the destiny that had been laid out for her since she'd stolen a roll of Bubble Tape at five?

She thought of her life here, her life at home. None of it had made sense before Julietta. Loving this girl had been the key that had come along to unlock everything she'd never dared to dream of.

Of course she could risk it.

Of course she would.

And so, with faith kindling to life alongside the destructive tendencies she'd been born with, Lola slid Professor Dropwort's sealing ring onto her finger, took her thick piece of lead pipe, and eased out into the hallway toward the east wing, smacking the pipe almost comically into her open palm.

The door to Principal Fornax's office was unlocked, and before Lola could talk herself out of it, the lead pipe was swinging. It connected with object after priceless object, sending shards of wood and glass and anything else that got in its way flying. The racket it caused was riotous; Lola imagined she'd soon be descended upon by anyone on the premises. She wanted to do as much damage as she could before that happened.

As each object in the office splintered, Lola pictured the beautiful girl she loved. The future they would have together when they were free.

And then the footsteps were coming, barely audible but definitely growing louder, and Lola wondered who it would be. The principal, perhaps, or any other teacher. One of the official-looking men who had been seen shuffling around the place? Even a student would be enough, as they'd surely run for the closest authority figure.

Lola didn't lessen the intensity of her destruction. This was it, her last act. She would make it count.

But when the door opened, it wasn't to reveal the principal, or a teacher, or some nameless suck-up who would turn her in and finally end this charade.

"Lola," whispered Julietta from the doorway. "Lola, why?"

The lead pipe, which she'd been so determined to keep swinging until the last moment, slipped from her fingers and clanged noisily onto the floor. "You're okay!" Lola said, relief and horror warring in her chest. "They let you go!"

Julietta's eyes were wide and confused. "My parents' lawyer got here an hour ago," she said, her voice hushed. "I've been looking for you, and people said . . . Lola, I would never judge you, even for the worst thing possible, and you know I have my own issues with Dropwort, but please tell me you didn't kill him because of me. Because the dagger isn't worth it, Lola. Nothing is worth this!"

Lola wanted to laugh. She wanted to cry. Julietta's family lawyer had gotten here *an hour* ago. She had never needed to resort to her last plan. But now it was too late.

"I didn't kill him," she said, needing Julietta to understand before anyone arrived. Before her horrible plan worked at last. "How could I have killed him? I was with you all night!"

"I fell asleep," Julietta whispered. "I thought . . . maybe . . ."

Lola shook her head. The clock was running out. "I was doing this to distract them, to force them to let you go, because I was afraid . . . I was afraid I was going to lose you. And I felt so helpless, not being able to tell them we were together last night, that I had to do *something* to help you."

Their eyes locked over the ruin in the room, calling back faint echoes of the night, the possibility that had unspooled between them like glittering thread.

"You did all this for me?" Julietta asked, those brown eyes warm and melting.

"I'd do anything for you," Lola said.

And then the footsteps were coming, and in the dead silence of the room it was clear that this was no lone student investigating a rumor. There were many of them, pairs and pairs of heavy shoes. And they were running.

"You have to go," Lola said at last, smiling inexplicably. "Take the window. Even your parents' lawyer probably couldn't get you out of this one."

"No," Julietta said, stepping forward and linking her fingers through Lola's. "No one killed anyone. I'll stay. I'll tell them I was with you last night. No matter what my parents say. It'll be all right as long as we're together."

"Aha!" came a voice from elsewhere in the room. Julietta didn't let go of Lola's hand. "Don't move, don't move! Are you seeing this?"

Faith was easier to come by with Julietta's hand in hers and a solid alibi between them.

"My gods!" Another voice joined the first, unmistakable as Principal Fornax's.

"Principal Fornax," Julietta said, stepping forward, her eyes on his. "Lola was with me last night. In my room. All night. She couldn't have killed Professor Dropwort."

"The letter!" the principal shouted, officers filing in behind him. He ignored Julietta entirely, pulling out Lola's letter and brandishing it like a cartoon weapon. His eyes were comically large in his sallow face. "Dropwort's ring! We have our culprit at last!"

"No!" Julietta insisted. "She wanted to *look* like she was guilty, but she's not, I swear. She's—" She might as well not have been speaking at all, for all the notice anyone took.

Lola had set her stage too well.

"Young lady!" came the principal's voice again, pitched dramatically low, like he was playing a detective on the stage. "You are to be taken into custody as the chief suspect in the murder of Professor Septimius Dropwort!"

Lola didn't fight as the officers pulled her away from Julietta.

"I'll call the lawyer back!" Julietta was saying now. "Lola, don't say anything. I'll get you out of there as soon as I can!" Julietta stepped forward as they bound Lola's wrists with some physical magic. This wasn't Lola's first time in handcuffs, by any means, but it was her first time in invisible ones.

Julietta was so close that Lola could see the tears clinging to her lower lashes.

"I love you," she said.

Lola smiled. "As if all this isn't proof enough, I love you too."

"Make the announcement!" shouted Fornax to any one of the lackeys behind him. "And, Miss Cortez," he said, "you will be coming with me."

CASE ID: 20-06-DROS-STK

Type:
[X] Communication
[ ] Audio recording
[ ] Spell residue
[ ] Photo or other visual reconstruction
[ ] Object
[ ] Form or record
[ ] Other: _____

Source: School announcement archives
Relevant Parties: Ladybird "Birdie" Beckley, vice principal; Beatriz Ruiz-Marín, vice principal; Suspect 3 (name withheld for privacy/age restrictions)
Description: Transcript of announcement broadcast to school at 3:47 p.m., following apprehension of Suspect 3

[Beginning of transcript.]

[Pleasant ding indicating start of announcement.]

Vice Principal Beckley: Attention, all students and staff. We wish to let you know that a culprit—

Vice Principal Ruiz-Marín: Suspect.

Beckley: [Muffled.] Same thing. [Clears throat.] A suspect has been taken into custody by the authorities in connection with the death of Professor Dropwort. Though this tragedy has brought some . . . unpleasant subjects to light, we are continually inspired by the dedication and service of the SNACC Enforcement Officers, and trust that justice will be served. That said, if you know *anything at all* that may provide additional insight into the case, it is your responsibility to come forward.

Nurse Fibula Smith: [In the background.] And if any snitches need stitches, you know where to find me.

Beckley: I swear, Nurse Smith—

Smith: You know, putting a clipboard over the microphone doesn't do anything.

Beckley: Don't you have an infirmary to run?

Smith: Just dropping off a note of absence for your aide. Caught a nasty hex this morning. Guess someone had a bone to pick—

Ruiz-Marín: We apologize for the interruption. With a suspect in custody, the school has been released to proceed to our next destination this evening. It'll be just like usual—all students report to their dorm towers after dinner, no later than nine-thirty p.m., and remain there until morning, when we've docked in Turkmenistan.

Beckley: Faculty will be doing a final sweep of the grounds to make sure there are no stragglers. The school will depart Stockholm at ten p.m. sharp. [Pause.] *Don't you dare.*

Smith: You said it, not me.

[Pleasant ding indicating end of announcement.]

[End of transcript.]

4:00 P.M.: MAXWELL ASTER, 16, CUPS

BY MASON DEAVER

Probable cause.

That was what the investigators had said about Maxwell Aster. That he'd had "probable cause" to murder Dropwort.

That was, until Lola had been apprehended.

It was shocking when he heard the whispers of her name, claiming that she'd been caught and arrested. Then again, Maxwell couldn't say that he knew Lola very well, or at all, for that matter. Perhaps he just didn't want to believe that one of his classmates was capable of murder. He wondered what the interrogation officers had said to her, if they'd asked her the same questions they'd asked him, what she'd given them, what proof they had to connect her.

They'd been *so* sure it was him, ready to pin even the slightest bit of circumstantial evidence they had on him. And they hadn't exactly been subtle about it.

"Did you have anything to do with the murder?" one of the

two SNACC officers they'd tasked with leading the investigation had asked.

He was a burly man with a squirrel for an upper lip, and a broad forehead. They'd given their last names, but Maxwell hadn't taken the time to remember them, simply referred to one as Good Cop and the other as Bad Cop.

Though referring to any officer as a "Good Cop" seemed irresponsible at best.

"Wouldn't that take the fun out of this interrogation?" Maxwell crossed his arms, his rolled-up sleeves the only reprieve from the heat of the desk lamp that shone in his face. Even his magically bleached blond hair was beginning to stick to his forehead.

"Maxwell . . . ," Kevin Vaughan-Crabtree, the school counselor, interjected.

For as long as Maxwell suffered in that room for the legally allotted half hour they were allowed to interrogate students, Kevin sat there longer, watching as each and every student gave their story.

"Please cooperate."

Maxwell respected Kevin too much to give a witty comeback. But even more, Maxwell knew that whatever sass he gave would make its way to Nora Vaughan-Crabtree, Kevin's wife, and Maxwell's head of house.

"We've already talked to several of your classmates, and all of them named *you* as a person of interest," Good Cop said. "Seems they don't like you very much."

This came as no surprise to Maxwell. Ever since the . . . circumstances of his birth had been brought to light, his classmates had looked at him with a certain ire, avoiding him whenever possible. Maxwell was all too happy to make that easier for them.

"I believe they're referring to the"—Kevin paused—"*spat* you and Professor Dropwort had the other day in the dining hall."

"I wanted to know what he stole from the gargoyles."

"Maxwell—"

"Your classmates claim that it became violent," Bad Cop said, looking at his notes. "That you threw food at Professor Dropwort and claimed that you'd 'get even.'"

"None of the students have said anything of—" Kevin began to say, but Good Cop shushed him.

"What did Dropwort steal from the gargoyles?" Good Cop took the chance to leap in. "What exactly are *you* accusing Dropwort of?"

"I . . ." Maxwell paused, suddenly feeling the dread of not having an answer. "I . . . don't know."

"But it was enough for you to challenge a teacher in the middle of the cafeteria?"

"He was sneaking around the Gargoyle Keep, acting suspicious. I saw him, and so did Sally. I called him out on it, but he told me to mind my business, that I couldn't tell him what to do. He called them 'beasts.'"

Then, not a full week after the confrontation in the dining hall, Maxwell had run into the professor on his way out of the Keep, a clear egg-shaped bulge in the chest of his robe. Maxwell had tried to stop the professor from leaving, but it had been pointless; and afterward, when Maxwell had counted Bronx's eggs half a dozen times and accepted that none of them were missing, he'd let the issue go, only telling Sally—the gargoyle keeper—and Professor Nora Vaughan-Crabtree about the incident.

"You believe that Dropwort stole an egg?"

"I don't know what he stole, but it looked like an egg underneath his robe," Maxwell corrected.

Kevin interjected. "Why didn't you tell anyone, Maxwell?"

"I did. No one ever listened. He just kept getting away with his behavior." Maxwell shrugged.

Good Cop went back to his notes. "And why would Dropwort want to steal a gargoyle egg?"

"How should I know?"

"But it was enough for you to go after him?" Bad Cop said. "To attack a teacher?"

"It wasn't an attack, it was an argument the week before, and I didn't *murder* him," Maxwell insisted. Though he'd certainly gotten far into his plan to dump a bucket full of gargoyle droppings onto Dropwort's head.

"Is there anyone who can account for your whereabouts when Dropwort was murdered?"

Maxwell leaned back in his seat.

There was no one.

He'd ended his day with a late-night session at the library, reading through material for a research paper that Dropwort would never collect now. The front desk had been empty, and there had been no one in the hallways.

So there was no alibi, no one to defend him, no one to prove that he hadn't been the one to kill Dropwort.

"No."

"Gentlemen," Kevin said, standing up quickly. "I'm sure

there are more questions for you to ask Maxwell here, but your time with him is up."

"He's our lead suspect!" Bad Cop said. "We can't allow him to leave."

"Actually, your thoughts on the matter are of no relevance." Kevin turned to Maxwell. "You may leave."

"No, you'll stay," Good Cop demanded.

Maxwell stood up and pushed his chair in without a word.

Bad Cop sputtered for a bit, pointing a finger at Kevin and then at Maxwell. "You will *stay* on campus until this is solved, young man."

As if he had anywhere to go.

He left the teachers' lounge as Kevin continued to argue with the police, and went back to the Cups dorm as instructed. He appreciated the time away from his classes; there were some papers he needed to finish, tests he needed to study for. Unfortunately, nearly his entire house joined him in the common area. He sat there in his studies, silently hoping that Delfina might make her way down to the common area, but he hadn't seen her all day. She was the one student on campus that Maxwell might be able to call a friend, who might be a comfort to talk to after the day he'd had.

Then the announcement blared through the PA system, alerting the students that a suspect had been apprehended, that they were allowed to leave their common rooms, and that classes would resume the following day.

Maxwell joined his classmates in staring at the PA system as the message ended. Then the whispers began.

And Maxwell took the permission it granted him, packing

his things and leaving the common room for the library. That was where he found himself when it happened, digging through the ancient leather tomes for his Gardening and Herbology homework.

That was when he heard the crying.

It was faint at first, but as Maxwell followed the sounds, he found a girl, hunched over, knees pulled close to her chest.

"Are you okay?" Maxwell asked, his voice low enough to his own ears that he wondered if the girl could even hear him.

Then she picked up her head, and he saw the face of Julietta Monroe. Her warm brown eyes were surrounded by raw red skin, her cheeks wet from her tears. Maxwell knew Julietta—not well, but they'd shared some classes over the years. She was smart, and Maxwell had no doubt she'd be the one giving the valedictorian speech at their graduation.

"Julie? Are you okay?" Maxwell stepped closer.

"Yeah . . . ," she said, but then her face contorted, and when she buried her face in her hands again, she shook her head.

"Did something happen?" he asked, feeling foolish, as the answer was obviously yes.

"It's nothing, Maxwell. . . . Just . . . It's nothing."

Maxwell considered stepping away from the situation altogether, relieving himself of this entire day. But he couldn't leave Julietta alone. She was one of the few students who'd shown Maxwell kindness, never insulting him or whispering things about him behind his back.

"Hey." Maxwell stepped closer to her and knelt down to her level. "It's okay."

"No, it's not."

"Do you want to talk about what's going on? I'm sure whatever it is, it isn't that serious." He added, "Like, what could've happened? Did you get a B on a paper or something?"

Julietta's continued sobs told Maxwell that humor was not the way to go.

"Listen." Maxwell swallowed. "Whatever's going on, you can tell me. I won't tell anyone."

Julietta dared to look up at him, her eyes bloodshot.

"It's . . ." She paused, and it was clear in her eyes that she was weighing her options. "It's Lola."

"Lola?"

"She's the one they arrested."

"For the murder?"

Julietta nodded solemnly.

"Holy shit." Maxwell sat there, dumbfounded. "Why? Why would she do that?"

"She didn't!" Julietta nearly shouted. Then she seemed to realize that she needed to keep her voice quiet. "She didn't. She . . . she's innocent."

"Well, then why was she arrested?"

"Because she admitted to the crime."

Maxwell went silent. "Julietta, I'm sorry, but this is getting a little confusing."

"I can't tell you why," Julietta said. "But she's innocent. She is, she told me so herself. And there's no way that she could've done it."

"Then why would she admit to the crime?"

"She did it to protect me."

"Julietta . . . did you—"

"No!"

"Well, I had to ask!"

"No, no." She shook her head again. "Lola was trying to defend me—there was a misunderstanding. And now she's probably sitting in a cell somewhere, and she's going to get charged with murder."

"Have you tried talking to Fornax?"

Julietta nodded. "No one will listen to me."

Maxwell chewed on his lip, thinking. Lola Cortez was another soul who'd always been kind to him, treating him like a person instead of a prophecy. What was happening wasn't fair.

He let out a sigh and stared at Julietta, knowing exactly what he needed to do.

"I'm going to help."

"What?"

"I'm going to help," Maxwell repeated, getting to his feet. "Lola's innocent, and Dropwort was up to something. There are pieces missing here."

"What are you going to do?" Julietta looked up at him.

Maxwell could've left the entire situation alone. He could've washed his hands of this entire day, gone back to his room, crawled into bed, and forgotten all about it. But there was something rotten going on at Galileo Academy, something that had Dropwort's name written all over it.

"I'm going to break into Dropwort's classroom."

With an arrest made, there was no one left to guard Dropwort's door, simply some yellow Do Not Cross tape that was easily ripped away. The door had been left unlocked as well, possibly due to the amount of investigators that had been making their way in and out of the classroom all day.

Maxwell couldn't begin to imagine what he might find about this stolen egg, or what information might clear Lola's name, though he doubted that he could just rummage through Dropwort's desk until he found whatever he might be looking for.

He watched the hallways carefully as teachers patrolled. After waiting just a few more minutes for the hallways to clear, Maxwell entered the classroom.

There didn't seem to be anything different about it, not that Maxwell could notice anyway. He'd been in here hundreds of times, none of them by choice.

Nothing seemed out of place in the rows of long tables that served as desks, fitting two students each; the tall windows that let in a ton of natural light but made the classroom unbearable for those unfortunate enough to have one of Dropwort's classes in the afternoon; the floor-to-ceiling bookshelves that seemed as stuffed as they could be; and an antique globe of a world that didn't seem to be their own. Dropwort's desk was large, made of oak, with ornate designs etched into it. Whereas other professors might decorate their desks with pictures or tchotchkes, Dropwort's classroom seemed devoid of personality.

Much like the man himself.

As he rummaged through the desk, Maxwell carefully avoided the switch to the PA system on the underside of the desktop, a feature on every faculty member's desk; the last thing he needed was his presence in the classroom announced to the entire school over the intercoms. He checked the drawers quickly, finding all of them locked.

"Nothing that can't be solved with a little chalk," Maxwell said to himself, pulling a stick of chalk out of the pocket protector on his shirt. His magic was mathematical, equations memorized from hours of studying, numbers and figures working together with Maxwell's goal in mind.

Unlocking the drawers was simple.

It took a few moments to calculate properly; he needed to estimate the force that would be required to open the drawer, be careful that he didn't overestimate. There had been one time as a child, before Maxwell had truly had an understanding of his own magic, when he'd made a few miscalculations and ended up with a doorknob smacking him right in the mouth and knocking out his two front teeth. At least they'd been baby teeth.

As Maxwell wrote down the final number, he could hear the lock click, and the drawer came loose.

Maxwell had always found math soothing; it was simple and easy to understand once you began to notice the patterns. And everything had a correct answer, a solution. Math was the law of the universe, with little deviation. Of course, as Maxwell began to explore many of the theories in mathematics, he understood that the subject was never ending, ever evolving, but he appreciated that as well. And it helped him in practicing his own magic.

Sometimes, though, there were invisible factors. Numbers that could be easily forgotten or left behind, steps in an equation that were missed.

Unfortunately for Maxwell Aster, his life was made of invisible factors.

The locks on the desk clicked open, but then a siren began to ring in his ears, nearly bringing him to the floor with its shrill volume. Maxwell watched as the door to the classroom slammed closed, the dead bolt audibly clicking.

Maxwell's gut told him that the door wouldn't be opening again anytime soon. At least, not from the inside.

He needed to work quickly.

No doubt the sirens were loud enough that the detectives were already on their way here. He needed to find *something*. Something of note, something about Dropwort's intentions.

At least the drawers had opened. Maxwell shuffled through paperwork, tests and papers that would go ungraded for who knows how long. There were notebooks that Maxwell took a moment to flip through, but there wasn't anything of obvious interest in the desk, other than—for some strange reason—a Magic 8 Ball.

Maxwell gave it a good shake.

"What was Dropwort planning?" he asked.

Ask again later.

Maxwell sighed.

He set the ball on the desk, and was unable to stop it before it rolled off the edge onto the floor with a thud.

A very hollow, loose thud.

Maxwell turned his attention to where the ball had landed. The floorboard seemed off. To anyone else it might've seemed entirely normal, but Maxwell looked at it with a close eye. The stain of the wood seemed darker by a few subtle shades, and it almost looked crooked. Maxwell had spent enough time analyzing and studying angles that he could see that it was slightly crooked from the rest of the floor.

Almost as if it weren't nailed down like the rest.

Maxwell grasped at the edges of the floorboard, shifting it slightly in its place. He just needed purchase, something to work it loose. Maxwell searched the desk. He emptied the drawers and eventually found a stash of apples and small cups of peanut butter in the last one.

And with them, a butter knife.

Perfect.

Maxwell shoved the dull blade under the floorboard and worked it loose so that he could finally grab on to it. There had to be *something* inside. There'd be no reason for Dropwort to have a secret hiding spot in the floor unless there was something he was hiding, and maybe—just maybe—that thing could clear Lola's name.

Whatever Maxwell had expected to find, some weapon or a stolen artifact, it didn't compare to what he *actually* found hidden inside.

There was almost *too* much stuffed into a space that seemed too small to hold everything.

But Maxwell knew that things that were bigger on the inside than the outside were mathematically impossible.

There were necklaces, gems, daggers, an *entire* sheathed sword, some old books that Maxwell could smell even without opening them. Rings with strange writing, mysterious-looking boxes, an empty vial with some green residue on the inside, empty glasses, stained fabric, similarly empty cups of the aforementioned peanut butter with some white fuzz growing inside.

Despite all that, though, Maxwell's eye focused only on one thing.

A note.

Lying carefully on top of a stack of the moldy books, as if it had been placed there deliberately.

On the outside, there was a date.

From last week.

Maxwell picked the letter up as if it might disintegrate in his hands—even though the paper seemed new—and he unfolded it carefully.

It was a mix of strange symbols, ones that Maxwell didn't recognize; in all his studies of math and the various formulas he'd read about, he'd never seen anything close to this. He didn't even think it could've been accidentally read as some ancient form of math or equations.

His mind immediately went to Delfina; she knew how to read, write, and speak more languages than Maxwell knew existed. Could she help? Would she know what all this meant? Should he get her involved?

These were all questions running through his mind as the alarm stopped ringing.

At first Maxwell didn't notice the noise was gone, he'd become so accustomed to it so quickly, but its absence finally knocked him out of his stupor. He stood quickly and raced toward the door in the hopes that it might've been magically unlocked. And indeed, it now swung open when he pulled on the knob, but instead of an empty hallway into which he could flee, or even two inept detectives waiting for him, there stood only one person.

The head of Maxwell's house.

Professor Nora Vaughan-Crabtree.

* * *

"I must say that I am disappointed, Maxwell," Nora said. They were the first words she said to Maxwell, after finding him in Dropwort's classroom and leading him on a walk of shame back to her own classroom, with a silent command issued only by the expression on her face. Nora prided herself on being stoic in the face of anxiety, able to keep her composure despite how messy things might get.

But Maxwell had been around her long enough to notice the signs, the careful ways her expressions changed, like her silence in the face of frustration, her brows furrowing when a student wouldn't listen to her, or how she made her hands busy when she was nervous, and at that moment she was playing with the silver letter opener every teacher had been given as a present some years ago. Maxwell had studied it once, out of sheer curiosity. It was a blank thing, with little decoration besides the initials of the owner etched into the hilt.

Maxwell felt the shame creep up the back of his neck, threatening to swallow him whole.

He never cared about anyone's opinion of him. Rumors about Maxwell and his birth had seemed to spread at this school the moment he'd stepped onto campus his very first day. Then again, if you believed that a child was meant to bring about the end of the world, all because of the time and circumstances of their birth, wouldn't you warn others as well?

"I'm sorry, Professor Vaughan-Crabtree." Maxwell hung his head, unable to even look at his house head.

Nora gave her student a lopsided smile. "I'm sure I don't have to tell you that breaking into a professor's classroom is wrong. Especially a *murdered* professor."

"Yes, ma'am."

"Good, I didn't have a lecture prepared," she said with a contented air. "It's . . . a strange time around the school. A professor has been murdered, he might've stolen something, detectives have been running around the campus interrogating my students." She pinched the bridge of her nose.

"Stolen something?" Maxwell dared for the first time to look Nora in the eye. "Was it the egg? The one I told you about?"

"Forget I mentioned anything," she said, putting her hands together.

"Professor, I feel like I should tell you that Lola didn't kill Dropwort."

"Oh? And how do you know this information?"

Maxwell opened his mouth, then closed it again when he realized that he probably shouldn't give Julietta away. There were pieces to this puzzle that were missing, and even if Maxwell trusted Nora above anyone else, he felt that he should keep some pieces to himself.

"I just . . . I know."

"Would it be because you have something to do with it?"

"What? I—no! I didn't—"

"Relax, Maxwell. I know that you don't have anything to do with Dropwort's death. And I'm inclined to agree with you about Lola. I don't think the girl has it in her to take a life."

For the first time since he'd been summoned into the teachers' lounge for his interrogation, Maxwell felt at ease. If nothing else, at least Nora knew his innocence, and that belief was worth its weight in gold.

"But you know that breaking into Dropwort's classroom sends the wrong message," Nora continued.

"I know."

"Good." She straightened in her seat. "Now, did you find anything?"

"I . . . What?" The turn surprised him.

"Did you find anything of interest? Anything that might . . . speak to Lola's innocence?"

Maxwell hadn't expected that reaction, clearly. With any other person, he might've withheld the note that was stuffed into his pocket. But this was Professor Vaughan-Crabtree. If there was anyone in this school who could help him, it was her.

"There—" Maxwell pulled the paper from his pocket. "There was a note, among other things. It was hidden under the floorboards. It's written in some strange language; I've never seen it before."

Nora stood quickly, took the note from Maxwell, and read it over carefully.

"Do you recognize the language, Professor?"

Nora waited a moment before answering, as if she were lost in her own thoughts. "No, I . . . I don't."

For the first time since he'd met her, Maxwell didn't believe what Nora was saying. There was something in the way her eyes moved, the way she bit her lip, something that told him that his head of house might not be telling the truth.

It seemed odd to him that a teacher at a school that traveled all over the world didn't at least *recognize* the language. Was it truly that mysterious?

Was she lying to him?

"I thought about taking it to Delfina. Maybe she knows?"

"Well, Delfina's knowledge of language is impressive for a girl so young." Nora paused, and Maxwell stared at his professor, the question on his tongue, unable to resist asking it any longer.

"Professor?" Maxwell broke the silence with a single word.

"Yes, Maxwell?"

"Do you know what happened to Professor Dropwort?"

"I don't."

Once again Maxwell wasn't sure if he could believe her. He didn't like the feeling; he didn't *want* to be suspicious of her. She'd been the first person to befriend him, during his second week of school, when the rumors had spread frighteningly quickly that Maxwell was an omen of something dark to come, simply because he'd been born under the sign of the Twins.

Ancient celestial beings that roamed the ether together, never leaving each other's side. In generations of birth records, children born under the sign of the Twins came out in pairs. Sometimes with matching faces, sometimes with features so distinct they didn't even look related at all; sometimes just minutes apart, sometimes hours.

But there were *always* two children. A girl and a boy.

Except when Maxwell was born. There was no lost sibling, no stillborn.

It was just him. His parents barely dared to name him. Of course, it was a name that he would later give away, one that never suited him anyway. "Maxwell" was a strong name, a name that he picked for himself when he transitioned.

Maxwell's birth had been seen as an omen. Prophets couldn't name what he might bring, each of them reacting in revulsion when his parents told them the truth, some of them casting Maxwell's parents away without any help at all. When Maxwell finally reached the age of thirteen, his parents sent him to Galileo Academy to live on his own.

Suddenly he wasn't their problem anymore.

The real shock came when Maxwell sent them a letter his first week of school, to let them know how he was adjusting. A letter came back, and Maxwell was so excited.

Then he read it.

A reply from a stranger who said they didn't know Maxwell, but they were glad he was enjoying school. Maxwell checked the address again and again. He'd gotten it correct; it was just that his parents no longer lived there.

That night, Maxwell hid. He discovered a cove deep in the school, in the secret tunnels. That was where Nora found him. She took him to her office, gave him a piece of cinnamon candy, and instructed him that the tunnels were dangerous and to be avoided. It was the first time anyone treated Maxwell with any kindness or offered him comfort.

"Maxwell," Nora said now. "We never discussed the argument you and Dropwort had in the cafeteria, did we?"

"No, ma'am. We didn't." He'd been ordered to her office after the argument, but she'd been so buried in paperwork of some kind that she'd dismissed him after he'd promised to stop bickering with teachers. It'd been an odd experience, to say the least, but Maxwell had tried not to think anything of it.

"You were convinced that he'd stolen an egg?"

"I saw him, in the hallways. He was cradling something, hiding it." Maxwell had to stop himself from standing, getting a little too ahead of himself. "Why would he even want a gargoyle egg?" Maxwell asked.

"I'm not so sure that it was a gargoyle egg, Maxwell. You said that there were no eggs missing from the Keep, correct?"

"Well, yeah, but what else—"

"There is a *something*. I feel like it's staring me right in the face and I just can't see it." She tapped her fingers on the desk, her long nails painted a soft lilac clacking on the wooden surface. Maxwell knew the look on her face well—it was the look of a person lost in thought.

"Professor?"

"I don't think I have to tell you that there's more going on here," she said softly, as if her words were a secret, as if Maxwell was no longer a student but a confidant.

"You think it has something to do with the egg?"

"I—" Nora opened her mouth to answer, but then there came a knock. Frustration colored her face as she watched the door carefully.

"Professor, we'd like to talk to you," a voice said, muffled behind the door. "We have a few more details to clear up." Maxwell recognized the voice of Bad Cop.

"They're here for me." Maxwell began to panic, his chest swelling.

"No, they're here for me. They don't even know you're here." Nora brushed Maxwell's shoulder carefully. "I'm not going to let them do anything to you, Maxwell. Please believe me."

That didn't mean his worries disappeared, or that he felt an immediate relief, but Maxwell *did* feel the comfort of Nora, and for him that was more than enough. He couldn't stop his twitching fingers as Nora moved to open the door, then stopped the detectives at the threshold.

"What is he doing here?" Good Cop asked.

"Maxwell is in detention."

Bad Cop sputtered. "Detention isn't exactly a fair punishment for murder."

"I was under the impression that you had a suspect in custody. Now, what is this visit all about?"

"We wanted to interview you about your colleague."

Nora waited a moment, looking toward Maxwell before she turned back to the officers. "Very well. Allow me to collect my things." Then she walked toward her desk and grabbed her bag. "Maxwell, as you're aware, you are being punished." She pointed to the door. "That door is not to be opened again until I return."

"Yes, ma'am," Maxwell muttered.

"And would you mind delivering this assignment to Delfina once your time is up?" She picked up a small stack of papers to show Maxwell. "I haven't had time to go to her dorm to deliver it, poor thing."

"Yes, ma'am."

Delfina? he thought. *She wasn't absent today.*

And as far as he knew, she wasn't sick.

"I think I'll have my fellow officer wait here at your door," Bad Cop said. "Perhaps he can escort Maxwell to his classmate to deliver these assignments."

Nora froze, watching Maxwell carefully.

Maxwell could see her thinking.

"Of course," she said with a cold smile. Nora took her purse, but before she walked to meet the detectives, she paused, eyeing the candelabras situated on the wall behind her desk. She licked her thumb, rubbed a spot away, and seemed dissatisfied. "I'll have to talk with Mortimer about getting rid of this rust spot . . ."

"Professor, our time here is limited."

"Yes, yes. I'm coming." Nora followed the officers and began closing the door. But before she did, she looked at Maxwell one last time. The door shut with the distinctive sound of a lock clicking.

And then he stood up.

Maxwell and Nora had known each other long enough to communicate simply through glances. It was a gift the both of them shared. Not anything explicitly magical, just a notion between two people who considered themselves family.

And when Nora had glanced at him, there had only been one word in her eyes.

Leave.

He looked at the papers she'd shown him, and just as he'd expected, the letter from Dropwort's hidden stash was folded between the pages. He took it carefully and placed it in his pocket.

She wanted Maxwell to have this note. To find Delfina and try to have her translate it. She'd told him as much. *Deliver this assignment to Delfina.* Then he turned his attention to the candelabra she'd polished. Maxwell walked over and tugged at it, pulling and pushing it in every direction.

He started to believe that it wasn't going to budge, but then he placed both feet against the wall, sure that he would be the one cleaning the prints from Professor Vaughn-Crabtree's walls later. He pulled and pulled, and eventually the candelabra gave way, Maxwell falling hard to the floor as the ornate decoration shifted.

"Ow." He rubbed his tailbone as the floor began to move underneath him. Maxwell watched as a square section of the wall began to slide back to reveal a secret opening, the stale air of the secret tunnels wafting into his nostrils.

Maxwell didn't know where it might lead or what might be inside, but it was clear to him that Professor Vaughan-Crabtree had wanted him to find this entrance.

And so, trusting her, he stepped inside.

Maxwell moved through the darkness of the tunnels. He didn't know why Nora had led him to the very place she herself had labeled dangerous. Did she think that there was a path to Delfina? Was Maxwell just supposed to hide from the officers? Was there another clue that she wanted him to find? He cursed her silently as he weaved through the cobwebs and dust, goose bumps creeping down his arms as he was *sure* that he heard a distant high-pitched laughter.

Does she know who killed Dropwort? She seems sure it wasn't Lola, Maxwell thought. *Or . . . did she . . .*

No, he didn't even want to entertain the thought. Sure, Nora hadn't liked Professor Dropwort. He'd made so many public attempts to embarrass her, using her identity as a Black woman and as the youngest professor in Galileo Academy history as weapons against her.

But she'd fought back every step of the way, never letting the man get under her skin. Maxwell could recall a conversation he'd had with Nora a few months ago, when he'd taken his lunch period to stay in her classroom to work on a project.

"People like that . . . they're a special breed of evil," she'd said. "Because there is no way to truly win against them."

"What do you mean, Professor?" Maxwell had asked.

"If he gets what he thinks he wants, which I suppose is seeing me fired, then that's the end of it—his fun would be over. For people like him, it's more exciting to see marginalized people stoop to his level, to get angry and be labeled 'irrational' or 'angry.'"

Maxwell couldn't recall any other professor speaking as frankly as Nora had in that moment.

"Never stop defending your right to be who you are, Maxwell."

He'd carried those words with him ever since.

Dropwort had been a sinister man. A man who'd encouraged bickering between students, who'd judged people on their skin color, where they came from, their sexual and romantic orientations, their gender identity. But the system that protected him was just as bad.

The world was better with people like Dropwort gone. Maxwell felt that guilt in his stomach, at being content with the murder of a man, but it was the hard truth he needed to face.

Whoever had killed Dropwort . . . they'd done a huge service to Galileo Academy.

Maxwell didn't think of the gust of wind as it blew by him. Not at first anyway. It didn't immediately occur to him that it might signal an exit.

He turned down one hallway, and then another, and then he saw light coming from a tiny crack in the wall, a cold, strong wind blowing through.

"Finally," he whispered.

He readied his chalk and drew the circle, writing out the formula carefully in the darkness, adding the numbers together in his head. Maxwell didn't care about where this exit would lead him, just that he'd be free of the darkness of these tunnels. He wrote the last number, allocating for the force required to move such a heavy stone door. The equation illuminated for a split second before going dull again, and the wall began to slide toward him. Maxwell moved out of the way, and took the first chance he got to step outside, breathing in the fresh air.

Except the air was anything but fresh.

He could tell where he was just based on the smell. Gargoyles weren't exactly the cleanest of creatures. Their keep was in the second-highest tower of the school, mostly so that they would have plenty of space to take off and land when it came time for them to patrol, or to simply just stretch their wings. Though Maxwell had always suspected that they were kept so high up to put the most distance between them and the students.

He wasn't sure if he was meant to come out this way; perhaps he was simply meant to escape the classroom, to find the quickest route to Delfina. For a moment he considered going back into the tunnels, finding the proper path to Delfina's house tower. What would he even say to her when he presented the note? What explanation could he possibly have? Would she look at him differently when he admitted to breaking into Dropwort's classroom? Would it incriminate him in her eyes?

Maxwell felt embarrassed to admit to even himself that he'd imagined a space in their relationship where they could become more romantic with each other, and yet, he was always too afraid of what might happen. If she would reject him, if he'd lose the only friend he had that was his own age, the first friend he'd ever met at school.

It was a nudge under his armpit that pulled Maxwell from the trance.

Bronx had made her way over to him, silently begging to be petted.

"Hey, girl." He scratched under her ears, where the soft fur that covered her head began to sprout.

So often when he was a child, Maxwell had heard gargoyles being called ugly and disgusting creatures, but their pictures in his textbooks at school had always fascinated him. His first time seeing them in the flesh had been from afar, watching as they took off from their tower to patrol the grounds of the place where the school had landed.

Maxwell had thought they were magnificent, their wings stretched out as they soared; the hard scales that coated their back, protecting them from poachers in the wild; the soft fur that covered their head, hands, and feet; the sharp talons they used for hunting prey.

He'd eventually worked up the courage to climb the tower, only somewhat fearful of what the gargoyles might do to him. Though he probably should've been more fearful of their keeper, Salbiah Hussein.

Rumors about her ran amok on campus. Students claimed that she was half gargoyle herself, or that she took unruly students and ground them up to make the gargoyle food.

She'd found Maxwell in the Keep, surrounded by the gargoyles, each of them wanting attention and food from the student. And while she had yelled at him at first, and he'd run away like a dog with his tail between his legs, she'd found him later and told him to come every day after class to spend time with the gargoyles.

It hadn't been a request; it had been a command.

"Are you ready for dinner?" he asked Bronx now, but really it was a question for all the gargoyles. He realized that there were more pressing matters to take care of, but the gargoyles always came first. They trusted him almost as much as they trusted Sally, and Maxwell would do whatever he could to keep that trust.

He double-checked their pens to make sure they hadn't already been fed, and then took some of the dried meats that Salbiah had prepared for them, and fed them by hand. Their tongues tickled his palms, like a horse eating a sugar cube.

How could anyone hate these creatures?

Of course, gargoyles were territorial, they were brash, some were hotheaded. But none of that mattered; if you simply offered them respect, they would return it.

When everyone was fed and back in their pens, Maxwell stopped to see Bronx once again. She lay on her side, letting her pups feed. They'd grown so much in just a few weeks.

"Hey, girl, how're you doing?" He squatted down, rubbing behind her ears once again. The pups looked healthy, though he'd have to check on them later; he didn't want to interrupt their feeding. The only boy of the litter had been running a fever for the last week, and if it persisted, they'd need to send for a veterinarian at their next stop.

One of the pups stopped feeding and bounced over to Maxwell. Her paws were still too big for her body, her wings not fully formed. She waddled over to him, and Maxwell let her sniff his hand, lick whatever flavor the dried meat had left on his palms.

Then she stopped, went over to the corner, and dug in the hay for a bit.

"What're you doing over there?" He stood and followed her. She turned, her paw in the air, as if she were pointing at something. "What is it, girl?" Maxwell bent down once more, pushing the bundles of hay out of the way.

Lying on the stone floor, as if it'd been buried, was a letter opener.

Maxwell picked it up carefully. It was much like Nora's—silver, thin—except this one seemed to be covered in a sandy residue, almost as if the sand were sticking to the blade, refusing to let go.

And there, on the hilt, where Professor Vaughan-Crabtree's letter opener would've borne the letters *NVC,* this blade instead had two letters.

SD.

Septimius Dropwort.

<u>**EVIDENCE EXHIBIT K9**</u>
CASE ID: 20-06-DROS-STK

<u>Type:</u>
[ ] Communication
[ ] Audio recording
[ ] Spell residue
[X] Photo or other visual reconstruction
[ ] Object
[ ] Form or record
[ ] Other: _____

Source: GAE Gargoyle Keep
Relevant Parties: Salbiah Hussein,
groundskeeper
Description: Photo of warning sign posted in
Gargoyle Keep

WARNING
BROODING GARGOYLE IN THIS AREA
DO NOT APPROACH

Gargoyle mothers are VERY aggressive
and VERY territorial.
You WILL lose at least one finger.
Authorized personnel ONLY beyond this point
until JULY 30.
—Salbiah

5:00 P.M.: JAMIE ELLISON, 17, SWORDS

BY VICTORIA LEE

Jamie Ellison wasn't dead, but he might as well be.

He couldn't get that thought out of his mind, walking down the gently curving stone hall between Swords Tower and the school infirmary. It echoed between his ears like a whispered secret: *not dead, but might as well be.* The other students had their easy smiles and friendships and laughter—muted somewhat, after the news of Dropwort's death, but still present. Jamie, on the other hand, was like a faded photocopy of a normal seventeen-year-old boy, the colors gone to gray and the light overexposed: no details, just lines and edges. The idea of a person but not the thing itself.

He had left kinetics class alone, but it hadn't taken long for Hamish to catch up. Jamie's despair must have shown on his face because Hamish said, "You always look at me like that."

"Has it occurred to you that it's because I don't want to talk to you?"

Jamie didn't bother whispering it, and so the words earned

him more than a few weird looks. Hamish was, perennially, unfazed.

"I'm sorry to say, you don't have much of a choice, my lord," Hamish told him. "I must beseech you once again, on behalf of the infinite dead—"

"Please don't."

"—to reconsider our petition."

Jamie groaned and fixed his gaze at a far point on the floor; maybe if he ignored Hamish, he would go away. Not that that plan had worked so far. He could *feel* people's eyes on him, their derision drilling into his skin, flesh, muscle, bone.

No. Epidermis. Fascia, myofascia, osseous tissue. Focus. If he focused on anatomy, he wouldn't focus on Hamish, and if he didn't focus on Hamish, Hamish might go away.

Surely Hamish had better things to do. A man had just been murdered right here at Galileo. Shouldn't Hamish be trying to solve the mystery or something?

"My lord," Hamish said again. Jamie ignored him. "*My lord,* please, you must be reasonable. You must embrace your power. You must shed the flimsy restraints of social convention and allow yourself to take your rightful place as Master Necromancer, Lord of the Grave. With the twitch of your finger, innocent souls might rise from the tomb. With the blink of your sacred eye, you could abolish death—"

"*Please* shut up," Jamie muttered.

A passerby flinched and glared at him; Jamie tried to apologize, but it was too late. They were already gone.

"I shall not," the specter of Hamish said solemnly. "Sir, it is my duty as one of the deceased to advocate on behalf of all lost souls for your merciful intercession."

"Hamish is right, you know," said a mournful voice from over Jamie's left shoulder.

Jamie had been startled by enough ghosts at this point that it didn't make him jump anymore—which was a relief. Once, he'd been so shocked by a ghost's appearance that he'd literally flung himself out of his desk in the middle of class, screaming, and had promptly tripped over his own backpack, to fall face-first onto the dirty linoleum. Some ghosts were visible to all students, but others—like Hamish—were invisible to all except necromancers. Jamie's absolute mental breakdown had looked even more sus because it had involved shrieking at empty air.

Invisible ghosts made it awkward.

But necromancy was an illegal forbidden art—albeit one Jamie had been cursed with since birth—and whether you dabbled in the manipulation of life forces or could actually raise the dead, the fact that necromancy was illegal made it dangerous.

Especially right now, in the wake of an unsolved murder.

"*Please* stop doing this," Jamie whispered, evading the wide dolorous eyes of Mariana Bocanegra, who had died in 1863 and spent the intervening years crying ghostly tears over metaphysical spilled milk . . . such as Jamie's insisting that he literally, positively couldn't help the dead reclaim their mortal coils.

"We cannot. Not until you listen," said Mariana. Then: "Wait. Weren't you a girl last year?"

And of course that was sufficient to make Jamie wish his secret magical talent was the ability to open up a hole directly to the center of the earth, so that he could disappear into it.

"No," he said, and luckily Mariana left it at that.

Jamie supposed it was too much to hope that the faded imprints of long-lost souls who'd died actual centuries ago would be incredibly well informed on trans issues.

"Do you realize," Jamie said when neither of them left his side even as he approached the infirmary, "a man is dead?"

The entire school was buzzing with the news, a collective feeling like being perched on the edge of a precipice. And then there was Jamie, refusing to look down, because if he looked down, he might get the overpowering urge to jump.

"Many of us are dead," Hamish said grievously.

"Many who don't have to be," Mariana added.

Great. Just great. Jamie had clearly made it worse.

But he'd just rounded the last curve of the circular Galileo hall, and the tall white doors of the infirmary rose up before them like a sanctuary.

"Well, would you look at that. Time for me to go. Lovely talking to you folks—*oh shit.*"

A spectral creature drifted toward Jamie from the other end of the arched corridor, trailing a tattered gray cloak, silvery blood dripping from the open wounds in his chest.

Professor Dropwort.

Jamie spun on his heel, prepared to dash away before Dropwort could notice him—but Mariana and Hamish blocked his path with their frigid forms, and it was too late, too late because Dropwort had seen him, and that was his detestably creaking voice calling *"James, James"* down the hallway.

The tide of students heading for dinner was impossible to fight against either. Jamie had no choice but to turn around and find himself face to face with the man who while living had occupied the dubious position of being Jamie's most hated person in the world.

"Professor," he muttered.

"Speak up, boy. I can't hear you," Dropwort snapped back.

Jamie felt a dull heat rise in his cheeks, had to remind himself that there was nothing Dropwort could do to him anymore—to anyone. He was dead. His cruel words were never going to be heard by anyone but Jamie, not ever again.

"I can't really talk right now," Jamie said. "I'm late."

"For what? Eating?"

"Well . . . yes?"

Jamie wondered, sometimes, what everyone else thought when they saw him talking to himself like this. Presumably illegal necromancy wasn't the first explanation on their minds. Maybe they just thought he really was that eccentric, or narcissistic, or oblivious.

"I'm dead," Dropwort said, "and you are, it seems, one of the only ones who can see me. I don't believe in coincidences, boy."

"Okay. . . ."

Jamie tried to edge around him toward the infirmary, but Dropwort quickly shifted to block his path. Jamie had walked through ghosts before, but it wasn't comfortable. It was rather like being submerged in half-frozen gray goo. Last time he'd tried it, he'd been sneezing ice crystals for days, and Fibula had told him that the next time he did something so *boneheaded* (her word), she would give him something to really sneeze about.

"You know something. I know you do." Dropwort leaned in closer, close enough that Jamie could feel the frost of the professor's not-breath on his cheeks.

"I really don't. I'm very sorry you're dead, but—"

"Don't pretend to mourn me, boy. I wouldn't let you into

my advanced courses, so you went and changed your whole damn gender hoping to be an exception, and I still wouldn't allow it. You're probably glad someone finally did your dirty work and killed me. Aren't you? Tell the truth!"

The last part was spoken with such force that Dropwort expelled a gust of sleet along with the words; Jamie gagged and wiped his face with his sleeve.

"So what if I am?" Jamie found himself spitting back. "What can you do about it now? Moan and rattle chains in the walls while I'm trying to sleep?"

"The least you could do is solve my murder. It's the decent thing to do. The human thing."

Jamie's mouth twisted in an expression that even tasted bitter. "I'm not human, remember? I'm a necromancer."

Dropwort flicked his ghostly fingers as if to dismiss the statement out of hand. "Don't flatter yourself. You aren't so special. You aren't even the only necromancer at this school. I spoke to another one of your ilk just this morning."

All at once Jamie's mouth felt like it was full of grave dirt. He stared at Dropwort, actually *looking* at him this time, with his filmy dead eyes and corpse-mottled skin.

It wasn't possible. Necromancy was rare—*vanishingly* rare, more myth than actuality at this point. If Jamie hadn't been cursed himself, he wasn't sure he'd have even believed in necromancers.

"You're lying," he said, and Dropwort shook his head, looking far too pleased with himself, in Jamie's opinion, for a man whose physical body was maggot food. "Who is it?"

"I don't think I'll tell you," Dropwort drawled. "Ungrateful wretch that you are."

"You have to!"

"I *have* to do nothing," snapped the ghost, and even Hamish and Mariana flinched. Jamie had to blink ice crystals off his eyelashes. "Not while my killer remains at large. Find my killer, and maybe I'll tell you the identity of your fellow grave-witch. No sooner."

Jamie rolled his eyes so hard, his skull bones hurt. "They say Lola Cortez did it. There. Mission accomplished. Your murder has been solved. Happy?"

"They're wrong," Dropwort hissed. "Foolish. Idiots. Nincompoops. I was killed in the Gargoyle Keep—I remember that much. That girl claims she killed me somewhere else entirely. It isn't her."

Jamie had already opened his mouth, ready to fight back, when it occurred to him: "Don't you already know who killed you? You were stabbed in the front."

And now that Jamie looked at Dropwort's stab wounds properly, there was something . . . strange about them. It was as if the blood dripping from his body wasn't blood at all but something else. In fact, it looked almost like *sand.*

Dropwort's thin lips curled into a grimace. Jamie wondered if he was a sociopath or something, because he kind of enjoyed the way Dropwort was the one on the back foot, dead and helpless. "I can't remember all the details of my death. It's all a blur. . . ."

"That is not uncommon," interjected Hamish with a compassionate chain rattle. "Perhaps it is a boon, to have the terror and pain of our final hours subsumed by the bliss of ignorance—"

Dropwort's filmy eyes focused on Jamie, gaze sharpening.

"What if it was you? You hate me enough. I've always thought you were a creepy, heartless little thing. Did you kill me, boy?"

The accusation was like a flung dart spitting poison into Jamie's bloodstream. Suddenly all he could hear was the pound of his own heartbeat in his head, a surge of something like fear rising within him. He was telling the truth, but that didn't matter. If Dropwort told the other necromancer—if he found a way to make himself visible to regular people like some of the other ghosts in this place—there would be very little Jamie could say in his own defense. He didn't exactly have an alibi. And people were always eager to blame necromancers for the world's evil deeds.

"No," said Jamie. "But I wish I had."

"*My lord,*" Hamish said, appalled, but then Jamie just rounded on him, hands balling into fists.

"You're wrong," Jamie said. "Both of you. *All* of you, begging me to use my power to resurrect everyone—don't you get it?"

Mariana and Hamish gazed back at him with round and frightened eyes, Jamie's living heart pounding so hard in his chest that he could hear it in his ears, could taste blood on his tongue.

"Some people deserve to stay dead."

The infirmary doors slammed shut behind Jamie, and for a moment he just leaned against them, eyes shut, sucking in shallow breaths that didn't taste like rotten ghost.

It wasn't until Fibula said his name that Jamie actually looked up. The skeleton nurse had clattered over from her desk to peer, concerned, at Jamie's face with empty black voids where her eyes ought to be.

Fibula was a relic of an old time, back when Jamie's magic was still legal and necromancers made a killing reanimating beloved—and unbeloved—dead. She didn't talk much about her living life, and Jamie knew better than to ask; some pasts, he knew, could be painful. Sometimes it was easier to believe one had emerged into the world fully formed, precisely as one was right now.

"I'm okay," Jamie said, pasting a smile onto his face for Fibula's benefit. "Just . . . you know." He didn't want to be too specific; there were curtains drawn around several beds, and he didn't know who might be behind them.

Fibula nodded understandingly. "Come on," she said. "Let's go sit down. . . . Let me rest these old bones . . ."

The comment was clearly angled to earn an eye roll from Jamie, so he gave her one, and she patted his shoulder with her slim fingers and guided him away from the door, toward one of the empty beds.

Jamie sat, the thin hospital mattress sinking beneath his weight. Fibula, when she lowered herself down next to him, barely made an indent.

"Tell me what's going on," she said.

"It's nothing, really. I got . . . waylaid, I guess you could say, by a few ghosts." He lowered his voice substantially for the last word, even though the infirmary was so silent that he doubted anyone else was even present—or awake, if they were. "Drop-wort was with them."

"Professor Dropwort!" Fibula, at least, had the decency to sound as shocked as Jamie had felt to see that wretched man floating toward him. "That must have been so terrible for you, Jamie."

Jamie grimaced. "Yeah, well, he all but accused me of murdering him even though they literally just arrested someone else, so . . ."

"That's absurd."

Jamie didn't know what to say to that. Really? Was it that absurd? Dropwort clearly knew Lola hadn't killed him. And that meant the murderer was still at large. It could be any of them. Which meant it *could* be Jamie, if Jamie didn't know for a fact that he'd spent the hour when Dropwort was killed in the library, curled in a depressive insomniac slump around a pile of books.

But who would believe that? No one had seen Jamie in the library. It wasn't a real alibi.

Maybe he should go there. To the Gargoyle Keep, that is. Maybe he could find proof that the murder had happened there . . . get Lola out of police custody . . . set the detectives on the *right* path.

It's what Fibula would do. It's what *Jamie* would do too, if he was the good, kind boy Fibula saw him as.

"That's what I told him," Jamie said, instead of any of the rest.

Fibula's osseous fingers squeezed his shoulder. "It sounds like you made a marrow escape." Jamie snorted, and that, of course, only egged Fibula on. "I would hate to encounter that god-awful man again myself. I truly don't have the stomach for it."

Once upon a time, Jamie had lived for Fibula's stupid bone puns. These days, they just made his heart ache, because Fibula was so . . . she was *so* nice to him, and she had no reason to be, and all he could give her in return was a forced laugh and a brittle smile. She deserved better than this. She deserved better than *him*.

"Well, I'm glad he's dead," Jamie said at last, turning his gaze away from Fibula's gaunt face and toward his own hands, pale fingers twisting together in his lap.

"That's a terrible thing to say, Jamie." Fibula's voice was gentle, reassuring—not horrified, the way Jamie had expected.

He lifted one shoulder and dropped it again. "Maybe. Still true. And clearly I'm not the only one who felt this way."

"You realize you're comparing yourself to a murderer."

Jamie kept looking at his hands. It was hard for him to conceptualize murder and murderers as evil the way everyone else seemed to—after all, for him, the grave was impermanent. Death might cause a period of temporary amnesia, and it certainly could be lonely if you didn't have an unfriendly local necromancer to harass, but it wasn't the end.

Plenty of evil people died. It didn't mean they couldn't stick around; it just meant they couldn't hurt anyone anymore.

He understood on some level that other people would rather stay alive; the afterlife, at least as far as Jamie had seen, wasn't exactly a picnic. But then again those people probably had actual lives that were actually worth living.

"I'm sure you're frightened," Fibula went on, massaging his shoulder with those skinny hands. "Everyone is. I've had so many patients in here today needing anti-anxiety tonics and Sleep spells. It's okay to be frightened."

Jamie knew it was okay to be frightened. In fact, maybe he'd feel better about himself ethically if he could muster *any* emotion regarding Dropwort's untimely demise aside from bitter, begrudging relief—or a fear that he might get blamed for it.

Maybe he wasn't normal. Maybe everyone who said necromancers were cruel, heartless, sociopathic monsters were right.

"I got a letter from my parents," he said, changing the subject.

"Oh?" Fibula, if she had eyebrows, would have raised them. "What did they have to say?"

"Not much. They wanted to know if I was going to be able to come home for the summer holiday at all. They don't really . . . You know, they're Neutrals, so they don't understand the schedule at Galileo. They still think I was supposed to come home in May and that it's some kind of human rights violation that I didn't."

"You know you're allowed to go home," Fibula said. "There are special dispensations for that. You could take a Leisure Week."

"You mean a Mental Health Week," Jamie said. That was what the students called it, anyway—snobbishly or with complete sincerity, depending on who was talking.

Fibula's bony phalanges squeezed his shoulder again. "I mean that it might do you some good, Jamie, that's all. It's nothing to be ashamed of. You know, I can feel a little lonely here too, working all by myself in this infirmary."

"You have the patients. You have the kinetics interns, sometimes."

"A skeleton crew," Fibula said, and Jamie groaned loudly enough that Fibula actually laughed herself, a horrible creaky sound that evoked a knife on glass.

One of the bed curtains was yanked aside at that, violently

enough that Jamie and Fibula both startled. A girl sat there on the cot—the most eye-stabbingly colorful girl Jamie had ever seen. She had a bright red top paired, for some reason, with shiny purple pants and orange Docs. Her neck was draped in what looked like six or seven homemade plastic bead necklaces, and her curly black hair was tied up in two buns with dramatically overlong pink ribbons. There was actual gold glitter swept across her dark brown skin, like she was on her way to some kind of pastel-Froot-Loops-themed rave. She had a lime-green cast on her left arm; presumably that was why she was in the infirmary in the first place.

"Wow," the girl said. "That's, like, actually *humerus*. Ha. Get it?"

"That's a good one, Shivanya," Fibula said approvingly, clapping her dead hands together.

The girl—Shivanya—grinned. She wore braces. Glittery blue braces, to be precise. "Thanks. Hi, by the way."

Oh God, she was looking at Jamie. He stared back at her, his mouth full of nothing but dust.

Shivanya nodded her head, as if in encouragement. *"Hi, Shivanya,"* she said. "That's usually the response."

Heat rose at the nape of Jamie's neck. It was bad enough to get made fun of in front of ghosts who already considered him *Master Necromancer* or whatever—it was far worse to be mocked in front of Fibula.

"I'm sorry," Jamie said. "I don't remember inviting you into this conversation."

"Jamie," Fibula gasped, but Jamie ignored her, pushing up from the bed and grabbing his backpack off the floor.

"I gotta go."

He fled the infirmary before either of them could try to gaslight him into staying.

Dropwort was lurking outside the infirmary when he emerged, somehow even bloodier (sandier?) than before and screeching about murder and devious creepy necromancer boys who were arrogant enough to think they'd get away with it. So instead of heading toward the library where he'd usually be seeking refuge from things he was trying to avoid, Jamie did the right thing, for once.

He headed for the Gargoyle Keep.

It was a long walk to get there, around the curving halls of Galileo, to the sturdy stone structure—fort, really—that was the Keep. He felt people looking at him as he went. He sensed it, like heat at the nape of his neck.

They think you're a killer, a voice murmured in the back of Jamie's mind—a voice that sounded suspiciously like Dropwort himself.

Only, that wasn't it. People had always looked at Jamie like this. He'd spent a long time trying to dissect his every interaction with the other students at this school, to diagnose precisely where the hell he went wrong. Because surely he'd done something. Right? He'd said the wrong thing, or disliked the wrong person, and the entire school had communally met up and decided that Jamie Ellison was a persona non grata.

Had to be. Because Jamie wasn't imagining it. Even Professor Dropwort had seen it—had said it to Jamie's face: *Back for another year, I see. . . . Although, why you keep inflicting your presence upon your poor classmates, I must admit I have no idea. . . .*

They were just waiting for a chance to say, *I knew he was a waste.* He wouldn't give them one.

"Mr. Ellison, is that you?"

The voice caught Jamie only a few feet from the north exit of the Cups Tower, the Gargoyle Keep less than a hundred yards away. It'd be easier to ignore it, but Vice Principal Beatriz Ruiz-Marín was one of the few people on the school grounds who seemed not to completely hate him. He turned to face her.

The vice principal had transitioned a year before Jamie had—although, whereas testosterone injections had left Jamie gangly and awkward and still hadn't managed to produce any noticeable facial hair, the vice principal's transition had transformed her into a statuesque beauty with soft features and perfect lipstick. It was kind of weird to be jealous of a girl for looking girly, considering, but Jamie *was* jealous. Not of the femininity but of how easy it seemed for her. How seamless.

"Hi, Vice Principal," he said.

"I told you, you can call me Beatriz." She smiled at him, displaying perfect white teeth. "Where are you headed?"

"Uh . . ." Jamie flailed around for an acceptable answer. He wasn't exactly known for his affinity with gargoyles—they scared him, if he was being strictly honest about it—and he doubted anyone would believe him if he said he was just heading to the Keep to spend some quality time with the school's stone sentinels.

Instead he shrugged. "Just going for a walk to get some air. You know. Clear my head."

Beatriz's mouth turned into a slight frown. "I'll join you." She gestured to the broad archway, and Jamie had no choice but to go, each crunch of the vice principal's shoes on the gravel behind him ratcheting like a countdown. "Jamie, I've been meaning to talk to you for a while now. Your teachers say you're struggling in classes. Missing some of them, failing to turn in work for others. . . . And I never see you go out whenever we make landfall. You don't explore any of these vibrant cities; you always stay in the library or your dormitory. I wanted to ask . . . is everything okay?"

Is everything okay? Why did that feel like such a cliché?

The worst part was, Jamie had no idea how to answer. Because no. Nothing was okay. Everything was messed up and wrong. People possibly suspected him of murder, everybody hated him, and frankly, Jamie didn't blame them.

He hated himself too.

A briny wind was blowing off the bay far below, and he tasted salt as he muttered, "Um . . . I'm fine. Thanks."

"Fibula told me you've been spending a lot of time in the infirmary," Beatriz said, drawing even with him. "Are you ill?"

She peered at him from behind her cat-eye spectacles, and Jamie already knew that she wasn't asking because she didn't know the answer. Of course Fibula had told her. Fibula, it seemed, couldn't keep her mandible shut these days.

"No. I'm all good. Just show up to get my hormones, or whatever. You know."

She nodded slowly. "I hope you know that you can talk to me, Jamie. Anytime. My door is always open. I've been where you are—transitioning is so hard, especially in these early days. And all those hormones can make you feel moody and depressed; they're literally a second puberty."

He knew that. He *knew* that. He wasn't an idiot. He knew there was a good reason why he felt so shitty all the time. Only, he felt like he was . . . like he was worse than he should be, if all this just amounted to being biochemically twelve years old again.

He felt like one of his ghosts, drifting through the world but never touching it. Never part of it.

"And the worst part is," Beatriz was saying, "you feel like you don't have a right to be upset anymore. After all, you got everything you ever wanted. You are finally becoming who you were always meant to be. So why aren't you happy? You should be euphoric, ecstatic, bouncing off the walls—right? But you aren't. So what does that say about you?"

All at once, Jamie's throat felt tight. He swallowed once, twice, trying to shove that knot out of his gullet. It was hard to breathe.

She was right. That was . . . she was exactly right. He felt so guilty. He'd literally only wanted one thing his whole life, and now that he had it, he had the gall to be miserable. It didn't make any sense.

"Yeah," he croaked out eventually—and to his surprise Beatriz reached for him and touched his elbow very lightly.

"It's going to be okay," she said. "It's going to get better. I promise you."

He wasn't sure he believed her, but he nodded anyway, earning himself a tiny smile and a squeeze at his biceps before her hand fell.

"I'll see you tomorrow, I'm sure," she said. "I need to go to a meeting now, unfortunately about this . . . horrible business, with Professor Dropwort. What a dreadful thing to happen." She paused, putting a hand out to stop him in his tracks so she could look him properly in the eye. "I'm always here if you need me. Understand?"

Jamie suddenly felt like crying. But he had to seem normal, especially now, he thought—especially with people talking about him taking *Leisure Weeks* and asking if he was *okay.*

He met Beatriz's eyes and said, "Thank you. For everything."

The sun wouldn't set for another few hours this far north, but the Gargoyle Keep still managed to tower ominously in the daylight, a bulging block of turrets and crenellation, gargoyles crawling into nests and taking flight like stone hornets swarming a hive.

He was steeling himself against the sight of them—and the smell, frankly—when a guttural voice spoke just behind him. "I've been searching for you."

Jamie didn't have to look to know who it was.

"Please go away," he said, shutting his eyes.

"Why?" Dropwort said. Jamie felt the chilly breeze against his neck as Dropwort shifted from behind him to float beside him, or in front of him. "Feeling remorseful? Developed a conscience in the hours since you murdered me?"

"I didn't murder you," Jamie said at last, blowing out a heavy breath. "I'm glad *somebody* did, but it wasn't me. More's the pity."

"I don't believe that," Dropwort said. His voice was a whisper, like winter wind rustling through fallen leaves. "All that time you spend in the library, all those hours in the infirmary with that ungodly bone woman. . . . I knew I was being poisoned. I suspected it. The skeleton gave it to you, didn't she?"

"What?"

"*Hourglass,*" Dropwort said, and finally Jamie opened his eyes to look at him. Dropwort was right in front of him, close enough that Jamie could see straight through his filmy eyes to the weathered stone walls behind him.

"I sincerely don't know what you're talking about," Jamie informed him bluntly.

"I was poisoned with hourglass. The symptoms match up—the timing—"

Jamie lifted his brows and pointed at the bloody mess on Dropwort's torso. "Um. Pretty sure you were stabbed, mate. That's why I'm here, right?" He gestured to the stone walls of the Keep. "You *literally told me* this is where it happened." Ghosts were often confused about the circumstances of their own deaths, but Dropwort ignoring the gaping wounds in his chest seemed like overkill. "Now, if you'll excuse me, I have to go figure out who did it so people will stop thinking I did."

He stalked up the staircase leading into the Keep, pointedly ignoring Dropwort's frantic sputtering from below, until the ghost's ranting faded. The dank musk grew more powerful the higher he climbed, a clingy smell that he knew wasn't going to wash out on the first try.

What are you even doing? What if Salbiah found him bothering her beloved gargoyles? What if one of them thought he was a threat and attacked?

Would it even make a difference, discovering the real killer, if everyone had already decided who it was?

He didn't see the flash of color against the grim stone until much, much too late, when he was already at the top of the stairs.

Slowly, very slowly, Jamie lifted his gaze to meet Shivanya's.

"Hi again," she said. "You know, it's kind of rude to just leave in the middle of a conversation like that."

"Okay." Jamie wasn't quite sure what he was supposed to say to this.

"I was just thinking that I've seen you around a lot," Shivanya continued. She tapped the hot pink nails of her un-injured hand against the banister. "You're James Ellison, right? From Swords house?"

"Jamie."

"*Jamie.* Okay, sorry. Jamie. Do you go to the infirmary a lot? Are you and Fibula good friends? Don't you think it's super weird that we have a, like, reanimated skeleton for a school nurse?"

"Um."

Shivanya kept going. "Like . . . the name 'Fibula.' What does that even mean? Isn't that a bone? Why is she named 'Fibula'?"

"She told me she just thought it sounded pretty," Jamie said.

"I mean, I *guess,* yeah, it's kind of pretty. And she does like bone puns. So it makes sense."

Jamie coughed. "Can I . . . ?" He gestured at the last few steps leading up to the Keep.

"Oh. Right." She moved aside. For a moment, the pungent musk of gargoyles was briefly alleviated by her orange blossom perfume. "So. What are you doing here?"

A perfectly natural question, and one that Jamie had ab-solutely no intention of answering. He didn't know Shivanya, didn't know her friends, didn't know which rumors she'd be feeding. He wasn't telling her a thing.

"What are *you* doing here?" he countered instead.

"Duh." She grinned at him. "I'm investigating a murder."

"What?"

"I know, I know, they arrested someone already, blah, blah, blah." She waved her hand dismissively in the air, and light bounced off the rhinestone pearls that dotted her cast, scattering patterns all over the walls. "But listen. I overheard this guy, Diego something-or-other? And *he* was saying—"

"Don't you have studying to do? Or food to eat?" Jamie cut in. The last thing he needed was her getting in the way. The sneer in his voice wavered embarrassingly. "Or . . . friends to hang out with?"

"I have a medical exemption from homework for the next week," Shivanya said, putting one finger up. "I ate Cheez-Its in the infirmary." Second finger. "And right now, I'm investigating a murder, while hanging out with you!" Third. And then her dark eyes widened with sudden realization. "That's why you're here too, isn't it?"

"No," Jamie lied, and turned to head back down the stairs.

Dropwort stood right behind him, dead eyes boring into his. *Jamie reeled back too quickly, feet catching on the steps.* "Shit—"

"Whoa." A hand caught his wrist, pulling him back up.

"Let go." He wrenched free, stumbling a few steps, adrenaline still wreaking hell on his pulse.

Shivanya held up her hands. "Sorry, no touching, understood. You okay?"

"Damn you, James. Make yourself useful," Dropwort rattled. Something told Jamie the ghost would block the way out until he got what he wanted.

"Fine," Jamie said heavily. "Yeah, I'm also here to investigate."

"Great!" Shivanya reached to link arms, then caught herself. "Two heads are better than one, or so they tell me. And your head is a particularly smart one, right? I see you at the library all the time. What do you know?"

There was something about her unconditional warmth that made it too easy to thaw. But what was he going to tell her? Dropwort's ghost had told him, and *only* him, that they'd arrested the wrong killer?

"Or I could go first." Shivanya spun a bright bangle around her wrist. "I heard that a guy found a note around here addressed to Dropwort, and I don't know how, but that letter was what a bunch of people heard this morning. I thought I'd see if Dropwort dropped anything else around here. Okay, your turn. Tell me *everything*." She smiled at him, eager.

Too eager, insisted part of him.

No. They had an agenda in common, that was all.

"Well. Um." He cleared his throat. "I got a tip from a . . . different source . . . that this is where Dropwort was murdered."

Shivanya's eyes gleamed with excitement. "You know, I heard that too! Keturah, you know her? Well, she was saying something about this weird sand trail that led here, and . . ."

"A *source*?" Dropwort rasped in his ear as Jamie's stomach sank. "How dare you, boy? I am *the* source! The only one that matters!"

"Would you shut up?" Jamie hissed.

Shivanya looked taken aback. "Excuse me?"

"Not you!"

"I was *poisoned*," Dropwort raged, so loudly that Jamie couldn't help but wince. "They'd been poisoning me for weeks by then. . . . Stabbed with my own silver letter opener . . . the silver. . . . Are you listening to me, boy?"

"Stop," Jamie said through gritted teeth.

Shivanya was gaping at him. Like . . . like he was exactly what they said he was. And just when he'd started entertaining the idea that he might finally have a friend here. So much for that.

Better to get this farce over with. "My source said Dropwort was stabbed with something silver. Why was Dropwort carrying a *silver* letter opener if he knew about the hourglass?"

"Impertinent boy," Dropwort thundered. "I had my reasons!"

Shivanya frowned. "What hourglass?"

"Hourglass poison," he told her. "It turns blood to sand when it comes into contact with silver."

"Oh." Shivanya twirled a strand of hair around one finger. Her cheer had yielded to a too-familiar kind of unease. "What does that have to do with anything?"

Jamie sighed. "Dropwort thought someone was poisoning him with hourglass."

"I *know* I was being poisoned!"

Shivanya had said something, but Jamie'd missed it, trying not to flinch at Dropwort's chill. "Sorry, what?"

There was that unease again. "How do you know that?"

"I—I heard—" Jamie faltered.

"You're wasting time!" Dropwort snarled, wheezing noxious

frost over the side of Jamie's face. The cold, the gargoyle musk, the questions, it was too much. "They have the wrong suspect! If the case is closed and the school leaves"—icy thorns prickled over Jamie's neck, and this time he couldn't help flinching away—"then they'll never catch—"

"*I KNOW!*" Jamie finally bellowed. "If you *want* me to find your killer, then you need to shut up and let me *think!*"

A horrible silence fell, even dampening the distant rustling of the gargoyles.

"Jamie," Shivanya said slowly, "who are you talking to?"

This was how it was always going to start. How it was going to get out. He'd been sloppy, he should have known better, it was all his fault—

Shivanya was staring at his face. No—lower. Slowly she reached out and touched a fingertip to his collar. Jamie knew what she'd find: frost.

Her eyes flicked to the empty space between them, where Dropwort's ghost coalesced.

"Can you *see* him?" she whispered.

This was worse than the infirmary, worse than tripping out of his desk, worse than Beatriz saying she understood his guilt. Lord of the Grave, Master Necromancer in the making, and he'd been caught because he couldn't even fake being normal.

All Jamie could croak out was, "Don't tell *anyone*. Please."

Shivanya shook her head. "Of course not." Then: "Oh my *God,* that's cool."

Jamie had braced for a myriad of reactions, but "that's cool" was nowhere close to among them.

"I mean, I'm not going to tell; that's your thing," she kept babbling. "It's just—wait, that's gotta be *terrifying* sometimes.

Do you see—okay, no, focus." Shivanya didn't seem to notice she was digging at the rhinestones on her cast. "Does Drop-wort know who killed him?"

Jamie could only stare. This was a setup, a trap—

But if it was, Shivanya didn't seem to be in on it. She waved her cast through the air where Dropwort's specter hovered. "Is he still there?"

"Yes," Jamie finally said. "He's still here."

They could solve this, and then . . . then, just maybe, Jamie could actually *talk* to someone. Someone with a pulse.

"Of course I'm here, you ridiculous children," Dropwort hissed. His ghostly pallor was infused with a strange sheen now, almost like sweat. "Should have flunked you while I had the chance! James. Listen, James. Avenge me. If you've ever been worth anything in your life, avenge me. I want justice. I want them to die my death, I want them to watch their blood turn to sand, I want them to feel the silver—"

"Silver?" Jamie pressed. "You mean the blade?"

Shivanya carefully poked his shoulder with a finger. Then she pointed down the hall. "You mean like *that*?"

All three of them looked to see Maxwell Aster standing at the end of the Keep's corridor, his eyes wide as he stared at them in shock, the evening light glinting off the letter opener in his hand.

EVIDENCE EXHIBIT TEXT-1
CASE ID: 20-06-DROS-STK

Type:

[X] Communication
[ ] Audio recording
[ ] Spell residue
[ ] Photo or other visual reconstruction
[ ] Object
[ ] Form or record
[ ] Other: _____

Source: GAE mass-messaging system
Relevant Parties: Beatriz Ruiz-Marín, vice principal
Description: Mass text sent to students June 29 at 5:30 p.m.

REMINDER

We will be departing for Turkmenistan at 10 p.m. on the dot! All students must be inside their own dormitory towers by 9:30 p.m., and remain so until morning. In the event of a medical emergency, please seek assistance from the nearest available staff member. For your safety, do NOT exit the dorms while we are traveling.

——Vice Principal Ruiz-Marín

6:00 P.M.: DELFINA MOORE, 16, CUPS/SWORDS

BY YAMILE SAIED MÉNDEZ

Delfina Moore had been sitting in detention so long, her butt was numb. The rest of her body, though, vibrated with anxiety, as she wondered what was going on in the school.

The overeager ghost who'd sent her to detention must have forgotten about her!

If only she could teleport or manipulate dimensions, or do something useful besides having an uncanny knack to learn languages . . .

But no. She had proven beyond a doubt that swearing didn't magically open doors, at least not in the twenty-seven languages she commanded.

"Hello!" she yelled, frustrated. "I'm still here. Please let me go," she added in a whisper.

In reply, a voice blared as if from the brick walls, announcing:

"All students are to report to their dorms immediately and remain there until they are called in for questioning."

When the last echo of the words died down, the door slammed open.

A person stood there, watching her.

Delfina jumped to her feet.

"Max?"

Maxwell Aster, also of Cups house, was the last person she'd expected to see.

"I finally found you." His words rushed out like they'd been little divers waiting to jump off the cliff of his tongue. "I've been looking for you everywhere. And I mean everywhere. I swear I'll never get the cobwebs out of my hair." He silently closed the door behind him. "Did you know gargoyles keep spiders as pets?"

She did.

On Delfina's first week at Galileo, Vice Principal Beckley had allowed her unlimited access to the storage area to get yerba mate. Tucked among the boxes of the tea leaves Delfina couldn't live without, she'd found a crate containing a Goliath birdeater spider one of the gargoyles had smuggled into the school after a stop in the Amazon.

She did a full-body shiver.

Max nodded and placed a hand on her shoulder. "I knew, but they still gross me out. The spiders, I mean. Gargoyles aren't that bad."

Delfina's friend Keturah called Max the Slenderman because of how tall and skinny he was, but Delfina had a crush on him. When he touched her, her mind short-circuited. All the languages she commanded vanished from her brain.

She wanted to kick herself. Now wasn't a good time to go all frozen like a comadreja, a "possum," when she was supposed to be cool and composed. She had a reputation to protect!

Max wasn't exactly considered the most attractive boy at Galileo Academy—that would be Diego, the quintessential bad boy. Honestly? She saw the appeal in Diego, but if she had a type, Max would be *it*.

He was a kind soul. She'd seen him around the gargoyles and had heard how he'd protected them from the vile Professor Dropwort.

Embarrassed, she looked down at his feet. His black shoes were splattered with mud and covered in spiderwebs.

Max tilted her chin with his index finger. "I need a favor from you. Please, Del!"

No one had called her Del in a long, long time. Memories of the love from people whose faces she couldn't really remember threatened to overwhelm her in a wave of grief. Because those people were long gone.

He looked over his shoulder, as if expecting someone to barge in. But the door remained closed.

"What is it?" she asked, his panic making her breath catch.

He took out a wrinkled piece of parchment from his pocket and handed it to her. Their fingers brushed, and he shivered a little.

"Open it," he said. "We don't have much time."

The clock on the wall had barely moved, but she felt a sudden prickling in the back of her mind. Was this what her ancestors had been trying to tell her this morning right before she got detention?

Delfina might not remember her real family or much about her life before she was eleven, when she was adopted by the Moores. PTSD, doctors said. But that didn't mean her ancestors had forgotten her. The Moores, a family who'd emigrated from Ireland to Argentina generations ago, might have given her a new identity and so many opportunities like education, but she'd never felt completely one of them. There were the obvious differences like their skin color and the way she felt the call of her land.

The ancestors kept a link to her, granting her magic, and with that a door into a world that would otherwise have been closed to her for being a girl, an orphan, and poor in a country still governed by the prejudices of a ruling class that revered whiteness and reviled magic.

Usually, once she could tune in to the vibrations she felt on her skin, she received warnings or revelations in the form of mathematical equations or celestial geometry that she loved to analyze like puzzles.

Now she felt the familiar sensation in the back of her mind, like the whirring of gears coming to life. Her ancestors never abandoned her.

She opened the parchment, expecting to find a mathematical equation, or a geometry diagram that he needed to decipher for a weird reason. What else would Max need her for? But that's not what she found.

The parchment was crisscrossed with words in Professor Dropwort's unmistakable handwriting.

"Ugh!"

Seeing the handwriting of her least favorite person in the school gave her a visceral reaction.

She doubted Professor Dropwort had ever known her name. Other than confiscating an ancient corn-doll from her—the only memento she had from her life before her memories had started—they'd had practically no interactions. He had claimed that no such objects were allowed on campus, which was a cruel lie. Keturah had told Delfina that he made a sport of stealing rare objects from students. But why the doll? She'd never know, now that he was dead.

In spite of her crushing her courses and entering the spotlight as one of the academy's best students, he'd pointedly ignored her. It was a well-known and documented fact that he detested that certain types of students had polluted his beloved academy. The type of students Delfina belonged to: poor, without a family, female, from a country most people ignored even though it was at the beginning of the alphabet.

Professor Dropwort had never written her one of the coveted notes to invite her to any of his exclusive gatherings, but she'd recognize his handwriting anywhere, even if it were in the Cyrillic alphabet.

"Where did you get this? How . . . ? Why . . . ?" She had so many questions, but Max was already shaking his head.

"There's no time."

"You need to tell me what's going on," she said. Her ears were whistling again, like a boiling teakettle; her first instinct if there was some danger was to get herself out of whatever mess they were in.

"I found it in Dropwort's classroom," Max said. "It might tell us who murdered him."

She could have danced with relief. If this note gave the authorities a clue as to who might have hated Dropwort enough to kill him, then she'd be off the hook. Maybe she could clear Lola of any suspicions too. Still, she remained outwardly calm.

"Besides Beckley, you're the only person I know who speaks and reads so many languages," Max said.

She tried to ignore the heat crawling up her neck to her face. "So why didn't you go to her?"

Delfina didn't believe in idolizing people, but she respected and admired Vice Principal Beckley, who had recruited her to Galileo. She represented everything Delfina wanted to accomplish one day.

Rapid, dainty footsteps were rushing in their direction. Someone was coming to the door.

"Professor Vaughn-Crabtree said to show it only to *you*," Max said.

The door slammed opened again.

Delfina hid her hands behind her back, ready to attack anyone who might even think of taking the note Max had entrusted to her. But it was just Ivy Barta from Coins house, preceded by her storm of bouncy curls. Unlike every other time Delfina had seen her, now there was no blazing smile on Ivy's face.

"What's going on?" Delfina asked.

"I could ask the same thing," she said, and then she looked at Max. "Beckley wants to talk to you."

"How did you know Max was here?" Delfina asked, taking a step toward Ivy.

Ivy held her ground and replied, "One of the ghosts saw him walk in here." Then she turned toward Max and snapped her fingers. "The professor needs you now. We can't keep her waiting."

Max sent Delfina a desperate look, but she was seething. What was Ivy playing at?

Delfina made her choice.

Casually she put her hand into her jeans pocket and tucked the note in with the tips of her fingers. She could see her reflection in Ivy's glasses when the other girl finally turned to look at her.

Trying to act like her cool, composed self, Delfina said, "Don't keep Professor Beckley waiting, Maxwell. If you need help with a protective barrier, I can suggest a couple of things later."

They'd been talking about this topic in class, so Ivy wouldn't think it was anything to remember. Also, Max's forte was arcane geometry; everyone knew that. Just like everyone knew that because Delfina's magic manifested in geometric shapes, the two had spent time discussing this together in the past.

Max seemed to get ahold of himself. He looked detached and cold as usual. But his pupils were dilated, pulsating as if reminding her to translate the parchment that seemed to burn in her pocket.

"You sure, Moore?"

"I promise," she said, hoping that Ivy wouldn't think she was being dramatic.

"Thanks," Max said, and he walked out of the detention room.

Before following Max, Ivy grabbed Delfina's arm and said, "You need to head to your dorm. Didn't you hear the announcement?"

She left before Delfina could shake her off or question her motives.

Ivy had always seemed innocent and transparent, but her attitude right now? It was unacceptable! What kind of authority did the girl have to act like this?

There were so many questions. So many mysteries.

Delfina was determined to find out at least what the note said, and the first course of action was to call for help from her ancestors.

She sat in front of the door, her back to it in case anyone else tried to barge in and interrupt her, and she smoothed the parchment in front of her. It had been torn from a larger sheet. Still, she could read the message as clearly as if someone were dictating its meaning in her ear, a real-time interpreter from the beyond.

She had learned to read the Cyrillic alphabet her second year at Galileo. She had been sick in bed for two weeks after, like every time she used her powers. Any suffering was worth it, though. Even now, she still felt the jolt of excitement and surprise when the meaning of the words jumped to her from marks that to other people didn't mean anything. It was like a window into a different world. Another language added to her collection was another tool, another weapon in her armory to free her people.

Now she read, soundlessly mouthing the words so not even the walls could eavesdrop on her. At Galileo, the walls had ears and eyes no one could see.

Gentlemen,

I understand your concerns and have done my best to answer your questions below. Please note that this is being written on indestructible parchment, so you may retain it for your records.

Firstly: I have authenticated the lost Fabergé egg myself by comparing it to similar samples from the same time period, you will find the mark of the House of Fabergé cast in gold at the base of the egg, and the magical signature reflects a completion date of 1911. I have also attached a record of the egg from the treasury of the Winter Palace under Tsar Nikolai II Alexandrovich in 1912, received as a gift for the 1913 celebration of 300 years of Romanov rule . . . mere years before the fall of the House of Romanov. It is a one-of-a-kind item, for not only is it an artifact of great significance to Neutral history but the concealed firebird egg within makes it extraordinarily valuable to the society of Sorcerers as well (see below).

Secondly: It was a fairly simple but foolproof process to confirm that the Fabergé egg conceals a firebird egg. When the proper mechanisms are activated, the decorative casing opens to reveal the distinctive shell of the firebird egg. Furthermore, a dormant firebird chick is uniquely able to absorb life energy from a nearby magical creature that's brooding. Upon receipt of the egg, I did not detect any signs of life, but after placing the egg with a brooding gargoyle for a week, a life signature was measured within.

Naturally, discretion must be exercised, given the significance of this being both a magical and Neutral artifact. However, I'm certain

"A firebird," Delfina whispered, and then quickly clasped a hand over her mouth.

Someone had killed Dropwort for this information.

She closed her eyes, for a second wishing she hadn't accepted the parchment from Max, that she hadn't read this note.

Already she felt looming over her head the doom that befell all those who tried to possess a firebird egg. But she wasn't foolish enough to even want to possess this *artifact*, as Dropwort had called it. So typical of him to talk about one of the most magical beings as a simple object to be possessed and used.

She'd known he was a fool, but not to this extent.

Delfina had never seen a firebird in real life, of course, but she knew about it. According to folklore, a firebird is like a breathing winged bonfire. Even a single feather could light up a room. Countless heroes had found their end in the quest for a single tail feather. The creature could be a harbinger of doom.

It was well known that after an initial flood of wealth and power, tragedy and disgrace followed those who possessed a firebird—or tried to.

So many people throughout history had sacrificed their personal safety for the greater good of their community. Some said that becoming a vessel for the firebird's magical and prophetic nature even for a few hours was worth giving one's life for.

An artifact like this in the hands of either Sorcerers or Neutrals could change the course of humanity. A firebird egg was more valuable than any precious stone, more than any money a country or group of people could hoard, or the promise she'd made for a boy she'd developed feelings for.

She imagined how her people's suffering would end with even one feather. No more darkness to haunt their nights.

Had Delfina's life been preserved so that she could be a pivotal player in this history-changing event? Was this why the witch of las pampas had prophesied her birth and why Matilde Moore had given her a home and an education? Even if she died, she'd give her people a life of freedom in the endless southern plains, as they were meant to have. She'd give them a chance, at least. *If* she could get ahold of the firebird egg. Or if she could help the right people find it first.

No matter what Max's reservations had been, Delfina trusted Vice Principal Beckley. She had to give her this note. Hadn't her benefactor Matilde Moore instructed Delfina to always trust in Matilde's old friend Beckley?

So many nights, Delfina had lain awake in her dormitory, wondering why the Moores had saved her, among the countless children who'd arrived at the estancia begging for some food. Why her? If she brought this egg back to Argentina, maybe she could help end a little bit of the inequity and injustice that quenched so many lives before the children had the chance to really live. True, she might have to deal with the eventual reckoning, but any suffering was worth it if it was for her people.

The Moore matriarch had always insisted that Delfina had been chosen for her gifts.

Beckley had even hinted that she was special, and the truth was, she'd always wanted to prove the professor right.

Now was her time.

If she helped discover the artifact, then maybe she could take it herself and return to Argentina with it.

A part of her winced that she'd have to abandon everything she'd worked so hard for.

But she'd made a promise to the Moores and her own ancestors to liberate her country from the dictatorship. The firebird was the key that would unlock her people from oppression.

She also had a debt with Beckley. She had to go tell her.

She peered out the door and saw the ghost still posted there, muttering in a language that was nothing like Italian. The little jerk! Delfina looked out the window. In her mind, she saw all her options, including climbing out the window. But if she miscalculated a single movement . . . No matter how she imagined her escape, all the scenarios converged in one probability: her ending up a splatter on the grounds if she fell to her death.

She felt the tug of another path. If she walked in a straight line on the bricks under the window, she could make it to the hallway that led to the library, and from there, it was just a few more steps to the administrative offices where she'd find Beckley. She didn't care that Max would be there. Vice Principal Beckley would know what to do.

But the library . . . She sighed. She loved books, but she hated the library here at the academy.

In her first year, a group of older students led by Dan Corbin's older brother, all part of Dropwort's posse of hand-picked prodigies, had locked her in the restricted section and sent the gargoyles after her. The boys had thought she couldn't speak English because back then she'd been so quiet. But they hadn't considered that she'd learned to say "please" and "thank you" to the sentinels of the school in their own language. That had earned her a reputation of being a respectful and kind kid. Which had saved her life because the gargoyles usually bit first, and then they asked questions.

Even though things had turned out well, she still broke out in a sweat and shivers when she went to the library. Something she'd never forget or forgive Dropwort for, because he'd laughed it off, claiming boys would be boys.

Holding her breath, clutching the piece of parchment like it was a lifeline, she balanced on the catwalk to the hallway, trying not to look down at the drop. The sky was a bright blue. This time of the year at this latitude, the sun wouldn't set until after ten, and she never tired of looking at it.

By the time she reached the administrative offices, her chest hurt for all her heart's frantic pounding. But a glance at her watch revealed to her that the hour was almost gone, and she had to warn her beloved Professor Beckley.

She was crouching behind a door when she heard people arguing. She recognized Fornax's annoying high-pitched voice. Who could the other person be?

From behind a marble column, Delfina craned her neck to see who he was talking to.

The other person had the look of an authority figure, like a police officer or something. "The school *must* remain in Stockholm," the officer said. "Even though Lola Cortez has been cleared."

Delfina could've collapsed with relief. She held on to the wall to sustain herself and keep listening to the conversation.

"There's still an active murder investigation, though. Galileo can't move out of our jurisdiction with a killer on the loose. Surely you understand this, sir?"

Fornax clicked his tongue like an old hen.

But when he finally spoke, his voice chilled Delfina's blood.

"The school *must* continue on its itinerary to Turkmenistan. The decision is final. It's already been announced."

"But, sir—"

"What part of 'no' don't you understand?" he spat. "We have investors and trustees to answer to. Just to give you an idea, the Moores in Argentina sponsored every event and trip in the next leg of our schedule. I'm not going to be the reason their money is wasted. Will you be the one to call them and explain? You must know how they respond to inconveniences such as unwanted news."

The man flinched as if Fornax had conjured a malignant entity by mentioning the name. Delfina's last name.

"But don't they care about the students? I know there's a Moore on the roster and another boy they're paying for," the man insisted.

Fornax scoffed. "The student you're talking about, Delfina, isn't a real Moore. She's what they called an arrimada, as they say in Castellano. Someone they took in as an investment. Delfina is nothing more than that to them. And to be honest, there are plenty of promising people if she doesn't work out according to plan. The little boy from Ceuta is very promising, I tell you. So as you can see, that argument isn't going to work with the Moores. They can replace whoever stands in their way."

There was a silence that only lasted a second but that sent Delfina into a downward spiral.

The words sank deeper and deeper into Delfina's heart and with them, they dragged down her faith in her adoptive family.

How many times had the Moore children called her arrimada before? And it was true that Matilde Moore had asked—

no, ordered—her multiple times to help Angel, the little student from Ceuta. She had reminded Delfina that her education was an investment the family was making.

Suddenly Delfina understood what they would want in return: everything, even her life.

She saw things as they truly were. She felt small and insignificant, a puppet in other people's hands. They had even brought in a replacement for her in case she didn't turn out as they had wanted. She felt so betrayed and used.

If the Moores and Fornax were on the same side, what did this mean? Had Matilde Moore lied to her and used her?

Who knew how many other kids had been tossed aside when they weren't needed anymore?

Fornax was just like Dropwort. Like the Moore matriarch. Like everyone with power that Delfina had ever met.

Delfina didn't know a lot of things, but she knew about the firebird.

This knowledge was power. She was going to prove to the world that they were messing with the wrong person.

Once the coast was clear, she'd find Vice Principal Beckley, the only person Delfina still admired and looked up to. She'd tell her what Fornax had said, and hopefully, she'd become the next principal when the time came. And maybe she could help Delfina figure out what to do, now that she'd discovered why the Moores had sent her to Galileo, to turn her into an obedient soldier they could use as they pleased.

A moment later, Fornax and the officer headed to the library.

Gingerly, her limbs aching from crouching in the shadows

for so long, Delfina left her hiding place and tiptoed toward the office. But before she could stop in time to hide again, she heard sounds as if someone were trying to force a door open.

She only had time to rearrange her facial features in one of innocence and subservience.

Her whole body resented having to pretend instead of showing the power inside her. But she'd learned from an early age to play the games of power, because one day, she'd turn things in her favor. She'd been chosen for this. The ancestors had shown her.

But when she looked up, her jaw dropped in surprise. She came face to face with Ivy. Again. Ivy trying to open Fornax's door.

In her hand she held a key. The multicolored glass of the chandeliers sent sparks all over the hallway. Blue like the sky in Los Teros, her home. Glinting golden like the Paraná River Delfina loved and hoped to see again soon.

Each girl held the other's gaze. But before Delfina could confront Ivy, Vice Principal Beckley opened the door beyond some filing cabinets and asked, "What do you two think you're doing?"

EVIDENCE EXHIBIT NF-8
CASE ID: 20-06-DROS-STK

Type:
[ ] Communication
[ ] Audio recording
[ ] Spell residue
[ ] Photo or other visual reconstruction
[ ] Object
[X] Form or record
[ ] Other: _____

Source: School records
Relevant Parties: Ivy Barta, student; Fibula Smith, school nurse
Description: Doctor's note for Barta, documenting Barta's attempt to enter restricted area

**GALILEO ACADEMY FOR THE
EXTRAORDINARY, INFIRMARY**
FIBULA SMITH, HEAD NURSE

Patient name: Ivy Barta
Date: June 29

MESSAGE: Please excuse <u>IVY BARTA</u> from their
classes on <u>6/29/2020</u> due to <u>RECOVERING FROM A</u>
<u>BAD CASE OF SIMMERING PUSTULES BROUGHT ON BY</u>
<u>THE LOCKED-ROOM CURSE APPLIED TO VICE PRINCIPAL</u>
<u>BECKLEY'S OFFICE</u>.

Signed,

Fibula Smith

School Nurse

7:00 P.M.: IVY BARTA, 16, COINS

BY JESSICA LEWIS

Ivy was in a mess.

Granted, she'd been in a mess ever since she'd solved her old chemistry teacher's murder last year, but this was worse than anything she'd dealt with so far. Getting caught trying to break into Bird's office? Her?! Humiliating. Oh, and of course there was the murder of Dropwort, but all of Ivy's meager sympathy for him had turned into shame at getting caught snooping. Uncle Perry would be so disappointed.

"So let me get this straight." Vice Principal Ladybird Beckley stared at Ivy with steely eyes. "You're not actually a student at Galileo—you're a detective. And you've been spying on our students for Principal Fornax. For the entire term."

"Yes." Ivy tried her best not to fidget. She'd weighed her options earlier and decided that telling the vice principal everything was better than said vice principal accusing her of breaking and entering. But she wasn't so sure that had been the right choice anymore. Not with ole Bird staring her down like she was a rotten piece of meat.

Bird pulled her gaze away to stare at the girl to Ivy's left, Delfina. "And you're saying you translated a note addressed to Professor Dropwort, and there's a firebird egg in the school?"

Delfina nodded, a note clutched tightly in her left hand. Ivy observed that the girl seemed less nervous than annoyed, as if discovering the school's dark secrets had personally offended her. Well, she wasn't ready for everything Ivy knew, she could tell her that.

"And you think Fornax may have something to do with Professor Dropwort's death?"

"It's possible," Ivy said, but she really meant "Yeah, definitely."

Bird was silent, staring down at her hands intently. Ivy took the time to study her surroundings. She'd never been in Bird's office—she was Fornax's hire, and apparently the vice principal hadn't even known of her existence. Interesting that the admin didn't share their secrets. She was disappointed that the office she'd tried to break into (and that had given her horrible, painful pustules) was so normal. Bird's office was decked out in extravagant and lavish decorations, from heavy ornate curtains that blocked out all light, to intricate vases and expensive china locked in a wooden case. She had framed certificates and awards all along one wall; Ladybird Beckley was everywhere in the room. Some certificates had "Ladybird Amboise" on them instead. A maiden name? Either way, she was quite proud of herself. Nothing wrong with a little pride, of course, but Ivy knew that that sort of thing was motive for more than a few cases she'd solved.

Bird suddenly stood up, startling Ivy out of her observation. "This is serious, girls. Ivy, you were trying to break into Fornax's office to secure evidence, correct?" When Ivy nodded, Bird smiled, a wide one that didn't quite reach her eyes. "I think we should continue that mission."

Delfina gasped in disbelief, but Ivy's eyebrows just rose a few inches. She wasn't opposed to old-fashioned B and E to get to the truth and satisfy her gut. That's what she'd been trying to do anyway. But usually that was something she and her Uncle Perry did, under the cover of darkness and with his coward's teeth chattering in her ear. Usually vice principals weren't approving of their methods.

"Really?" Delfina's voice was full of surprise and dread. "We're just going to break in?"

"Of course." Bird strode to the door, like she would leave them behind if they didn't hurry. "Ivy's allegations are serious. We need to confirm his part in Professor Dropwort's death."

Delfina glanced at Ivy. Ivy met her eyes. She knew Delfina wasn't a detective, but she wondered if her classmate was feeling the same thing she was . . .

Something wasn't right.

Nevertheless, Ivy followed Bird out of her office and across the hall to Fornax's office. She could figure out the vice principal's weird behavior later—Ivy first had to figure out if Fornax was the murderer after all. Delfina caught up with Ivy, muttering curses under her breath.

"You can leave, Delfina," Bird told her. "I will need your assistance, though, Miss Barta."

"No way," Delfina said, a little too loudly. She cleared her throat. "Sorry, I just mean, I want to come with you. Just to see if it's true."

Ivy could admire that. Delfina was curious, something that had ruined Ivy's life continuously for over a year now. Maybe Delfina was interested in becoming a detective . . . ! That would be very cool, since Ivy was usually alone and no one could understand her explanations without her writing them down—

"This is so nuts," Delfina muttered. "How'd you get wrapped up in this anyway, Ivy?"

Now *that* was a loaded question. How could Ivy tell her that she'd been at home, minding her own business, when suddenly a private school had written her a letter, wanting to hire her to spy on some rich, spoiled kids and their crooked admin? *We have reviewed your talents and hope you'll be interested . . . blah, blah.* You solve *one* little murder in your spare time and everyone's breathing down your neck all of a sudden. She'd thrown the letter into the trash. And the next one. And the one after that. But when the fourth letter had come in the form of an owl who'd then transformed into an irritated short white man, Ivy had known she was in trouble.

Galileo Academy for the Extraordinary not-so-politely requested that she join them. She tried to say no, but Uncle Perry (who she had the misfortune of putting up with after her parents decided to take a trip to Paris and just not come back, the lucky bastards) was so delighted. What the hell was Ivy supposed to do at a private school? A magic private school at that! She'd been born with the ability to do spells and whatever, but no one else in her family had a lick of magic, so she'd never even held a wand before. She said no, obviously, but then they offered her a fat paycheck. And, well, it was a lot harder to say no after that. She was still waffling, but then Uncle Perry threw a tantrum and said she had to go or else he was gonna give her collection of shoes away.

A low blow, even for him. A girl couldn't even have one thing to herself. Jesus. But, hey, with the amount they were paying her, she could just buy her own shoes. And a house far away from Uncle Perry and Paris and this infernal school. And Ivy thought she could learn some cool magic tricks to help with the detective work. So she took the job, vaguely hopeful, but honestly it was a nightmare. Fornax told her to spy on the students and secretly report to him any major transgressions so they could be dealt with "in house." Ominous wording, but Ivy did her best. Still, most of it was painfully boring. Julius cheating on his exams, Mac skipping class to brew illegal potions in his room, Greta sneaking a dragon onto school grounds. Annoying, petty stuff she didn't bother to report but couldn't help noticing. Learning about Dropwort's smuggling was moderately intriguing, but even as she meticulously gathered evidence against him, it wasn't really worth all the trouble of buying new clothes and moving to a new school. And then her moderately interesting mark had to get murdered.

Remember the "solving one murder" thing? Well, guess what? Now they wanted her to do it again. At least, that was what she thought they'd want. But after she heard about Dropwort's death, she popped up at Fornax's office, ready to blow an actual interesting case wide open . . . and he told her to forget it. He was sweating like a pig when he said that too, and didn't look her in the eye. Let the police handle it, he said. That's when her alarm bells went off. If the police were so trustworthy, why had he gone through the trouble of bullying her into spying for him? Wasn't it he who'd said that the reputation of the school had to be protected no matter what? Oh no, there was something else afoot, something big, as her gut told her. The gut never lied. And curse her curiosity, but she couldn't let that go. So, she spent the day rummaging and sleuthing and ruining her new Jordans in gargoyle drool. An absolute nightmare. Had to yell at a kid for starting a random fire at five in the morning; and then the classroom holding Dropwort's body *hexed* her (she'd be scarred for life, literally and figuratively, from a hex that caused her to hear screaming in her ears for an hour and a half.) And *then* she had to question a kid about a suspicious knife, which went nowhere. And of course old Bird's office hexed her again, with pustules. Hell, absolute hell. All the clues were coming together, and her gut was nearly satisfied, but her brain, body, and new shoes were weeping. God, why couldn't she just have stayed at public school?

Delfina stared at her, and Ivy realized she hadn't said anything for a full minute. She didn't have time to explain her life story to this girl. They were at Fornax's office, waiting for Bird to finish doing whatever to the door. No time for life stories. They had to hurry.

"I'll tell you later, okay? I would do it now, but—"

"Shh!" Bird hissed at them as she fiddled with Fornax's door. "No noise. I need to concentrate."

Ivy and Delfina watched as Bird muttered a chant and the area around the door glowed bright red. She tried the door and . . . nothing happened.

"That's not good, right?" Delfina glanced anxiously from Ivy to Bird, who was trying a number of spells to unlock the door, none of which was making any impact.

"Vice Principal Beckley? Can I try?" Ivy smiled at Bird, and she backed away, a dark look on her face. Ivy tugged at the golden doorknob. Locked. She tried her secret magic key that was reserved just for her . . . but that didn't work either. Why would he lock his office if he had nothing to hide? Not looking good for you, Fornax.

"What now?" Delfina asked. She glanced nervously behind them.

"No problem," Ivy said cheerfully, and rummaged in her backpack for her student ID. Both Delfina and Bird looked a little horrified as she slipped the card into the space between the door and the lock, and popped the door open with a few jiggles of the card.

"Magic makes y'all lazy," Ivy told them, stuffing the ID into her backpack. "All sorts of magic wards on it, but no one springs for a dead bolt. Pitiful."

Ivy opened the door, and Fornax's office swung into view. It looked the same way it always did, his messy desk full of papers, the massive stained-glass window covered by a blackout curtain. She'd been in there a ton of times, listening to his boring lectures about nonsense she didn't care about. Bird breezed past them as Ivy dug into her backpack again, this time for latex gloves. She wished she still had her silk gloves that made her look supercool, but they'd been ruined by Dropwort's sandy bloodstains earlier, so RIP to them. The sooner she got done with this case the better. She passed a pair to Delfina and put some on herself. "Have to be careful! Can't mess up evidence! Do you want some, Vice Principal Beckley?"

Ivy paused, observing Bird's behavior. She was ruthlessly rummaging in Fornax's desk, scattering papers everywhere. The evidence! "Bird, stop! You're destroying potential evidence!"

The vice principal froze, looking up at Ivy like she'd forgotten the girl was there. "Oh, I'm sorry. I was careless. Wait, did you just call me 'Bird'?"

"I'll help you check the desk!" Ivy offered, ignoring that last part. She let Delfina give Bird the gloves while she scanned the desk. Detention forms, confusing-looking admin paperwork, half-eaten snacks. All normal. The lower left-hand drawer was annoyingly rummaged through, thanks to Bird. Even non-detectives should know you can't just throw shit everywhere when you investigate! Uncle Perry would have had a heart attack. Ivy carefully put everything back in place as she remembered it (which she was pretty confident in), and then wandered to the filing cabinets near the door. Delfina was staring into a potted plant, which normally Ivy would disapprove of, but who knew what could be hiding in a magic school?

Ivy was halfway through the B last names when Bird gasped. "Oh my goodness! Look at this!"

Ivy turned, surprised. Bird was standing next to the desk again, but this time she clutched an ornately decorated egg. "The firebird egg?"

"And the Fabergé egg," Delfina gasped. "It's beautiful."

Bird's face was grim and her mouth was a thin line. But Ivy watched her eyes carefully. They didn't seem nearly as distraught as the rest of her expression. "Ivy, you were right. Principal Fornax must have killed Dropwort to get to this."

"Or took it off the body after he killed him," Ivy said, but she wasn't really paying attention. How had she missed an egg in the desk? "Where'd you find it?"

"It was right here, next to these." Bird motioned to the desk, now holding a pair of silver-studded black leather gloves. Ivy came to her side and paused. The left-hand drawer was wide open. The same one Ivy had carefully examined after Bird had rummaged through it a few minutes ago with no results.

The tingling feeling that Ivy had had earlier—the sense that something was off—came back in full force. Ivy met Delfina's eyes. She'd expected Delfina to be overjoyed by finding evidence, but she was eerily quiet.

"You girls keep looking," Bird babbled, oblivious to their silence. "I'll take these to the SNACC-EOs before any real damage is done. Be right back!"

Ivy watched as Bird scurried from the room, leaving the office wide open. She crossed the room and closed the door carefully with a soft click.

"Delfina," Ivy said, still staring at the door, "something isn't right."

"Yeah," Delfina said. "The plant, right?"

Ivy turned around. "What?"

"What? Oh, sorry, I thought you were talking about this. You go first."

Ivy glanced at the plant Delfina had been staring at earlier. It was just a nondescript fake houseplant as far as she could tell . . . but wait, investigation first. "No, I'm talking about Bird. I didn't see an egg in that desk when I looked."

"Maybe you overlooked it?"

"I'm a detective."

"So . . ." Delfina's eyebrows rose. "What are you saying?"

"Let's back up. Review what we know." Ivy paced the room in a small circle. She rubbed her face with one hand. This was so much more than she was getting paid for. And she might not get paid anyway, because of all the mess they were in. Ivy picked apart the tangle of clues and discoveries in her head so she could form a half-decent explanation. "So, you know Dropwort died, right?"

"Right."

"He was murdered. I mean, obviously. That guy was too mean to die on his own. But that also means a lot of people wanted to kill him, huh?" Ivy paced faster, her mind whirring with clues and evidence and two administrators' suspicious behavior. "It's all connected. The egg, Dropwort, Fornax. Maybe Bird, but I haven't confirmed that yet."

She wasn't making sense. Delfina was silent, confusion all over her face. Ugh. Ivy hated this part. Uncle Perry was always good at the explanations, which was why she'd *told* him she wouldn't be good at this—

"Okay. Let me back up. Dropwort equals dead. But the big question is why, right? I've been investigating him for months, and I turned up some real unpleasant stuff. Smuggling, specifically, which is really lucrative if you know the right people. Jewelry, ancient artifacts—"

"And priceless Fabergé eggs," Delfina said, understanding dawning on her.

"Yes!" A surge of gratitude filled Ivy's chest. Maybe Delfina could follow her explanation. Usually she had to write it all down for the cops to get it. "And I just got done telling Fornax about the smuggling. Had a whole PowerPoint and everything. And he seemed real interested, thanked me, and I thought it was all done and I could concentrate on not failing physics. But then BAM! Dropwort drops dead. So now my job's even harder, because I gotta find out who killed him."

Ivy shifted from foot to foot, getting excited. Delfina was listening closely, actually following what she was saying! That never happened!

"But Fornax didn't want me to see the body. Why not? He knows I'm a detective. He's the one who hired me. So I'm suspicious now, and I sneak into one of the classrooms to see the body anyway. Had to do all kinds of spells and shit, you wouldn't believe . . . Anyway, I saw the wounds, and they were made by something thin and sharp, maybe a knife, maybe not. But the interesting thing is that there was sand all around the wound."

"Sand?" Delfina's frown deepened.

"I know, that's what I said! This girl Keturah showed me sand all over the loading docks, where they found him, and the same sand's outside the Gargoyle Keep, where there's evidence of a scuffle. So I do some more digging, and there's this poison—"

"Hourglass." Delfina's voice was a hushed whisper. "No way. It's banned all over the world."

Ivy was stunned into starstruck silence. No one had ever interrupted her explanation and finished her deduction. She had to convince Delfina to be her detective partner. Or maybe marry her. Ivy cleared her throat, scrambling to get back on track. "Yes, it's illegal, but that doesn't matter. That's what the evidence says, so we have to follow it. Hourglass turns the blood to sand, so that's where the sand around the wounds had to come from. Would love a forensics team to confirm that, but gotta work with what we got and all that."

"But why stab him if he's being poisoned?"

"Bingo bango, however that saying goes. If you're a murderer, you don't need to kill Dropwort two different ways. Then how does a stabbing and a poisoning make sense?"

Delfina frowned. "Maybe the murderer was just being careful?"

"I don't know yet. But I'm saying there's more to this case. Just have to figure everything out." Ivy stopped, a little winded. Delfina had made it all the way through her explanation! She was kind of moved. Maybe Delfina really had major detective potential. Which reminded her—"What was that about the plant?"

"Oh yeah, come here." Delfina led Ivy to the plant, which looked like an ordinary plastic plant. "Doesn't it look weird to you?"

"Uh . . ." No, it really did not. "What kind of weird are we talking?"

"It's plastic, but it's wet around the bottom. See?" Delfina pointed to the bottom, and sure enough, dark patches of water stained the bottom of it.

Wait, water, right? Ivy touched the substance, but it wasn't water. It was a sticky blue residue, almost grainy in texture. "What is this? And why is Fornax watering a plastic plant?"

"I think it might be that stuff we learned about in potions. Glamour, right? It hides stuff."

Ivy looked at Delfina, stunned for the second time that day. "You're some kind of genius, aren't you?"

Delfina laughed, a deep sound from her gut. "No, I just pay attention in class. You're always asleep!"

True, because when was she ever going to need a potion as a detective? Though this proved how wrong she was about that. "Okay, how do we get rid of the glamour?"

Delfina studied the blue goo closely. "I think we just have to move the plant. This is almost dry, so the glamour effects should be weak."

Ivy nodded, readjusted her gloves, and tugged at the base of the plant. It was *way* heavier than it looked, which made it even more suspicious. Ivy tugged one more time, and when she dragged it a few inches to the left, there was a loud pop. The plant disappeared in Ivy's hands. And in its place . . .

. . . was a girl, bound with tight rope and gagged.

"Huh," Ivy said as Delfina gasped and the tied-up girl's eyes widened. "Well, this is a surprise."

Delfina rushed to untie her, but Ivy took a moment to observe. She was a short Black girl, hair in twin puffs on either side of her head. She was wearing a strange gray shirt made out of a material Ivy had never seen before. Her shoes (which were red with black lightning bolts on the side and *so* cool, holy shit Ivy needed some immediately) were dirty, and a bit sandy. Ivy had never seen her before, and though Ivy was terrible with names, she hardly ever forgot a face. Curiosity tugged at her gut. *Interesting.*

Delfina finished with her wrists, and the girl rubbed them, wincing. The skin under her hands was raw and red. Probably been there for hours. Or struggling for hours. If she'd been there that long, that meant Fornax might be coming back soon . . . and they did not need to be there when that happened. Ivy glanced at her watch—7:48. Surely he'd be on his way back soon. Or Bird. And both of them weren't the people Ivy wanted to see. This was not ideal at all.

"You could help, you know," Delfina grumbled at Ivy, shaking her from her thoughts.

"Sorry." Ivy leaned down and untied the girl's ankles while Delfina ungagged her.

"Thanks," the girl said as soon as she could talk. She coughed, a harsh, throaty sound. She should probably go to the nurse after this, just in case. If Fornax or Bird didn't catch and kill them all, of course. "Who are you? How'd you know I was here?"

"Delfina's a genius," Ivy said, tugging the knots loose. They'd been hastily tied. Sloppy. She was starting to think this imprisonment hadn't been planned. "We came to see if Fornax is a murderer, but he's definitely a kidnapper!"

Delfina frowned at Ivy. "Sorry, I know this is a lot. I'm Delfina; she's Ivy. What's your name?"

The girl seemed a little rattled but answered anyway. "I'm Sydney. What were you saying about the murder?"

"Long story, but a guy died, and something's funny about this case. Which reminds me, I was so weirded out by Bird and the egg, I didn't find anything to prove Fornax was behind this. . . ." Ivy crossed her arms, staring at Fornax's wooden cuckoo clock. "We don't have forever. Either one'll be back soon. Although, Fornax didn't kill you, so that's a plus. We could maybe plead for our lives if he gets here first. But the bigger question is *why* didn't he kill you?"

"Don't mind her," Delfina said to Sydney. "She's a detective. It's not personal."

"Yeah . . . ," Sydney said, but she looked like she wanted to be anywhere else.

"Why'd he tie you up? And make you look like a plant?" Delfina asked. Ivy listened while she pulled out fresh latex gloves from her backpack. Delfina really was a good partner. Ivy didn't even have to ask her to help gather witness statements! Though finding evidence of Fornax's behavior was more important, maybe Sydney could reveal something too.

"I don't know. I don't know what's going on. I'm not from this dimension—long story. I was chasing a perl named Uno—and I ran into this Fornax guy. He started talking, and I couldn't move. It was awful. He said something about needing a body?"

Ivy gaped at Sydney. "A different dimension? Are you serious? Tell me more. Tell me everything."

"Focus, Ivy," Delfina muttered.

Ivy's gut was going haywire. She *had* to know about this different dimension where they had soft-looking gray shirts and hella cool shoes. But murder first. Ivy took a deep breath, the facts running through her brain. Fornax had something to hide, and he was in a hurry. Sydney had to be an accident; there's no way he could have predicted that an inter-dimensional traveler would be looking for her lizard-cat today. But then, what did he want with her anyway? He could have let her go. Maybe he was feeling the pressure. Maybe he thought a convenient inter-dimensional traveler would make a good fall guy if things got sticky. Oh, now that was interesting indeed.

"I don't know if it'll help," Sydney said, still rubbing her wrists, "but I've been here all day, and there's been a ton of people coming in and out. Cops were doing interviews or something? I guess I know why now, the murder. But anyway, the guy who jumped me put a little camera up there." Sydney pointed directly above her. Ivy gasped; it was disguised as a housefly.

"Delfina—"

"On it." Delfina practically ran to the computer on Fornax's desk.

"Won't it have a password?" Sydney asked.

"They're all on a sticky note. In the first drawer." Ivy smiled when Delfina withdrew a pink sticky note full of ink. "I saw them earlier. What a dummy. And he made *me* go to cyber-security training!"

Delfina didn't answer, probably engrossed in the video footage. Ivy normally would hover over her, scanning for a crumb of evidence, but her gut told her to trust Delfina. She had this. So, Ivy would make herself useful elsewhere.

"Sydney, will you act as lookout?" Ivy didn't wait for her to answer before starting her search. She rooted around on top of his desk (gum, some magical pain reliever, pens), in the drawers (paperwork, her own report on Dropwort), and finally in his closet. She picked through each piece of clothing meticulously, until she found a heavy black coat hidden at the back. It was a soft texture, expensive . . . and had sand all over it, and a gargoyle tooth snagged in one of the button holes. Bingo bango.

Ivy emerged from the closet, gut singing with happiness. Here it was—solid proof. The sand had to be from Dropwort's hourglass-poisoned blood, and gargoyle teeth didn't appear out of thin air! Ivy practically wanted to dance. "Delfina, I think Fornax killed Dropwort."

"Yeah, me too," Delfina said. "Well, I know he did."

Ivy was taken aback. Had she seen the coat? No, Delfina's eyes were glued to the monitor. Ivy carefully draped the coat over a chair and joined her at the computer. Sydney was on her other side, which annoyed Ivy a little. She needed to be lookout.

A grainy black-and-white video was playing on Fornax's monitor. "I couldn't find the footage from that camera, but I found this. It's from the Gargoyle Keep."

Weird that Fornax had access to security footage, but she'd seen worse. "Okay, what's on it?"

Delfina just pressed play, her mouth set in a grim line. Ivy watched as Dropwort appeared on the grainy screen, checking his watch and cradling something that looked suspiciously like a firebird egg. Delfina skipped ahead a few seconds, and stopped when another figure joined him. Tall, gaunt, wearing a very nice black coat . . . Ivy's stomach sank. She knew what she was about to see.

There was no audio on the video, so the only sounds in the office were tense breathing and the ominous tick of Fornax's clock as the two figures argued, and Dropwort shoved Fornax, and Fornax withdrew a shiny silver letter opener from Dropwort's own coat pocket. Ivy winced as Fornax plunged the letter opener into Dropwort's chest and streams of sand fell out of the wounds. Dropwort fell, and Fornax just stood above him for a second, seemingly in shock. Then he tossed the letter opener to the side and dragged the body toward one of the loading docks, out of frame. Delfina skipped forward in the recording, and stopped when a curious gargoyle peeked its head into frame. It poked at the sand, but when it noticed the sheen from the letter opener, it grabbed the murder weapon and retreated toward its nest again.

"Well." Ivy paused to collect herself. She never liked seeing the murders; she preferred cleaning up after. It was kind of shocking to see a murder before her eyes. "Your evidence is much better than mine. I feel kind of silly now."

"What do we do?" Sydney chewed on her thumbnail nervously. "That guy who tied me up is a murderer. Like, not a suspect but for real."

"Let me think." Ivy ran through the facts. They had definite, concrete proof Fornax was the murderer. And normally that would be enough, but Ivy's gut sang a warning. There had to be more to it. Fornax was panicked in the video. Dropwort surprised him, there was a struggle, and he stabbed Dropwort. Dropwort had also tied up Sydney to be his fall guy, but he couldn't have predicted that someone from another dimension was coming. If he had been poisoning Dropwort, he'd have had a fall guy all picked out months ago. This whole murder was hasty. Sloppy. Unplanned. Compared with how long it takes to poison someone with hourglass, it just didn't make sense. There were two MOs—one sloppy, panicked stabbing and one meticulous, careful poisoning. They didn't match up in the slightest. Which meant . . .

"I know Fornax stabbed Dropwort, but I don't think he poisoned him," Ivy announced after a full minute of silence. "I think we have two perps."

Delfina raised her eyebrows. "Why do you think that?"

Ivy started to explain, but she shook her head. They had to hurry. "I'll tell you later. Did you find anything else on his computer?"

"Actually, yeah. There's another video of him and the egg." Delfina clicked out of that video and loaded another. It was of one of the loading docks, and a hooded figure appeared on the screen. Ivy leaned closer to the screen, frowning. The figure was wearing a black coat, so it looked like Fornax, but . . .

"This must be him grabbing the egg," Sydney said. All three of them had their noses inches from the screen.

"Why didn't Fornax get it after he killed Dropwort?" Ivy asked.

"Must have forgot it because he was so freaked out?" Delfina said.

Ivy said nothing, watching the video with narrowed eyes. The figure's posture was all wrong; calm, self-assured. They were wearing gloves, and nice leather ones that felt familiar somehow. The figure bent, grabbed the egg, and tucked it under their cloak. Wait a minute—it was a cloak, not a coat. The demeanor, the posture, the clothing were all wrong.

"This isn't Fornax."

Delfina looked at Ivy in surprise. "What? I mean, it's kind of hard to see, but how do you know—"

"Look at the gloves." Ivy was so close to the screen, her vision was slightly out of focus. "There's writing on them."

"Looks like . . . LA?" Sydney said.

LA. Definitely not Fornax's gloves, then. LA . . . Ivy had seen those initials before. She racked her brain, reviewing every detail of the case. Fornax had acted suspiciously, but someone else had too—

"Ladybird Amboise," Ivy said out loud, remembering Bird's certificates in her office. She hadn't found those gloves in Fornax's desk—she'd planted them. "LA is ole Bird."

Delfina gaped at her. "So you think—"

"She's the one in this video? Definitely. I also think she's the one who poisoned Dropwort. That's more of a 'probably,' but my probablies are usually right."

Delfina's eyes were huge. She started to say something, but she was interrupted by a pointed cough. Ivy looked up sharply . . . straight into the cool eyes of Bird herself.

Ivy was stricken. She'd been so engrossed in the computer that she hadn't even heard Bird come in. How long had she been standing there?! Uncle Perry would be so disappointed. And dammit, now she had to outwit a murderer. She was *definitely* not getting paid enough for this.

"Sounds like you girls have stumbled onto something you shouldn't see," Bird said. She looked more annoyed than threatening, but Ivy knew that could change in an instant.

"We can forget it," Ivy said breezily. She met Delfina's eyes briefly; the other girl was clutching a pair of scissors in a tight fist under the desk. Ready to rumble. Ivy hoped it wouldn't come to that, but she was glad Delfina was ready. "We have evidence pinning Fornax. Can't convict two people for killing him."

"But if you kill us, you're definitely going to jail," Delfina said. Her voice trembled, but only a little.

Bird watched them for a few seconds, her sharp eyes boring into the group. Finally she said, "True. But I need you to stay out of the way for a while until I decide what to do."

"We'll just go to our dorms," Ivy said. "Won't tell a soul—"

"Nope." Bird pointed at the corner they'd found Sydney in. "All three of you, sit down right here. You're going to be potted plants for a while."

Delfina clutched the scissors, but Ivy shook her head. It was too dangerous. They outnumbered her, but Sydney was injured and Ivy had the upper body strength of a noodle. Bird was a murderer, which was bad enough, but she was also skilled with magic, and that was something unpredictable and dangerous.

"This is the worst school ever," Sydney muttered under her breath. Still, she followed Bird's instructions and sat in her original place. Bird used magic to tie her wrists and ankles, and stuck duct tape over her mouth. Ivy joined her, smiling up at Bird to (hopefully) inspire some mercy.

"Not too tight, please," Ivy joked. Bird frowned and tied Ivy up the same way she had Sydney, the ropes around her wrists extra tight. Delfina stood at the desk still, hesitating. "Come on, Delfina," Ivy said, looking into her eyes. "I'm sure we'll be fine."

Delfina sighed but joined them. Bird tied her up too, and then smeared disgusting blue goop onto their foreheads. Ivy felt it go from cool to warm in a few seconds, and then Bird smiled down at them.

"Loveliest ferns in the whole school! Now, sit here and be quiet. I'll be back to deal with you later."

Ivy said nothing as Bird ripped Fornax's CPU from under his desk, shrank it to pocket size, and left the office, shutting the door softly behind her. She looked at Sydney's forlorn expression and Delfina's pissed-off one and smiled. Well, she tried to, but it was hard due to the duct tape. She waited a minute more before wriggling her bound wrists to her ankle, where she withdrew a pocketknife. Delfina's eyes widened in surprise while Ivy tried to smile again. Bird was amateur hour; always check your kidnap victims for weapons!

It took Ivy ten minutes to saw through her wrist bindings, but after that it was easy to untie herself, Sydney, and Delfina. Delfina sighed when she eased the tape from her mouth. "This has been the worst day."

"No way! I solved a murder and a poisoning!" They both glared at Ivy, so she laughed awkwardly. "Okay, well, getting tied up sucks. And she took the computer. We can't prove she did the poisoning without it."

"Oh, don't worry about that." Delfina reached into her pocket and withdrew a flash drive with tiny skulls on it. "As soon as I saw that video, I copied it."

Ivy stared at her, starstruck again. "Do you want to get married?"

"What?"

"Nothing. Never mind." Ivy cleared her throat and wiped the goo off her forehead with her sleeve. She felt a slight pressure in her ears, but otherwise felt fine. Not bad for a run-in with a perp. She stood and stretched, then smiled at her budding detective agency. "Let's get out of here and catch some criminals."

CASE ID: 20-06-DROS-STK

<u>Type:</u>
[ ] Communication
[ ] Audio recording
[ ] Spell residue
[ ] Photo or other visual reconstruction
[X] Object
[ ] Form or record
[ ] Other: _____

Source: Ladybird "Birdie" Beckley, vice principal
Relevant Parties: Ladybird "Birdie" Beckley, vice principal; Nicolas Fornax, principal
Description: Gloves planted by Ladybird "Birdie" Beckley in the office of Nicolas Fornax

[IMAGE: a pair of black leather gloves with a pattern of metallic silver rings on them, emblazoned with the initials LA]

8:00 P.M.: LUPITA AUGRATRICIS, 16, COINS

BY NATASHA DÍAZ

You don't have much time, Lupita. Lupita's great-grandfather's voice, ripe with tobacco and hibiscus tea, ran through her mind as Lupita's secrets stitched themselves together, preparing to turn her inside out.

No shit, Sherlock, Lupita thought.

I can hear you, Lupita.

"Sorry," she whispered.

Her great-grandpa might have taken his last breath over a hundred years ago, but in Lupita's world, you never disrespected an elder.

Focus, Pa commanded.

Focus. Under normal circumstances, Professor Dropwort's death would have been good news. He had been a black-finned beetle in Lupita's butt since her first day as a Galileo student, but there hadn't been a celebration; instead she'd been casing the halls of the orbiting campus to find what he had taken from her before it was too late. But the sand in the hourglass had just about emptied. No matter how hard she tried to hold on, she had at best an hour before life as she knew it was lost. Even when he was deader than a low-rise jean fad, Dropwort would still be the end of her.

Focus.

The school vibrated around her as she speed-walked through the Coins lounge and up the stairs. Lupita slowed as she turned the corner to Dropwort's office. Someone was crouched before his door, blocking her entry. Lupita inched closer; she didn't have time for this. She had a plan:

1. Break into the office.
2. Find what had been taken from her.
3. Get back to her dorm and hope she did it before anyone figured out the truth.

The plan had not accounted for anyone else at Dropwort's doorstep, but she would have to turn this roadblock into a shortcut. Whoever was trying to break into Dropwort's office was going to get her in as well.

"Ahem." Lupita announced herself, but she barely had time to finish clearing her throat before Vice Principal Ruiz-Marín had her wand pointed directly at the tip of Lupita's nose.

"Lupita?" The vice principal released her fighter stance as recognition dawned.

"Vice Principal Ruiz-Marín . . . what are you doing here?"

"I was . . . well, just standing guard, of course. I could ask you the same question."

Lupita's brain was already half-scrambled, but even through the fog, she couldn't make sense of what the vice principal was saying. Lola had been taken into custody as the prime suspect in Dropwort's murder. If the killer had been caught, why would anyone need to stand guard?

"I heard a suspect was in custody already—Lola?"

Lupita had heard a lot more than that as she'd loped through the school all day. Her classmates weren't convinced the authorities had arrested the right person, and she was inclined to agree. If she'd had a moment, she might have investigated further; there was nothing that made Lupita's blood boil more than innocent people being punished for crimes they didn't commit. Anyone could have wanted Dropwort gone, but Lola didn't seem the type.

The vice principal placed a hand on her hip, looking Lupita up and down. "Well, yes, but frankly, that isn't your concern. Now, I am going to ask you again. What is it that *you* are doing here?"

"I . . . uh . . . just came to pay my respects." Lupita spoke slowly to keep herself calm. She had to get inside Dropwort's office; she shuddered at what might happen if she didn't.

"Is that so?" Ruiz-Marín asked with a curious nod. "I never got the impression you were such a fan of his."

As much as Lupita wished she could make the vice principal disappear, she couldn't help but admire how stunningly fierce she looked in her electric-blue pantsuit. The truth was, she liked Vice Principal Ruiz-Marín; everyone at Galileo did. She listened to the students. She cared about their interests more than climbing the ladder of academia. Under any other circumstance, Lupita might have gone to Ruiz-Marín for help—but not with this. It wasn't worth the risk.

"Oh. Well, you know, a tragedy is a tragedy. A few of us planned to hold a vigil here tonight. Like, right now." Lupita bit her lip to keep the flames inside her from bursting out.

"Lupita, you heard the announcement. Everyone is to wait for questioning."

"Perhaps if you just open the door . . . I need to pay my respects!" Lupita felt the panic in her voice leap out.

Vice Principal Ruiz-Marín straightened herself, adding a couple of inches to her height, and raised her eyebrows even higher.

"Are you all right, Lupita? You look unwell."

"Uhh, I'm . . ." Lupita reached into her back pocket for her wand, begging for a miracle of strength. Overpowering such a skilled Sorcerer would be practically impossible, but the vice principal was giving her no other choice but to try.

"There you are!" Lupita and Ruiz-Marín turned to find Beth Andromeda, Lupita's roommate, otherwise known as the ingrown hair personified that, no matter the amount of tweezing and steaming, always grew back with a vengeance. Beth was racing toward them with such haste, you would think a ring-tailed lynx had caught her scent.

"What now?!" Ruiz-Marín burst out. If she caught on to what Lupita was up to, there was no telling what could happen.

Keep your wits about you, Lupita; that man is dead, but he is not worth dying for, her pa cautioned from inside her mind.

Lupita stepped between them before Beth could do or say anything.

"The vigil, right?" Lupita spoke so loudly, she was practically shouting. "Rescheduled apparently. Sorry to bother you, Vice Principal!"

"Whaaa—?" Beth began to ask, but Lupita dragged her away.

"Aghh!" Lupita bent over as soon as the door to the stairwell shut. A pain coursed through her, so sharp and powerful that she had to count her breaths to keep her body from exploding like a firecracker. There was only one last option—to give in to her fate and hope she wasn't found. At this point, it would be a miracle if Lupita even made it back to her room in time. But if she did, she could hide. Maybe once the commotion died down, she could find a way into Dropwort's office and get back what he had taken from her. Protect her secret. But for now, she had to disappear.

"Lupita!" Beth cried out.

Quicker than she knew she had the energy for, Lupita jumped up and covered Beth's mouth with her hand.

"Whatever it is, Beth, just drop it, okay?" Lupita spoke through gritted teeth. "And find somewhere else to sleep tonight."

Lupita turned on her heel and left Beth in the stairwell. She walked into the Coins lounge. The ornate room was brimming with nervous teenagers. Lupita couldn't deny that despite the pain and panic she was suffering, the chaos unraveling around her was welcome. Dropwort's death had broken a levee of secrets across the orbiting campus, and she felt comfort in knowing that for once she wasn't the only one looking over her shoulder, wondering if she had been figured out. As long as everyone was preoccupied with the murder, her secret was safe . . . but how long until someone uncovered what Dropwort had taken from her? How long until everyone was searching for *her*?

"Lupita!" Upon hearing her name, Lupita turned to Beth, red-faced and determined, marching toward her. "We need a plan."

"There is no 'we,'" Lupita snapped. "What I need is in that office, and now I can't get to it."

"That's the thing! It isn't!"

"What? How do you—"

"That's why I came to find you. Apparently all the confiscated items have been moved to his classroom, and students will be able to recover what he stole in the morning."

Lupita froze. She had never lived with a roommate at Galileo until this year, when Beth had shown up at her doorstep after a mix-up with the registrar. The start had been rocky, what with Beth mistaking "roommate" for "friend" and Lupita having to give her the cold shoulder, but she had been careful. So how did Beth know what she needed? But before she could ask, Beth chimed in.

"Us living together wasn't a mistake—I requested you. I've been trying to tell you all year! You weren't the only one avoiding Dropwort outside the physics lab once a month, Lupita. I know you have this whole 'I'm a grumpy loner saving the world' vibe, but you need someone on your side. Trust me."

Trust was the only thing Lupita had never learned how to fake. It was why she had no friends. No confidants. But Beth knew about the lab. She knew what Dropwort had taken from her just hours before he'd died. If Beth was the same as Lupita, it would mean there were *more* of her. It meant that there was someone else who understood what it meant to straddle the line between two worlds every single day. It meant that maybe Lupita wasn't as alone as she'd thought she was.

Focus, Lupita! Pa's cry in her head brought her back. None of this would matter if she was arrested . . . or worse.

A sharp pain struck her, and Lupita fell into Beth's arms as her ribs fractured slowly, like ice cubes floating up through a cup of warm soda. Lupita could feel the eyes of their classmates on her back; people were starting to take notice.

If Beth was right, perhaps Lupita could still fix this. But if she was going to make it, she had to go now.

"Beth. Go back to the dorm room."

"But—"

"Beth, I don't know if this will work, but it's the best chance I've got, and I wouldn't have it without you, really. I just can't put you at more risk than I already have. If I'm not back in the room in twenty minutes, go find Vice Principal Ruiz-Marín. Tell her everything. Promise?"

Lupita waited for Beth to nod in agreement, and then without another word, she ran.

By the time Lupita made it to Dropwort's classroom, she was in agony, but no one was around to see her writhe. No one stood guard outside the classroom. Not so much as a carriage-mouse or a flicker-fly kept watch. The silence was her only audience when the door swung open after just a few minutes of magical maneuvering. It was too easy, too perfect, she knew, but she had no other options.

"Maybe, for the first time, the universe is looking out for

me," she half whispered, half prayed as she lifted one foot to cross the threshold into the room.

Lupita! No! her pa shouted from within her just as a hand reached out from the dark classroom and pulled her inside.

"Lupita Augratricis," said a familiar voice. "I thought I might be seeing you tonight, what with the full moon and all."

"Who are you?" Lupita cried, but it was too late. The moment the door closed, her head began to swim. Her skin began to tear. The pain was blazing, but instead of stars, all Lupita saw was the bright full moon. And as she resigned herself to the shift, everything went black.

The werewolves had been deemed illegal more than two centuries ago, after Sorcerers betrayed the peace treaty that had been agreed upon by all the species and coordinated a global attack on the werewolves, determined to exterminate them all. But they didn't succeed, and the wolves who escaped lived in hiding, dependent on the Lualoba elixir to prevent their turning, passing as Neutrals among those whose parents and grandparents and great-grandparents had wanted them dead. Within Lupita's secret community, it was forbidden for werewolves to mingle with Sorcerers beyond what was necessary to survive; for centuries the wolves abided by this rule, until one fell in love with a Sorcerer and made Lupita.

Brash, unbothered, too smart for her own good, leather-ankle-boot-wearing even in the hottest of summers to cover the pawprint birthmark with four claws on the side of her foot. Lupita.

Half happenstance, half romance. Half wolf, half Sorcerer. Half creature, half conjurer. Half midnight, half moonlight. Hidden in plain sight, carrying the weight of her history on the shoulders of her faded silk jacket. Passing as a Sorcerer to infiltrate and broker the wolves' much-deserved peace. To free the rest of her pack to stand in the shadow of the stars and howl. To mourn those lost in the genocide. To be together on the patches of the universe that had been stolen from them.

Well, that had been the plan, until Dropwort had figured her out.

Pasty, hateful-ass, uncultured-ass, tight-ass, decrepit-ass, crooked-ass Dropwort.

He hated the wolves for existing at all. For desecrating the earth. For daring to have power of any kind, even if they had never intended to share what they had with anyone but themselves. He'd been on Lupita's case from the start. Making his snide remarks, trying his best to catch her with anything that could bring truth to his suspicions.

Lupita!

Pa's voice only spread the flame inside her. If it weren't for the Dropworts of the world, she would have more than just a disembodied voice popping up at the most inopportune times. She would know how to relish the pain she was now convulsing under.

Lupita!

The magnitude of her purpose could at times be insurmountable. Everyone rushed around Lupita worried about themselves, about their studies, their love lives, their grades. She was worried about saving a part of the world.

Lupita!

Under normal circumstances, the cry that whipped through Lupita's head would have barely registered, but not tonight. Thanks to Dropwort, who'd finally caught her as she'd rushed out of the physics lab the night before the full moon and confiscated her Lualoba, tonight the cry echoed from the back of her throat to her ear tips. A warning. A cloak of danger that wrapped itself around her neck. An itch in that unreachable spot at the center of her spine. A cloying, festering, unshakable scream. The deepest howl.

"Lupita."

When Lupita opened her eyes, she was no longer standing in the hallway outside Dropwort's classroom—she was sitting on the floor in front of his desk. The pain as her body transformed should have been enough to knock her out again, but something strange kept her lucid: her body was frozen. Lupita tried with all her might to rise from her seated position, but when she peered down, her hands, now half paw, sat motionless in her lap. The elixir had kept her wolf at bay for years, but she knew what it meant to turn—and this was not part of the process.

Footsteps interrupted Lupita's thoughts as Vice Principal Beckley revealed herself. She winced at the sight of Lupita mid-transformation. "A Binding spell," she explained, pointing to Lupita's immobile limbs. "In your state, I couldn't take any chances, you understand, but we mustn't worry about such trivial things. I want to help you, Lupita. That's why I am here."

"You do?" For the first time, Lupita felt hope.

"Of course! I know how it feels to be discriminated against.

They laughed at the idea of a female professor when I started. You couldn't imagine what I've been through. I could tell you stories that would make your fur mat."

Beckley preached at Lupita, waving her finger in her face, and began to pace a few feet in front of her.

"I personally don't see the big deal about wolves. You should have heard Dropwort go on at the holiday parties—he was obsessed. They always are, aren't they? These mediocre Sorcerers clinging so desperately to the past and the power they once wielded . . . Anyway, best not to talk ill of the dead. I marched against the injustice your kind face; I'm on your side. That Dropwort, well, I can understand how he pushed buttons. It's what he deserved. We both know that. We can get ahead of this."

"What—what do you mean?" Lupita stammered.

Beckley reached into her pocket and placed the vial in the open air so that it hovered inches from where Lupita sat. The unmistakable glow of the moon on the sea. The Lualoba. Her elixir. She went to reach for it but then remembered she couldn't move at all.

"This is what you came here for, is it not? The proof Dropwort had been searching for that proved illegal wolves still roamed our world. The threat to you and no doubt countless others you know are hiding. Tsk, tsk, tsk. You had no choice but to kill him." Beckley shook her head as her tongue clicked against her teeth.

"What? No. No! They already arrested—"

"I know, but it would seem they did not find the right suspect," Beckley said, cutting her off. "I'm going to make sure they do."

Lola was innocent! That was why Ruiz-Marín was outside

Dropwort's office. She was trying to figure out who the real killer was. . . .

"You see, Lupita, they will go easier on you if you come clean. I can vouch for you—lessen the sentence."

"Please! If you just give me some time, I can figure this out. I'm innocent, I swear! I just need to make it to the next moon."

"I have heard the process of turning can boggle the brain. It makes sense that you would be confused, but I can help you, Lupita. Perhaps we can write it all down so you have your story straight."

"It wasn't me, Vice Principal Beckley. You have it wrong."

Beckley twitched with frustration at Lupita's pushback.

"I've figured it out it down to the final minute. Quite the clever ruse, if I do say so myself, but not clever enough. Dropwort stabbed by the silver letter opener—"

"I didn't stab anyone," Lupita protested, but Beckley spoke louder.

"That triggered the poison YOU gave him to protect YOUR lies—"

"Vice Principal Beckley, please! If you want to help me, you have to believe me. I didn't do this!"

"And on the eve of the full moon, no less! Lupita, it could be no one else! You are making this harder for yourself than it needs to be. Do you take me for a fool?"

"Of course not, but what you are saying isn't true! It's a good story, I will give you that, but it is not mine."

"ENOUGH!" Beckley roared, and sent Dropwort's chair into the chalkboard in a rage. "Constantly undermined and disregarded by the staff, by you children, who think you know better than everyone else."

A school-wide announcement from Vice Principal Ruiz-Marín echoed through the room and interrupted Beckley's tirade. "This is a reminder to students that we will be departing shortly. All students must remain inside their dorm tower for the rest of the evening."

"I will not debate this any longer, Lupita. Whether you remember or not, I have told you what happened. You will not take this moment from me."

The fire and desperation in Beckley's eyes finally made sense. After all these years of hiding who she truly was, if there was one thing Lupita knew, it was what it looked like when someone was covering for themself. Lupita could beg and try to reason with her all she wanted, but it didn't matter. Beckley wasn't trying to help. She knew Lupita was innocent.

"You will come with me, Augratricis, and you will do so quietly . . ."

Beckley's tirade faded into the background as Lupita tuned her out. She felt the hope seep out of her with every labored breath she exhaled. The pain was too much. The exhaustion was too much. She had been caught, exposed. Beth would carry on for her, for them. For all the wolves. While Beckley continued to rant, Lupita scooted under the desk and hugged her knees. She felt her paw's fur on her cheek as she lowered her head, resigned—

"Oh!" Lupita gasped quietly, covering her mouth as she regained control of her body. Beckley's Binding spell must have only worked if she held her focus, and right now, she was having a Neutral-at-the-department-store-level tantrum. Lupita could move, but to where?

Pa, I'm scared. I don't know what to do. Please help me, Lupita begged inside her heart.

If they can hear, they will listen.

What does that mean?! she cried with her thoughts, hoping an ancestor could read the room and give a prophecy that was a little clearer.

If they can hear, they will listen, he repeated, echoing from every corner of her body.

Pa, Lupita called within herself again, but he didn't respond.

She was losing control of her body, and time wasn't running out—it was done. If she reached out to grab the elixir, she could take it to slow the turn, but she was already half there. That was all the proof Beckley needed.

Lupita searched through the haze and the hot oil pulsing through her veins. She could run, but she wouldn't make it halfway to her room before she was seen.

She was cornered. This was it.

"I have already alerted the Swedish authorities, Lupita. I don't want to have to tell them you threatened me—that would look very, very bad for you," Beckley warned in a singsong voice.

Focus, she snapped at herself, looking around wildly for an answer. As she did, she banged her head into something cold and hard just under the desktop. Lupita was bracing herself for whatever Beckley was planning to do to her, when her pa repeated himself.

If they can hear, Lupita, they will listen. IF they can hear.

This time, she understood. The speaker system.

The switch to turn it on was pressing against the back of her head. Every professor had access to the speaker system at their desks. It was the only thing that connected the entirety of Galileo, and after years of complaints from professors about echo and feedback, they had upgraded the system so the room where the broadcast came from was the only one that couldn't hear it. If she turned it on and let the school hear the truth, she was giving herself up . . . but maybe that was what she was meant to do. For her whole life the Dropworts and the Beckleys of the world had made her feel like she couldn't be who she was. They were the reason she and her family had been hiding. Well, they might have won in the past, and they might win this time, but they weren't going to take her pride along with them.

Lupita took a deep breath and flipped the switch to activate the broadcast, just as Beckley pulled her from her hiding place. The vice principal materialized a silver bullet at the tip of her wand and pointed it at Lupita's chest.

"There we go. Nice and easy, Lupita."

For the first time in her life, Lupita felt peace. She closed her eyes and swallowed the lump the size of the moon in her throat. She saw her pa beside her and drank in his smile as she counted the cracks in his face, his fur the same shade of the earth as her own mother's. After carrying hundreds of years of grief and strife, she would stand here in her power until the end. If she succeeded, she would do so as her true self. If she failed, she would do so as her true self.

No more hiding. No more pretending. Half heartache, half daybreak. Half chosen, half found. Half yesterday, half tomorrow.

Lupita gathered what little strength she had left from every second of the history that had been stolen from her, and spoke.

"Vice Principal Beckley, let me go. Please. I haven't hurt anyone. Yes, I'm a werewolf, but I'm also a Sorcerer. I have every right to be here, and Dropwort hated that, but I didn't kill him. I'm sure you had a good reason for what you did to Professor Dropwort. I won't tell anyone. I swear I won't—"

Beckley threw her head back with a cackle, unhinged.

"You think anyone will believe you, a filthy werewolf, over me?"

CASE ID: 20-06-DROS-STK

Type:
[X] Communication
[ ] Audio recording
[ ] Spell residue
[ ] Photo or other visual reconstruction
[ ] Object
[ ] Form or record
[ ] Other: _____

Source: School announcement archives
Relevant Parties: Septimius Dropwort (dec.);
Nicolas Fornax, principal; Ladybird "Birdie"
Beckley, vice principal; Fibula Smith, school
nurse; Beatriz Ruiz-Marín, vice principal;
Lupita Augratricis, student
Description: Transcript of school-wide
announcement broadcast to students at 8:23
p.m. from the classroom of Septimius Dropwort
(dec.)

[Beginning of transcript.]

Lupita Augratricis: Vice Principal Beckley,
let me go. Please. I haven't hurt anyone.
Yes, I'm a werewolf, but I'm also a Sorcerer.
I have every right to be here, and Dropwort
hated that, but I didn't kill him. I'm sure
you had a good reason for what you did to
Professor Dropwort. I won't tell anyone. I
swear I won't—

Vice Principal Beckley: [Laughs.] You think
anyone will believe you, a filthy werewolf,
over me? You think *I* made a mistake?

Lupita: Vice—

Beckley: *Vice. Principal.* [Sighs.] That's the
only mistake here. I don't make mistakes. I
clean up Fornax's. I knew—the moment I set foot
in my first class here, I knew it would be
me. Ladybird Amboise was born to be the first
female principal in Galileo's history.

Lupita: Amboise?

Beckley: Maiden name. "Beckley" now. Principal
Ladybird Beckley. They were *supposed* to pick
me! I was supposed to be . . .

Lupita: . . . Chosen.

Beckley: *I* earned it! I gave this school
decades of my life, and the board just—just

435

hands the job to some discount Elon Musk they scraped off the good old boys' club. If I were calling the shots, Dropwort would have been canned months ago, but *nooo,* Fornax wanted *diversity of thought.* What does that even mean?

Lupita: [Slowly.] Nothing. Literally nothing.

Beckley: See! You get it. Do you know how much overtime I clocked mopping up after Dropwort? All the parent complaints, all the arbitrations, all the confiscated property he kept "misplacing"? Turning Galileo into his own personal smuggling hub? It was a full-time job just protecting my—my school's reputation, and that's not what I signed up for. Even the trustees were pissed that Fornax let it get this bad! Do you know how sloppy you have to be for a bunch of rich old white men to get mad at their golden boy?

Lupita: So you *poisoned* him?

Beckley: I resolved an ongoing issue.

Lupita: You could have just turned him in to the police.

Beckley: And make another mess *I'd* have to clean up? Really, Lupita, aren't you here on a scholarship?

Lupita: [Significant, frosty pause.] No.

Beckley: I must be thinking of someone else. Whatever. It wasn't even supposed to be like this. The hourglass was supposed to crystallize in his bloodstream last night. He was showing all the symptoms. I *saw them.* [Sounds of rapid pacing.] He was going to drop dead after dinner. Then I'd find the firebird egg in his possession, Fornax would sink with the scandal, and . . . Oh.

Lupita: What?

Beckley: Fornax. That miserable dunce. Of course. He hired that little spy as my "assistant," and she wound up actually documenting all Dropwort's trash and making a paper trail the school's trustees couldn't ignore. Fornax might have faced a single consequence in life for once, so he panicked. That's why he stabbed Dropwort.

Lupita: You saw the principal stab Dropwort?

Beckley: No, Lupita. *You* saw the principal stab Dropwort. And then you took the firebird egg off Dropwort's body and brought it to Fornax.

Lupita: I don't unders—

Beckley: I think you do. I have two witnesses to say I found the firebird egg in Fornax's office, along with these gloves. LA. . . . Your initials.

Lupita: Ladybird Amboise.

Beckley: Lupita Augratricis.

Lupita: No. I never touched the poison—

Beckley: [Rustle.] This poison? *Oops.* Guess I forgot to fill out the confiscation form when I took it off you. Beatriz will get over it. All you have to do is tell everyone Fornax made you poison Dropwort. You can even play the werewolf card and say Fornax was blackmailing you. You were just keeping your secret safe. It might get you dropped to manslaughter.

Lupita: . . . Or.

Beckley: Or?

Lupita: You're asking me to take the fall for a murder—

Beckley: To do what's *best* for the school—

Lupita: That usually comes with an "or." What if I say no?

Beckley: [Voice shaking.] Th-then I scream and call for help and tell them I was so *scared,* a w-w-werewolf tried to kill me, and— [Voice abruptly steadies.] You'll have a hell of a time arguing them down to manslaughter.

[Silence.]

[Thud.]

Beckley: What did you . . .

Lupita: That wasn't me.

Beckley: Don't lie to me. I saw that book— *Agh!*

[Louder thud.]

Lupita: What's happening?

Beckley: Turn the lights back on. *Right now!*

Lupita: I didn't—the bookcase—

[Sounds of cursing, papers flapping, heavy thumps.]

[Loud crash of furniture.]

[Distant thud.]

Beckley: *I SAID STOP, LUPITA. THAT'S AN ORDER.*

Lupita: It's not me, I swear!

[Wood splintering.]

[Thud, closer.]

Beckley: *ENOUGH!*

[Series of thuds, crash, sound of glass breaking.]

Lupita: The *gargoyles*?!

[Sound of door splintering; muffled thuds.]

Beatriz Ruiz-Marín: Yes, Lupita. Their job—
our job—is to protect our students. Thank you,
Castelli. Amityville Protocol has ceased.
Please return to your normal post.

[Indistinct murmuring of antiquated Italian.
Silence.]

Beckley: Beatriz. I was just . . .

Ruiz-Marín: What? Rehearsing for a play?

Nurse Fibula Smith: Only if it's *Bye Bye Bir—*

Ruiz-Marín: *DON'T.* [Aside.] It's trademarked.
[Louder.] Vice Principal Ladybird Beckley,
there are some officers in the hall who would
like to speak with you. Since you've been
broadcasting this entire chat over the PA
system, I imagine it's going to be a very short
conversation.

Beckley: You don't understand. I'm doing this
school a favor! I'm getting rid of Fornax *and* a
werewolf, and—

[Series of thuds.]

Ruiz-Marín: [Coldly.] Again, Beckley.
The gargoyles are here to protect our
students . . . and you saw what they did to
Professor Dropwort. I suggest you get away from
Lupita before they have to be more encouraging.

<u>Beckley</u>: But I—

[Cone of Silence incantation spoken by Ruiz-Marín.]

<u>Ruiz-Marín</u>: *Out*.

[Thuds accompanying shuffling footsteps out the door.]

<u>Lupita</u>: Can I cut the mic now?

<u>Ruiz-Marín</u>: Yeah. There are going to be some questions, but . . . it's over. You're safe.

[End of transcript.]

FROM THE OFFICE OF THE PRINCIPAL

To the new students of Galileo Academy
for the Extraordinary:

When I first came to Galileo, the school board called it an institution. They were so proud of their traditions, their rich history, the long lineages of their faculty; they boasted of the elite, the chosen, the boys who walked their halls and emerged as leaders among men. But they were too enamored of their institution to consider the shadow it cast on others. They forgot how, and why, it was founded.

When we're asked why the school chose to uproot itself, both physically and in our academic approach, the answer is simple. Galileo is an academy, not an institution. We are here to bring out the best in you, to ask old questions and new ones, and to seek out answers beyond even our ancestors' dreams.

The school's history, its legacies, they do not make it extraordinary. You, our students, do. Not because you were chosen but because of who you choose to be. It is our honor to be your home, and to lift you to even greater heights.

Eppur si move, the words of our founder. Galileo Academy for the Extraordinary moves forward, and so do we.

Your new principal,
Beatriz Ruiz-Marín

ACKNOWLEDGMENTS

There are many people we need to thank for their help in making this massive undertaking a reality, but none deserve it more than our agent, Victoria Marini, who always listens to our wildest ideas and somehow doesn't go running for the hills.

We are immensely grateful to Krista Marino for the faith she put in us and our vision for the *Grimoire,* and to Hannah Hill for her willingness to take us on and bring the project home. Our thanks also to Beverly Horowitz, Wendy Loggia, Barbara Marcus, Tamar Schwartz, Colleen Fellingham, Alison Kolani, Melanie Muto, Alison Impey, Trisha Previte, Kenneth Crossland, Dominique Cimina, John Adamo, Kelly McGauley, Elizabeth Ward, and Adrienne Waintraub from Delacorte Press/RHCB; this book would not exist without you.

And lastly, we want to thank our contributors for listening to our pitch, saying yes —we still can't believe you did—and then putting up with our seemingly endless notes and revisions. We are so proud of what we all put together, and we hope you are too.

ABOUT THE CREATORS

Hanna Alkaf is the author of the Freeman Award–winning *The Weight of Our Sky,* the *Kirkus* Prize finalist *The Girl and the Ghost, Queen of the Tiles,* and *Hamra and the Jungle of Memories.* Hanna lives near Kuala Lumpur with her family.
hannaalkaf.com

Margaret Owen is the author of the critically acclaimed Merciful Crow duology and the award-winning Little Thieves trilogy. In her free time, she enjoys exploring ill-advised travel destinations and raising money for social justice nonprofits through her illustrations. She lives in Seattle.
margaret-owen.com

ABOUT THE AUTHORS

Preeti Chhibber is an author, speaker, and freelancer. She has written for SyFy, *Polygon,* and *Elle,* among others. In 2022, she made her Marvel comics debut in Women of Marvel #1 with a brand-new Black Cat story. That same year also saw the release of *Spider-Man's Social Dilemma,* the first installment in an original upper-middle-grade Peter Parker trilogy from Marvel Press. You can find her cohosting the podcasts *Desi Geek Girls* and *Tar Valon or Bust.* She's appeared on panels at New York Comic Con, San Diego Comic Con, and on-screen for SyFy. You probably recognize her from one of several *BuzzFeed* "look at these tweets" lists. Visit her online at PreetiChhibber.com.

Kat Cho is an internationally bestselling author who loves to incorporate her Korean heritage in her writing, especially if it involves describing food. She also loves anything that encourages nerding out, including reading, K-dramas, K-pop, and anime. She's the author of the Gumiho duology (Penguin) and *Once Upon a K-Prom* (Disney). Find her on Twitter at @KatCho, on Instagram & TikTok at @KatChoWrites, and at KatChoWrites.com.

Mason Deaver is the bestselling award-winning young adult author of *I Wish You All the Best, The Ghosts We Keep,* and *The Feeling of Falling in Love,* as well as a contributor to several anthologies and the horror novella *Another Name for the Devil.* They currently live in San Francisco, where they watch too many horror movies and struggle to find a place to fit their lightsaber collection.

Natasha Díaz is an award-winning author and screenwriter currently living in Brooklyn, New York. Her debut novel, *Color Me In,* is out now.

Hafsah Faizal is the *New York Times* bestselling, award-winning author of *We Hunt the Flame, We Free the Stars,* and *A Tempest of Tea* and the founder of IceyDesigns, where she creates websites for authors and beauteous goodies for everyone else. A Forbes 30 under 30 honoree, when she's not writing, she can be found designing, playing *Assassin's Creed,* or traveling the world. Born in Florida and raised in California, she now lives in Texas with a library of books waiting to be devoured.

Victoria Lee grew up in Durham, North Carolina, where she spent her childhood writing ghost stories and fantasizing about attending boarding school. She has a PhD in psychology, which she uses to overanalyze fictional characters and also herself. Lee is the author of *A Lesson in Vengeance* as well as *The Fever King* and its sequel, *The Electric Heir.* She lives in New York City with her partner, cat, and malevolent dog.

Jessica Lewis is a Black author and receptionist. She has degrees in English literature and animal science (the veterinarian plan did not work out). She lives with her way-funnier-than-her grandmother in Alabama. Her debut novel is *Bad Witch Burning*. She also writes contemporary middle-grade novels under her pen name, Jazz Taylor.

Darcie Little Badger is a Lipan Apache writer with a PhD in oceanography. Her critically acclaimed debut novel, *Elatsoe*, was featured in *Time* magazine as one of the Best 100 Fantasy Books of All Time. *Elatsoe* also won the Locus Award for Best First Novel and is a Nebula, Ignyte, and Lodestar finalist. Her second fantasy novel, *A Snake Falls to Earth*, received the Newbery Honor and the Nebula Award, and is on the National Book Awards longlist. Darcie is married to a veterinarian named Taran.

Kwame Mbalia is a husband, father, writer, *New York Times* bestselling author, and former pharmaceutical metrologist, in that order. His debut middle-grade novel, *Tristan Strong Punches a Hole in the Sky*, was awarded a Coretta Scott King Author Honor, and it—along with the sequels *Tristan Strong Destroys the World* and *Tristan Strong Keeps Punching*—is published by Rick Riordan Presents/Disney Hyperion. He is the coauthor of *Last Gate of the Emperor* with Prince Joel Makonnen, from Scholastic Books, and the editor of the #1 *New York Times* bestselling anthology *Black Boy Joy*, published by Delacorte Press. A Howard University graduate and a midwesterner now living in North Carolina, he survives on dad jokes and Cheez-Its.

Named one of *The Root*'s and BET's 100 Most Influential African Americans, **Leatrice "Elle" McKinney, writing as L. L.**

McKinney, is an advocate for equality and inclusion in publishing, and the creator of the hashtags #PublishingPaidMe and #WhatWoCWritersHear. Her love of all things geek and nerd is clear in her body of work, from writing for Power Rangers, Wonder Woman, and Black Widow to dropping Easter eggs about anime and video games in her books. She's the author of the Nightmare-Verse series and the highly anticipated (or already released depending on when you're reading this) novels *Escaping Mr. Rochester* and *Splintered Magic.*

Tehlor Kay Mejia is the bestselling and award-winning author of the We Set the Dark on Fire duology, the Paola Santiago series, and other books for young adult and middle-grade readers. She lives with her daughter, partner, and two small dogs in Oregon, where she grows heirloom corn and continues her quest to perfect the vegan tamale. Find her on social media at @tehlorkay.

Yamile (sha-MEE-lay) Saied Méndez is an Argentine American author. She lives in Utah with her Puerto Rican husband and their five kids, two adorable dogs, and one majestic cat. An inaugural Walter Dean Myers Grant recipient, she's also a graduate of Voices of Our Nations and the Vermont College of Fine Arts MFA Writing for Children and Young Adults program. She writes picture books and middle-grade, young adult, and adult fiction. Her book *Furia* is a Pura Belpré Award winner and an Amelia Elizabeth Walden Book Award finalist. Yamile is a founding member of Las Musas, the first collective of women and nonbinary Latine children's authors.

Cam Montgomery (nonbinary she/her) is a born and raised Angeleno. She is the author of two YA novels—*Home and Away* and *By Any Means Necessary*—and the newly minted editor of the anthology *All Signs Point to Yes*. Cam's daytime gig involves working with foster kids, and all spare time is spent at the local boxing gym or dreaming up her next romancey work in progress. You can find her on Instagram at @camstagram.jpg or on TikTok at @hey.itsCam. Having ditched LA, she now lives in Seattle with her rescue pup Sébastien ("Bash").

Marieke Nijkamp (she/they) is a #1 *New York Times* bestselling author of novels, graphic novels, and comics, including *This Is Where It Ends; At the End of Everything; Critical Role: Vox Machina—Kith & Kin; Hawkeye: Kate Bishop; The Oracle Code;* and *Unbroken: 13 Stories Starring Disabled Teens.* Marieke lives and writes in Small Town, The Netherlands.

Karuna Riazi is a born-and-raised New Yorker, with a loving, large extended family and the rather trying experience of being the eldest sibling in her particular clan. She holds a BA in English Literature from Hofstra University and an MFA in Writing for Children and Young Adults from Hamline University and is an online diversity advocate and educator. She is the author of *The Gauntlet* (S&S/Salaam Reads, 2017), *The Battle* (S&S/Salaam Reads, 2019), *Ghostwriter: The Jungle Book* (Sourcebooks Wonderland/Sesame Workshop, 2019), and *A Bit of Earth* (HarperCollins/Greenwillow Books, 2023).

Randy Ribay is an award-winning author of young adult fiction, including *An Infinite Number of Parallel Universes, After* *the Shot Drops,* and *Patron Saints of Nothing,* which was a National Book Award finalist. He earned his BA in English Literature from the University of Colorado at Boulder and his master's degree in Language and Literacy from Harvard Graduate School of Education. Born in the Philippines and raised in the Midwest, Randy lives in the San Francisco Bay Area with his wife, son, and catlike dog.

Kayla Whaley is the author of the chapter book series A to Z Animal Mysteries. Her essays and short fiction have appeared in numerous anthologies, including *Unbroken, Vampires Never Get Old, Game On,* and *Allies,* as well as in publications like *Bustle, Catapult,* and *Michigan Quarterly Review.* She holds an MFA in creative nonfiction from the University of Tampa and is a graduate of the Clarion Workshop. Kayla lives outside of Atlanta, where she drinks too much coffee and buys too many books.

Julian Winters is the author of the IBPA Benjamin Franklin Gold Award–winning *Running with Lions,* the Junior Library Guild Selections *How to Be Remy Cameron* and *The Summer of Everything,* and the multi-starred *Right Where I Left You.* A self-proclaimed comic book geek, Julian currently lives outside of Atlanta, where he can be found reading or watching the only two sports he can follow—volleyball and soccer.